Dirt Road Secrets

ASHLEY JAMES

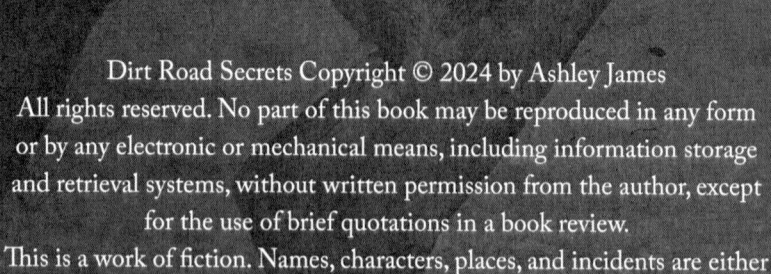

Dirt Road Secrets Copyright © 2024 by Ashley James
All rights reserved. No part of this book may be reproduced in any form or by any electronic or mechanical means, including information storage and retrieval systems, without written permission from the author, except for the use of brief quotations in a book review.

This is a work of fiction. Names, characters, places, and incidents are either products of the authors imagination or used in a fictitious manner. Any resemblance to actual persons, living or dead, or events is purely coincidental.

Cover Design: Fortuitous Designer
Interior Formatting: Wanderlust Formatting
Editing: Nice Girl Naughty Edits

For anyone who has ever felt *different*, who worried something was wrong with them because they didn't feel things in the same way their friends or their peers did.

There's nothing wrong with you. You're perfect just the way you are.

To all the Copeland Murphy's of the world... this one's for you.

PLAYLIST

Full playlist can be found on Spotify.

Good Time by Niko Moon
Somethin' 'Bout A Truck by Kip Moore
Something in the Orange by Zach Bryan
Blindsided (Yeah, Sure, Okay) by Kelsea Ballerini
Redneck Love Song by Morgan Wallen
Find Your People by Drew Holcomb & The Neighbors
I Don't Know About You by Chris Lane
Forever and Ever, Amen by Randy Travis
How Country Feels by Randy Houser
A Little Lime by Jordan Davis
The Replacement by Kae
Bless the Broken Road by Rascal Flatts
White Horse by Chris Stapleton
Down on the Farm by Tim McGraw
Rumor by Lee Brice

Copper Lake Disclaimer

This series takes place in the fictional small town of Copper Lake, Wyoming, and it follows cowboys who compete in the professional rodeo. The use of the Professional Rodeo Cowboy Association (or PRCA as it's frequently referred to as in the books) is a work of fiction. I did my best to keep the organization as accurate as possible with regards to the rules, regulations, circuit schedule, etc., but there are instances where I had to take creative liberties for the sake of the storyline. Names, characters, businesses, places, events, and incidents are either the products of the authors imagination or used in a fictional manner. Any resemblance to actual persons, living or dead, or actual events is purely coincidental.

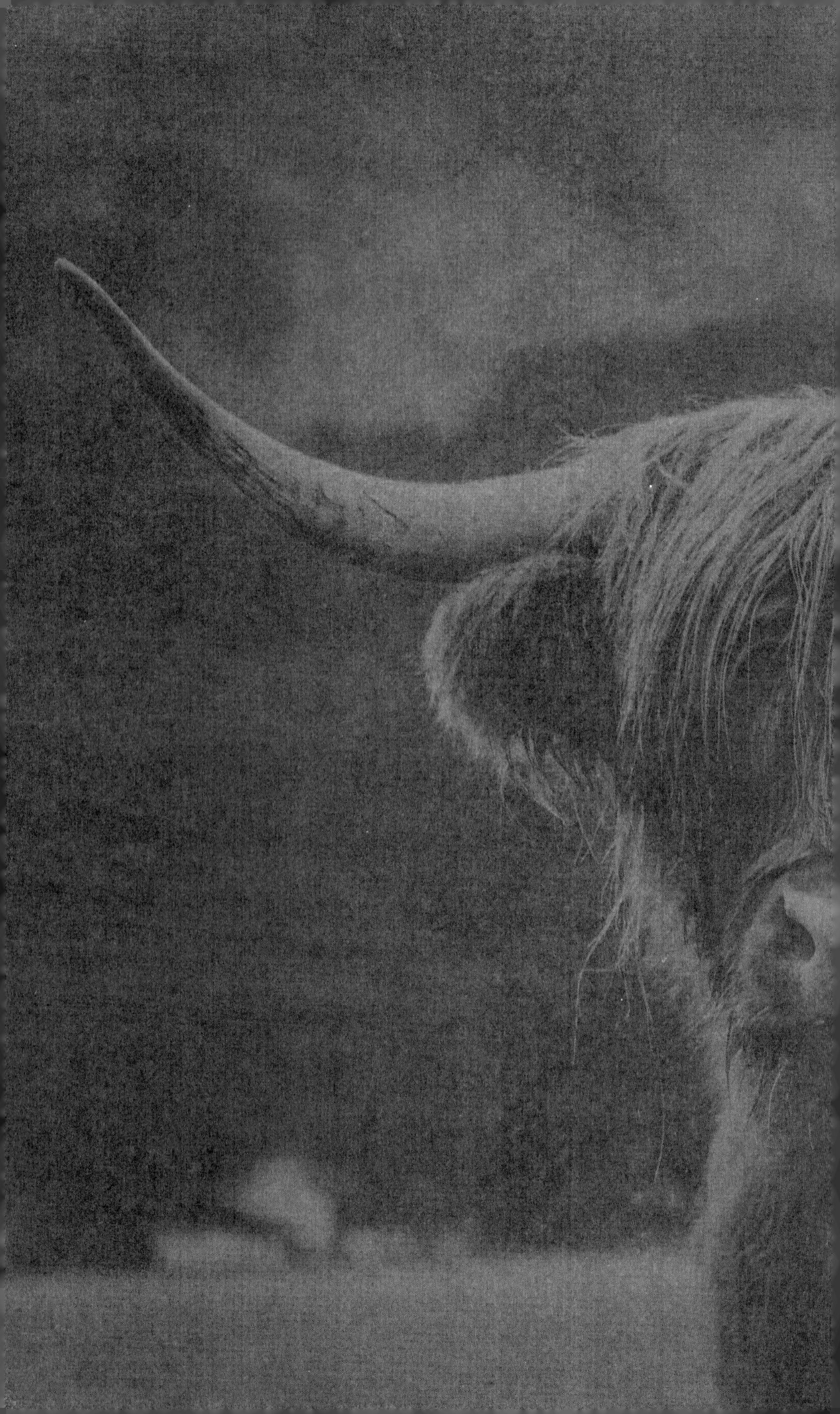

Chapter 1

Cope Murphy

Fall is by far my favorite season. I know there are the die-hard summer lovers, with the beach and the heat and the bikinis, and then there're the winter wonderland fanatics who go ape shit over the snow, the holidays, and the cold weather, sitting in front of a fire with eggnog.

Eggnog is disgusting, first of all.

And the snow is nothing more than a nuisance. Yeah, it's pretty to look at until it comes time to drive in it, and then you're surrounded by a bunch of idiots who don't know what the hell they're doing. Then the snow turns into sludge, and suddenly, it's not so pretty anymore. Growing up in Copper Lake, I'm quite acquainted with the snow and the cold during the winter months, but that doesn't mean I like it.

Spring's okay. It's the start of the rodeo season after all, so it deserves its recognition. But fall is where it's at. The crisp, cool air, the leaves changing colors, all the hoodies that can come out of hibernation. Not to mention it's the perfect season for hard cider around a campfire. You just can't beat it.

It's early October, the season fully upon us, and I'm in my element as I'm driving home from the gym this afternoon. The sun is shining down, the temperature a comfortable sixty-four degrees, the driver's side window is rolled down in my pickup, and Zach Bryan is singing through the stereo. Taking a right onto the dirt road that eventually leads to my property, I take in the trees surrounding the road, the animals grazing in the grass to the left and right. Mr. and Mrs. Timmins just got a couple of new cows that are hanging out in the pasture right now, and I make a mental note to go over there this week.

When I bought my house, I did it with the intention of one day having a family to fill the inside and some animals to occupy the yard. That day is not today, and while my house may be a little big for just myself, I loathe the process of home buying and moving in general, so when given the opportunity to go big or go home, I chose to go big. It's nothing huge and outrageous, but I definitely don't need four bedrooms and fifty acres for just me—but I work hard and deserve it, okay? And besides, I'd rather have room to grow than to outgrow my home.

My house is toward the end of this long, narrow dirt road. It's a couple of miles long, and it's one of those where you have to pull off to the side if someone else is driving down the opposite direction. Which is why it's not unusual for there to be a car pulled over on the shoulder as I near the end of the road. What *is* unusual, though, is that I've never seen this car before, and typically, it's the same several vehicles going up and down this road on a daily basis, and the fact that this car's hood is lifted and the driver's side door is swung open, a foot coming from inside planted on the ground.

Curiosity has me coming to a stop behind the car. It's a dark green Nissan Altima that's seen better days with Washington plates on the back. I leave the truck running as I hop out, shoving my phone into my pocket just in case, and approach the open door. A guy with black shaggy hair beneath a hot pink beanie sits in the driver's seat. He's wearing a black hoodie and a pair of ripped jeans with Vans on his feet. When he hears me approach, he turns his head, our gaze colliding. Ice-blue eyes meet mine, and there's a furrow in his dark brows, most likely from frustration over whatever's going on with his car, if I had to guess. He looks to be a little bit older than my twenty-five, but I could be wrong.

"Oh, uh, hi. Hey." His head turns, and he looks into the rearview mirror before returning his attention to me. "Am I in your way? I'm so sorry. My car broke down, and I don't know what to do. I'm the least car savvy person I've ever met. It started smoking, and it freaked me out. I didn't know if it was going to catch on fire or what. I'm not even that far from where I'm supposed to be going, but the stupid thing won't start." He lets out a disgruntled sigh, the stress he's feeling damn near emanating from his pores.

I breathe out a small laugh at his rambling before I can stop myself. "No, you're good. I could easily get around you, but I wanted to make sure you were okay?"

He looks at me like I've grown a second head. "You're... You stopped to see if I—a stranger—was okay?"

"Yes?"

"Why?"

"Um..." I frown, my brows pinching together in confusion. "Because you're clearly having car trouble, and it's the least I can do."

"No, I'm a complete stranger to you. The least you could do is drive right on past me and get to wherever you need to be because you don't owe me—again, a *stranger*—anything."

The wind's kicked up in the last few minutes, and his pale cheeks have turned pink. I glance around him into the car. Starbucks cups take up both cup holders, and there's even one in the door, and it looks like his back and passenger seat are filled with shit. "You're not from around here, are you?" I ask him, ignoring his weird comment from before.

"What makes you ask that?"

"Well, it looks like everything you own is in the car with you," I reply plainly, indicating behind him. "And the Washington plates are kind of a dead giveaway."

"Right," he mutters, but offers nothing else. His hands are in his lap, fingers fiddling with one another and picking at the skin around his thumb. Chipped black polish litters a few of the nails, while others seem to have none.

"If you're this far down the road, you're probably heading one of three places. My house, Ms. Dawson's, or the Hendrickson's. And seeing as how I've never seen you in my life, I'm assuming it's not my place. So, which of the two is your destination?"

He tosses me a look I can't decipher. "Dawson," he supplies. "My aunt."

Taking a step back, I say, "Come on. I can give you a lift." Motioning my arm toward my truck, I watch as bewilderment takes over his face all over again. He doesn't move. "I'm her neighbor, and once we get back there, I can grab the stuff from my garage to hook your car up to the back of my truck and tow it to her place."

When he still doesn't make any attempt at getting out of the car, I trudge back to my truck before pulling out my phone and checking the time.

"Come on. I swear, I don't bite, and it's on my way anyway."

I open the door before adding, "And once we get your car back, I can call my buddy, who's the mechanic in town. He can probably come take a look at it this evening."

This finally gets him to slide out of the car and stand up. "But you don't even know me," is all he says.

Is he concerned because I'm a stranger? Like, worried I'm going to chop him into a million pieces or something? It's literally, like, a mile down the road, if that.

"I don't need to know you to give you a lift down the road," I say slowly. "You're stuck, and I want to help. It's not a big deal. If it makes you feel better…" I walk over to him, extending my hand. "I'm Cope, and you are?"

Surprisingly, he slips his hand into mine. I notice how warm it is, and how much softer it is than my own. "Xander."

"Okay, Xander, nice to meet you. See, not strangers anymore. So, get in."

"I've got a cat," he announces, pointing his thumb over his shoulder toward the car. "He's in a carrier."

"Grab him and come on."

Xander doesn't look any more assured, but after he plucks the carrier out of his car, he rounds the front of my truck and pulls open the passenger side door, climbing into the cab, setting the cat on his lap. The opening faces away from me, so I can't see the animal, nor is it making any noise. Maybe it's asleep. I join him, not bothering to put my seatbelt back on since we're not going very far. I do, however, turn the music down.

"It smells good in here," Xander mutters, dragging his gaze around everything.

"Thanks. It's some air freshener I picked up the other day." Putting the car in drive, I go around the Nissan, and head toward his aunt's house. "What's your cats name?"

"Larry."

I shoot a look over at him, a smile tugging on my lips. "Your cat's name is *Larry?*"

Much to my surprise, he breathes out a laugh. "Yeah, I don't know. He just looked like a little wrinkly Larry when I brought him home."

"Alright, I like that," I murmur, bringing my attention to the road in front of us again. "I didn't know Ms. Dawson had a nephew. Are you visiting?"

"Yeah, I've never been here. Any time we've seen each other, she's always come to Washington. But yes, I'm visiting, kind of."

"Kind of?"

Xander's hands are back in his lap, but this time his fingers are twirling around a bracelet he's wearing around his wrist. It's black, and it's one of those types you can cinch together using the two end pieces. I wonder if he made it himself. "She's having surgery on her hip soon. So, I'm coming here to help out with her animals while she's recovering."

That's nice of him to do. Ms. Dawson has quite a few animals that I know of. A couple of horses, some cows, goats, chickens. I think she's even got a few ducks running around too. "You're from Washington?"

"Mhm."

"Like, Seattle?"

"No." He chuckles. "Not like Seattle. I live in a town just outside of Pullman in eastern Washington."

"That's cool. Do you have farm animals there that you take care of?"

"No."

"Have you ever?"

He shakes his head. "Just my cat."

"So, you have no clue what you're doing?" I ask, my brow arched in question.

"Pretty much." His lips lift into a small smile that doesn't reach his eyes. In fact, it looks forced. "But she said she'll show me what to do. I'm a quick learner, so I'm sure it'll be fine."

"Yeah, it'll be great," I reply—even though I *highly* doubt it will be—as we pull in front of my house. It looks fairly similar to his aunt's, except where mine's more dark, neutral colors, hers is a bright yellow. "Wait here. I'll grab the stuff and be right back."

Because I'm so neurotic about how things in my garage are organized, I find what I need right away, bringing it back out to the truck and sticking it in the bed before climbing back inside. Xander is fiddling with that bracelet again, and he looks over at me as I shut the door.

"Thanks for helping me," he mutters, throwing a quick glance my way. "I'm not normally this much of a basket case, but everything about this trip has been hell. This is just the icing on top of the fucked-up cake. So, thank you."

Nodding, I say, "Hey, no problem at all, man. We all need a little help every now and again."

Putting the truck into reverse, I back out of my driveway before heading back to where his car's at. It's easy enough getting it hooked up to my truck, and when we get to his aunt's place and I unload it, I give him the number to my mechanic before also plugging in my number.

"If you need anything, just give me a call or text me. I'm very well acquainted with farm animals and how to take care of them, so just let me know."

"Uh, thank you. I appreciate it." He takes his phone back,

stuffing it into the pocket of his hoodie, tossing me one more smile that seems more genuine this time, before he climbs out of my truck. After he grabs a few things from his car, he heads toward the front door, but not before glancing back and giving me a wave.

    Well, he's…different.

Chapter 2

Xander Dawson

There's no Starbucks around here. No coffee stands. There isn't even a Dunkin'. When I asked Aunt Colette where to go to get an iced coffee this morning, she laughed at me and pointed to her coffee pot.

Coffee. Pot.

I don't think I've even seen a drip coffee pot since I was a child. It's not even a Keurig. I burned the first pot I tried to make. Didn't even know that was possible. Pot number two, I finally got it right, but then realized that Aunt Colette doesn't have any creamer in the house, and when I thought about going to get some at the store, I remembered my car is as good as stationary right now, so I can't. She left about twenty minutes ago for some pre-surgery appointment. Her doctor is all the way in Cheyenne since she had to see a specialist, and there aren't any of those here.

Copper Lake, Wyoming.

I knew this town was small and figured it would be a lot different from where I'm from in Washington, but I haven't even been here a full twenty-four hours yet, and the differences are painstakingly obvious already. What kind of place doesn't have a Starbucks? Isn't that a universal place, like a post office or a McDonald's?

Hell, there's probably no McDonald's here either.

Non-burnt cup of coffee, sans creamer, in hand, I pad out onto the back porch. It's a partial wraparound, with a couple of rocking chairs and a little circular table in between them. Her house is nice, but this property? Insane. Beautiful. There's so much of it, and it's like right out of a damn Hallmark movie. I remember in high school when my aunt told my mom she was moving here, my mom was beside herself. She didn't understand why anybody would want to move to somewhere as small as Copper Lake. And honestly, I kind of agreed at the time.

Desert Creek, the town I live in, isn't large by any means, but it's still centralized and has everything you need, and if it doesn't, then it's a short drive to the city to get it. This is… something way different. I wouldn't be surprised if I saw people getting around via horseback here.

"Hey, honey, can you run to the store and get me some flour?"

"Sure thing. Let me grab a saddle and hop on the back of Ryder. Be right back!"

Yup. Could totally see it.

Setting the coffee cup on the table, I reach into my pocket, wrapping my hand around the contents, and pull them out. Opening up the small, rectangular tin can, I pluck out one of the pre-rolls before placing it between my lips, and bring the blue BIC up to it. The lighter sparks to life, a flame burning the end of the paper until a sour, earthy scent wafts around me and fills my lungs.

The first hit in the morning is always the best. A slow,

steady calm settles over me, a wave of relaxation feeding my mind. An iced coffee with a joint is my favorite way to start the day—it's how I've started every day for as long as I can remember. Bringing another glaring difference between home and here; Washington is a very weed legal state, while Wyoming is *not*. So legal, in fact, that I own and run a dispensary back home. Something I'm grateful for in situations like this, when I needed to up and leave for who knows how long. I didn't have to worry about getting fired or not having the money to make ends meet while I was gone. The shop doesn't make a huge profit, but it does make enough that I can easily support myself, which is a plus.

After I'm done with my coffee, I need to get started on this list of chores my aunt left for me. I'm happy to be here, and to help her out during her surgery and the recovery, but I'd be lying if I said I wasn't feeling very in over my head. The closest I've ever come to farm animals is going to the petting zoo or the occasional pony ride at the fair as a kid. I have Larry, but he's about as low maintenance as they come and lives strictly indoors. All I have to worry about is the litter box and making sure he's fed every day.

Aunt Colette has a whole damn herd of animals, so this should be interesting.

Taking one more hit off the joint, I put it out before placing it back in the tin can. I grab my phone, checking it to see if there're any missed calls or texts, but of course, there isn't. Although, I am an hour ahead of Washington time, so it's still extra early there. However, I didn't hear from him last night either, but I refuse to go there. Not first thing in the morning, and not when I already have so much on my plate. I don't have time to worry about why I haven't heard from my boyfriend or what he could be doing that keeps him from texting me.

I told myself I wouldn't obsess over this while I was here. And I mean it.

My eyes catch on my most recent text message, and memories of my shitshow of a day yesterday come barreling through my mind. My car has been on its last leg for quite a while now, and I knew it was risky driving it here from Washington. I considered flying, but I didn't want to either be without a car the whole time or have to rent one or borrow my aunt's, so I chanced my luck and drove. In its defense, it did just fine up until I crossed the Wyoming state line. When I stopped for gas, it didn't want to start back up, and at stoplights, it was idling weird. I don't know shit about cars, but even I knew none of those were good signs. Then, when I turned onto the road that was supposed to lead to my aunt's house, the hood started smoking bad enough for me to panic and think the damn thing was on fire.

Car trouble is so stressful, especially if you know nothing about them. The mechanic is coming to look at it today, and I'm praying it doesn't cost an arm and a leg to fix. Is it even worth it for me to fix at this point, or should I just get rid of it and buy a new one? Hopefully, the mechanic isn't a price gouger. Some of them can be so sleazy, after nothing but your money. If he's anything like Cope, though, then I'll bet he's nice and polite. That's one major plus about back home. My best friend's fiancé is a mechanic, so I always get the best deals, and I know my car is in good hands with him.

I'm still beside myself at how nice and helpful Cope was yesterday. And for no reason. He doesn't know me from Adam, yet he stopped when he saw me broken down, and immediately offered to lend a hand. Who does that? Back home, you see someone pulled off the side of the road, you drive on by and mind your business. It's not even to be rude either. You just never know who you'll run into in situations like that, and you can't be too careful. I was raised to always have my guard up and to never be too trusting.

Apparently, the residents of Copper Lake were not taught that same mindset. Or at least, Cope wasn't. I wonder if I'll see him again. He *does* live next door, and he *did* tell me to reach out if I needed anything, so I'm sure the chances are likely.

Deciding I should quit wasting time, I heave a sigh before standing up and stretching my arms over my head, and grab my mug, bringing it back inside. After rinsing it in the sink, I collect the list Aunt Colette left for me, stop and pet Larry, who looks positively grumpy this morning, where he's sitting in the windowsill, and head out back. Her cursive handwriting is nice, and it reminds of an elementary school teacher. Before she left this morning, she told me there was a pair of rubber boots out in the barn I could wear while I worked if I wanted, but glancing down at my Vans, I don't really see why I'd need them. It's not like it rained yesterday, so the lawn wouldn't be wet.

I should be fine.

I'm not fine. Not fine at all.

Very quickly, I realized why my aunt suggested wearing the boots. It's not for fear of getting my shoes wet from the damp grass. Well, it kind of is, but it's more than that. These damn shoes don't have good traction, and even though the grass is mostly dry, there's still mud near the troughs, and there's poop *everywhere*. I've been out here twenty minutes, and I can't even count how many times I've almost slipped and fell on my ass.

My white shoes are covered in mud, my socks are wet, and everything stinks out here. The food, the grass, the shit, the *animals*. Why does she have so many fucking animals in the first place? What one person needs this many? Horses, chickens, ducks, goats, donkeys, cows. There's even a fucking *mule*. Who the hell needs a mule?

I've let all the chickens out of their coop, gotten everyone food and fresh water, swept the barn, and now I need to turn the horses out… Whatever the hell that means. Aunt Colette has three horses, Meadow, Blanc, and Bertha—don't ask me who's who, because I don't have a single clue. She gives written instructions on how to put on the halters and walk them out to the pasture, but I'm feeling very out of my element looking at these giant beasts.

I'm sure the instructions make sense to someone who understands horse lingo, but to someone like me, who thought the only meaning for a halter was a type of shirt before today, they're about as good as useless to me. I guess I could look it up on YouTube or something, watch a video on how to do it. I have always been more of a visual learner anyway. But I left my phone on the porch. Wiping my hands on the front of my jeans, I leave the barn and head toward the house.

The sun's finally out, and while it's not overly hot, it is still getting warmer, especially with me doing physical work. I'll probably ditch my jacket when I grab my phone. What happens next happens so fast, I don't even see it coming. I take a step, the grass a little muddy, and I completely lose my footing, my legs flying out from underneath me as my entire body catches air. I land straight on my ass with a loud *thunk*. The air's knocked out of me, and in an instant, my entire back is soaked in the muddy water seeping between the strands of grass. I'm left staring up at the sky, sucking in large gulps of air, wondering what the fuck I was thinking, agreeing to come here and help my aunt when I don't have a fucking clue what I'm doing.

It's day two, and already things have gone horribly. My car is broken down; I'll probably have to buy a new one, my whole fucking back is soaking wet with mud and who knows what else. It's probably animal shit. Wouldn't be surprised.

A deep, masculine chuckle reaches my ears, and I fight the urge to melt farther into the ground. Especially when I look up and find Cope stepping up to me, his form now blocking the sun from my eyes. "What're you doing down there?" he asks, an amused grin lifting his lips.

"I obviously fell," I deadpan, finally sitting up.

Cope extends his arm to me, silently offering to help me stand. I slip my hand into his, and just like yesterday when he introduced himself with a handshake, I notice how calloused and rough his palms are. *Hardworking hands.* I wonder what he does for a living to have hands like that. Now isn't the time to ask, but I make a mental note to ask later when I'm not covered in mud, with cheeks burning hot from embarrassment.

When I get to my feet, I don't even bother trying to wipe off my ass. I already know it's futile. "What are you doing here?" I ask him.

"Coming to see how you're holding up. Clearly, you need the help more than I thought." He chuckles again, and I can't help but let out a little one of my own because, from the outside, I'm sure I do look ridiculous.

"What would give you that idea?" I tease. "I'd like to think I'm handling all of this quite well."

"Right." He nods. "Because a day on the farm is never

complete without a back full of mud."

Shrugging, I say, "Heard it's good for the skin."

His whole face lights up when he laughs. "Sure, farmland serum. I think I've heard of that." Cope glances down for a moment. "Why on earth are you wearing shoes like that out here?"

I groan. "Have I mentioned I don't know what I'm doing?"

"Don't worry, I'm here to save the day." He waves his arm out in front of him like he's Prince Charming. "You'll be a fully functioning cowboy in no time."

"Ahh, I don't know about that."

Cope nods toward the house. "Go get changed and get on some actual boots, and I'll help you with whatever else you have left to do."

My brows clash together. "Why?"

"I mean, if you want to work covered in mud, by all means—"

"No, I mean, why are you going to help me?"

Now it's his turn to look confused. "Because you need help, and I want to…"

"Why are you so nice?" First, with my car, and now this. He barely knows me—no, he doesn't know me at all, aside from my name and what state I live in—and yet, he's so willing to lend a helping hand. I don't get it.

He flashes me a wide grin. "I'm being neighborly. Now, quit being weird and just do as I say. Go get changed before I change my mind."

Okay, bossy.

As quickly as possible, to not keep him waiting too long, I get changed and slip into the boots I should've put on originally, and I meet him back outside. I allow myself a moment to take him in as he stands there, not paying me any mind while he pets one of the cows. This one is much fluffier than the other one—fluffier than any cow I've ever seen. It looks like a cow that's gone to the hairdresser and gotten a blow-out.

Cope's dressed in a plain white V-neck t-shirt, a pair of light denim jeans that fit him *damn* well, and some dark brown cowboy boots. He's also wearing a trucker hat with some logo on the front that I can't quite make out. He's a bit taller than I am; maybe six foot or six one, and while his build is lean, it's more than obvious in the way his shirt clings to him that he works out. His skin is a golden tan like he spends a lot of time in the sun, and his face is peppered with scruff that's a little bit more than a five o'clock shadow but not quite a full beard, a little darker than the dirty blond atop his head.

He's the embodiment of a country boy, and up until this very moment, it was a look I didn't realize I was attracted to, but I don't know…this is kinda doing it for me. I manage to wipe the drool from my chin by the time he glances up from the cow to me, that same warm grin plastered on his face from before.

"Ready?" he asks, walking over to me with his hands shoved into the pockets of his jeans.

"Yup, let's do this."

We head into the barn, and he walks me through how to halter the horses. I was right, seeing it done helps much more than the written instructions, and it's not even as hard as I was making it seem. Once we're done with that, we walk all three of them out to the pasture.

"How long are you here for?" Cope asks after a few minutes of us walking quietly.

"I'm not sure. My aunt goes in for surgery Monday morning, and depending on how long it takes for her to heal up enough to handle all of this by herself, I'd guess at least a few weeks. Maybe more."

"That's nice of you to offer to help her out. Are you guys close?"

"Not really," I reply truthfully. "I mean, we aren't estranged or anything, and any time she comes into town, me and my sister enjoy visiting with her. She comes to Washington a few times a year, mostly for holidays."

"Do you just have one sister?"

"Yeah, Gemma. She's two years younger than me."

"And how old are you?"

I glance over at him as we walk. He meets my gaze, and I notice his eyes are a rich dark brown, like a milk chocolate color that looks gorgeous when the sunlight hits them. He's asking a lot of questions, but it doesn't feel like filler or like he's being nosy. It's like he genuinely wants to learn more about me. It's different.

"I'm twenty-eight—twenty-nine in a few weeks. What about you?"

"Twenty-five." He grins. "So why are you here taking care of your aunt's farm instead of your sister?"

We reach the pasture and let the horses go. One of the cows is in the field on the other side of the fence, chomping on grass. She doesn't even look up when the horses trot away. This one looks like the typical cow that I've always thought of in my head; black and white spots, no horns. No Brazilian blowout.

I return my attention to Cope and the question he asked. "Gemma's married, and she's pregnant," I offer. "And I'm not… on either account. So, it made the most sense for me to come."

"Makes sense," he murmurs. We watch the horses for a moment before turning to head back toward the house.

"What about you?" I ask. "Any siblings?"

"Nope," he replies. "I'm an only child."

"Did you like that growing up, or did you wish you had brothers or sisters?"

"Eh, half and half probably. Sometimes I wish I did, but other times I was fine with it. Mostly because I was so close with the other kids in town since our parents were all friends, that it felt like they were siblings sometimes. For instance, my best friend, Shooter, and I have been friends since we were really little. Our dads competed together, so our families were all very close. Shooter and his sister, Daisy, have always felt like family to me."

"Competed?"

He nods. "In the rodeo."

"Like bull riding?"

"Like bronc riding." My brows pinch together at that.

"What's the difference?"

Head dropped back onto his shoulders, Cope groans to the sky. "Oh my God. What are we gonna do with you? You might just be hopeless after all." Leveling me with a stare, he asks, "Are you serious right now?"

I can't help the chuckle that sneaks out. "Uh, yeah. What the hell would I know about the rodeo? Washington, remember?"

"There's rodeo in Washington, my friend."

"Well, not where I'm at. So, enlighten me."

Cope clutches at his chest. "I'm hurt. Disappointed."

"And dramatic," I add, rolling my eyes playfully.

After he manages to pull himself together after I clearly broke his heart with my lack of rodeo knowledge, he says, "Bull riding is just that—riding a bull. Bronc riding is very similar, but instead of a bull, it's a horse. A bronco."

I nod. "Got it." I don't got it, but I'm not going to further exasperate him. "So, your dad is a professional bronc rider?"

"Was," he corrects. "He's been retired for quite a while."

"And he was…good?"

"Clint Murphy was the greatest." Pride radiates off of him. "Until I came along," he adds with a haughty little smirk and a shimmy of his shoulders.

My eyes widen at that. "So, you're a… I mean, you ride broncs too?"

His grin is blinding, more pride rolling off of him, except now it's an inward type that seems to make him glow. It makes me want to know so much more. "Sure do."

"Wow, that's so interesting. I've never met someone who does anything like that before. What's that like?"

"Wild, crazy, and fun as hell."

So many questions swarm my mind; I don't even know where to begin. I don't get a chance to ask any of them, though, because as we approach the house, I notice my aunt sitting in one of the rocking chairs. She's wearing a warm smile as she glances between me and Cope.

"Hey, you just get back?"

"A few minutes go, yeah." Looking over at Cope, she asks, "You help my nephew with his chores?"

Holding up his thumb and index finger about an inch apart, he laughs and says, "A little bit."

"Alright, I did a lot by myself before you came over, thank you very much."

"Yeah, a lot of something." He chuckles. "Xander was ass over tea kettle when I got to him, bathing in the mud like a hog on a sunny day."

Aunt Colette cackles, throwing her head back. Mouth hanging open, I drag my gaze from her over to him, where he's looking mighty proud of himself. "Did you just call me a *hog*?"

"Oh, relax, city boy. I'm just giving you shit." He waves as he steps back. "It was nice to see you, Ms. Dawson. Xander, I'll catch you later. I gotta hit the gym for a while."

After he leaves, I grab my phone off the table and head inside, wanting to take a shower. I still feel all gross from the mud earlier. Probably stink too. Checking my notifications, I'm disappointed but not surprised to find none from Henry. I roll my eyes, pulling up his contact and send him a text, even though I told myself I wouldn't be the first to reach out.

I'm always the first to reach out. What's new?

Me: Hey. Let's FaceTime tonight. I miss you. Xo.

Hitting send, I lock the screen and set it on the counter, jumping in the shower, all while wondering if he'll respond.

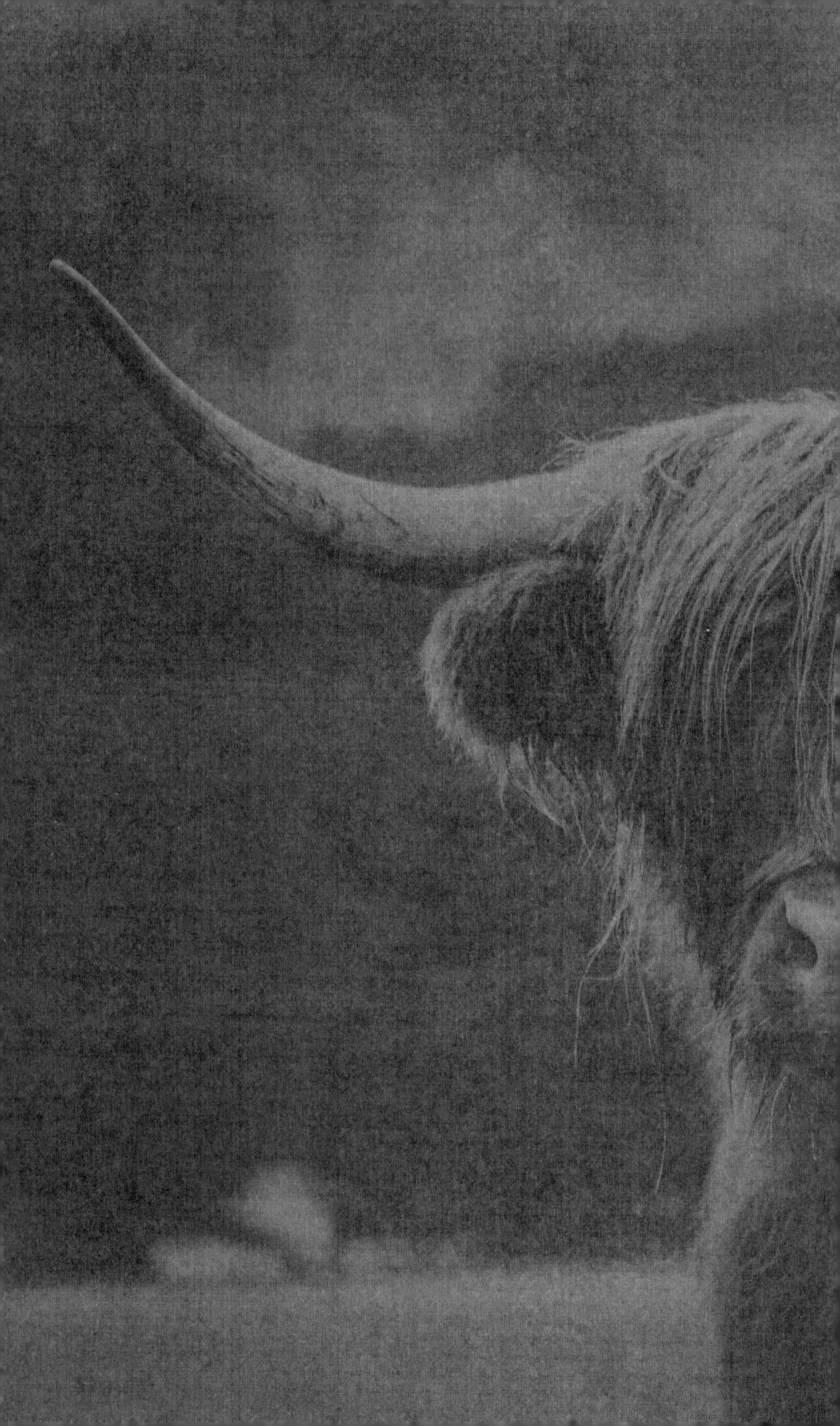

Chapter 3

Cope Murphy

Something I love about being from a small town is how everybody knows everyone. You drive around the lake and see Mr. and Mrs. Flatcher from down the road walking their dog. You wave, they wave back. You pass by Ms. Shephard, your old third-grade teacher, in the produce section at the grocery store, so you stop and say hi, catch up a little.

We're a tight-knit community, and we always have each other's backs.

Yeah, everybody may always know your business, but they'll be the first ones to show up at your door, ready to roll up their sleeves and get to work if something happens and you need anything. I remember a few years back when Henrik and Catherine Strauss passed away unexpectedly, the entire town rallied together to help Conrad with the ranch and all the responsibilities that came with it while he took the time he needed to grieve the loss of his parents. It was such a beautiful thing in the midst of something so tragic.

Almost everybody I'm friends with now are people I've

known since elementary school. Sure, I have friends who I haven't known my entire life, like Sterling, my best friend's boyfriend, but for the most part, they're people I played hide and go seek with, or who saw me go through puberty and my horrible acne stage. And honestly, I love it that way.

The friendships you can make in small towns are some of the best you can find. At least, in my experience. Those are the thoughts flitting through my mind as I sit around the roaring fire with an ice-cold beer in my hand and a handful of my closest friends surrounding me. It's my buddy, Colt's, birthday tonight, so we're all at Grazing Acres—Conrad's ranch, and where most of our get-togethers take place—celebrating him the only way we know how; with liquor, loud music, and large bonfires.

Shooter is to my right, the birthday boy to the left, and some Koe Wetzel song is blaring from the speakers of someone's truck over near the barn. The sun set hours ago, nothing but moonlight and the fire keeping the area lit.

When I left Ms. Dawson's place earlier today after helping Xander with the animals, I went to the gym for a few hours, took a piping hot shower there, then went home and wasted away the rest of the day lying on the couch fucking around on my phone and half-watching re-runs of reality TV. Don't ask why I took a shower at the gym when I have a perfectly good one at my house. They hit different after a hard, sweaty workout. I don't make the rules.

At the reminder of Xander and the mess I walked into earlier, I lean over and bump Shooter's arm with my elbow. "Hey, I forgot to tell you. You know my neighbor to the left, Ms. Dawson?"

His brow arches as he asks, "The one with the mule named Moscow?"

"Yup, that's the one." I laugh. "She's apparently having surgery soon. Her nephew is visiting from out of state to help her take care of all the animals. I met him the other day when his car broke down on the side of the road."

"Like, a kid?" he asks with pinched brows.

"No, no. He's around our age. He seems pretty cool." As the words leave my mouth, I realize how pointless this whole conversation is. Where am I going with this? Why did I feel the need to tell Shooter about him in the first place? To what, tell him I made a new friend?

My cheeks heat without my permission, and I'm thankful for the darkness surrounding us, so maybe it's not as noticeable as before.

"You should've invited him tonight, man," he says coolly, oblivious to the internal spat I'm having with myself.

And you know what? I should've. He's new in town, clearly doesn't know anybody aside from his aunt, and well, now me. I said I was being neighborly earlier by coming over and helping him, but I should've also been neighborly and invited him out, so he has a chance to make some friends while he's here.

I consider pulling out my phone and shooting off an invite, via text, to him right now, but that seems weird. Oh well. Next time, I guess.

We all sit around the fire for a little while longer, sipping on our beers before the lot of us get up and do a round of Jell-O shots for the birthday boy. Clementine, or Clem, as most of us call her, makes some of the best Jell-O shots I've ever had. They're never anything extravagant, just basic flavors like blue raspberry or strawberry, but they're the perfect mix of Jell-O and vodka. I've had some *nasty* ones in my day, so I always love when she brings a big ol' batch.

After we toss back a couple of shots, I walk away from the crowd for a minute to have a smoke. It's a nasty habit I picked up when I was a teenager, one I've never kicked. It's become a comfort for me at this point. Something to do with my hands or something to keep my mouth occupied when I don't know what else to do. I've always been into chewing gum or sucking on mints. This is kind of like that…but way different. A shitty kind of comfort, but hey, it could always be worse.

Scanning the property, I notice how many people are here tonight. It's much more than our normal get-togethers, but if I had to guess, it's probably because Colt invited a ton of people for his birthday. He's a social butterfly. Being a professional bull rider gets him a lot of attention. To be honest, we all get a ton of attention from being part of the pro rodeo, but some of us—Colt, and up until recently, Shooter, specifically—enjoy and relish it much more than others.

A couple of girls walk up to me as I'm taking a drag from my cigarette. I nod at them by way of greeting, and they smile at me.

"You're Copeland Murphy, right?" the brunette with big, bouncy curls, asks.

"The one and only," I reply with a grin. "But please, you can call me Cope."

She giggles. "Okay, Cope. Well, I'm Bridget, and this is my friend, Miya. We're big fans of yours."

Eyebrows lifting, I say, "Is that so? Well, thank you very much. You ladies having fun tonight?"

They look young. Not too young, but if I had to guess, they're probably barely old enough to drink. Copper Lake U students, I'm sure.

"Yeah, we are," Miya replies, lifting her red Solo cup to her lips and taking a sip of whatever liquor is in there.

"When we heard about this party tonight, we knew we had to come," Bridget practically purrs as she steps closer to me. "We were hoping to get to meet you."

The sweet scent of vanilla and coconut wafts over to me from her. I know what she's insinuating—what they're both probably wanting—and while they're very attractive girls, I have no interest in going there tonight. Deciding to nip this in the bud, I grin at them both before taking another drag. As I blow out the smoke, I tell them, "You know who'd really love to see you beautiful ladies?" When their eyes widen in question, I point behind them. "The birthday boy. Colt would love to celebrate tonight between the two of you."

Somehow that works, and they prance away excitedly. After I finish my cigarette, I grab a bottle of water and take a seat by the fire again. Shooter and Sterling are back there, too, except Sterling is now propped in Shooter's lap. They're in the middle of a heated discussion about football, and I sit back and enjoy listening to them bicker back and forth about it.

By the time the fire starts to die, my eyes are scratchy and I'm ready to climb into bed and call it a night, already mentally rearranging my morning in my head, knowing I'm going to get up extra early to help Xander with his farm chores. Doing a quick round, I say bye to everybody before I jump into my truck and take off. On my way out, I spot Colt with those girls who were talking to me, and I chuckle to myself. He'll be nice and busy, it looks like. Similar to how Shooter was before Sterling came around, Colt is a natural flirt. He loves the attention, and there's never a shortage of buckle bunnies around to keep him occupied. I love that for him.

For many years, I thought there was something wrong

with me. Unlike my friends, the idea of dating and hooking up never appealed to me. I lost my virginity much later in life than everybody else I knew—at almost nineteen—and I think I only did it to say it was done, not because I was dying to do it. Sure, it was nice, and it felt good in the moment, but it never seemed like something I couldn't do for myself.

I've never struggled with being alone. I happen to enjoy my own company, and I don't know… I never felt the pull toward finding someone to fill my bed for the night to be all that alluring. That's not to say I don't hook up from time to time, especially when we're on the road for the season, but it's usually after a few too many drinks, and by the morning, I'm internally rolling my eyes at my actions.

There was a period when I thought maybe it was a relationship I wanted, and that's why hooking up never appealed to me, but any time I've tried to have a girlfriend, I just never felt overly connected to her deeper than a friendship. I know it's not because I'm turned off by relationships or commitment, because I *do* want to settle down with someone and start a life with them. Hell, it's the whole reason I bought my house. But I want that person to be someone who makes me feel like I couldn't imagine living without them. Not someone I have to question if I even have romantic feelings for, or if it's just a friendship, that'll eventually lead to sex.

That girl's out there somewhere, I'm sure, and I'll find her one day. In the meantime, I'm in no rush. I'm cool being alone, riding out this rodeo career, and letting whatever's meant to happen, happen. Maybe I'm just a sappy romantic with unrealistic expectations over what a relationship is supposed to feel like, but after watching the way my parents love each other unconditionally, how they still to this day are playful and flirty with each other, and how vibrant their adoration is for one another after so many years together, I don't think my expectations are that crazy.

My house is about twenty minutes from the ranch. This time of night is my favorite time to drive. The stars are out, the moon is shining, and nobody is on the road. I can cruise with my windows down, my music turned up, and just let the road take me. Sometimes when I can't sleep, I'll hop in the pickup and drive with no destination in sight. Typically, I'll just make a loop through town, and be good to sleep after, but sometimes, I'll drive through the outskirts of town and get myself lost for a few hours. I don't know what it is about backroads in the dead of night that's so comforting.

Thankfully, be it the few beers I had or the farm work I helped Xander with, tonight isn't one of those nights when sleep escapes me. As soon as I'm home, I brush my teeth, strip down, climb into bed, and I swear I'm out before my head even hits the pillow.

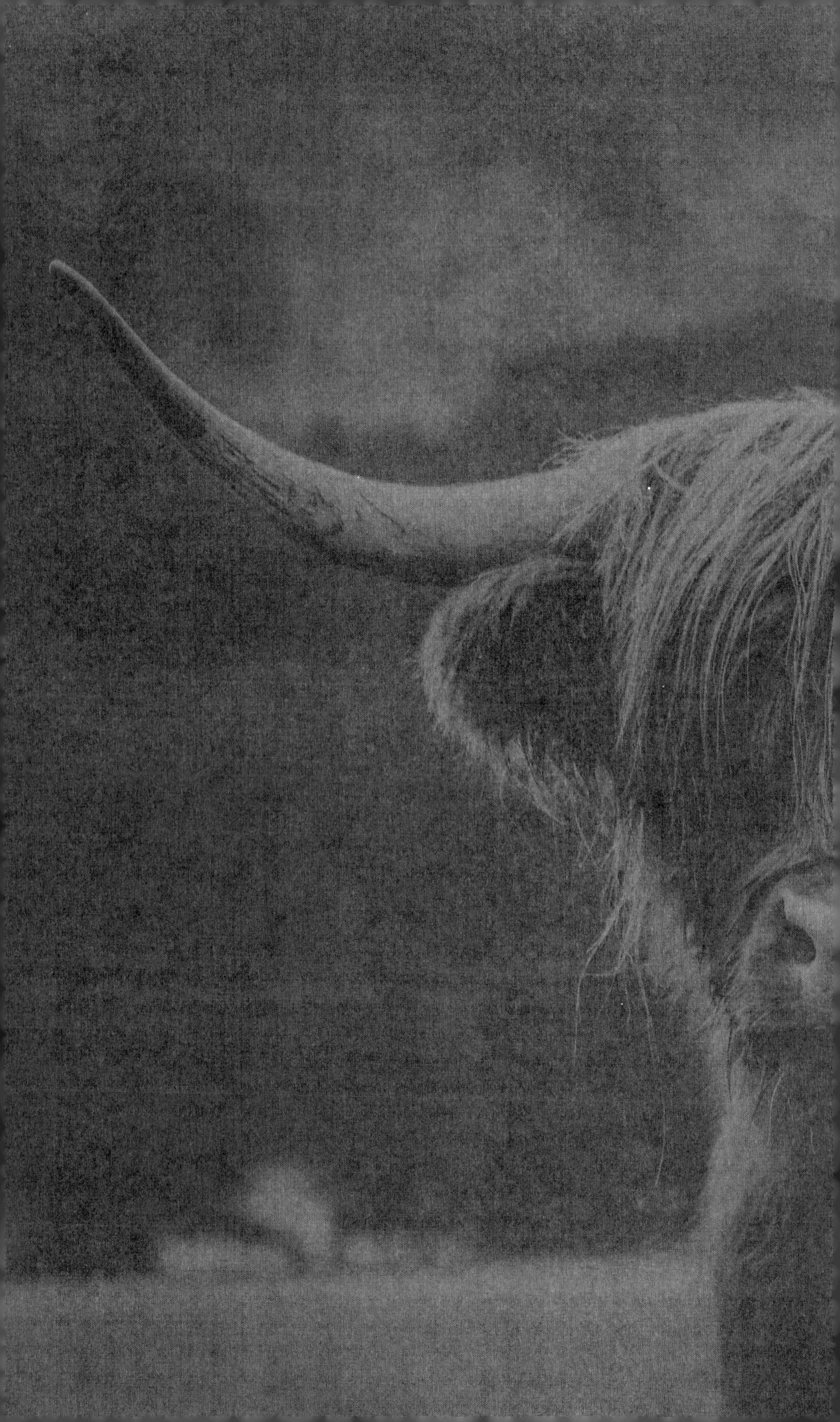

Chapter 4

Xander Dawson

Sunrises here are unreal. I've never seen anything like it. The entire sky burns a rich orange, blanketing everything beneath it in the vibrant color before it fades to a pastel pink as the sun finds its proper place in the sky. Everything feels fresh, like the world is truly waking up. You can't help but watch it, enthralled by its beauty. Which is exactly what I've been doing every single day for the almost week since I arrived here.

Each morning when I wake up, I brew a pot of coffee—thankfully, now I have creamer—and take the steaming hot cup of joe out onto the back porch. As of the last couple of mornings, the fluffy brown cow who looks like she just got a blow-out, whose name I've learned is Agatha, trots up to the house and stands on the edge of the porch beside my rocking chair while I sip my coffee and scroll through my phone.

Unlike the black and white dairy cow named Tootsie, who for the most part remains in the pasture at all times unless it's time to milk her—which is an interesting fucking experience—

Agatha doesn't have to follow the same rules. When I asked Aunt Colette about it, she compared Agatha to Houdini, and said when she was a calf, she always found a way to escape the pasture. All she ever wanted to do was be in the yard where the chickens were, so eventually, my aunt stopped trying to contain her.

Essentially, Agatha thinks she's an oversized dog, and to be honest...I don't disagree. She's really fucking cute and soft, and sometimes, it's like she forgets she has huge horns coming out the side of her boxy head because she'll bump them on this or that on the porch or in the yard. She's started following me out to the barn as I feed the animals—including her—and get the horses out to pasture. When it comes time to muck the stalls, she'll hang out at the door of the barn, observing as I go from stall to stall. If I didn't know any better, I'd think she was a robot my aunt put into place to make sure I was properly caring for her animals.

Like clockwork, I've been out on the porch for about ten minutes, and up walks sweet Agatha. Her hair is flattened on one side of her head, like bedhead, further proving my guess that she strolls up here upon waking up.

"Good morning, Aggie girl." I've found myself speaking to her like I would a baby. She seems to like it. "Did you sleep well last night? Get up to any trouble after lights out?" She, of course, doesn't respond, but I continue as if she did. "No trouble for me either."

My aunt's been in the hospital for all of two days, I've been in town for five, and I'm already speaking to animals like I'm Dr. fucking Doolittle. Lord help my sanity when it's time to leave this town.

Another new constant that seems to have made its way in

my day-to-day since arriving strolls up the steps to the porch, dark brown cowboy boots pulled up over a pair of sinfully fitting gray sweatpants. Baseball cap flipped backwards on his head, Cope's rich brown eyes light up as they meet mine, a blindingly white grin pulling on his lips. "Morning, city boy."

As if this were his own porch, and he has all the right in the world, he plops down in the rocking chair beside me, reaching down to run a few stroking pets up and down the side of Aggie. In his lap is a clear Tupperware container with a red lid, the contents inside could be anything.

"You know you don't have to come check up on me every morning, right?" Which he has. Monday rolled around when my aunt left for the hospital, and here showed up Cope, bright eyed and bushy tailed, ready to help. He also brings some sort of breakfast pastry each day, too. Yesterday, they were bagels that tasted so fresh, I could've moaned with each bite.

Cope chuckles, the sound deep and gruff, as he eyes me, a lazy shrug lifting his shoulder. "But if I don't, nothing'll ever get done properly. You city boys don't know how to do nothing right," he teases.

"Right," I reply with a small laugh. "I was sure after Meadow kicked you yesterday, making you fall nearly in a pile of her shit, you'd never come back."

He scrubs a hand down his face, fighting a smile, almost looking…bashful? "It was my fault for spooking her like that. I know better than to approach a horse where she can't see me."

"Yeah, rookie move," I reply in a taunting tone. "I thought one of us was supposed to be a professional horseback rider."

"*Bronc* rider," he groans. "There's a big difference."

I know that. Teasing him is just really fucking fun. Seeing him get all exasperated and huffy; it's too cute to pass up.

Guilt hits me thick and heavy at that thought. I shouldn't be doing anything to cause a *cute* reaction out of anybody who isn't Henry. We've talked a few times over the last several days, finally. A few text messages throughout the day, some phone calls, we even FaceTimed the other night like I'd wanted. He's busy with work; I get that. It just seems like ever since I told him I was coming here for a few weeks, things between us have been…distant. And I don't just mean geographically.

Whatever. I can't sit here and stress over the status of my relationship. Not when I currently have a million and one things to do on a daily basis.

Nodding toward the container in his lap, I ask, "What treat did you bring me this morning?"

Glancing down like he forgot it was there, he grabs the Tupperware, handing it to me. "Muffins," he replies. "Apple cinnamon. I made them last night."

"You…made them?" Taking them from his offering hand, I peel open the lid, the sweet scent wafting out, making my stomach grumble. I'm not normally a big breakfast person, but all this food he's been bringing every day may just turn me into one. "These smell *sooooo* good."

"It's nothing special," he replies, clearly trying to downplay himself. "They're from a box."

I take a bite out of one, the flavor exploding on my taste buds. A moan slips out before I can stop myself, and I fall back into the rocking chair. "Holy fuck, Cope. These are delicious."

When I glance over at him, he's watching me intently. Almost studying me, and when he swallows, I can't help but track his Adam's apple as it bobs in his throat. "Glad you like 'em."

Holding out the open container toward him, I ask, "Want one?"

Cope nods, taking one. "Thanks."

We eat a couple while I finish my coffee, and when we're done, we head out to the barn to get started. He's been coming here for several days now, and I feel like I'm getting the hang of what I'm supposed to do, so we work together and check everything off the list efficiently while still chatting. I've started to look forward to these mornings. When I first made up my mind to come here, I thought everything about this trip would be dreadful, but between the gorgeous sunrises, Aggie, and Cope coming to help me, there's nothing dreadful about this.

As we're walking the horses out to the pasture, Cope asks, "What's Washington like?"

"Nothing all that special," I reply with a laugh. "I live in the eastern part of the state, which is desert-like. It gets hot as hell in the summer, and really fucking cold in the winter. It's also flat and brown and boring. Not anything like the Seattle area where it's lush and green and wet."

"Have you traveled a lot?"

"Nah. I went to college in the next city over, and I've, of course, visited Seattle a few times in my life, but aside from coming here, I've only been to California once. And that was only because I went with Henry on a business trip he had to go on. It was pretty there, but too damn expensive."

"Who's Henry?" Cope asks curiously, and I freeze.

I didn't even realize what I said. What if he's a homophobe? Cope seems like a nice, genuine guy, but you never know, I am in the country after all. I could lie…but I kind of suck at lying, and the idea of not being truthful with him makes a pit grow in my stomach that I don't quite understand.

Fuck it.

"Henry's, uh…he's my boyfriend."

I've known I was gay since I very first started having crushes as a kid, and I've been out just as long. My mom has always been more than supportive, and never made me feel like it was something I needed to *come out* as. Not to mention, Washington is a very accepting state, so I've never had to deal with hate regarding my sexuality, but I know next to nothing about Wyoming and how they handle things.

Cope turns his head, looking at me, but I won't meet his gaze. I keep walking straight ahead, the weight of his eyes enough to make me squirm. "Oh, boyfriend." He says the word like he's trying it out on his tongue. "So, you're gay?"

I can't help but laugh as I finally turn my head and meet his gaze. "Yup. So, I'm gay."

He smiles, nodding. "My best friend is gay. So is his boyfriend." He pauses before adding, "Well, obviously."

Sniggering, I reply, "Well, in your defense, he could've been bisexual, so not totally obvious."

We let the horses go, watching them for a moment. Glancing to my left, I spot Tootsie, where she likes to stand in the morning near the fence.

"How long have you guys been together?" Cope asks. "You and Henry."

That's such a hard question to answer. Henry and I are complicated, and we've always been complicated. What started out as a random hook-up here and there turned into a friends-with-benefits type deal that lasted entirely too long, then ended up with me getting hurt, and after we went through all of that, we finally got into a semi-functioning relationship.

So, I give Cope the most simplified answer I possibly can. "On and off for about two years."

"How'd you meet?"

Internally, I scream. He's asking the worst questions, and he doesn't even know it. I hate telling this story because it shows off—what most people see as—a power imbalance. But again, I'm a shitty liar, so I give him the simplified version. Which, I guess, *technically* would be a white lie.

"We met at my store. He came in as a customer, and ended up becoming a regular."

"Store?" he questions, sounding confused. "I just realized I've never asked you what you do for work."

"Oh, I own a marijuana dispensary back home."

His head snaps in my direction, brows lifted clear into his hairline. "What? You do?"

I nod. "Yeah. It's legal in Washington to purchase, consume, and even, in some cases, grow marijuana."

"That's so fucking wild to me," he mutters. "It's illegal here, I think."

"It is," I confirm. "Checked before coming here. Gotta say, it's a little weird being in a place where it's not legal when, for most of my life, it's been a normal thing to be around."

"That's so cool. So, you own your own business then?"

"I do! Well, I have a business partner, but yeah."

"Badass," Cope exclaims as we start walking back toward the barn. "How does that work with you being here, though?"

"I've got employees who work the store, and my partner. I'm taking somewhat of a leave of absence, but I can still handle a lot of the paperwork and stuff from here, since it's digital."

When we make it back, we spot Aggie taunting some of the chickens. It's kind of funny the way she'll stalk them around the yard, pissing them off until they chase her. I've never seen a cow run before, but she sure does.

"What about you?" I ask, finally voicing the question I've

been dying to ask for days now. "Any girlfriend for you?"

Normally, I wouldn't assume someone's sexuality. No matter how straight presenting someone looks, you just never know. I don't necessarily scream homosexual from the outside. But the way he specified that his best friend was gay leads me to believe Cope, himself, is not queer…as disappointing as that is.

"Nah, I don't have time for all that," he replies.

"Sure, sure. You probably get enough action on the road that you don't have to worry about that," I murmur, both wanting and not wanting to know more.

Yesterday, when we were working on morning chores, I asked a little bit about how his bronc riding works. He explained how he and his friends—whom are also in the rodeo—travel for several months out of the year, competing in various shows. All sounds very nomad. I don't feel like I'd enjoy traveling that much. I'm no introvert; I enjoy being around people, but I also very much enjoy my own bed.

Cope chuckles. "Yeah, no. I'm not really the hook-up type of guy, to be honest."

Hearing that calms something inside of me. Something that has no business feeling calm. The idea of him hooking up with random people makes my stomach turn.

You have a fucking boyfriend and he's a straight cowboy from Wyoming, Xander. You shouldn't fucking care what he does between the sheets.

We finish up what we're doing, but not before we eat the rest of the muffins he brought. I'm dying for a shower, and as soon as he leaves, I'm taking one. Which I don't have to wait long, because about twenty minutes later, he's wiping off his hands on the front of his pants and telling me, "Welp, I gotta hit the gym." He goes to the gym every single day. It's insane.

"I don't think I'll be back this evening. I'm going fishing with a couple of my buddies, but I'll see you in the morning?"

One thing about having farm animals is you have to do everything you did in the morning in reverse at night.

"You really don't have to keep coming over here," I tell him. "I'm sure you got better things to do."

He pins with me a stare that makes me want to laugh. "Knock that shit off. I don't mind, and I wouldn't do something I didn't want to do anyway."

"Somehow, I don't think that's true, cowboy," I mutter.

He shrugs, chuckling. "Okay, you're probably right. But this isn't one of those times. I like helping you out. We're friends. And friends help each other."

Friends. Right.

I nod wordlessly before letting a smile slip through when he jabs me on the arm with his elbow playfully. "I mean it," he says sternly. "I'll see you in the morning, city boy."

"Okay, okay. Have fun fishing. Although that doesn't sound fun at all."

"Hater," Cope calls out over his shoulder as he leaves the yard. I can't help but watch him go. His long legs. The way his ass looks oddly perfect behind those sweats. The damp strands of hair sitting at his nape, hanging out from under his hat. He's so fucking good looking. *And nice.*

Since when am I swoony at *nice*?

I'm in trouble.

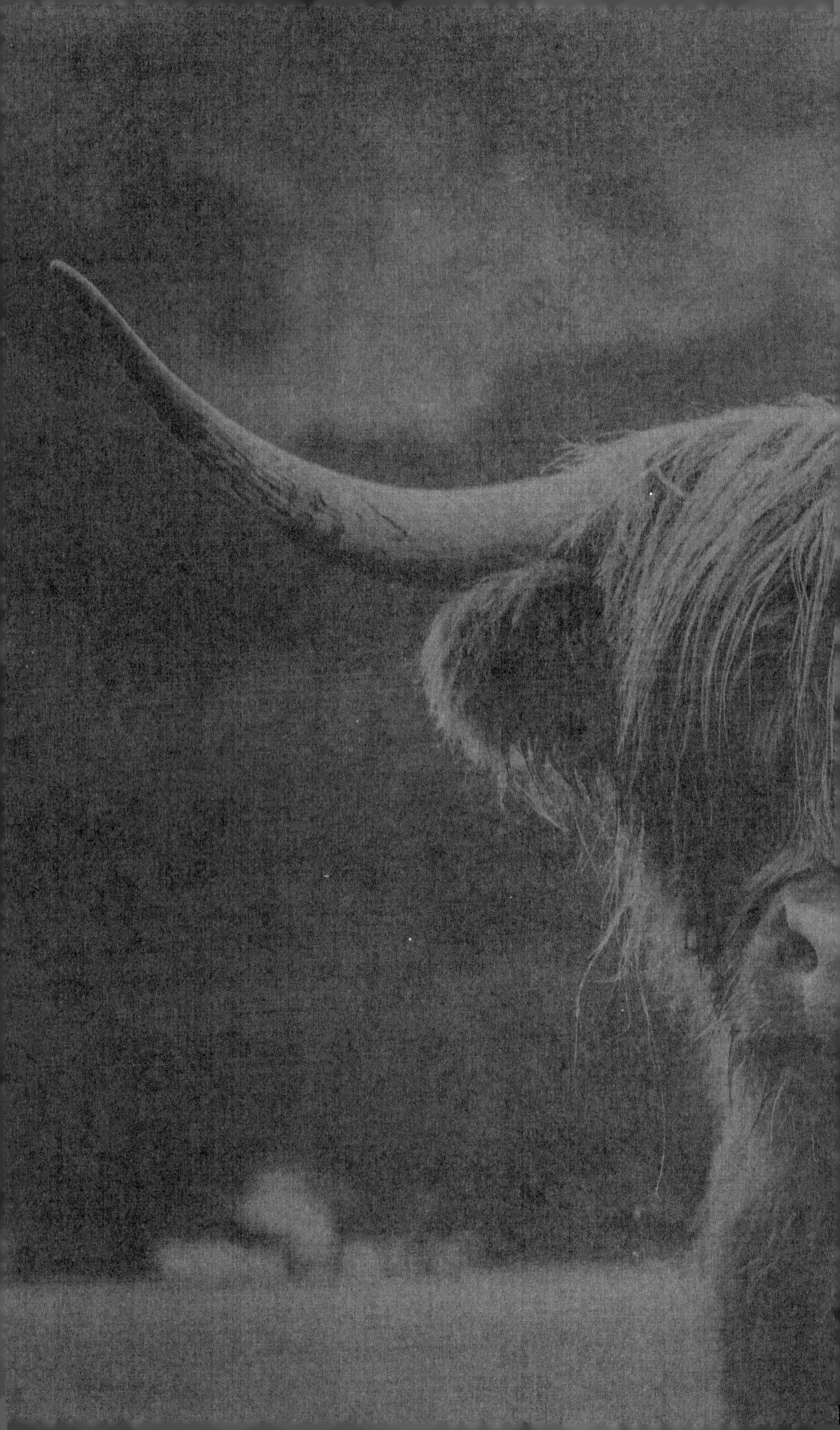

Chapter 5

Xander Dawson

"Will you sit down and let me make you some lunch?" I ask with a huff.

Aunt Colette got home from the hospital this afternoon, and she's being difficult as all hell. She fought with me at the hospital when I tried to take her bags and put them in the trunk for her, then she fought with me when we got home and I tried to take them inside for her, and now she won't sit down and fucking relax. The doctor said she needs to take it easy for a while, and she's getting around with crutches, for Christ's sake. Those can't be comfortable propped under her arms. You'd think she'd want to give her pits a rest.

"Boy, don't you tell me what to do. I changed your diapers."

I roll my eyes where she can't see me. "Has literally nothing to do with what I'm asking now, Auntie."

"I can make my own lunch," she grumbles, wobbling toward the kitchen. Intercepting her, I place my hands on her shoulders, leveling her with a stare.

"You *just* had hip replacement surgery, and the doctor

stressed the importance of taking it easy. I'm here for a reason—to help you. *Let* me help you." Her features soften a tad, and I know I'm getting through to her. "Please, go take a seat at the table, and I'll bring you a plate when I'm done."

Lips pressed into a thin line, she nods. "Yeah, alright. Thank you."

My mom and my aunt are two of the most stubborn people I've ever met. I truly don't understand where I got my laid-back nature from. In the kitchen, I fix us both turkey and Swiss sandwiches on this French bread I found at the store yesterday, with some sliced cantaloupe and watermelon and chips on the side. I don't know if she'll be able to stomach all of that, but I want to give her enough just in case.

Once my aunt went to the hospital, I finally caved and took her up on her offer to borrow her car. Mine's in the shop, who knows how long that'll take, and not having a mode of transportation wasn't logical. I don't like borrowing stuff from other people or accepting help. I should be able to do it myself.

Hmm…maybe I'm more like my mother and my aunt after all.

After I pour us each a glass of ice water, I bring everything to the table and sit across from her. She thanks me again before we dig in. The bread is so good. It's fresh, and it's so soft.

"How have things been going around here?" she asks between bites.

"Great. I'm basically a pro now. Could run this shit in my sleep." I flash her a smile.

"Copeland still helping you out?"

I've never heard his full name before. And then I remember she saw us working together before she went to the hospital.

"Yup."

She nods. "He's such a nice boy."

"That he is," I agree, willing my mind to not focus on him. It doesn't work, so instead, I try to change the subject. "Auntie, can I ask you something?"

She arches a brow questioningly. "If you must."

"Why here? Like, what made you decide to move from Washington to Copper Lake?"

Taking a few bites, she seems to think over her answer before she speaks. "I don't know if you know this, but when your mother and I were little, we lived in a town very similar to here. We didn't own any farm animals or anything, but I remember loving the small-town feel. The country life. I don't have one set reason why I chose here specifically. But I'm glad I did. I love living here, love taking care of all the animals. All of it brings me great joy. A joy I didn't find back in Washington."

"So, you don't miss it?"

Shaking her head, she replies, "No, I don't. Of course, I miss being able to see you, Gemma, and your mom any time I want, but as for the location and living there, not at all."

After we finish eating, I take our plates and put them in the dishwasher before helping my aunt to her room. She's pretty tired, probably from the medication, so she ends up taking a nap for a few hours while I sit on the porch in the rocking chair, doing crossword puzzles. I've enjoyed them for as long as I can remember. One of my earliest memories is sitting in my mother's lap and working on these on weekend mornings before she had to go into work.

Later on, when I'm doing the evening farm chores, I decide to call Henry. I feel like I should miss him more than I do. That thought makes me feel guilty enough that I'm popping my ear buds in and dialing his number as I feed the animals. It rings a few times, and I think he might not pick up. Eventually, he does.

"This is Henry?" I don't know why he always answers the phone like it's a business call. He knows who's calling.

"Hey, babe," I say softly. "What're you up to?"

"Hey, Xan. I'm driving to a meeting. How's things over in bumfuck Wyoming?"

Clenching my jaw, I grind my molars together. Something about his question is rubbing me the wrong way. Maybe it's his tone, or just his overall distaste for the town he has no clue about.

"They're fine. My aunt came home today."

"So, you're coming home?"

My brows pinch together, because I don't know how many times I went over this with Henry before I left, but I thought I made it clear. "No, she still needs to recover. I'm staying until she's able to take care of everything around here by herself."

"I don't understand why she didn't just hire someone," he grumbles. "It's a little unrealistic to expect a grown man to put his life on hold just to help her out."

It's moments like this I have to remind myself that Henry isn't close with his family. He doesn't understand doing things that may be a little inconvenient to help those you love. He's a very cut and dry type of person. Everything he invests time into has to have some sort of a gain from it. He's a businessman, through and through.

Trying to change the subject because I know if I don't, I'll just end up getting annoyed like every other time we've landed in this conversation, I say, "I miss you. Maybe you can come visit soon?"

He sighs into the phone, and I already know it's not going to be favorable. "Xan, you know how busy I am. We all can't have jobs we can just drop whenever we want."

Ouch.

"Well, my birthday is next month. Maybe you can make an exception for me," I say in the sweetest voice I can muster up, despite the frustration building in my chest.

Henry scoffs into the phone. "You think you're still going to be there in a *month*? That's ridiculous, Xander."

I roll my eyes. "I'm just trying to think ahead. Do you think maybe you could?"

"We'll see. But, babe, I gotta go. I just got to the office, and this meeting is important."

They're always important.

"Okay, I love you."

The line disconnects, and disappointment flares. Henry's been much more distant from me since I left Washington. I figured it would happen, but thinking it and seeing it come to fruition are very different things. I go to shove my phone into my pocket so I can finish these chores, but before I do, I notice I have a new text message. My stomach flutters as I read the name.

Cope: Hey, it's supposed to be a nice, cool day tomorrow. Wanna go for a trail ride after we finish with the chores? I know a really cool place we can go.

The first thought that pops into my head is, *aww he wants to take me on a trail ride?* The second, more blaring, thought is, *I have no fucking clue how to ride a horse.*

Surely, it can't be that hard, right? You hop on up and hold on tight… I can do that. Hell yeah, I can do that.

Me: Sure. That'd be fun. :)

He responds immediately, and I re-read it about a dozen times before putting the phone away.

Cope: Sweet. Can't wait.

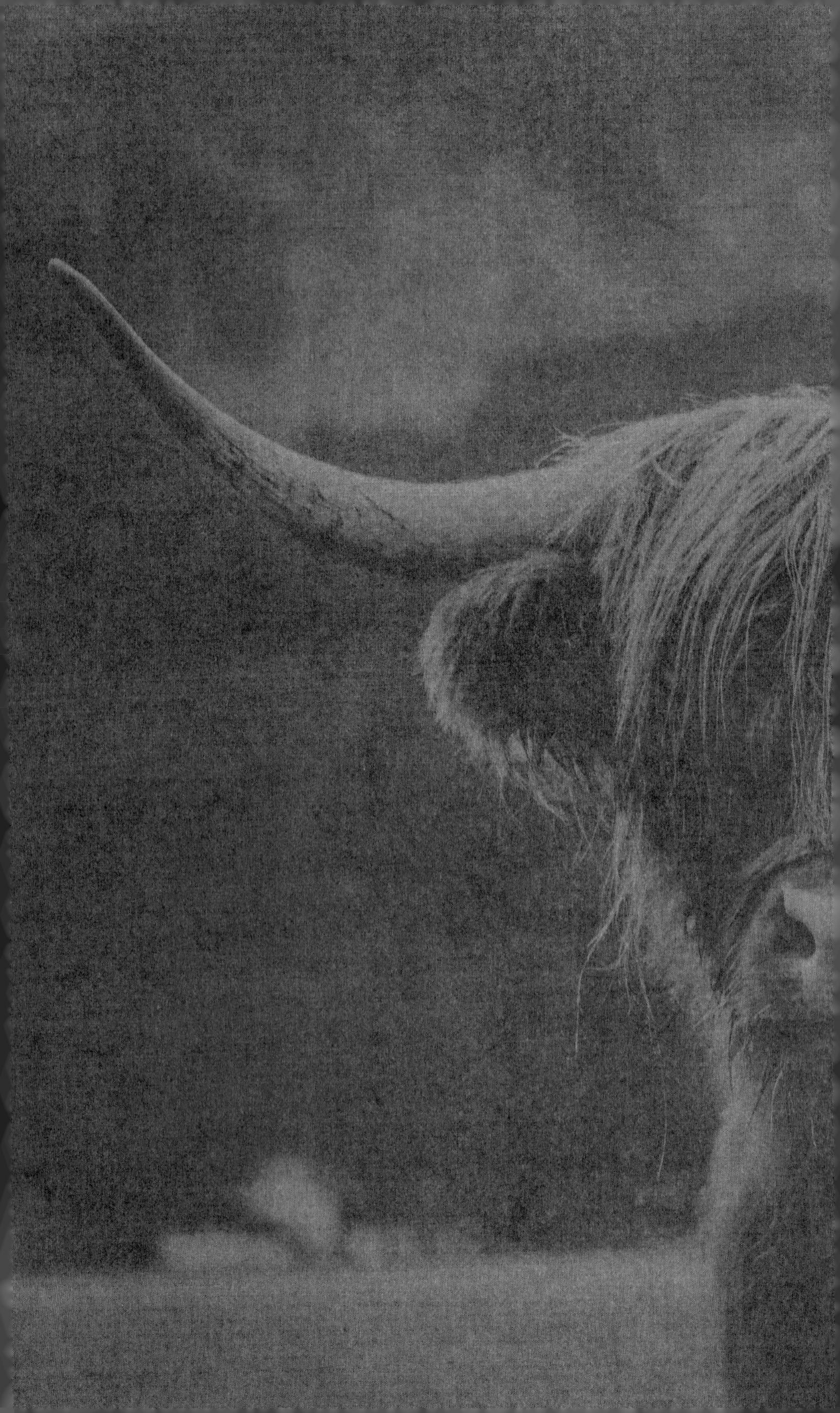

Chapter 6

Cope Murphy

"You've seriously *never* been on a horse before?" I ask in disbelief. "The first time I rode a horse, I had probably just learned to walk."

Xander rolls his eyes, leveling me with a stare. "Cope, your father was a famous bronc rider. Of course, you rode a horse at a young age. My mother was a bartender who barely made enough to get by. Horses weren't the first thing on her to-do list when it came to my sister and I."

"Okay, but as a teenager or as an adult… Never?"

"Oh, my God," he grumbles. "Are you going to show me how to get on this fucking horse, or stand here and judge me all morning?"

"Sheesh, somebody is touchy." I can't help the smirk that fights to break free. I can tell he doesn't like not knowing how to do things. I saw it initially when I helped him on the farm that first day. He's somebody who wants to be great at everything he does, so in turn, learning new tasks is frustrating. Shooter is the same way. "It's easy. Here, I'll help you."

I walk over, positioning myself behind him, placing my hands on his hips. He freezes for a moment, his breath audibly hitching. "Is this okay?" I ask, not wanting to make him uncomfortable.

He lets himself relax before he nods. "Yeah, it's fine."

Tapping his hip with my hand, I say, "Take your left foot and stick it in the stirrup. Put your left hand there—yup, like that—and now, putting your weight on that left foot, hoist yourself up and throw your right leg over her."

Xander goes to do as I say, and I tighten my grip on his waist, helping him up as best as I can. He's pretty light, so it doesn't take much to get him positioned on the horse the right way. His scent wafts around me as he jumps up; fresh, clean, and almost sweet. It smells nice. When he gets into place, he peers down at me, his cheeks flushed and his bottom lip tucked between his teeth.

My stomach does a weird flip at the sight of him, and I suddenly feel flustered. *What the hell?* Clearing my throat, I push past that and grin up at him. "See, that wasn't so hard, was it?"

He shakes his head, returning the smile, but it looks forced. Almost like a wince.

"Are you okay?"

"Yeah, it's just..." He blows out a breathy laugh. "I'm nervous. I've never done this, and she's massive. But I'm okay."

Something inside of me melts at his honesty. "I'll ride right beside you. It'll be good," I assure him.

Before we saddled up the horses, I went over how to ride them—how to get them to go, to stop, slow down—so once I climb up on my own horse, I go over that one more time before we get started. True to my word, I stay beside him the whole time, but at first, I stay a few feet back so I can keep him in my sight. He's a little wobbly and a lot stiff. It's more than clear he's nervous, but it's endearing to watch.

Growing up in Copper Lake and being around the rodeo as much as I was all throughout my life, it's not often I meet people who've never ridden horses. So, getting to show Xander the ropes—literally and figuratively—and watching him find his footing is fun for me. Glancing over at him, I can't help but smile to myself because he very much looks like somebody not from around here, and I don't mean that in a negative way. It's just the facts.

Everybody here is either a cowboy or a farmer. It's rare to see someone with a style like Xander's. I wouldn't go as far as to say he dresses emo, but it walks that line. He's currently wearing ripped, dark-wash skinny jeans that seem entirely too tight to ride in, a white band tee—don't ask me what band; I don't have a clue—a black zip-up, and the same Van's he's always wearing. He must've washed them after they got dirty last week when he was doing his chores.

His black floppy hair has a slight curl to it, and it hangs over his forehead in a way that has my fingers itching to brush it back. *That's interesting...* A few of his fingers are adorned with rings, and the black polish on them is still chipping away.

Xander doesn't look like a cowboy or a farmer, but I like that about him.

The farther down the trail we get, the more comfortable he looks. His lithe body sways ever so slightly as the horse walks, and I can't help but be mesmerized. It's weird, the way Xander holds my attention the way he does. From the moment I saw him on the side of the road, I've felt enamored by his presence. This constant need to be around him is new. Sure, I have friends who I enjoy being around from time to time, but

I also thoroughly enjoy my alone time. I'm not even this way with Shooter, who's my best friend.

With Xander, it's like I've had this urge to be near him. To help him, and learn as much about him as I can. He fascinates me. It's why I've come over every morning to help him out. Of course, I'll always help someone in need. It's just the gentleman in me, but I don't think I'd go this out of my way to make sure someone gets the help they need.

It's all so unusual, but I'm choosing to not think too hard about it because, while it's different, it also feels right. Xander is new here. He needs friends, and I want to be that friend. Why not? Nothing wrong with that.

We ride for a couple of miles before getting to where I want to be. The scenery and the view here are picturesque. It's one of my favorite places to go when I want to be alone and with nature. I've never run into anybody else here. The sounds of the river pattering by down below and the birds chirping in the distance are calming. Relaxing.

"Holy shit," Xander says as he maneuvers his way to the ground. "This is gorgeous."

His ice-blue eyes are wide as he takes in our surroundings. Clear skies surround tall mountain ridges as far as the eye can see, and the sun blankets the view, giving everything an early afternoon glow. It's fifty-five degrees right now, and while we're both wearing jackets, the warmth from the sun is enough to keep us comfortable.

"I found this place shortly after I bought my house. Isn't it great?"

We attach the leads to a nearby branch so the horses can relax and graze without risking them getting away from us and potentially lost. I shoulder off the backpack I'm wearing, unzipping it before pulling out the food I have stored in there.

"What're you doing?" Xander asks quietly, standing a few feet away from me.

"Packed us a lunch," I reply. "Can you lay the blanket down that I have draped on the back of Blonc?"

When Xander doesn't respond or move right away, I glance up and find him watching me with an expression I can't place. He nods when he notices me looking at him. "Sure."

Once the blanket is on the ground, I kneel down. Ham and cheddar sandwiches wrapped in tin foil get set down as I grab the bags of Doritos and water bottles I placed in the bag. A Tupperware container filled with baby carrots and cucumbers and containers of strawberry yogurt join the bunch. I hand Xander a plastic spoon as he sits down across from me, and he smiles warmly as he takes it.

"You didn't have to do all this," he mutters.

"It's no big deal." I shrug. "You've made lunch for us before."

"Yeah, but you bring me breakfast nearly every morning," he replies with a chuckle.

"You could just say thank you," I tease back. Tossing him a wink, I hand him a sandwich before grabbing one of my own and unwrapping it.

Rolling his eyes, he bites off a large chunk before saying with a very full mouth, "Thank you, kind gentleman."

Laughter bubbles in my throat, and I nearly choke on the bread. "Now, that's more like it."

He waves his hand in front of him in a way you would when greeting royalty. It makes me snort, almost spitting out the drink I just took.

After I nearly hack up a lung coughing, and I'm sure I'm not going to die, I ask, "How's Larry? He adjusting to the new house?"

Xander glances over, a look crossing his face I can't place. "You remembered his name," he mutters with something like disbelief in his voice.

"How could I forget a name like Larry?" I laugh.

He shrugs. "Touché. He's doing good. He adapts pretty well, I'll give him that. He's not too fond of my aunt, but he enjoys watching the animals frolic outside from the window perch, so long as they don't come up to the porch." He laughs as if remembering something funny. "A few days ago, he was cleaning himself in the window when Aggie came up the steps and stuck her snoot right against the window. It scared Larry half to death. I was walking through the living room as it happened, and I've never seen him jump so high."

I join Xander in laughing, the image in my mind hysterical. "It's nice of your aunt to let you bring him when you came here."

He nods. "She wasn't crazy about the idea, honestly, but I think she knew it was the only way I would be able to come."

We fall into a comfortable silence, eating our sandwiches as Xander looks around the area, taking it all in. "This really is beautiful up here. It's insane that places like this are real."

"Washington has some beautiful places, too. I've seen them online before. The mountains and the crystal-blue lakes. Gorgeous scenery up there."

"Yeah, but that's mostly all in western Washington. Where I'm from is a whole lot flatter and browner." He guzzles down some water before continuing. "Don't get me wrong, it has its own type of beauty, but it's nothing like this. This is…stunning."

Xander takes another large bite of his sandwich, a glob of mayonnaise smearing on the corner of his mouth. I watch him chew and swallow, then once he's done, the tip of his pink tongue pokes out to lick up the mess, and my mouth goes dry.

Like I've just been caught with my hand in the cookie jar, I dart my gaze away before he can catch me eyeing him like a lunatic. My heart thumps, the blood roaring in my ears as I work on steadying my rapid breathing.

What the hell was that about?

I'm so stuck in my head that I completely miss when he says something, only catching the tail end of it. Glancing back over at him, he's watching me with a weird look on his face. Probably waiting for me to respond to whatever it was that he said.

"What'd you say? Sorry, was zoning out."

He smiles, the gesture brightening up his whole face. "I asked when you start your rodeo stuff again?"

The way he says *"rodeo stuff"* makes me chuckle. "The season starts in the spring, but finals are in December, and I'll be participating in those."

"Where's that at?"

"Las Vegas. It's a huge national event."

"And what do you do there? Do you just..." He gestures his hand in front of him in a circular motion like he's trying to find the right words. "Ride the horses?"

Throwing my head back, I half-laugh, half-groan before tossing my balled-up foil at him. "How many times do I have to tell you, it's *bronc* riding."

His smirk tells me he knows exactly what he's doing. He shrugs, though, like he has no idea. "So sorry, Mr. Cowboy. *Bronc riding.*"

Something about the way he says that has my stomach bottoming out. The way he affects me is so strange. I don't feel like this with any of my other friends, and plenty of them give me a hard time, just like he's been doing.

"But yes, it's a ten-day event where the best of the best go up against one another in each sport. There're nightly winners and prizes given, but at the end of day ten, an overall winner is crowned in each category, and they take the prize and the title."

Xander's thick black brows furrow. "Prize? Like money?"

"Yup, like money."

"Is it a lot of money?" His eyes go wide as soon as the words leave his mouth. "Shit, am I allowed to ask that?"

Chuckling, I wave him off. "It's fine. I don't mind. But yeah, it can be a lot of money. We have the ability to earn throughout the season too, depending on where we place, but NFR is a much larger pool of money, and it's what most of us live off of year-round. Well, that and sponsorships."

"NFR?"

"National Finals Rodeo," I explain. "It's the name of the event."

He nods, downing another sip of the water. "Think you'll win?"

"Shit, I hope so." I laugh. "I got close last year. Took second place, but I'm gunning for the world champ title."

We fall into a comfortable silence as we finish our lunch, taking in the view. I need to hit the gym after this, and I told Shooter I'd come over and help him build a fence later on today, but being right here is so relaxing and nice. There isn't a part of me that wants to end this.

Eventually, once Xander's done, he looks over at me and says, "I looked you up."

It takes me by surprise, and I couldn't hide the grin that grows on my face even if I wanted to. "Oh, yeah?" I ask, quirking an eyebrow. "And what did you find?"

"It, uh…" He threads his fingers through his hair. "It looks dangerous."

I nod. "It can be."

"Have you ever gotten hurt?"

"Oh, plenty of times. When I was first learning, I'd end up black and blue for days. Once—it was my first year pro—I didn't have a good enough grip on the reins, and ended up getting bucked off. I landed wrong and dislocated my shoulder when I fell. Hurt like a motherfucker."

The color drains from Xander's face as he stares at me with widening eyes. "Jesus," he mumbles. "Why do it if you can get hurt?"

"Why do anything?" I throw back. "You can get hurt doing anything in life, whether that be physically or emotionally. I enjoy bronc riding. The thrill is unlike anything I've ever experienced before. When I'm out there, I feel unstoppable. On top of the world. I'd rather get to experience that high than stay on the sidelines where it's quote-unquote safe. Life's too short to play it safe, in my opinion. Not to mention, I'm damn good at what I do."

A slow smile creeps up on Xander's lips as he nods. "Your passion is…inspiring."

"It's intense," I mutter with a laugh. "You can say it. I can get a little intense about rodeo."

"Well, yeah, but it's also really cool to see how passionate you are about it. It's not often you see people go after what they want and what truly makes them happy."

"What about you? How'd you get into your line of business?"

It's still mind-blowing to me that he owns a marijuana store. Stuff like that doesn't exist here, at all. You get caught buying weed, you get in trouble. It always takes me back to see how other places in the country do things differently.

Xander snorts. "I've been a pothead since I was a teenager. When the legalization of weed happened, I wanted to own my own store, eventually. At first, it was a pipe dream, but then I got into college, and realized how good I am with numbers and all that. Suddenly, my pipe dream didn't feel as far-fetched anymore."

"So, you just decided to do it?"

"Well, in simple terms, yes. But there's a lot more that goes into it than just deciding to do it. We had to come up with a solid business plan, find the right location—which, there are tons of restrictions. It couldn't be near schools, parks, daycare centers, libraries, anything like that. Then we had to find investors and apply for the right loans. Once we had all that set, we had to apply and present it all to the Washington State Liquor and Cannabis Board. It was a long process that felt never ending."

"Damn." That's way more elaborate than I would've thought. But then again, what the hell do I know? "Is your boyfriend your business partner? What's his name again?"

"Henry," he offers, and something about his stupid name leaves a sour taste on the back of my tongue. I don't know why. "And no, he isn't. He is one of our investors, though."

Henry's a rich boy, then.

My brows lift at that. "Did you guys start dating before or after he invested?"

"After. It's a long story, but like I told you before, he came in as a customer for a while. That's how it started."

Xander's told me very little about this guy, but there's something about him I don't like. I just can't put my finger on what it is.

"How's he feel about you being here?" I ask, pushing down the growing distaste I feel in my gut.

"He thinks it's stupid that I'm here. That my aunt should've hired someone." Resting his arms behind himself, he extends his legs, probably trying to stretch them since he's been sitting crisscross for so long. "I think he's flying down here in a few weeks for my birthday."

I grit my teeth, not understanding this bubbling annoyance flaring inside of me. "Do I get to meet him?" I ask.

Xander's eyebrows furrow. "Do you want to?"

No. "Well, I think as your new best friend, I should meet the boyfriend, don't you?"

"Best friend, huh?" A smirk splits his face, a matching one reflected on mine.

Shrugging, I say, "I mean, I'd say we're well on our way. Wouldn't you?"

He laughs. "Obviously."

We hang out for a little while longer before the horses get restless. When we get back to his house, I help him put them out in the pasture before I head home to get changed for the gym. The entire time, I feel more confused than ever.

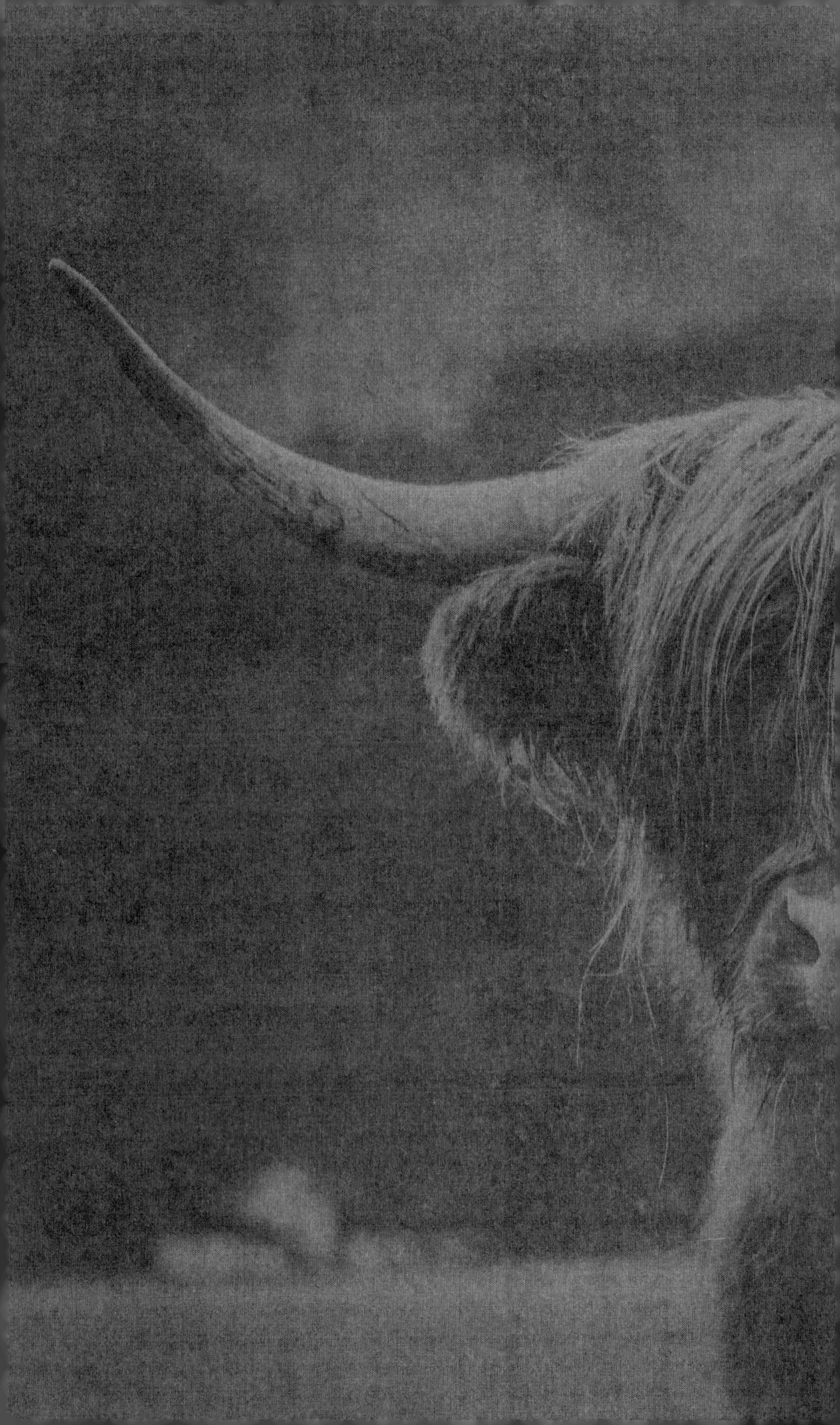

Chapter 7

Xander Dawson

Aunt Colette is starting to move more and do things around the house again. She's slow, and she tires easily, but she's doing it. And *boy*, is it annoying as all hell. Over the last several weeks, I've developed a nice routine when it comes to the chores and the housework. I can get everything done in a decent amount of time in the morning, and again in the evening. Well, now, all that's flown out the window. She *insists* on helping, and lord save my ass if I try to do it all myself.

I got my ass chewed out this morning after telling her she should go back inside and rest while I finish the chores. How dare I try to make things easy on her. It's not the whole fucking reason I'm here or anything. She's getting on my last goddamn nerve, and staring down at the text message I just got, I should be more excited, but instead, I stare at it like I don't know what to do with it.

Cope: There's a bonfire tonight up at my buddy's ranch. Wanna come?

Do I want to go? *Uh, yes.*
Should I go? *Probably not.*

It's been about a week since he took me on that trail ride turned picnic with a view, and it's a day that's been on my mind on a constant loop. Ever since he placed his hands on my body and helped me get on that horse, this slow-brewing crush I've felt toward him has intensified tenfold. It's like his fingertips burned their memory into my hips, even over my clothes, and the way I swear he was looking at me with some sort of desire while we ate.

I'm ninety-nine percent sure I'm making it all up, though, because as far as I know, Cope identifies as straight. Falling for a nice, straight cowboy from Wyoming is about the dumbest thing I could do, *especially* when I have a boyfriend, and shouldn't be developing feelings for anybody—straight or not—except him.

Although, it's not that anybody would know I have a boyfriend with how little Henry and I communicate. Honestly, that's neither here nor there. Yet still…I can't help but wholly want to accept Cope's offer to go hang out with him *and* his friends tonight.

Raking my fingers through my messy hair, I grumble before doing the only logical thing one can do…FaceTime my best friend for advice. It rings a few times before the line connects, his bright face taking up most of the screen, dirty blonde hair longer than usual.

"Xan, long time no see," he teases with a smirk.

Travis Barnes is somebody I met at the beginning of undergrad, and we quickly became close. We even lived together for a while in college, and then briefly a few years ago when he broke up with his cheating asshole boyfriend.

"How's it going?" I ask as I take a seat in the rocking chair on the porch. It takes Aggie no time at all to spot me from where she's at by the water trough and amble over.

Propping his phone on something, it becomes clear he's sitting at his desk at work. "Pretty good." He shrugs. "Just working. What about you? How are things where you're at?"

"Not too bad, actually. Well, up until the last few days, when my aunt decided it was time to get back to her normal."

"Already? Didn't she just have surgery, like, two weeks ago?"

Nodding, I say, "Yeah, dude. She's one stubborn woman."

"Hmm, must be where you get it from," he teases.

"Don't have a clue what you mean."

We both laugh, then his eyes lift to somewhere behind the phone. A dopey smile pulls on his lips. "Hey, what are you doing here?" he asks.

A deep, gruff voice fills the line. "Wanted to bring you lunch, *cariño*."

Travis's fiancé, Mateo, steps into the frame, his eyes meeting mine through the screen. He's a big, tall brute of a man with gorgeous brown skin and miles of black ink. Truthfully, when they started hooking up, I wasn't his biggest fan, but I'll admit, he's grown on me over the years. He's obsessed with Travis and has never been able to get enough of him, and that's exactly what Travis deserves.

As much as I hate to voice the thought, even if only inside my head, Travis's ex-boyfriend reminds me a lot of Henry, with the way he treated Travis during their relationship. It's a thought that makes my stomach twist.

It was a nice change of pace when Travis met Mateo, even if they met under less than stellar circumstances. I couldn't be happier for them.

"*Hola, pendejo,*" Mateo drawls. "Milk any cows and fuck any farmers yet?"

Travis whacks him in the chest as he laughs, and I can't help but let out a chuckle too.

"Actually, that's kind of why I called you today…" I wince as I look at Travis, his eyes going wide.

"Holy fuck. Mateo was joking, but *did you*?"

"No." I shake my head. "Well, yeah, I've milked a cow, but that's not what I mean."

Mateo leaves the frame, coming back a moment later with a chair that he pulls right up next to Travis. "This is going to get good," he says with a smirk.

"Tell us," Travis pushes after a moment.

Blowing out a breath, I dive in, telling them everything about mine and Cope's… friendship, starting with the way that we met, right down to the picnic the other day, and the invite I just received.

When I'm finished, they share a look before Travis says, "This is the cutest fucking story I've ever heard."

"What?" I balk. "No, it's not. It's a disaster."

"Why?"

"Uh, have you met Henry? My boyfriend."

"Yeah, we have," Mateo chimes in. "And he's a fucking douchebag in a stuffy designer suit. I say ditch him and fuck the cowboy."

Travis sniggers beside him while I gape at him. "He is not—"

"Don't you dare even say he isn't a douchebag," Travis blurts out, cutting me off. "You know damn well he is, Xander. He's a douchebag who treats you like garbage, and you deserve better."

I scoff, but I can't even pretend to be surprised. Travis has made no efforts at concealing how much he dislikes Henry, and my relationship with him. Similar to how I was with his ex.

"You wanna know what I think?" Mateo asks. When I tell him *no*, he waves me off. "Well, I'm telling you anyway." *Of course he is.* "You know exactly how much Travis hates Henry, so I think you knew, even if only subconsciously, that he wouldn't dissuade you from this. You knew he'd be on board."

"That is *not* true," I argue, knowing full well it is.

"Right," Mateo mutters. "Whatever helps you sleep at night."

Travis's eyes soften around the edges as he looks at me. "I'm not saying go cheat on your man, because trust me, I'm not."

"Sensing a 'but' coming on."

"But I think you should accept the invite. It sounds like fun, and you deserve a little fun. Then maybe later on, figure out what you truly want with Henry."

I blow out a breath, rolling my eyes, and feign annoyance. "You guys suck."

"We will if you ever let us off the phone," Mateo grumbles, his insinuation about office sex loud and clear. Travis whacks him in the chest again, trying to hide a smile, but I take the hint, and we quickly get off the phone.

Somehow, even if I feel no less confused, I manage to feel a little lighter. Deciding to take his advice, I pull open my phone and respond to Cope's text, telling him I'd love to come tonight. It only takes a few seconds before a reply comes through that makes me smile like a fucking fool.

Cope: Awesome. Meet me at my place at 5, and we'll drive over together. ;)

Cope's truck smells *just* like him, and it's making me dizzy. Whatever cologne he wears does it for me. We left his house a few minutes ago, and I'm staring out the passenger side window, avoiding looking at him. He looks so fucking hot, there's no way to do it without drooling all over myself and making it abundantly clear that I'm into him. So, to be safe, I just won't look.

I've never met anybody before who can make tight jeans and a t-shirt look so fucking good, but Cope does. Pair it with the cowboy boots he's always wearing, and he's a walking wet dream. When he admitted to me that he doesn't hook up all that often, I was shocked. For one, *look at him*. He's insanely attractive, carries himself with a thick air of confidence, and he's genuinely nice. Secondly, I've seen his rodeo videos…more times now than I'd care to admit out loud. He's great at what he does, and people go feral for him on social media.

"You okay?" Cope asks, breaking me out of my highly inappropriate thoughts about him in nothing more than his cowboy hat and those chaps he wears when he competes.

My face heats like he can hear my thoughts as I flash him a smile. "Yeah, I'm good. Just had a long day with my aunt."

Concern etches his features. "Is she okay?"

"Yeah, she's a stubborn old bat, is all." His worry makes my chest tighten. "I think she's getting back to things too quickly, but she says she's fine."

When Aunt Colette started insisting she help with chores again, she shooed Cope away, and said she didn't need his help, so this is the first time we've seen each other in a few days.

"But she's not in pain?" he asks, eyes straight ahead on the road.

"Nah. Well, at least not that she tells me. I don't think she'd tell me even if she was, though."

"Hmm, I wonder who that's like," Cope mutters, tossing

me a sly look.

"Why does everyone keep saying that?" I laugh, knowing exactly what he's insinuating.

"Oh, I don't know." He pretends to think for a moment, fingers caressing his chin. "Maybe because you act like you don't need help, even when you don't know what the fuck you're doing, and when you do accept help, you get all huffy and puffy because you're not the best at it right away."

Reaching over, I shove his arm. "I do not do that."

"Riiiight, sure you don't."

Cope hangs a right, turning onto a one-lane gravel road. I'm assuming this is the road that leads to where we're going. Before we left his house, he told me it was his friend, Conrad, who owned the ranch. It was handed down within his family, and he raises bucking bulls—the bulls that are in the rodeo, I guess. We drive for a solid few minutes before he parks in front of a picturesque red barn. It looks like something straight out of a Lifetime movie. There're already people here mulling about and, suddenly, the nerves I've been pretending don't exist flare to life all over again.

I'm about to meet all of Cope's closest friends. If they're anything like him, they'll be plenty nice and welcoming, but something about wanting his friends to like me weighs heavy. Which is kind of silly. I'm going to be in Copper Lake temporarily, and then probably never see Cope or these people again, so why care what they think of me?

Maybe because you have a ridiculously inappropriate crush on him, dumbass.

As if Cope can sense my unease, he reaches over and grips my thigh, squeezing a few times—as if that helps *at all*. "Ready?"

I swallow thickly, tamping down the way his touch radiates

throughout my entire body, especially about four inches *up* from where he's holding. Nodding and feigning a confidence I don't feel, I say, "Mmhmm, let's do this."

Chapter 8

Cope Murphy

He fits right in with my friends. When we were getting out of my truck earlier, I could tell Xander was nervous. Which I can understand. It's intimidating going to a place where everybody knows everyone except for you, but I knew he had nothing to worry about.

About a half an hour ago, Shooter and I decided it would be a good idea to set up a beer pong table, because why not play drinking games like we're a bunch of frat boys? So, it's currently Xander and me against Shooter and Sterling, and it's neck and neck. A nineties country playlist pulses through the giant speaker Conrad has hooked up out here, and the sun is well on its way to setting. Thankfully, the lights from the outside of the barn are bright enough to illuminate the beer pong table once it eventually gets fully dark.

It's our turn, and Xander tosses the ping-pong ball. It dunks right into one of their cups, Shooter immediately groaning, like the sore loser he is, while Xander and I throw our hands up and cheer, turning to bump our chests together. Which only ends up making us laugh.

Shooter downs the beer, setting the can down, and wipes his mouth with the back of his hand as he narrows his eyes on Xander. "You're a little too good for my liking, fucker."

Xander throws back a laugh before putting on a serious face. "Uh, sorry?"

"Yeah, you better be sorry," Shooter drawls, turning to point a finger at me. "Your little boy next door is on my shit list."

Sterling and I can't hold back our laughter even if we tried. One look at Xander, and it's obvious he doesn't know if Shooter is serious or not. The confusion furrowing his brow as he looks at me and mouths, *Boy next door?* is comical.

Thankfully, Sterling pulls himself together far quicker than I do. "Don't listen to him. Shooter has always, and will always be, the world's biggest sore loser there is. He doesn't actually mean anything he babbles off when he's getting his ass kicked."

Xander throws a glance at me, and I'm still chuckling, but I nod in a way that I hope's reassuring. The game continues, throw for throw, and we're tied right up until the end when Shooter somehow pulls some magic out of his ass and takes the game. He's, of course, gloating like a motherfucker. He comes over and shakes both of our hands like a giant tool.

"Forgive everything I said before, boy next door. You're cool, especially when you lose."

"Uh, you too," Xander replies back to him, biting the inside of his cheek to hold in a laugh.

I bump Xander's arm with my elbow. "C'mon, grab us another couple beers, and we'll go over here. You mind if I smoke?"

This is the first social setting we've hung out in together, so it's really the first time I've been in a position where I want to smoke, and I'm not sure how he feels about that. I know he smokes weed, but still, cigarette smoke is different for some people.

He shakes his head, gaze meeting mine as he hands me an unopened, ice-cold beer. "Nah, I don't mind."

A quick glance around the area, and I find Colt, Jessie, Daisy, and Whit all sitting around the fire. They look to be in a pretty intense conversation. Conrad's chatting with Clementine over by the front porch, and who the hell knows where Shooter and Sterling went. Probably up to Sterling's barn loft to fuck, if I had to guess.

I drop the tailgate to my truck, and we hop up and sit in the bed near the front, our backs up against the cab. Cracking the beers, we both take a sip before I reach into the pocket of my jeans and pull out my pack of smokes. At the same time, Xander reaches into his zip-up pocket and pulls out a rectangular tin can before shooting a look at me.

"Would you be bothered if I smoked too?"

A stray strand of black hair hangs over his forehead, covering one of his brows. The urge to push it out of his face is strong, similar to when we were horseback riding. It takes me by just as much surprise as it did the first time.

"No, not at all," I rasp. Placing the cigarette between my lips, I bring the lighter up to the end and light it. Inhaling deeply, I let the smoke fill my lungs. I offer Xander my lighter, but he gives me a quick shake of his head as he holds up his own. My head drops back onto the back window as my gaze lifts to the sky. "Thanks for coming tonight."

He's quiet for a moment, but based on the flame burning bright in my periphery, he's lighting up his joint. Blowing out the smoke, the sour, earthy scent of the marijuana wafts around me. "Thanks for inviting me. Your friends are nice."

"Yeah, they are," I agree, taking another drag. "Think they like you."

"Well, look at me," he teases. "How could they not?"

We both laugh, and when I glance over at him, gaze locking onto his icy blues, this fluttering feeling dances through my lower stomach. The type of feeling you get when you get to the very top of a rollercoaster and you're beginning your descent. Or like when I bust out of the chute that very first time of the season. I've always chalked it up to a feeling of euphoria…but why would I be feeling euphoria with Xander's eyes on mine?

"I think your friends and this backwoods party are the stuff country musicians sing about," Xander says with a chuckle. "It's feeling very *Down on the Farm*."

My shoulders shake as I let my head fall back onto the truck window, my hand coming up to cover my face and the laughter I can't hold back at the Tim McGraw comparison he just threw at me.

"You're laughing like I'm wrong."

"No, it's pretty spot on, actually," I admit. "I'm laughing because a country music reference is about the last thing I expected from you."

Xander gasps, clutching his chest in mock offense. "Are you stereotyping me based on my appearance?"

Leaning over, I give him a playful shove. "You mean, kind of like you just did to all of us?"

"Touché," he says, and when I glance over at him, he tosses me a crooked grin that makes my stomach bottom out. It's boyish and cute. It's innocent with a side of flirty that makes my pulse kick up.

He brings the joint up to his lips, and they purse around the paper as he inhales, the cherry pulsing bright red and orange amongst the dark night. It's the first time I'm really noticing his lips; how nice they are. They're full, soft pink, and they stand out nicely against the fairness of his skin. That area above his lip that connects to his nose—I have no clue what it's called, but it's like two little lines leading up to his nostrils—it's defined in a way that's pleasing to the eye. In fact, his entire face is oddly proportionate, but in a good way. Like the angles and curves that make up Xander's face scratch something inside my brain.

Wow, I should never, ever say those words out loud unless I want him to think I'm some sort of freak.

I'm not sure how long we stare at each other, but he's the first one to break the connection, clearing his throat, and glancing down at his lap. He takes another hit off the joint before putting it out on the top of the tin can. Shoving the roach inside, he pockets it before tossing me a quick glance. There's no lingering to his gaze this time.

"Should we get back to everyone?" he asks, his voice a little raspy now. Probably from the smoke.

I nod, taking one last drag. "Yeah, sure, let's go." Even though that's the last thing I want to do.

Standing up in the truck bed, I'm the first to jump down. Xander follows right behind me, but as soon as his feet touch the ground, one of his legs gives out and he falls forward, a garbled sound leaving his mouth. Thankfully, I'm right there to catch him, but the moment he's in my embrace, it's like the oxygen around us is sucked away.

Xander looks up at me, his hands curled into fists on the front of my t-shirt, his floppy hair now fully in his face. The energy around us thrums with something I don't understand, and my heart hammers against my ribs. His tongue pokes out, wetting his lips, and probably because of our proximity, my eyes immediately drop and track the movement, a zap of… something else entirely shooting down my spine at the sight.

I don't…I don't understand it. All I want to do is lean in and close the distance, to taste those lips he just licked.

I. Don't. Understand. It.

But I want to do it. To try it.

What would he taste like? Feel like? How would I feel kissing him? A man. Would I like it? Want to do it again?

All these questions swarm my mind, and in the end, I think…I'm going to do it. Like he heard the decision be made in my mind, his eyes drop down to my lips, and I watch as he swallows hard before meeting my gaze again.

I'm distantly aware that everybody is on the other side of the yard. Aware there's music playing, and a fire burning, and people dancing and talking and having fun. I'm aware of it all, but it doesn't exist in my world right now. I lean in a little closer, Xander's breath hitching as I do.

Our faces are so close, our lips nearly brushing. I'm breathing him in, and him, me, but before I can seal my mouth to his, Xander's fists press down on my chest. "Cope." He breathes my name so quietly, I almost don't hear it. "I can't."

Right.

Taking a small step back and putting some much-needed distance between us, I clear my throat, dragging a hand over my mouth. "I'm sorry about that." I huff out a laugh that sounds forced even to my own ears. "Don't know what came over me."

"No, please don't be sorry," he replies, reaching out to touch my forearm, and then deciding better of it, dropping his hand altogether. "If it weren't for, well, you know…"

"Henry," I say, his name like glass on my tongue. "I get it. I shouldn't have done that. Wanna head back over there?"

"Yeah." Xander nods, fingers nervously toying with the bracelet on his wrist. "Let's do that."

What the fuck was that? Why would I try to kiss him? And now it's fucking awkward. Way to go, Cope.

Walking in silence, we take a seat beside each other in front of the fire. Shooter and Sterling must've finished their quickie because they're across from us, and based on the way Shooter's watching me, I'd say he caught part, if not all, of what just went down over by my truck.

Lovely.

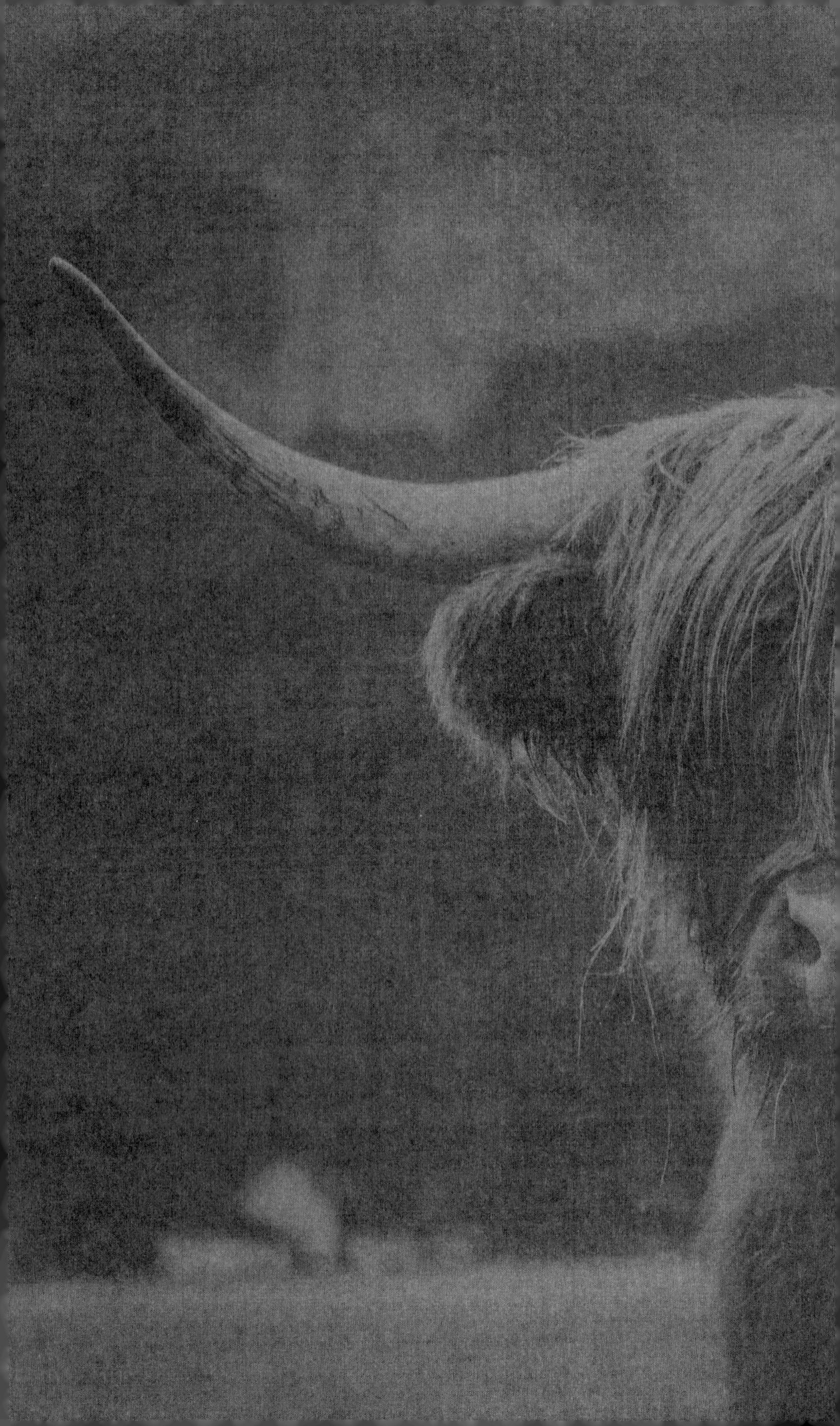

Chapter 9

Xander Dawson

Glancing at the time on the dash, I urge the car ahead of me to go a little bit faster because I'm running late. Henry's plane lands in twenty minutes, and I'm still about thirty-five minutes away from the airport. No surprise to anybody, there's no airport in Copper Lake, so I had to go all the way into Cheyenne to pick him up. I'm driving my aunt's car. I got mine back from the shop last week—it cost a pretty freaking penny to fix, but I still don't trust it to drive long distances.

Thick, dense dread sits unmoving at the bottom of my gut the closer I get to picking Henry up, which is stupid. He's my boyfriend, whom I haven't seen in almost a month. I should be excited to see him.

No, you know what? I *am* excited to see Henry.

I am.

But there's also a large part of me that's consumed with guilt. I almost cheated on him last week. Almost let Cope kiss me. And if I'm being honest with myself right now, it pained me to stop him. I wanted him to kiss me. Wanted it like I've never wanted anything before. Having his eyes on me the way that they were was thrilling. Seeing even a sliver of the attraction I feel for him mirrored back at me that night was nothing short of intoxicating. Not only that, but when I almost fell, he caught me, and having his strong arms holding me, his scent wafting around me, it made it damn near impossible to do the right thing.

And I think *that's* the part that suffocates me with the guilt... Not that it almost happened, but the fact that I didn't want to stop Cope. I wanted it to happen, and had he not backed off immediately when I stopped him, had he tried again, I would've let him.

I feel like Henry's going to be able to read it all over my face when he sees me. I've never been a good liar; I wear my emotions right there for everyone to see all the time. Over the last week, I've contemplated coming clean to Henry. Telling him what happened. In the end, I decided against it for two reasons. One, nothing happened. I stopped it. And two, I'd only be doing it to alleviate my own guilt. All it would do is upset him and cause him distress. So, in a way, it feels selfish to tell him. And it's not like it's going to happen again. It was a one-time lapse in judgement on both of our parts. We'd both been drinking, and then when I fell, our adrenaline was rushing.

It would've happened to anybody. It's not like Cope *actually* wants me. He's straight. And even if he wasn't, it wouldn't change anything. I have Henry.

Henry, the man who's about to land in Wyoming, to visit me for my birthday. The man who I've been with for years now—even if only off and on. He deserves my loyalty.

Yes, things between us feel more unstable and rockier

than ever before, but he's here now. Or well, he will be. And that's gotta count for something, right? I'm sure once we're together again, things will feel normal. The distance will be long forgotten. Cope probably won't even be on my mind.

I'm not going to be wondering what he's doing. Or what he's wearing while he's doing it.

I definitely won't be remembering the way his deep brown orbs looked at me like they were really seeing me for the first time that night a week ago in the back of his truck…after he introduced me to all of his friends. Or the way those same eyes drifted down to my lips more than once.

And while I'm compiling a list of things I *won't* be thinking about while Henry is here, I absolutely won't be thinking about all the times he came over and helped me with Aunt Colette's animals while she was in the hospital or healing. How patient he was when showing me what to do. How he never made fun of me for being utterly clueless. How he taught me to ride a horse, packed me a picnic lunch to eat over a stunning view of the river and the mountains, and how when we got back to my aunt's house, he explained in great detail how to take care of my legs and my groin area that were going to be sore later—which they were, and his tips helped greatly.

Zero thoughts about how kind he is. How good looking he is. How talented he is.

None of that.

Fuck! Snap out of it, Xander. He's just a guy. A straight *guy.*

Hitting every single red light on the way to the airport, I end up getting there even later than I thought, and when I pull up, Henry is already waiting on the curb, suitcase in hand, a scowl on his face. Putting my hazard lights on, I pop the trunk and hop out of the car, rounding the back to meet him.

"I'm so sorry I'm late," I apologize as I take his luggage from him, placing it in the trunk. "There was traffic, and I'm not used to my aunt's car."

The furrow in his brow softens slightly. "It's okay. I wasn't waiting that long."

Henry pulls me into a hug, bergamot and orange filling my nostrils as he places a kiss on top of my head.

"Missed you," I murmur, pulling back and taking him in.

His dark brown hair is longer than it was when I left, almost down to his chin now, and his green eyes are on the darker side today. He's tall—significantly taller than my five-foot-ten stature—and his features are sharp; etched from stone, making him appear fierce at all times. Like always, he's dressed impeccably in a tailored dark gray suit. It doesn't matter that he just spent the last several hours in an airport and flying on a plane. If there's one thing to know about Henry Darby, it's that he will always look professional and put together wherever he goes.

When we first started dating, I was convinced he even slept in those suits.

"Missed you, too, honey." He lets go of my shoulders as he rounds the car, sliding into the passenger side while I do the same on my side. Aunt Colette drives a Subaru Outback that's only a few years old. It's a much nicer car than mine, but watching the way Henry looks around with disgust curling his lip, you'd think he just climbed into a rat-infested pile of junk. When he notices me looking at him, he erases the look off his face before saying, "I see your car's still out of commission."

"It is," I confirm, pulling away from the curb.

"I can't believe you haven't gotten a new car yet, Xan. That thing is a hunk of garbage."

"Well, we all can't drive around in brand new Teslas now,

can we?"

"You could if you wanted to," Henry counters. "It's not like you don't have the money."

How has he been in the car for less than five minutes, and we're already about to have a money spat?

"How was your flight?" I ask, changing the subject, refusing to go there. It's an age-old argument between us.

He shrugs, fingers clicking away on his phone. "It was alright. Not a full flight, so there was plenty of breathing room."

"Well, that's nice," I reply. I get a "mmhmm" back from him, and that's pretty much where the conversation dies. Another thing there is to know about Henry is that he is the definition of a workaholic. I'd bet my left nut he's currently responding to emails right now because God forbid he takes a vacation.

The drive back to Aunt Colette's doesn't take nearly as long as the drive to the airport, and by the time I'm pulling into the garage, she's waiting for us. This'll be their first time meeting. Every time she's flown to Washington to visit since Henry and I started dating, he's always been out of town or too busy to meet her. She wasn't feeling the best when I left for the airport this morning, and she still looks like she isn't. Her skin's pale, and the bags under her eyes are darkened and prominent. She must be coming down with a cold. I feel bad for her. First, she had major surgery, and now she's getting sick.

Much to my surprise, Henry shoves his phone into the pocket of his suit jacket before climbing out. I pop the trunk and grab his suitcase while Henry and my aunt are doing their introductions. We all head inside, and I drop his stuff off in my room before meeting them both in the kitchen. She's grabbing him something to drink, and it looks like she made up a meat and cheese tray for us to eat.

"How are you feeling?" I ask her.

"I'm fine, dear." She waves me off like she always does when I ask her that. Like it's absurd that I care about her wellbeing. "Why don't you boys eat? I'm sure you're hungry after your flight."

"Thanks, Auntie."

She disappears, probably going to lie down.

Henry and I eat a little bit before I put the rest away in the fridge. Then I take him outside to show him around and introduce him to the animals, especially Aggie, who's already waiting for me when we step out onto the porch. He isn't all that thrilled or excited to meet them, but I figured he wouldn't be. It took him nearly a year before he warmed up to my cat, and I swear, that's only because he doesn't have any fur so there's zero chance of it getting on Henry's expensive suits. Speaking of suits, he looks comical out here on the farm, even more out of place than even I do. Thankfully, I convinced him to at least change into a pair of rubber boots, otherwise he'd probably chew my ass out for the mud ruining his shoes.

"This is what you're doing every day?" he asks as we walk out of the barn. "Hang out with these animals, and clean up after them?"

"Well, I mean…yeah."

He pins me with a look. "Your aunt seems fine, Xan. You can probably come home soon. You've been here almost a month."

"Henry, she's healing from a hip replacement."

"Again, she should've hired somebody."

I blow out a sigh, my frustration growing. "Can we not do this again? She's my family, and you take care of your family."

He shakes his head, and I'm sure he has so much he wants to say, but instead, he pulls out his phone. "I'd like to take you to dinner tonight," he says matter-of-factly. "Somewhere nice.

Is there anywhere around here like that?"

"Not really. There're a few diners, but not really anything up to your standards."

Henry looks appalled as he glances over at me. "Nowhere?"

"Not in town, no. We'd have to drive back to Cheyenne." I take him by the hand, leading him back inside. "Come on, let's go lie down together."

Exhaustion has hit me strong out of nowhere—probably because I was up half the night worried about him being here, and somehow finding out about the almost-kiss—and nothing sounds as good as a nap does right now. I highly doubt Henry will take a nap, but hopefully he can do some work on his phone or something so I can get some sleep.

For as weird and distant as things have been between me and Henry lately, it feels oddly comforting to lay my head on his chest and have him wrap an arm around me. I've always been a cuddler, physical touch very much my love language, so when I don't get that, it's easy for me to feel a deep void between me and my partner. Cuddling and being intimate are very important to me, and they help me know things are okay.

It's been well over a month since we've seen each other. He was in New York on business when I left for Copper Lake, so everything going on with me is most likely just from that. I need this—this cuddling, this reassurance that everything is okay. It's nothing more than that. It's where my misplaced feelings for Cope came from. I just need to feel connected to my boyfriend, that's all.

Peering up at him, he glances from his phone to me, and he smiles. It's warm and genuine. *Yeah, I just need to feel an emotional and a physical connection to Henry. That'll make me feel better.* I reach up, cupping his cheek in my palm as I press my lips onto his. He turns his body so it's facing me a bit more, his hand coming to my hip to hold me close. When his lips part, I slip my tongue inside, brushing along his.

I'm so right. I don't have a crush on Cope. No matter how nice, cute, and smart he is. He's just a guy. A hottie cowboy in tight Wranglers and boots. He is not *my amazing, successful boyfriend, who is here, and who loves me.*

Henry tugs on my thigh, bringing me onto his lap as he positions himself onto his back, and it's like my body is coming alive. For someone with as high of a sex drive as me, it's been a long time since I've had sex. Sure, I have my hand, and that works fine, I guess, but it never beats the real thing.

Fingers drifting down the front of Henry's shirt, I slip each button through the holes until his chest is exposed to me. My hands roam the wide expanse of flesh and muscle. Henry's hands round my hips until they're palming my ass, and I groan into his mouth as I roll my hips into his. Suddenly, the memory of how calloused Cope's palms felt, a vision of how they'd feel gripping my ass, similar to how Henry is doing it right now, pops into my mind. I bet he'd be rougher with me, his grip bruising as his full pink lips would devour mine.

Fuck, that image is hot. My dick thickens as I think about what else he could do to me. An erotic movie plays through my thoughts—Cope bending me over the bales of hay in the barn. Cope fucking me in the bed of his truck, or letting me suck his cock while he drove down the backroads. *Or* Cope letting *me* fuck him. How tight his ass must look outside of his jeans, how thick and muscular his thighs have to be from riding broncs all the time. He probably looks heaven sent without his clothes on.

Henry glides his hands from my ass up my back, underneath my shirt. The softness of his palms is like a bucket of cold water on my fantasy. The guilt builds all over again that I'm thinking about another man while fooling around with my boyfriend. God, what the hell is wrong with me?

His lips leave mine, trailing down to my neck. I'm trying my hardest to be in the moment with Henry, not in my head, thinking about Cope. It's not working.

This is so fucked up.

A loud crash sounds from somewhere in the house that causes us both to pause. "What was that?" Henry asks, his lips still hovering above my throat.

I jump off his lap, feet pounding against the floor as I reach for the doorknob. "I don't know."

Without thinking, I take a right, somehow knowing it came from Aunt Colette's room. My heart thunders in my chest as I reach the closed door, my fist coming up to knock.

"I'm fine," my aunt grumbles from the other side. She's full of shit.

"Better hope you're decent because I'm coming in," I warn, giving her a few moments before I twist the handle and enter. She's sprawled out on the floor right in front of her bed. She must've scraped her forearm on the nightstand when she fell because she's bleeding, but it doesn't look terrible. "Fuck, are you okay? Did you fall on your hip? Does it hurt?"

I kneel in front of her, grabbing her uninjured forearm and bringing my other hand up to her back to try to help her up. She's drenched in sweat and burning up. The heat is practically radiating off her skin.

"Xander, goddamnit, I am *fine*," she grits out as she stands up.

"You're not fine," I counter, tone firm. "You've got a fever and you just fell."

"I tripped coming back from the bathroom. It's not a big deal."

"Even if that's the case, you're still burning up. I specifically remember the doctor saying something about that."

Aunt Colette huffs out a disgruntled sigh as she sits on the edge of the bed, her blue eyes that match mine narrow as she glares at me. "Knock it off!" Brushing her hair out of her face, she drags in deep breaths. It's clear she's struggling. "I'm a grown woman, and when I say I'm fine, I mean I'm fucking fine. Now, get out of my room before I beat your ass."

Taking a step back, I cross my arms over my chest, leveling her with my most serious, I-mean-business look. "No."

"No?" She balks at that.

"Yeah, no. I'm not leaving. Either you get up and come with me to the emergency room now or I'm calling the ambulance, and you'll have to pay that bill. The choice is yours. Either way, you're going in."

My aunt's face twists up in annoyance as I watch her weigh her options in her head. Finally, she groans before standing up. "You're such a little shit and a pain in my fucking ass. What the hell was I thinking asking you to come here anyway?"

"You were thinking that you needed help, and I'd have to agree. Now, move it, lady."

"You keep talking, and I'll hit you upside your pretty little head."

"Yeah, if you don't stroke out from the fever first."

She throws me a scowl over her shoulder, and if I wasn't so worried about her right now, I'd probably laugh. She's insufferable. As soon as we get into the hallway, my gaze snags on Henry, who's standing in the doorway to my room, eyes watching me questioningly.

"She's got a fever and she's not feeling well. I'm taking her to the emergency room," I tell him. "You can stay here or come with."

He nods. "I'll come."

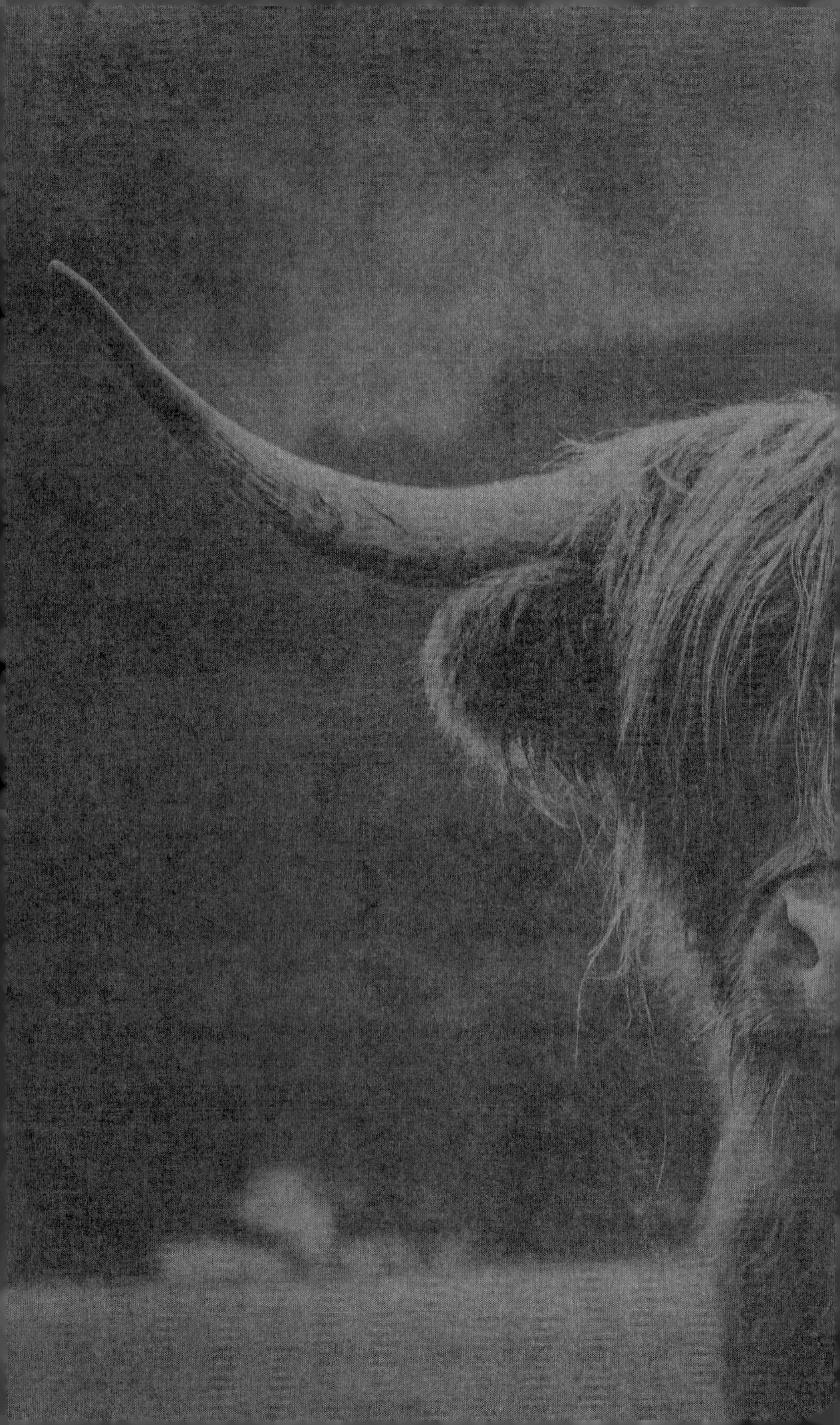

Chapter 10

Xander Dawson

For how sick my aunt is, it took us an awful long time to be seen at the ER. We've been here for a couple of hours now, and she's finally back in a room, hooked up to IV antibiotics. The doctor used a whole lot of big words and terms I don't know the meaning of, and won't be pretending to, but the word I do understand: *infection*.

Apparently, it's a risk with all types of surgery, and she's just one of the unlucky ones who gets to experience it. After they got her hooked up with the antibiotics and something for the fever, she fell asleep. Probably exhausted after the fall, and I'm sure she's going to have one hell of a bruise later.

Henry's behind me on the couch by the window, while I'm sitting in a folding chair in front of her bed. I know he's getting antsy and wanting to leave for the dinner he planned to take me to, but I don't really feel comfortable leaving town—even if only to Cheyenne—while she's sick in the hospital. Not to mention, I'm going to have to head home and do the evening chores soon. The animals need to eat, and I have to bring the horses in from the pasture.

Going out to dinner is the least of my concerns, but when I tell him that, he's going to be pissed. I know he doesn't mean to come off like a dick, but when he comes up with plans in his head, he has a really hard time straying from them. He doesn't do well with change or things not going his way.

A phone rings behind me, startling me. I glance over my shoulder as Henry pulls it out of his pocket. He meets my gaze before standing. "I have to take this. It's work."

I nod but say nothing as he steps out into the hall. Glancing at my aunt, she's peacefully asleep. Pressing the back of my hand to her forehead, it feels like the fever's gone. With a relieved breath, I pull out my own phone, opening up social media. After scrolling for a few moments, my finger takes me to the one account I shouldn't be looking at, but I can't seem to help myself.

Cope's.

There're a couple of stories posted. A few from the gym, and then a few that were posted after. It looks like he's at some diner, like maybe he went out to lunch after he worked out. One's a selfie with him and Shooter, and the other is of his plate of food. I snort to myself at how basic the pictures are. I'm tempted to text him. We haven't spoken much since he dropped me off the night he tried to kiss me. It was awkward, the drive home. When we parked at his place, he apologized *again*. I'm not sure if the silence is him giving me space, or him freaking out. Maybe both.

He is busy, though, too. The finals event he told me about in Vegas is less than a month away, so he's been preparing every day. I'm not entirely sure what goes into training for something like that, but I know he's at the gym a lot more than usual. So, between that, the almost-kiss, and Henry being in town, we just haven't really crossed paths, but I'd be lying through my teeth if I said I didn't want to.

Several minutes pass before Henry steps back into the room. He's tucking his phone into the pocket inside his suit jacket, green eyes lifting to meet mine. "You about ready to get out of here? It sounds like she's going to stay for at least the night, so we don't need to be here. If we leave now, we can still make it to the restaurant."

Releasing a sigh, I sit up straighter, preparing for the fight that's bound to come.

"Henry, I'm not going out to eat tonight." In my mind, it's obvious that going out to dinner isn't an appropriate thing to do, but based on the scrunched-up face he's giving me, I'd say it's not that obvious to him.

"Why not? Your birthday is tomorrow. I want to take you out for it."

It's my turn to look at him like he's lost his mind. "Oh, I don't know, Henry. Maybe because my aunt is in the hospital, suffering from a fucking infection from the surgery she had."

"She's sleeping," he blurts out, entirely too loud. "It's not like we can do anything here."

I take a deep breath, not wanting to explode on him, especially not in this hospital room. Once I'm sure I can talk without yelling, I look at him and ask, "Will you come outside with me, please?"

He looks confused, but nods anyway.

The air is chilly when we step out into the night, and it's already dark, the moon shining big and bright in the sky. We walk to the back of the parking lot as I pull out a pre-roll, lighting it and taking a hit. I could use the weed to calm my frazzled nerves. I'm anxious over what's going to happen with my aunt, I'm on edge over the impending argument I can feel coming on with Henry, and even though this shouldn't be on my mind at all, I'm still so uneasy over the way I feel toward Cope. I hate it. It feels like the weight of the world is on my shoulders, and I'm not strong enough to hold it up.

I take a seat on the sidewalk as I bring the joint up to my lips again. I'm surprised when Henry sits beside me. Normally, he wouldn't ever dirty one of his suits by doing something like sitting on the ground. We're quiet for a moment. The sound of cars passing by on the highway behind us fills the air. It feels like this is the start of a conversation that should've happened a while ago. It's heavy. It's uncomfortable. But we need to do it.

"What's going on with us?" I finally ask, my voice quiet. We're both staring straight ahead at the hospital, neither of us wanting to face this head on.

Henry heaves a sigh before saying, "I just want to take you out for your birthday. I came here for you."

It's an effort to not roll my eyes. "I know this is hard for you to comprehend since your family isn't close, but I don't get to worry about myself and my birthday right now. She's sick and could get a lot worse. Not to mention, I have to help with the animals at the house while she's in the hospital. I didn't come here for no reason, even though I know you think I did." Taking one last hit, I put the joint out before continuing. "I'm here to help her with things around the house. And believe it or not, it's hard work."

"Then what was the point of me coming at all?" he asks, not as harshly as I was expecting.

This time, I do look at him. Turning my head, my eyes clash with his, brows pinched tightly. "Because I missed you,

Henry, and I wanted to see my boyfriend for my birthday. It's not like I planned for this to happen while you were here. Why is that so hard to understand?"

"Yeah, but we're not even able to spend any time together."

"We can still spend time together, even if it's not exactly how you envisioned it."

He doesn't reply, and I'm not surprised. Henry's never been that great of a communicator, so I can't even hold it against him. Not only do I know it, but I've accepted it and put up with it for years now. How can I expect him to be different when I've never asked as much from him? But something about this feels different. Something about his apathy toward my aunt doesn't sit right with me. It has me not wanting to look past it. Not give him a pass simply because he doesn't know any better.

"We're different," I say, no louder than a whisper. "Things between us are different. We've barely talked since I came here, and when we do, it's like you'd rather be doing a hundred other things than talking to me."

"Well, I'm busy, Xan." The passive aggressiveness behind those four words is enough to knock me on my ass if I wasn't already sitting, and I don't even think he realizes it. "This is nothing new. You know how my job goes, you know how busy I am. What, did you think I'd drop my responsibilities to sit on the phone with you for hours out of the day just because you left the state? Be real, Xander."

Looking back on this conversation later, I'll probably realize that it was more than just my aunt that fueled my frustration. Fueled the seemingly rash decision I come to. Looking back, I think I'll realize it wasn't so rash after all. It was a long time coming, but I'm too much of a people pleaser to listen to my own wants and needs until my irritation and resentment build and build, until I'm so full with it, I could explode. Until I *do* explode.

"No, *you* be real, Henry," I spit back at him, the vexation in me rising. "You do realize being in a relationship is work, right? It's not just going to run smoothly because you'd prefer it to. You give me the bare minimum and expect me to thank you for it." Standing up, I start to pace in front of the sidewalk. He remains seated, but he looks up at me as I go on. "I'm fucking aware you're a busy man. I'm aware you have to work, and your schedule looks different than most. I get that, and trust me, you never let me forget it. But what I also get is that when we first started dating, you somehow made time for me in between your crazy work schedule. I mean, fuck, Henry, you made time for me in the middle of your divorce! Do you think because you got me now, you don't have to work to keep me? Think I'll always be here? Is that it?"

"Don't be ridiculous," he scoffs, raising to stand, coming face to face with me. His words drip with condescension. I see the flare of anger flash in his eyes, and I know I hit a nerve.

When Henry first started coming into the dispensary, he was married. Well, separated. The divorce was ugly and messy. They owned a lot of property together, and dividing all their assets was a disaster. Against my better judgement, for a reason I still to this day don't understand, I offered to be there for him through that time.

Our relationship has never been easy, but I think I made myself believe things were better because the idea of losing him hurt too much. I'm not exactly sure when that changed for me; probably around the time my aunt asked me to come help her, and I didn't even bat an eye at having to leave him. When you dull down who you are and what you want for so long, eventually it becomes impossible to do it anymore. I watered down what I wanted from Henry because I knew he'd never be able to give it to me, but now I just resent him more than ever.

I glance down to where my fingers play absentmindedly with the bracelet around my wrist. It's a dinky bracelet I made once with my sister that I've just never taken off. "I think you should go," I mutter, lifting my eyes to meet his. The surprise from my statement is evident on his face; it's probably the last thing he expected me to say.

His eyebrows shoot straight up. "Excuse me?"

"It was a mistake having you come here."

"All of this because I wanted to take you to dinner for your fucking birthday?"

A laugh bubbles up my throat, but it's lacking any humor. "It's not about that, Henry, and you know it. That was just the catalyst to the end we both knew was coming."

"You're breaking up with me?" he balks, eyes wide as saucers.

Dragging in a deep breath, I scrub my hand down my face. "I just... This isn't the most ideal place to have this conversation, Henry, but yeah, I guess I am." I level him with a stare, trying my hardest to get him to reason with me. "You can't honestly say you're surprised by this or you don't agree. We've barely spoken for the last month."

Henry's lips part, but he shuts them again, seemingly at a loss for words. I cross the space between us, taking his hand in mine as I feel something inside of me fracture. Something that's been slowly cracking for a while. Or maybe it's not breaking... Maybe what I'm feeling is it healing. "Coming here has made me realize how much our relationship really is more like a friends-with-benefits situation than a real relationship."

"I'm not sleeping with anybody else, and I haven't the entire time," he replies, shaking his head like he can't digest what I'm saying. "How is it friends with benefits?"

My eyes fill with moisture, the pressure behind them building. I don't want to cry. I give myself a moment to breathe before I say, "I'm only interesting to you when it's convenient for you. This"—I point between us—"isn't a real give-and-take relationship. That's why it was so easy for you to ignore me when I came here."

A tear falls. And then another. Henry's features have softened, but he remains quiet.

"I think subconsciously when I decided to come here, I hoped you'd realize in my absence how much you needed me, but that's not the case." Wiping my cheek with the sleeve of my jacket, I clear my throat, wanting what I say next to come out strong and clear. "It's not your fault, and it's not mine either. Our expectations were different about what this was and what we wanted out of it. I'm seeing that now, and I'm coming to terms with it. Coming to terms with how it won't change—it can't—because I can't ask you to be any different in the same way you can't ask that of me. But I want more, Henry. I want more out of my partner, out of a relationship, and you can't give that to me, and that's okay."

He looks like he wants to argue, but if I had to guess, I'd say it was a knee-jerk reaction, not because he truly disagrees with what I'm saying. No matter how self-assured you are, and no matter how independent you are, you don't go days at a time without talking to your partner who you've been with for years, the one you supposedly love. That's not healthy, and it should've been a dead giveaway of a problem. Henry knows it; I know it. This is a shitty time for me to decide to do this, but what's done is done. I can't take it back, especially not when it feels like a thousand pounds has been lifted off my shoulders.

The silence stretches on, but in it is a sense of clarity.

"Why don't you book a flight, and I can drive you to the house to grab your stuff, then take you to the airport," I offer when he doesn't say anything.

"Jesus Christ." Henry breathes out a laugh through his nose. "I haven't even been here twenty-four hours, and we're already breaking up."

A pang of sadness fills me.

"I'm going to head back up to my aunt's room." I point a thumb in the direction of the hospital. "Come back in when you get that settled, okay?"

He nods, green eyes meeting mine, and it's like understanding flows between us. Putting one foot in front of the other, I walk back into the hospital, and go up to my aunt's room. She's still sleeping, but I think that's to be expected. It's getting late, so I'm not sure if she'll wake up at all tonight.

This entire day took a turn in a way I never saw coming… in more ways than one, and I don't know how to feel about it all. But the one thing I do know with certainty is that I did the right thing. It's something that I probably should've done a while ago, but at least it's done now.

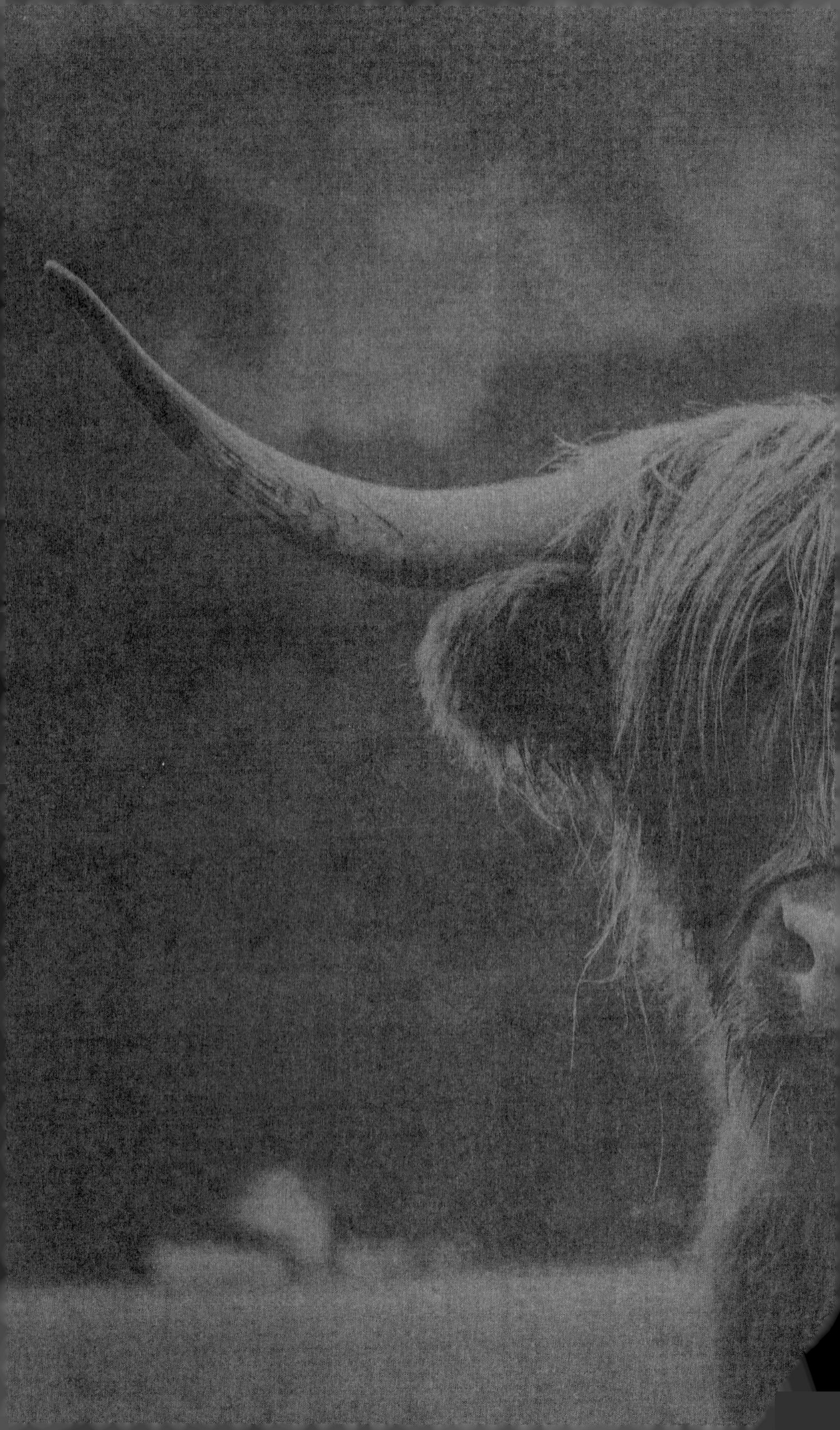

CHAPTER 11

COPE MURPHY

Me: Happy birthday, city boy!
Xander: Thank you! :)
Me: Doing anything fun today?

Hitting send, I shove the phone into my pocket before heading into the diner where I'm meeting Shooter for lunch. It's been pouring rain all morning, and I'm drenched by the time I reach the front door to the establishment. I wipe my shoes off on the mat that's sitting on the other side, gaze meeting Ginny's, the server who works here.

"Morning, Ginny."

"Good morning, Cope," she greets back, a warm smile sliding onto her face. "Shooter's already in the back waiting for you."

Me, Shooter, and a group of our friends come here weekly for lunch. It's something we've done for years now. But that's not until later on this week. Today, it's just Shooter and I. Mostly because I need to get some shit off my chest, and I know he'd never judge me or make me feel like an idiot. Not that our other friends would, but out of everyone, he and I are the closest.

He spots me as soon as I stroll through the back. "'Bout time you got here, man."

"Says the one who's notoriously late," I tease as I take a seat across from him.

"I don't know what you're talking about," he replies dryly, with a shrug and a smirk.

Ginny drops off a glass of ice water and a Coke for me before taking our order. We come here so often, we typically always get the same thing every time, and today is no exception.

"Where's Sterling?" I ask Shooter as Ginny steps away.

"He went with Conrad to Piston to pick up a couple horses."

Shooter's boyfriend, Sterling, is another bronc rider. It was his first pro season this year, and he fucking killed it. He moved here from Texas at the start of the season, and has been staying at the ranch ever since. He helps Conrad out a lot with the chores that need to be done there.

I pull out my phone, checking to see if Xander responded to me, and my stomach tightens when I see nothing waiting for me. Blowing out a breath, I decide to get it over with already. I came here wanting to get all this shit off my chest. If there's anybody who would never judge me, it's Shooter. After I put my phone away, I meet his gaze from across the table.

"Oh, shit. What's wrong?" he asks with a smirk, like he knows whatever this is, is about to be juicy.

"How did you..." I groan, my face growing hot. This is a lot harder to bring up than I thought it would be, a lump forming in my throat. Swallowing thickly, I continue. "How'd you know you were into guys?"

If Shooter is surprised by my question, he doesn't let it

show. "I've always known, I think," he replies, leaning forward with his elbows on the table. "For as long as I can remember, I've been attracted to guys."

I nod. "Oh, right. That makes sense."

"It's not like that for everybody, though," he goes on, raising a brow. "Why do you ask?"

I have a feeling he knows exactly why I'm asking, but I appreciate him playing dumb.

"Remember Xander?"

Shooter's lips tip up as he nods. "How could I forget your little boy next door?"

"Stop calling him that," I grumble.

"That won't be happening." He chuckles. "But yes, I remember him."

Teeth clenched, I glance over, meeting Shooter's gaze. His blue eyes are much darker than Xander's. They're soft as they watch me right now.

"I think I might be into him," I mutter quietly. "But I don't…really know."

"You think?" Shooter laughs. "Bro, I didn't miss how you tried to kiss him at the bonfire last week."

Groaning, I say, "I had a feeling you caught that."

"So, what's the problem?" he asks. "He not into you? He did dodge the fuck out of that kiss."

I frown, starting to regret confiding in him. "You're such a dick, you know that?"

"Of course, I do," he replies with a wide tooth grin. "Now, spill, Copey."

"I don't know how he feels," I mutter honestly. "There have been a few instances where I felt maybe there was something there, but then, like you said, he didn't let me kiss him. Which

I understand. He has a boyfriend, and I shouldn't have even tried." Although, it hasn't escaped me that Xander *did* say that night if it weren't for Henry, he wouldn't have stopped me... Or maybe I'm reading too in between the lines there. I don't know. I've latched on to it and haven't stopped thinking about it. Heaving a sigh, I go on. "Just... I don't know. Something came over me in that moment, and I had to."

Shooter seems to mull over what I said for a moment. "Where's his boyfriend at?"

"They both live in Washington State."

"How long have they been together?"

"I don't know. A few years, on and off, he said."

He nods. A few moments later, Ginny steps up to the table, setting our food down in front of us. We dig in, and for the time being, the conversation comes to a stop. I got a regular cheeseburger and some fries, but fuck, they're good. Hitting the spot. For the majority of the time, I make a conscious effort to eat at home. It not only saves me a shit ton of money, but it's also important for me to eat healthy and balanced to stay in shape for the rodeo. Getting to come here at least once a week is nice, though, because the food is always top-notch, especially for a small town diner.

Shooter wipes his mouth with a napkin before asking, "This the first guy you've been attracted to?"

I nod. "Yeah. Well, I mean, of course, I've noticed that men are attractive before in the same way I'm able to tell when a woman is attractive. But you know me, I'm not big into hooking up, so it's never like I'm out searching. Besides, looks aren't always the most important thing to me anyway. Like, yes, I find Xander incredibly physically attractive." My cheeks heat up with that confession. I'm sure Shooter can see it. "But I'm also very attracted to his personality. Hanging out and spending time with him is fun and easy. We get along really well."

"Fucking sucks that he has a boyfriend," Shooter drawls as he shoves a French fry into his mouth.

"Yeah, you're fucking telling me."

My phone goes off in my pocket, and when I pull it out and check the screen, my stomach flutters at seeing Xander's name flash on the notification.

Xander: Probably not. My aunt is in the hospital with some sort of an infection from the surgery. I'll probably head back up to the hospital here in a few hours and spend most of the day there.

Me: Damn, is she okay?

Xander: I'm sure she'll be fine. She had a gnarly fever yesterday before I took her in, but she was resting when I left her this morning.

Me: Are you at your house now?

"Why're you staring down at your phone like that?" Shooter asks, my head snapping up.

"Xander's aunt's in the hospital with an infection. She had a hip replacement done a few weeks ago."

"Shit. She okay?"

"I don't know."

My phone buzzes with his response.

Xander: Yeah, I am. I'm going to take a shower, make some food, and then head back up there.

Me: I'll bring you some lunch before you head back up there. I'm at the diner with Shooter right now anyway.

Ginny comes by to check on us, and I put in an order for Xander before she walks away.

"What the hell are you doing?" Shooter asks, brow arched as he watches me like I've lost my mind.

"Bringing him lunch." I shrug. "He's probably stressed out and hasn't eaten all day. And it's his birthday."

"Boyfriend, remember?"

"I can platonically bring him lunch," I scoff.

"Riiight."

Xander responds, the phone vibrating in my hand.

Xander: You don't need to do that, Cope. I'm sure you have tons of other things to do.

Me: I don't have to, but I want to. And I already ordered the food, so it's done. I'll be there soon.

The text bubbles appear and disappear a few times before a simple 'thank you' comes through. Shooter and I finish up eating before Ginny brings us the bill and my to-go order. The entire drive over to Xander's aunt's house, my stomach is in knots. This is the first time we're seeing each other since the bonfire last week. We've texted a little bit here and there, but nothing face to face.

Truck parked in front of the house, I take a deep breath, grab the bag of food off the seat, and climb out. Xander answers almost as soon as I knock, neither of us saying anything for a few moments as we take each other in. His black hair is still a little wet from his shower, and he's in a black ribbed tank top and a pair of red athletic shorts.

"Hey," I finally murmur, my heart thumping hard.

"Hey." Xander offers a small smile, stepping to the side. "You can come in if you want."

We head into the kitchen, where I set the food on the counter. I pull a plate out from the cupboard and unbox the order onto it. Xander pulls a Gatorade out of the fridge, setting it beside the plate.

"You really didn't need to do this."

"I know, but I wanted to," I reply, shoving the plate in front of him. "Besides, maybe I also kind of wanted to see you."

Xander bites the inside of his cheek, and I take that as a sign I didn't say too much, or fuck up too badly. He takes a seat on one of the bar stools, and I pull out the one next to him. "Well, thank you. I haven't eaten all day."

"I figured you hadn't."

He digs in, and in between bites, he tells me what happened yesterday that led to going to the hospital, and he explains what the doctor had said about her infection.

"Do you know how long she'll have to be in the hospital?" I ask him, stealing a fry off his plate and popping it into my mouth.

He shakes his head, glancing over at me. "No, I don't really know anything either. Like, all of this is practically a foreign language to me.

It's written all over his face how nervous he is. It's in the shaky way he talks and the troubled look in his eyes. My gut twists, and I hate that he's dealing with all of this. That he's her only family here. Moving on instinct alone, and with the comfort I'd want if this were me, I cover his hand with mine, squeezing. "Hey, you did the right thing," I tell him in what I hope is a reassuring tone. "I wouldn't understand a thing either, but it sounds like you acted fast and did everything right. She's going to be fine."

Xander doesn't remove his hand from my hold, but he also doesn't say anything for a moment. I chance a glance at him, finding him already looking back at me, a quizzical expression on his face that I can't quite place.

"Thank you," he finally says, voice barely above a whisper, like if he talks any louder, he'll break down. "For bringing me lunch when you really didn't have to, and for trying to make me feel better. I really appreciate it."

Giving his hand one last squeeze, I let go, even though I'd rather hold on to it all day. "Anytime, Xander."

Once he finishes, he tosses the bag in the trash. "That was so good."

"Have you been to that diner yet? The one right in town."

"No, but I've wanted to."

"I'm going there again later on this week if you want to come? Me and my friends meet there for lunch every week."

"Uh…yeah, maybe. It depends on how my aunt is doing."

"Of course." A stifling tension wafts around us as we watch each other, the need to say something growing by the second. "Listen, about last week—"

Xander shakes his head, breathing out a laugh. "Don't. It's fine, really. I'm sorry I've been so distant since. I've just been busy, and kind of in my own head. I'm not mad or anything."

My brow arches. "You sure?"

"Positive. That moment at the bonfire was…intense. I felt it too; it wasn't just you. We're cool, I promise."

Nodding, I stuff my hands into my pockets. "Okay, thanks for that. So, you heading back to the hospital?"

"Yeah, I think so."

"Want company? I don't have anything else going on today."

Shit, maybe I shouldn't have offered that. But the idea of going home, and not getting to hang out with him some more, sounds about as unappealing as getting bucked off a bronc right about now.

Xander's thick dark brows lift. "What? You don't have to

do that."

"Why do you keep saying that?" I laugh. "I'm well aware I don't have to. I want to. Your aunt is the only family you have here, and it's probably stressful dealing with this all by yourself. If it were me, I'd want company."

Xander's shoulders relax, a soft smile tugging on his lips. "Uh...I mean, sure, if you want to, that'd be really nice."

Grinning at him, I say, "Sweet. We can take my truck."

After he changes into some jeans and puts on some shoes, we head out. As soon as we climb into the truck, his sweet scent fills the cab, and I try my hardest to not obsess over it. Easier said than done.

Boyfriend, Cope. He has a boyfriend.

Confiding in Shooter about how I'm feeling—or how I think I'm feeling—helped, but I also feel like it opened a can of worms, These feelings I thought I had for Xander seem to be amplifying, which is the opposite of what should be happening.

What I said to Shooter is true, though… I can be there for him platonically.

I can.

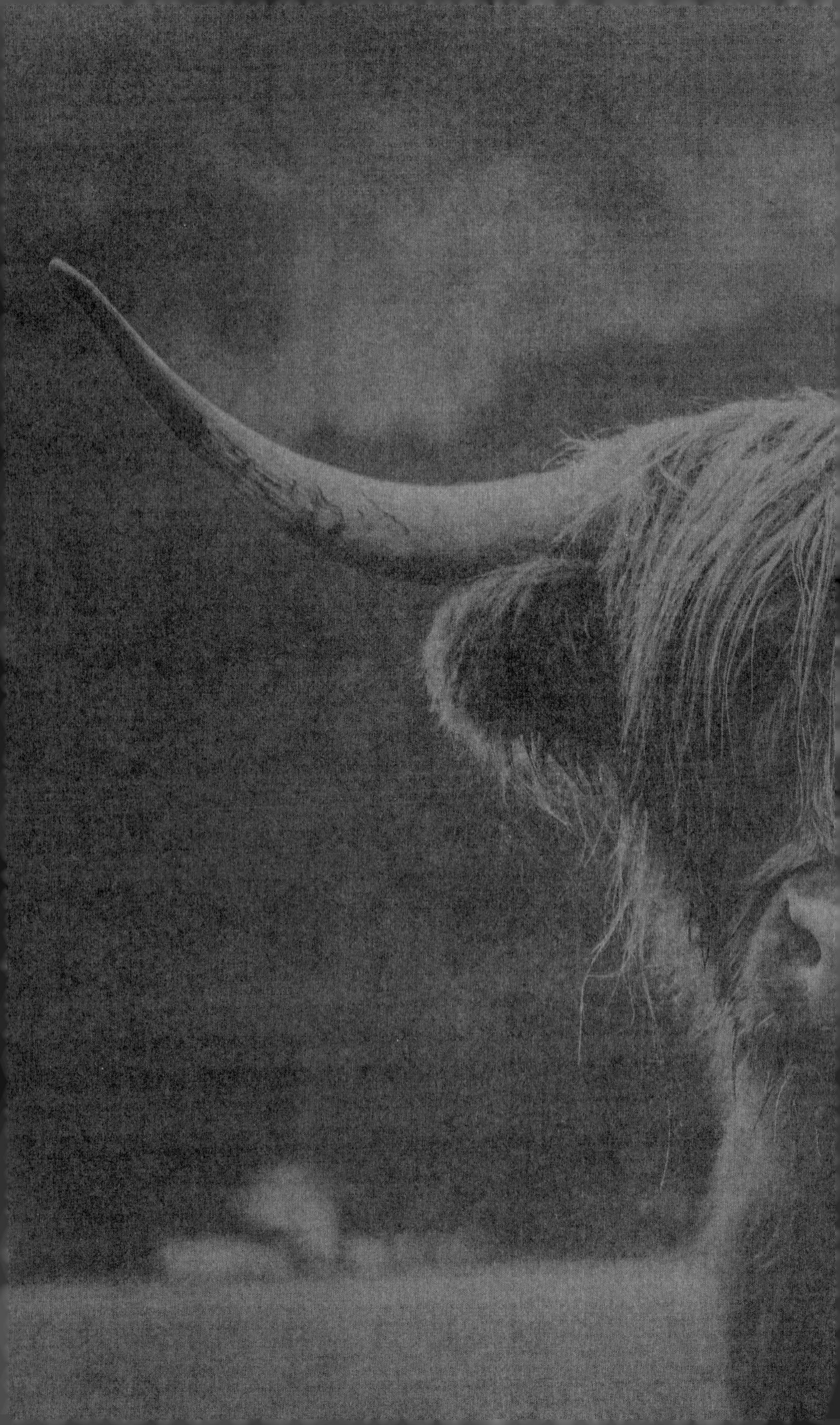

Chapter 12

Xander Dawson

"Are you comfortable?" I ask my aunt as I climb into the driver's seat, buckling my seatbelt.

"I'm fine, Xander."

"Okay, but are you cold? We can turn on your seat warmer."

I reach for the button to turn it on, but she slaps my hand away before I can. "Boy, I am plenty capable of turning on my seat warmer if I should want it. I'm not incapable."

Wincing at her brash tone, I put the car in reverse and back out of the spot. Discharge at the hospital took much longer than either of us anticipated. The nurses had told us she should be out of there by noon. Then something came up—some other surgery or complication or something—and the doctor was unable to make his way to her room. It's after five in the evening, and we're just now leaving. They were going to keep her another night since it was getting so late, but she bit their heads off and demanded to be let go.

The medication she's on can apparently cause mood swings…and it shows. Which, I get it; she's been cooped up in the hospital, hooked up to monitors and IVs for days. I'd want to be at home, in my own bed too.

Thankfully, there's no traffic on the drive. I'm already mentally going through my to-do list for tonight that I'll need to start as soon as we get home and I get her settled. Farm chores will need to be done, we're both going to need to eat, and I don't think there's anything in the house that's easy to throw together, so I'll have to cook something, I'm sure. If I didn't think my aunt would chew me out for it, I'd stop and pick up burgers and fries somewhere. But it's getting dark and the animals are probably confused about where we are and where their dinner is, so that takes precedence.

Still, I know by the time I crawl into bed tonight, I'm going to be so physically and mentally exhausted. I'm glad she's coming home and she's okay, though. That's all that really matters. The plus side to all of this is that it's helped me keep my mind off my breakup with Henry. And the fact that he hasn't, not once, texted me to check in and see how my aunt is, or how I am. Not that I necessarily want to talk to him—because I don't—but it would be nice to show that he cared enough. We were together for a significant amount of time, after all. If the roles were reversed and it were his family in the hospital, breakup or not, I'd still want to check in and make sure they were doing okay.

And then, of course, my mind drifts over to Cope, and I can't help but compare the two of them, even though there's no comparison. The entire time my aunt's been in the hospital, he's been texting and checking up on me. Offering to bring me food. Asking what the doctors were saying and how she was feeling. He's just so attentive and caring, and he has no reason to be.

He's Henry's polar opposite in every single way, and as much as I appreciate all that he's done and the kind words he's given me when it's clear I'm anxious, it also makes me uncomfortable because I've never had this from anybody. Sure, Travis has checked in and made sure everything is okay because he's my best friend, but this is different. We, essentially, barely know each other, and Cope is going above and beyond, simply because he wants to.

It's like my brain doesn't know how to process that and accept it. How pathetic is that? Knowing I've been treated so poorly in past relationships that I don't know how to accept being treated with no-strings kindness. Because yes, after the almost-kiss at the bonfire, it's clear that, despite how straight I thought Cope was, he feels *something* for me a bit more than friendly, even if it's only physical. But I don't at all get the vibe that he's doing all of this because he's trying to get with me. He's doing it because he's simply a genuinely nice guy...and my mind can't make sense of that.

Finally making it home, I park in front of the house and turn off the car. Before I can even get out and attempt to help my aunt, she's already gone. *Stubborn old bat.* As I'm getting her discharge paperwork and her bag of stuff from the back seat, I hear her talking, but I can't make out what she's saying. Shutting the car door, I'm about to ask her to repeat what she just said to me, when I glance over the top of the car and see she isn't talking to me at all.

She's talking to Cope...who is standing in front of the house, with what looks to be a slow cooker in his hands. His head turns in my direction and our gazes lock for a moment. He gives me a quick nod of his chin before he follows Aunt Colette inside.

Okay...what the hell is going on?

Befuddled, I use the key fob to lock the car, and I follow them inside. Cope's in the kitchen with my aunt as I enter, and he's plugging the—yup, I was right—slow cooker into the wall.

"Hey, what's this?" I ask, setting everything on the table. My chest feels tight and my throat aches as I take Cope in, standing in my aunt's kitchen, clearly bringing her food.

Before he can respond, my aunt chimes in. "I'm going to change and wash my face."

Cope and I both watch her leave.

My stomach clenches and my palms are sweaty as I nervously drag my gaze back to him and ask again, "What's this?"

He smiles, and even though it's small, it does something to my insides. He's wearing a pair of gray sweats, and a Carhartt jacket over a plain black t-shirt. From seeing him on the porch, I know he was also wearing a pair of boots, but he must've toed them off before coming inside...because he's a fucking gentleman like that. The backward hat on his head completes the mouthwatering, rugged cowboy look he's got going on.

"Figured you guys might be hungry, and after eating only hospital food for days, I thought something hot and homecooked might be nice."

He...cooked for us. "You didn't—"

"Have to do that," he finishes for me, breathing out a laugh. "Yes, city boy. I know I didn't have to. I wanted to."

The blood roars in my ears as my body feels light. "It smells good," I say, meaning it.

"It's nothing special," he mutters with a shrug. "Just a beef stew, and I made some cornbread."

Just some beef stew and cornbread. I swallow around the crater sized lump in my throat. "Thank you," I practically whisper as I try to slow the pounding of my heart. It's like it's trying to crack through my ribs and fly right out of my chest. Maybe toward him.

Cope holds my gaze, the eye contact strong and heady. My knee-jerk reaction is to look away, but I force myself to do the opposite. "You're welcome. Oh, and I took care of the evening chores, so you don't have to worry about that. You can just eat and relax tonight."

Clenching my jaw, pressure builds behind my eyes, the tip of my nose burning. I don't know whether I want to kiss him or cry…maybe a little bit of both. And honestly, I don't know where these emotions are coming from. Probably exhaustion, or the stress of the last week catching up to me, but this is so fucking nice. And so thoughtful. Why would he do this?

Cope takes a couple of steps in my direction, probably worried I've had a stroke with how silent I've gone. He stops in front of me, but not too close. "You doing okay?" he asks gently. "I'm sure the last week has been a lot for you."

I nod, wetting my lips with my tongue. "Thank you for doing all of this. You have no idea how helpful it is, and how much it means to me."

"It's no big deal. I had the free time and I wanted to do something to help."

"Don't do that," I mutter with a quick shake of my head. "Don't downplay it. Thank you, really."

The urge to slip my arms around him and bury my face in his neck for a hug is overwhelming, but I resist. I probably already look a little nuts with how speechless I am. I don't need to make it worse by plastering his body to mine. I probably wouldn't let go.

"You're welcome, Xander." He smiles. "I'm going to head

home, but give me a call or text if you need anything. And I mean it."

Saluting him, I say, "Yes, sir."

Heat flares in his eyes briefly before he blinks and it's gone. "Goodnight."

"Night, Cope."

I watch him leave, every bone in my body screaming at me to ask him to stay. To tell him I broke up with Henry. Beg him to try to kiss me this time. But I don't. That seems unfair to him somehow, like he'd be a rebound—which he absolutely wouldn't be. Instead, I take a scalding hot shower, change into some pajamas, then grab a hearty bowl of the stew that smells heavenly and a couple of pieces of cornbread, before I sit at the table and eat it all, while thinking of how good Cope is. How deserving. How he's unlike any other guy I've ever been interested in…and how maybe that's exactly what I need.

Chapter 13

Xander Dawson

"How's she doing?" my sister, Gemma, asks as I'm switching the clothes from the washer into the dryer.

"She seems fine. Not that she'd ever tell me if she wasn't."

It's been a week since Aunt Colette came home from the hospital, and she *does* seem like she's doing fine. There haven't been any more fevers, she doesn't look to be in any pain, and surprisingly, she's taking it easy like the doctor said. Maybe a week-long hospital stay was enough to knock some sense into her that she isn't superwoman and she can't do everything. Her stubbornness is incredibly frustrating.

"And how are you?"

I can hear Gemma's concern all the way through the phone. Rolling my eyes, thankful she can't see me, I reply with, "I'm fine, Gem. Just like all the other times you've asked."

"Well, sue me for being concerned about my brother," she mutters.

"I appreciate that, Gemma. I really do, but Henry and I

were at the end of our road. I did us both a favor by breaking it off."

"Yeah, but you're isolated all the way out there in that small-ass town with nobody but Aunt Colette to keep you company. Forgive me for wondering if you're slowly losing your mind."

Grabbing the laundry basket filled with the warm, clean clothes, I carry them to my bedroom. "I'm not isolated," I scoff. "Yes, I have Auntie, but I've also made a…friend."

I don't know why I paused like that, but I know my sister caught it, and is about to latch on like a shark that's scented a whiff of blood.

"Friend?" she asks, a hum to her tone. "What friend? And why haven't I heard of this friend until now?"

Snorting out a laugh, I say, "Well, maybe because, despite what you believe, not everything is always your business."

"That's just rude."

"His name is Cope," I offer while folding the clothes. "He's the neighbor, and he's really nice. He's helped me a lot when it comes to the animals, since when I got here, I had no fucking clue what I was doing."

"That's nice of him. How old is he?"

"Twenty-five."

"Is he cute?"

"Very." The word slips past my lips before I can stop myself, and I regret it immediately. *Way to open the nosy floodgates, Xander.*

"Oooooh, snap. Is he the real reason you broke up with Henry?" she asks, and I can hear the smirk in her words.

"I'm about to hang up on you right now," I grumble. "Do I really strike you as somebody who would leave a multi-year relationship on a whim for some guy I just met?"

"Okay, grumpy."

"The truth is, yes, Cope is cute—*really cute*—and extremely nice. He's also the one who helped me on my first day here when my car broke down. But I ended things with Henry because it was time, and because I was unhappy. As far as I know, Cope is straight, except for that night he tried to kiss me, and even—"

"I'm gonna stop you right there, brother," Gemma cuts in. "He tried to *kiss* you?"

"Yes. It's not a big deal, and I stopped him before he could."

"But you still think he's straight?"

Raking my fingers through my hair, I let out a sigh. "I don't know, Gemma." *No, but I'm not ready to admit that, is what I don't say.* "I'm beginning to regret calling you."

"Oh, hush. You love me." She chuckles. "But lucky you, I have to cut this call short because I just got to my appointment."

"Is everything okay?" I ask, my hands pausing on the washcloth I was about to fold.

"Yes, calm down," she replies soothingly. "It's just my monthly checkup."

"Alright, I'll talk to you later. Love you."

"Love you, Xan."

We hang up, and I finish folding the laundry. As I'm putting away the towels in the hall closet, my aunt comes out of her room. Her hair's wet and hanging down her back like she just got out of the shower.

"Hey, how're you feeling?" I ask, giving her a smile.

"I'm fine," she grunts. "Quit asking me that, boy." She pads down the hall, taking a right, probably going into the kitchen.

Is this how Gemma felt when she asked how I was and I bit her head off?

"I'm getting a little hungry," I holler after her. "Thinking of making lunch. Want some?"

No response.

Sure, let's ignore me.

I head back into my room and grab the now empty clothes basket, bringing it back into the laundry room, and setting it on top of the dryer. Once I'm done, I meander into the kitchen, where—yup—she's brewing a pot of coffee and munching on one of the muffins Cope brought over this morning.

For the most part, I've kept to myself over the last two weeks. Despite knowing the breakup was for the best, and not regretting it, it's still a lot to process. We were together for several years, and it still feels like a loss I needed to grieve. I guess it's not so much Henry that I'm grieving, but the future I subconsciously grew to expect—even if foolishly. As I inch closer to thirty, I can't help but wonder what the fuck the future holds for me. Am I going to get married? Have kids? Or am I going to be single forever, hopping from one relationship to the next with no stability?

The latter is depressing.

I don't even know if marriage and kids are something that I necessarily want, but as time goes on, it's the stability I crave, and the love of somebody special, even if we don't technically get married. Just knowing I have a future with somebody would be nice.

Cope's respected my withdrawn behavior, but he's still been coming over in the mornings to help with chores since my aunt was in the hospital, and then on bedrest. Having him here is a relief when it comes to everything that needs to be done, and he's always bringing some type of breakfast treat with him. My aunt's eating that shit up—literally and figuratively.

"Want a cup?" she asks as I pull open the fridge, looking

inside at what my options are.

"Nah, I'm good. Thank you, though."

She hums as she finishes fixing her own. "I want to make dinner tonight," she announces.

"Oh, yeah? Like what?"

"My lasagna."

My ears perk up at that. I don't know what it is, but Aunt Colette makes the best lasagna I've ever tasted. It's my favorite thing she makes. "Well, you won't hear me telling you no," I mutter, breathing out a laugh.

"Invite your friend," she blurts out, holding up the rest of her muffin, a mischievous look on her face. She keeps referring to Cope as *"my friend,"* as if she hasn't known him longer than I have.

My stomach lurches into my throat at that suggestion. "Ah, I don't know. He's probably bu—"

"Ask him," she replies, more firmly this time. "You never know until you ask. He's a nice boy, and it would be lovely to have more than just us at dinner tonight. Besides, he made us that delicious stew. We should return the favor."

I snort. "Auntie, he's twenty-five. That's hardly what I'd consider a boy."

"Xander, you better text him already before I smack you upside your stubborn-ass head with my slipper."

"Okay, okay. Jeez." I hold up my hands in mock innocence. "So abusive around here."

Reaching into the pocket of my sweats, I grab my phone, and pull up the message thread between Cope and I. Heart galloping against my rib cage, I type out a text.

And promptly delete it because it sounds stupid.

Then type it out again, before erasing it all.

Third time's a charm, as I press send before I can talk myself out of it.

Me: Hey, my aunt is making lasagna for dinner tonight, and wanted me to invite you. I'm sure you're already busy. It's late notice, so no worries if you can't come.

Staring at the message, I attempt to swallow the lump in my throat, to no avail. Why does it feel so weird inviting him to dinner? It's not like I'm asking him on a date; my aunt will be here. Hell, it was her idea, but it still feels…oddly vulnerable.

It's probably all in my head.

Stomach grumbling, I get back to the task at hand—making some lunch. I pull out a loaf of bread, some ham, cheese, and the tub of butter. A grilled ham and cheese sandwich sounds good, so I make that, all while trying to keep my mind off the phone on the counter, and whether Cope responded to my invite yet. It takes all my willpower not to look the entire time I'm cooking, and by the time I sit down with my hot sandwich in front of me, my hands practically fumble with the phone, trying to check it.

Heart skipping a beat in my chest, I click on the new message from him.

Cope: I love lasagna. I'll be there. ;)

Jesus Christ. These flutters in my stomach need to chill out.

After I finish my lunch, I try, but epically fail, to continue with my afternoon without anxiety twisting up inside me. I do more laundry—I do *all* the laundry—go for a walk around the property with Aggie, Facetime Travis, and then shower…all while my mind is pinpointed to the fact that Cope will be here, in this house, and I don't know how to process that.

We've hung out so many times now. Why does it feel so different?

Probably because it's dinner and not chores, and probably because you're still *avoiding telling him you broke up with your boyfriend.*

A quick look at my phone shows that I have about an hour before he's supposed to arrive. This is going to be the longest night of my life if I don't figure out how to calm the fuck down. After I throw a little bit of gel into my hair, I head out to the porch to smoke a quick J, knowing it'll ease my nerves some.

There's a whole boatload of shit on my mind and on my to-do list. In the near future, I need to get all of my stuff from Henry's place, and I really need to sit down with Bastian, my business partner, and figure out a plan for the dispensary. Henry's still one of the investors, and while we both agreed to keep our relationship out of business, I'd still like to buy him out. That's a goal I've been wanting to achieve for a lot longer, though.

For about the last year now, Bastian and I have been toying with the numbers and seeing if it would be possible to buy out *all* our investors, not just Henry. We want to open other locations, but we don't want to do that while indebted to people. Maybe this breakup is the push I need to finally make that happen.

A large part of me isn't ready to go home yet. Yes, my aunt is doing well, but I would hate for me to get home, and she has nobody here if something were to happen. It just doesn't seem logical for me to leave any time soon. Although, I could fly back home for a few days, get my shit from Henry's, and sit down with Bastian, before flying back here. That's always an option, I guess.

I don't know. Maybe I'll text Bas tomorrow and see what he wants to do.

Taking a hit off the joint, I watch with a grin as Aggie ambles across the grass toward the porch. I've noticed when it's just my aunt out here, Aggie doesn't usually come over here unless she's got treats or something, so I'm not sure why she seems so attached to me. I love it, though.

She comes up on the porch, standing right beside my chair. The way she waits for pets reminds me of a dog or a cat. I never knew cows enjoyed being pet the same way house animals do. Maybe it's just her, I don't know. Tootsie doesn't mind if I give her pets, but she doesn't go out of her way to ask for them.

"Hey, Aggie girl," I coo, running my hand up and down the side of her, the thick brown coat brushing through my fingers.

My phone vibrates inside my pocket, and when I pull it out, I see a text from Cope, palms instantly slicking up.

Cope: I'll be heading over soon. You guys need me to bring anything?

He's so thoughtful and sweet.

Me: We got everything here, but thank you.

Cope: Alright. See you soon. :)

"Uh-oh, he's coming over here," I mutter to Aggie as I put the joint out and stand up. "Pray for me, girl. I may not survive."

Aggie tosses me a look over her shoulder that, no shit, looks like she's judging my dramatics. I chuckle to myself like a psycho.

"Trust me, I'm judging me too."

Chapter 14

Cope Murphy

"You're white as a ghost, dude. Relax." Shooter pats me on the back before taking a seat on the loveseat across from the couch I'm on.

"I'm relaxed," I lie.

Shooter chuckles. "Bro, you're more tense than a bronc locked up in the bucking chute, waiting to be released."

"Shooter's right," Whit chimes in as he strolls in from the kitchen. He hands his new boyfriend, Reggie, a beer. "You look awfully pale. What are you nervous for?"

Shooter, Sterling, Whit, and Reggie have all been over since late this morning watching football. Meaning they were also here when I got the text from Xander inviting me over. I ended up telling them everything I already told Shooter, about how I thought I was starting to have feelings for Xander, and that it confused me. Mostly because Whit is probably one of the most level-headed ones out of our friend group, and I figured he'd have some good advice.

"Honestly, I don't even fucking know." Blowing out a

breath, I rub my hands on the top of my thighs, my palms annoyingly sweaty.

"Have you hung out with him since you admitted your growing feelings to yourself?" Whit asks.

I nod. "Yeah, but also, not really."

His brows pinch. "Elaborate."

Breathing out a laugh, I go on. "Well, we hung out at the hospital for several hours while his aunt was there, but that was a high-stress type situation, so these feelings weren't really on my mind. And then I saw him briefly when they got home from the hospital. I'd brought them dinner, but it was more of a drop-off-and-go scenario, so we didn't actually hang out. After that, the only times we've hung out are the mornings when I go over there to help him with his farm chores. We're busy when we do that, so again, it's easy because my mind is occupied with other things. This is dinner. I won't have anything to occupy my mind. And it feels like the more I try to convince myself we're friends and nothing more, the more my brain latches on to everything about him I find way more interesting than a friend would. Whenever we're around each other, it feels intimate… not friendly."

"Do you think your nerves are coming from the fact that Xander is a guy?" This time, the question comes from Sterling.

It's a genuine question, and it's one I've asked myself. "I don't think so," I reply honestly. "Shooter and Whit can vouch for me on this, but I've never really dated a lot. I haven't had feelings for more than a few people. It just hasn't been my thing. I've been so busy with other stuff, like finishing high school, going pro, and then, as we all know, once professional rodeo comes into play, it's easy to take up a lot of your time."

"So, the feelings are what make you nervous, and not who

they're directed toward?"

Meeting Sterling's gaze, I nod. "It feels silly because I'm twenty-five years old, and it seems like something I should've experienced already, but the way I feel around Xander is unlike anything I've ever felt. Being around him is easy. It's fun. But it's more than that, too. I don't know, I can't explain it. I don't understand it, but he just feels *different*, and I don't know how to handle that, especially since he has a boyfriend. Why couldn't I feel this way about somebody who was available?"

The thought has crossed my mind more than once, that if Xander didn't have a boyfriend, I'd have no trouble pursuing him. I'd want to claim him. Make him mine. It has nothing to do with him being a guy and everything to do with having feelings for somebody I shouldn't, given their state of being unavailable.

"Life and love are never that simple," Whit cuts in.

"I don't love him. I hardly know him."

"I'm not saying you do. I just mean relationships and feelings; they happen even when they aren't supposed to. We've all experienced it," Whit says with an almost sad smile.

Somehow, without him even saying it, I know he's referring to Conrad, his ex-husband. It's in the faraway look in his eyes. I remember the shock I felt when I heard they were splitting up. It's been a couple of years now since the divorce has been final, and Whit's now moved on to Reggie, but everybody in town thought Whit and Conrad were end game.

Glancing over at the clock, I raise off the couch, my legs feeling a little like jelly. "Well, as fun as this conversation about feelings has been, I have to go if I want to be on time. Lock up when you guys leave."

"Good luck!" Sterling calls out to my retreating form right

before Shooter says, "I want details if you bang the boy next door." I glance over my shoulder, flipping Shooter off before I step into the laundry room, where I keep my boots.

Slipping my feet into them, I check my pockets and make sure I have my keys, wallet, and phone before I step outside. With Xander's house being so close, and it being a dry day today, I decide to walk. I pull out a cigarette and place it between my lips, lighting it, and hoping the smoke will help calm my nerves and clear my head. The walk over takes no time at all, and after inhaling a few drags, I put it out and slip the butt into the pack, as to not litter on their property.

Trudging up the steps, I knock on the door, my heart thumping rapidly as I wait to be let in. When the door's pulled open, it's Xander's bright, smiling face waiting for me. As discreetly as possible, I run my gaze over the length of him. He's dressed simply in a plain brown t-shirt and a pair of tight dark jeans, his curly black hair looking extra bouncy today. I don't know how else to describe it. It looks soft, like I could easily thread my fingers through it. He's not dressed up, by any means, but he looks *really good*. And relaxed.

"Hey," he breathes out with a wide grin. "Come on in."

The house smells delicious as soon as I step inside. My stomach rumbles, and I already know dinner tonight will be the best I've had in too damn long. While I prefer to cook at home versus eating out, I'm still not the greatest cook, and usually stick to simple things that don't take much time to make. I'm a much better baker.

A true home-cooked dinner isn't usually something I get unless I go to my folks' house. Since they've been traveling a lot now that they're both retired, dinners at their place are few and far between.

"Thanks for coming tonight," Xander says, tilting his head to look at me as we walk through the house. "I know it was kind of short notice, but she sprung it on me earlier."

I smile, nudging his arm with mine, trying to ignore the spark that ignites under my skin from the contact. "Thanks for inviting me. I probably would've just had delivery pizza otherwise."

That's a lie. Whit's cooking dinner for everyone over at my house, but there's no way I'm missing this.

"My aunt's always been an incredible cook, but she doesn't do it often. It's like a treat when she does."

The hallway opens to the kitchen, where she's working away at the stove. She glances up as we walk in, setting her spoon down and wiping her hands on the front of her apron, before crossing the space and pulling me in for a hug. "Hi, Cope," she murmurs, the sound muffled by the hug. She smells like herbs and spices, making it clear she's been in the kitchen for a while. "Happy to have you here."

"Thank you for inviting me, Ms. Dawson," I reply. "It smells incredible."

"Hope you're hungry." She pulls back with a smile. "I've made plenty."

I take a seat beside Xander at the bar, and we all fall into an easy, light conversation as she works on the meal. Eventually, she asks Xander to get the salad ready. Watching him cut and spin the lettuce, then dice up the tomatoes, onions, and cucumbers is far more mesmerizing than it oughta be. Every once in a while, he'll glance up from his task, gaze meeting mine, and it's like a moment passes between us. A wordless one that feels significant.

When he's done making the salad, I help him set the table. Through all of this, we weave around each other effortlessly.

Sure, there's conversation flowing between the three of us, but it's small talk—Colette asking me about the rodeo, we all discuss her farm, Xander talks a little bit about his business and how it's going from here, that kind of thing. As far as Xander and I go, there's not really room for us to talk about anything meaningful or heavy. It doesn't feel awkward or uncomfortable, though. It feels…nice.

Once the lasagna is finished, we sit down and dish up. My stomach is now steadily growling, and when I take the first bite, it's an effort to not groan. "Colette, this is amazing."

"Well, thank you, dear. I'm glad you like it."

The three of us fall into a comfortable silence while we take our first few bites. There's the lasagna, a fresh garlic bread, and salad, and I can't get enough of any of it.

Xander is the first to speak. "When do you go to Vegas?" he asks me, wiping his mouth with the napkin.

"In about two weeks."

"And you're gone for a week?"

"Ten days," I correct him. "Well, it's a ten-day competition event, but I'll be there for closer to two weeks. There're a bunch of panels and events we participate in prior to the main event."

"What's in Vegas?" Colette chimes in, curiosity swimming in her glinting eyes.

"Rodeo finals, ma'am."

"Oh, enough with the ma'am." She waves me off, and I can't help but chuckle. "Now, that sounds fun. Do you do it every year?"

"If I make it to finals, yes." It's my turn to wipe my mouth with the napkin, setting it in my lap when I'm finished.

"Which he always does," Xander chimes in, a wide grin on his face.

"Not *always*," I counter, a matching smile on my face.

"Don't be modest," he teases. Turning his attention to his aunt, he says, "From what I've seen, Cope is incredible at what he does. You said you were close to winning the world title last year, right?"

I nod. "Right." Pride swells in my chest at hearing Xander tell his aunt about me. About what he's learned from listening to me, but also from what he's watched when he looked me up online. "During the regular rodeo season, we compete in our event at different rodeos, earning points. The better you do, the more points and money you earn. By the time the season ends, the top fifteen for each event are chosen based on earnings to go to NFR, which is the grand finale of the year for professional rodeo. It's held in Vegas every year, and it's a huge event. People from all over the country travel there to watch it."

Colette smiles and nods. "How fun! I've never been to a rodeo, but I want to. I know how big they are here. Do your family and friends get to come and watch you in Vegas?"

"They can." I nod. "Several of my friends will already be there competing themselves. My folks usually fly out, but this year, they're traveling around Europe, so they won't be able to come."

"All sounds so very exciting," she mutters with a grin.

We finish eating, then Xander and I clear the table. Colette immediately starts on the dishes, instructing us to head out and do the evening chores instead of helping her in here.

"I'll be right back," Xander says, glancing at me. "I'm gonna run to the bathroom, and then we can go."

He disappears down the hall, and I can't help but watch him go. It's so different how drawn to him I am. Normally, I'm never this hooked on somebody and every little thing they do. Sure, I can acknowledge my attraction, but it's never this compulsive need to keep eyes on them whenever they're in the same room as me, like it is with Xander. Not to mention the fact that he's a man, and I've never even looked twice at another man before him. I feel like I should be freaking out more than I am about it, but my attraction to him almost feels…I don't know… Like a special circumstance, maybe.

"Thank you for all the help you've given Xander," Colette says, pulling my gaze back into the kitchen and onto her, where she's standing in front of the sink. Hot, soapy water fills one side of the sink as she rinses dishes before putting them in the dishwasher. I wonder if she saw me checking out her nephew just now.

"Oh, it's nothing," I reply, shaking my head. "Happy to help."

"I don't know what I would've done without him here during my surgery, and then again when I was in the hospital." She eyes me, like she has more to say, but it takes her a few moments before she continues. "I do wish he got out a little bit more, though, and didn't worry about me so much."

"He cares about you. I get the feeling that Xander has a big heart and wants to help those he loves."

"You're not wrong about that." She chuckles. "But I'm starting to feel a little better, and I just wish he'd take some time for himself. You know, get out and do something that made him happy."

I can't decipher the look she's giving me, but I don't have time to even try to figure it out because Xander strolls back into the room.

"Ready?" he asks, a baby blue beanie on top of his head that wasn't there when he left.

"Yup, let's go."

Chapter 15

Xander Dawson

I'm hyperaware of Cope's every move. The way his feet sound as they trudge through the grass. The softness of his breathing as we work side by side, feeding the animals. The way I can see him looking at me in my periphery when he thinks I'm not paying attention.

Especially that last one.

By the time we finish everything up, it's dark. The crickets are loud tonight, and the stars seem brighter than usual. There's not a cloud in sight. We're all done, so logically speaking, there's no reason for Cope to stay here. It only makes sense for him to go back home now…but I don't want him to. And based on the way he stayed to help with the evening chores after dinner, even though he didn't have to, I'm inclined to say he doesn't want to either.

I want to draw this out for as long as possible. Soak up all of him that I can get.

"Wanna have a beer before you head home?" I ask, and then very quickly add, "It's alright if you don't want to, or can't.

It's getting kind of late, so I totally get it if you'd rather—"

"Xander, slow down." Cope chuckles. "It's not even eight yet; I'd hardly call that late. I'd love a beer."

My shoulders relax a little at hearing him say yes. "Cool. I'll go grab them from inside if you want to wait out here?"

I don't know why I phrase that as a question, but he nods anyway. "Okay."

When I walk inside, it's quiet and all the lights are off. I doubt my aunt is asleep already, but I'm sure she's in bed, probably reading or watching some TV, so I keep it quiet as I cross through the house and grab a couple of cans out of the fridge. By the time I step outside, Cope is sitting on the edge of the porch, a cigarette lit, while he pets Aggie, who is, of course, still up here with us.

I don't know why Cope didn't sit in the rocking chair behind him, but I'm not complaining as I sit down beside him. We're close, but not close enough that any part of us is touching—much to my disappointment. Cope is so not somebody I'd normally be interested in. The cowboy, country boy thing has never done it for me. He's also more dude-bro than I usually care for—not that he's over the top or anything. Which is hilarious because my college ex-boyfriend was a frat guy.

Cope's multi-faceted. Had I not met him the way I did, had I seen him for the first time on TV for bronc riding, I'd probably assume he's a douche. Or at the very least, an asshole. His handsome face and the confident way in which he carries himself in the arena give off cocky vibes. Cope's just not at all who I would've expected, and I like that. I *really* like that.

"You made my aunt's whole week," I say with a breathy laugh, breaking the bubble of silence we've put ourselves in. "I think it made her happy to get to cook for people."

"I'm glad you invited me. It was delicious, and I'm glad I got to spend some time with you."

He glances over at me, and even in just the light from the moon, I can see the sincerity in his dark brown eyes. It makes my chest squeeze and my stomach flutter. It makes me want to lean over and beg him to try to kiss me again, so this time I could let him. I wonder, not for the first, or the second, or even the tenth time, how it would feel to kiss Cope. How his lips would feel against mine. How his mouth would taste. How our bodies would feel lined up together, hands roaming and grappling. Would he be confident in his movements, or nervous and unsure?

"So," I say, my voice coming out a little croaked, "your parents are in Europe right now?"

Cope nods, taking a drag of his cigarette. My eyes drop, shamelessly watching the way his lips pucker around the filter. The way they part, and I catch a glimpse of his tongue when he pulls it away. The way his eyes squint against the smoke. His nostrils flair slightly. "Yeah, they're both retired now, and have been making an effort to travel together more."

I lick my lips, trying to bring some moisture back to my dry mouth. Suddenly, I'm parched, like I haven't drank anything in weeks. My throat feels like sandpaper, and I can't rip my eyes away from him. Remembering he said something and is probably waiting for some sort of a response, I nod and smile. "That's fun. Good for them. Where are they now?"

"When I talked to them last, they were in Paris. It's somewhere my mom has always wanted to go, but for many years, my dad's one and only focus was rodeo. It doesn't leave much time for other shit, you know?"

"Yeah, but you don't compete the whole year, do you? Like,

you have time off to do whatever you want?"

"Yes, and no." Taking one last drag, he puts it out, sticking the butt in the pack and shoving it in his pocket. "With the exception of NFR, we're in off-season from about mid-September until about early May. However, most of us are still training and practicing weekly, if not daily, during that time. It's rare for us to take any real time off from that type of schedule. It's a year-round commitment if you want to be pro, just like any other sport."

"How often are you training?"

"I go to the gym every day, and I'm practicing at least two or three times during the week on top of the gym training."

"And how do you practice?"

"On broncs," he replies plainly, and my cheeks heat because that feels a little obvious. "But also in other ways, like mechanical horses. This helps me practice my form and keep my core muscles strong outside of the gym."

His passion and his dedication are such a turn-on.

Over the last several weeks, I've discovered how much I enjoy listening to Cope talk about the rodeo and about bronc riding—two things I never thought I'd find interest in. And truthfully, if it weren't Cope talking about it, or Cope riding, I probably wouldn't give a shit. But something about watching and listening to him explain something he's so visibly passionate about makes me warm all over. It's clear to anybody with eyes and ears that Cope loves what he does. It's not just about title or money or whatever else they do this for. He's talented and he genuinely enjoys it.

"I'd love to see you ride one day," I announce softly, and when he turns his head, gaze meeting mine, his wide smile makes my heart skip a beat. *Was that a stupid thing to say?*

"We can make that happen," he replies, nudging my arm with his. The touch is electric, making my breath hitch. We hold eye contact, and the world disappears beyond us. I wet my lips with my tongue, and my blood heats as his eyes dip, tracking the movement before mimicking it with his own.

Fuck. Kiss me. Please. Fucking. Kiss. Me.

I could honestly laugh at how ridiculous I sound inside my head right now. Why the hell would he kiss me when he still thinks I have a boyfriend? When I turned him down the first time?

But you don't have a boyfriend anymore, dipshit. So, tell him that.

Then it would seem like I was only telling him because I want him to kiss me.

Well, you do *want him to kiss you.*

Oh my God. I'm losing my mind. How am I arguing with myself?

Internal me is right, though. I need to tell him. Hell, I *want* to tell him. So, why does it feel like such a big deal?

Because I'm me, and I always make things way larger than they need to be.

For fuck's sake, Xander.

Dragging in a deep breath, I clasp my hands together in front of me, staring out into the night, my pulse a jackhammer, as I finally say it. "Henry and I broke up."

Cope sucks in a breath, and I can see his body tense up beside me, but I don't dare look at him. "When?"

"When he came to visit for my birthday."

The questions and confusion radiate off of Cope, and I don't even have to look at him to know it's there. I can *feel* it. "But I saw you on your birthday, and he wasn't here."

"Yeah, uh…" *Spit it out already.* "I broke up with him the

night my aunt went back to the hospital. He got on the next plane back home."

"Why? Ah, I mean, you don't have to answer that," he blurts out with a quick shake of his head. "I don't know why I asked that. It's none of my business. Are you okay?"

When I finally look over at Cope, his brown eyes are soft, watching me with curiosity and something that vaguely resembles care. It turns my insides into mush.

"It needed to happen. We wanted different things, and the distance between us made that painfully clear. I'm okay."

And I *am* okay.

Cope clears his throat and runs a gentle hand down the side of Aggie, where she's still standing in front of us, chewing on some of the tall strands of grass near the edge of the porch. "What are the things you wanted that he didn't?" he asks quietly.

This was the one question I was hoping he wouldn't ask. The answer can feel heavy. But I'm also not going to lie to him.

"A future," I reply, as if it's so simple. "I want to know that I have a future with my partner. That I'm not just wasting my time and dating only to date. I want to know I'm important to them—and not just be told that, but to *feel* it."

"And you didn't feel important to Henry?"

"Sometimes I did." A deep sigh leaves my lungs, knowing this probably won't make any sense. "What Henry and I had was very convenient for both of us for a lot of the time. At least in the beginning. It worked for me because, at the time, I had just gotten out of a relationship that had hurt me more than I expected it to. So, when we first got together, I wasn't looking for anything serious. Then I grew to want more. But he didn't." I laugh sadly. "I remember this one time, about a year into our relationship. I'd asked if he wanted to meet my mom. It had been bugging me that she hadn't met him yet."

"He said no?"

"He said no," I confirm. "I believe I told you he's not close with his family. He couldn't grasp why it was so important for me, even when I explained it to him. I brought it up again about six months ago. Told him I thought it was the right next step for us, and how much it meant to me." The memory of how much that conversation sliced me open hits me in the chest. "He still wouldn't, and he got weird about it. Made me feel like *I* was the weird one for wanting such a thing. Looking back, I think that was probably the first time I really started to realize he could never give me what I wanted. What I *needed*."

My chest feels flayed open, sharing all of this, but when I glance over at Cope, he's giving me a look, filled with something like understanding, that makes me feel okay to continue.

"All that to say, it was for the best, and it needed to happen, but it still sucks. Dating someone for so long and having it go nowhere, especially at my age."

"Because you're so old," Cope teases with a chuckle, somehow managing to lighten the mood.

Rolling my eyes, I shove him playfully as I let out a laugh of my own. "That's not what I meant, asshole." I glance over at him, the smile on his face brightening his dark eyes. "I'm getting close to thirty. Meaningless dating isn't as appealing as it was in my early twenties."

"Well, I'd say I'm sorry it ended, but I'd have to agree, it sounds like it was for the best," Cope mutters. "I am sorry it's caused you pain, though."

"Thank you." The sincerity in his tone is like a balm to any nerves I was feeling.

"I should probably head back home." Cope pushes to a

stand, and I do the same. "I've got an early morning, and it's getting late."

"Of course. I'll walk you out front." We move in silence around the side of the house, side by side. My whole body tingles with what I want to happen when we part ways. I'm not sure it will, though.

We come to a stop in front of the house. "Thanks for inviting me," he says softly.

He turns his body so it's facing mine, and the energy around us shifts as we lock eyes. Butterflies swarm in my stomach, and a light tingling feeling takes over my chest, spreading down my arms until I can feel it in the tips of my fingers. It's electric, the way he's looking at me.

It could be all in my head, but I hope not. It feels shitty of me to be craving another man's kiss when I just told Cope about the ending of my relationship, but I can't find it in me to care. Especially not when Cope's hand comes up, palm cupping the side of my face, his thumb rubbing along my cheekbone. Everywhere he touches, it lights up. Leaning into the touch, I stand on bated breath.

Except he doesn't make any move.

"I want to kiss you, but I won't. Not yet." I can't deny the disappointment flushing through me at his words, but then he continues. "I'll be respectful of your relationship ending for now, but I need you to know that I plan to make you mine in due time, city boy."

And with the weight of that declaration in the air, he turns on his heel and walks away into the night while I'm left here, stunned silent. Replaying his words in my head, a smile upturns my lips, so wide I'm thankful that it's dark enough that if he turned around, he wouldn't be able to see it.

Did he really say that?
Yes…yes, he did.

After a few minutes, the night's chill catches up to me, and I head inside. Once I lock up, I meander into the kitchen to grab some water before going to my room for the night. My aunt's in there, sitting at the counter, scrolling through her phone. She glances up when she sees me, a grin forming on her lips.

"What's got you smiling like that?" she asks, almost knowingly.

Opening the fridge, I grab a water before closing it. I shake my head. "Nothing," I lie. "I'll be in my room watching TV if you need me."

"Mmhmm," she hums. "Goodnight, Xan."

"Night, Auntie."

With a quick pit stop to the bathroom to wash my face and brush my teeth, I head to my room, where I strip down to my boxer briefs, and slide into bed, all while anticipation and a nervous type of excitement swirl through me. By the time I'm settled and have the TV turned on, I grab my phone, noticing a new text notification, the sight spiking my pulse all over again.

Cope: This is probably a long shot, but I'd love if you were able to come to Vegas for NFR. Even if it was only for a few days.

Another one comes in before I have a chance to respond, and it brings a smile to my lips.

Cope: Don't answer tonight, but please think about it. It could be fun. And I know it may not be possible with your aunt and all, but if you can swing it, I'd love to have you there. Goodnight, city boy.

For the next several hours, I watch TV without ever actually watching anything, a permanent smile on my face as I replay every minute of tonight, from start to finish.

This is either really bad...or really fucking good, and my wildly beating heart hopes it's the latter.

Chapter 16

Xander Dawson

I'm slowly becoming obsessed with my mornings here in Copper Lake. Sitting on the back porch, watching the sun rise in the sky. The calm quietness that comes with the air of each fresh day. Aggie joining me when she wakes up and wanders over to this part of the yard. Even the roosters crowing.

This type of early morning relaxation isn't something I get back home.

Sure, I have a porch I enjoy sitting on while I drink my coffee, but instead of crisp, fresh morning air and the sound of the farm animals waking up, I get polluted air and the sound of morning traffic. Don't get me wrong, I love my little house back home. It has never done me wrong, but it's never crossed my mind that maybe I'd enjoy country living.

Growing up, it always seemed boring; living in a town so small, you can drive through it in under twenty minutes, having so much land that you can't even see your neighbors from your porch, and not having several fast-food joints at your disposal every other block. Having been in Copper Lake for about a month so far, I can wholeheartedly say that I don't miss those little conveniences as much as I thought I would. Not when the alternative is all of *this*.

I'm in my head, watching Aggie chase the chickens around the yard, when the backdoor opens. Glancing over, I watch my aunt step outside, a maroon robe tied around her waist and a pair of black, ankle-high rubber boots on her feet. Her hair is wrapped up on the top of her head in a towel, like she just got out of the shower. A steaming cup of coffee in hand, she sits down in the rocking chair next to me.

"Morning, dear." Aunt Colette's voice is soft and warm.

"Morning. How'd you sleep?"

"I slept fine, honey. How about yourself?"

In the yard, one of the chickens turns on Aggie, chasing her around. Aggie moos loudly as the chicken squawks. Aunt Colette and I both chuckle at the sight.

"I slept fine, too," I tell her. My stomach twists as I consider what I say to her next. It's been on my mind since I got his text, and while I know I can't go, it still makes me giddy, and I need to tell someone. "Cope texted me when he got home last night, and invited me to Vegas."

Her grin grows as her eyes slowly shift over to mine. "Did he?"

"Wait, did you tell him to ask me?" She looks way too evil genius right now.

Chuckling, she shakes her head. "No, I didn't ask him to invite you to Las Vegas, Xander." Taking a slow sip from her coffee mug, she looks at me over the lip of the cup and adds, "But I think you should go."

My brows clash together tightly as I look at her like she's lost her mind. "I can't do that, Auntie."

Her face screws up. "And why the hell not?"

"Uh…" I motion between us with my hand. "Maybe because the whole reason I'm here is to help you?"

"Oh, for heaven's sake," she mutters. "I'm not a damn child, you know?"

"No, just stubborn as hell," I toss back, rolling my eyes.

"You're one to talk."

Scoffing, I narrow my eyes on her. "What the hell is that supposed to mean?"

"It means that it wouldn't kill you to take some time for yourself. Do something for *you* for once. I'm not going to wither away and die if you're gone for a few days."

She doesn't give me a chance to respond because she gets up from the rocking chair, grabs her coffee mug, and goes inside without another word. She's ridiculous.

After I finish my coffee, I get moving on with morning chores. As usual, Aggie follows me around for every task, even when I take the horses out to the pasture. Tootsie glares at her from her side and, if I didn't know any better, I'd assume there was some cow animosity going on between the two of them. I make my way back toward the main part of the yard, coming to an abrupt stop at the sight.

Elvis, one of my aunt's two mini donkeys, is chasing Pepper, one of the goats, around the front of the barn. Pepper *hates* Elvis and Bogart, the other donkey, because they love terrorizing the goats. Elvis is hot on Pepper's tail, while Pepper screams for his damn life.

"Elvis! Knock it off." I step closer to them, clapping my hands loudly to deter Elvis. "Pepper doesn't like you, you fool. Leave him alone!"

He doesn't listen. Chasing Pepper around and around,

weaving through the flowers, around the trough. I can't help but laugh at the sight—and the sound—of it all. Elvis is braying as he chases a yelling Pepper. Finally, Pepper runs past me, and I put myself in between Elvis and him, cutting Elvis off.

It's never a dull moment here.

Once I divert Elvis's attention elsewhere, I finish up my chores, getting them nearly completed by the time my phone goes off in my pocket. Grabbing it out, I'm surprised to see a call from my sister so early. I hit accept, putting her on speakerphone.

"You're up early," I mutter as I waltz back into the barn to put my stuff away.

"Can't sleep," she rasps. "I've got heartburn like I've never had it before."

"Fuck, I'm sorry." I wince.

"So…" Gemma says, but doesn't go on.

"So, what?"

"I just talked to Aunt Colette."

"Ah, fuck. Of course, you did." I blow out a breath, already knowing where this is heading. "Go on… What'd she say?"

"Don't get all huffy with me, big brother."

"Gemma…"

"Fine, fine." She giggles, and my irritation grows. "She told me about your invite to Vegas from the hottie cowboy from next door. She also told me you won't go."

"Uh, yeah. Because I'm here for a reason. Not to gallivant around the country."

"Okay, gallivant is a tad dramatic, don't you think?"

"No."

"Alright, well, I just wanted to let you know that right before I called you, I booked my flight to Copper Lake for the second week of December."

"You what?" She can't be serious.

She hums. "I'll be there to help with whatever auntie needs. Meaning you don't have to be."

"Gemma, you're pregnant."

"I am barely twenty weeks along. I will be okay."

"Yeah, but you don't need to do that. You have Lucas, and your whole life there."

She snorts. "Xan, I'm not moving there. I'm coming for a week. Lucas will survive on his own. In fact, he's about to head to New York for the next month to get their new office set up. He won't even be here. Stop trying to talk me out of it. I'm coming, and you're going to Vegas with the hottie cowboy."

Groaning, I say, "Stop calling him that."

"You *did* say he was cute. I'm honestly a little disappointed I won't get to meet him while I'm there."

"She is such a meddler," I mumble, crossing through the yard toward the porch.

"Who? Aunt Colette?" Gemma asks rhetorically. "Of course, she is. This isn't news."

My stomach's in knots at the thought of actually taking Cope up on his invite.

"Listen, I gotta get up and go to the grocery store," Gemma says, cutting through my thoughts. "But you're going. End of discussion."

"Thanks, Gemma."

"Anytime, brother."

I can hear the smile in her voice before she ends the call. Suddenly, my hands are all shaky and my heart is racing a mile a minute. *Holy shit.* I'm doing this.

After I kick my shoes off by the door, I walk inside, and

find Aunt Colette standing in the living room, a shit-eating grin on her face. "You're welcome."

"I hate you," I grumble, but we both know I'm full of shit because as soon as I brush past her, a huge smile takes over my face.

"You better text him and tell him you can go," she calls out after me.

It takes me an entire shower and approximately twenty minutes of sitting on the edge of my bed, talking myself into it, before I finally pull out my phone and send the text.

I can't believe I'm doing this.

Chapter 17

Cope Murphy

Shania Twain's *Any Man of Mine* blasts from the subwoofer near the back of the parking lot as a black Honda Civic pulls up. Shooter's got a navy-blue bandana tied around his neck, a pair of too-short matching athletic shorts on, and he lost his white t-shirt about an hour ago after Sterling drenched him with the hose. Which I'm beginning to suspect was on purpose, given the way Sterling's been making googly eyes at Shooter ever since.

Powder Ridge Arena, the arena we all train at, and the place where Copper Lake hosts rodeo events, is holding a car wash fundraiser this afternoon for the rodeo club at the local high school. It's an annual event, and it's usually held in the spring before we leave for rodeo season, but this year, the arena parking lot was getting repaved so we couldn't.

It's an unusually warm and dry day for early December, and that's the only reason this damn car wash is acceptable. Well, that, and the fact that the arena has a bunch of industrial grade heaters blowing on us. The water is still freezing, though.

My nipples are so hard, I'm surprised they haven't fallen off. Yet, here's Shooter, willingly getting soaking wet to turn his boyfriend on. I'm not even surprised.

The driver of the Civic rolls his window down. Sterling goes over the cost and takes payment before we begin washing. I spray the car with the hose while Shooter makes a show of dunking the large sponge in the bucket of soapy water and wringing it out—but not before letting some run down his bare chest. I can't even count how many cars we've washed so far in the few hours we've been here. It seems like everybody in town is in this parking lot.

Once we're finished cleaning the Honda, he drives toward the other side of the parking lot to pick up a complimentary glass of lemonade and some cookies from Daisy and Jessie, our two barrel racers. We've got the system down pat at this point, working this car wash like a well-oiled machine. By the time the next car pulls up, I'm so in the zone with what I gotta do, I don't even notice who it is that's pulled up until I hear Shooter holler my name.

"Copey!" When my eyes lift to meet his, he's got a roaring smile on his face. "Looks like your cute little boy next door came to get his car washed."

I glance down, taking in the Subaru that belongs to his aunt before looking through the windshield, gaze locking with Xander's bright blues. A wide grin splits my face as I round the hood. "Hey. Fancy seeing you here," I say, tossing him a wink.

"Cowboy Car Wash," he drawls with a chuckle. "Really?"

"Catchy, don't you think?" I shrug. "I'm glad you came."

Things between Xander and I have always felt easy, but it feels like ever since finding out he broke up with Henry, any nerves I'd been experiencing, any guilt I held on to for feeling a way I shouldn't, have completely dissipated.

"Yeah, well, when you asked me to meet you here, you conveniently left out the wet t-shirt car wash going on." Xander shamelessly rakes his gaze down my body, and it feels good having his eyes on me. Knowing he's into me too.

"Thought it'd make for a nice surprise." Running a hand down the front of my soaked and nearly see-through t-shirt, I add brazenly while waggling my brows, "You like?"

Xander's cheeks pinken as he allows his eyes to quickly roam down the front of my abdomen again before coming back up to my face. Clearing his throat, he nods. "I definitely like."

"Knew you would."

"Okay, listen up Cowboy Casanova," Shooter cuts in, slapping a cold, wet hand on my shoulder. "While I love watching you flirt with your hottie neighbor, the line is getting longer, so can we get on with the show?"

Xander sniggers softly, eyes alternating between me and Shooter. "How much?" he asks, gaze settling on me.

I flash him a toothy grin. "It's on the house."

"Uh, it very much is *not* on the house," Shooter blurts out behind me. His presence is suddenly annoying me, but it only makes Xander laugh harder. "This is for the high school's rodeo club. That'll be ten bucks, Xan-man. Will that be cash or card?"

Shooter all but shoves me out of the way as he takes the money from Xander, and I don't think I've ever wanted to smack the shit out of Shooter as much as I do right now. An idea coming to mind, I grin as I twist up the wet rag in my hand before snapping at Shooter's shirtless back.

He jumps up and spins around, eyes narrowed on me. "Ow, you cocksucker," he grunts. "The fuck was that for?"

I lift my hands, shrugging innocently as I take a step back.

He flips me off before returning his attention to Xander. Once he's finished giving him his change, Shooter steals the hose from my grip, spraying the Subaru. Scowling at him, I reach into the bucket and grab the sponge, wringing it out. Before I even have a chance to wash anything, Shooter turns the hose on me, drenching me from head to toe in three seconds flat.

"What the fuck, man?" I balk at him.

Smug look on his face, he tilts his head toward Xander. "Thank me later."

I roll my eyes, but get to work scrubbing the dirt and grime off the car. Every once in a while, I'll glance up and find Xander watching me from inside. His eyes alternate between my face, my hand that's holding the sponge, my arms, and my chest. They roam, somehow being everywhere all at once. His full lips are parted, and he's not even trying to hide the fact that he's checking me out.

Biting the inside of my cheek to keep my smile from breaking free, I focus on cleaning the car in the most attractive way possible. Everyone in this parking lot fades into the background as I lean over the hood of the car, internally smirking at the fact that my t-shirt rides up, giving Xander a view of my bare skin. Using the sponge, I rub wide circles onto the car, ensuring I get every inch. His window is rolled up for obvious reasons, and how I desperately wish I could hear him. Hear the way his breath probably hitches, or how it speeds up the more he watches me, hopefully enjoying the view. Or better yet, I wish I could hear the thoughts streaming through his mind as his eyes take me in.

Does he like what he sees?

Does he want to watch me do this with less clothing on?

Maybe he wants to watch me do something else entirely…

maybe to him.

For the most part, I was pretty good about not allowing my mind to wander toward inappropriate and intimate thoughts regarding Xander—and Xander and me—since I knew he had a boyfriend. But ever since he told me last week that he broke up with him, my mind has been on overdrive. The images filtering through, the desires clutching at me, are intense. At first, I wondered if it would be weird, since Xander is a guy, and my only experience is with women.

The more I think about it—which, I'm not kidding, is *a lot*—the more I don't think it'll be just fine. Everything with Xander is different. From the moment I met him, I was enthralled with him in a way I've never been before. The easiness that comes from being around him, the comfortable way I feel when we hang out, the voracious attraction I feel toward him, and the way it feels like I might perish if I'm not near him, close enough to feel his body heat at all times…it's all new. I've had feelings for other people before, sure, but they've all felt, I don't know, surface level, maybe? They all pale in comparison to him. I think being with him intimately would feel right.

"Bro, hurry the fuck up," Shooter hisses at me, pulling me out of my thoughts. "The line is damn near wrapped around the fucking building. I think the car is clean enough."

Groaning, I roll my eyes, and begrudgingly finish up the wash before Shooter rinses the car off. Once we're done, Xander drives down and grabs the lemonade and cookies from the girls before he parks. I smile to myself, knowing he's staying. The next car pulls up, and like we have every other time, we work in a system, washing, rinsing, and then repeating with the next car. And the next. Until finally, they're all finished.

The temperature has dropped significantly the later in the

afternoon it's gotten. It'll be dark soon, so we all hustle to put everything away before we all head inside. Each year, the owner of the arena hosts a barbecue for all the volunteers who help with the fundraiser. It's a thank you for spending our entire day doing this. Since it's freezing and nearly dark this year, they're doing a buffet style meal inside the arena. Xander climbs out of his car, crossing over the parking lot until he's standing right in front of me.

"Is it okay that I'm still here? I can go."

"You're not going anywhere, city boy," I tell him, nudging him with my arm, and loving the electricity that flows between us at the small touch. "You hungry?"

He nods, lips tugging into a grin. "I could eat."

Inside the arena, there's a vast array of food laid out on several different folding tables. Whit and his entire veterinary clinic staff are here, making sure the food is out, silverware and plates are available, and they're helping direct people on where to go. Xander and I each fix ourselves a plate, sneaking the occasional glance at each other, before heading over to the bleachers and take a seat. Scarfing down a bite of the pulled pork sandwich, I groan, the flavor smoky and delicious. I had a half-ass breakfast before coming here this morning, so I could easily eat another four of these.

Xander breathes out a laugh as he takes me in. "You got a little…" Instead of finishing his sentence, he reaches over, and with the pad of his thumb, wipes away a glob of barbeque sauce left on the corner of my mouth. My heart stutters in my chest and a lick of heat swims through my veins as I watch him bring the sauce-covered thumb up to his own mouth and suck it clean. His eyes meet mine, and he must see the heat in my gaze, and it's as if he just realized what he did and what it did to me, because his cheeks flame a bright pink and he looks away quickly, shoving a bite of sandwich into his mouth.

Good God...now is not the time for my dick to give an appreciative twitch.

Shooter and Sterling come up and sit beside us once they have their food, and given the look Shooter sends my way, I know that fucker caught what just happened. I swear, he never misses anything. Eventually Colt and Boone come and sit down, too. Suzy, Boone's daughter, is right on his heel, carrying her own little plate full of food. Instead of sitting beside her dad, she positions herself right in between Shooter and Sterling, setting her plate on top of Shooter's thigh. She's always been his biggest fan, and he has a soft spot for her. It's cute. I've never seen Shooter interact with little kids the way he does Suzy. Older kids, sure, he's great with them, especially if they show an interest in rodeo and bronc riding.

"Petition to never do a car wash in the winter ever again," Sterling says right as a shiver wracks through him. We're all still dressed in our wet clothes, and even with the heat of the arena, we're all probably chilled down to the bone.

"Amen," I mutter before taking another bite. "That was fucking cold."

"Maybe Xan-man, here, can warm you up after," Shooter drawls, waggling his brows. "I know I plan to bury myself so deep—"

"Don't even think of finishing that sentence in front of my daughter, man," Boone cuts in, and we all laugh as Shooter glances down at Suzy, who's already watching him, and he shrugs.

"I was going to say bury myself so deep under my covers." He rolls his eyes dramatically, and Suzy copies the act.

"Mmhmm, sure you were," Boone quips.

"Tough crowd," he whispers to Suzy, loud enough for everybody to hear. She giggles and nods.

Boone shakes his head, rubbing a hand over his mouth to hide the smirk there. He glances over at Xander and says, "So, Cope says you're coming to Vegas?"

"Yeah, I think I am." He smiles. "Just for a few days, probably."

"It's a fun time," Boone offers. "I think you'll enjoy yourself. Have you been to any rodeos before?"

Xander shakes his head. "This will be my first."

His eyes skirt over to mine, and we share a quick look before he smirks and looks away again. My entire body is hyped up from having him here, anticipation and what I can only describe as *need* for him vibrating inside of me.

"Well, this'll be quite the rodeo to pop your cherry," Shooter chimes in. "NFR is a fucking wild time. It's my favorite event of the year."

"How are you feeling about not competing in it this year?" Colt asks Shooter.

Shooter is a three-time world champion at bareback bronc riding, but earlier this season, he left the circuit for mental health reasons. Because of that, he wasn't able to qualify to make it to finals. A few of the guys were worried he'd snap before the event, but I don't think so. He's the happiest I've seen him in a long time, and he's very much at peace with his decision to step back this year.

"I'm feeling great, man," Shooter replies to Colt. "There's always next year, and now, this way, I stepped aside so my man can win his first world title." He grins.

Sterling groans, rolling his eyes beside him. "Riiight. Keep telling yourself that, baby."

This is Sterling's first year pro, and he kicked serious ass this season, qualifying himself for finals. It's not often that happens during your rookie year, but Sterling earned it. Even before Shooter dropped out, he was neck and neck with him when it came to scoring. We all know—even Sterling—that Shooter is just shooting the shit, but we like to give him a hard time anyway. Nobody is as cocky and full of himself as Shooter is. Sterling's the only person I've ever seen knock him down a notch or two. Honestly, I think it's part of why Shooter is so crazy about him.

A few hours later, once we've all finished eating our body weights in pulled pork and fruit salad, we help Whit and his team clean up the food before we pile out into the parking lot. Shooter winks at me as he and Sterling pass by, heading toward his truck. I rode with them this morning, but I have other plans for tonight… Hopefully, at least.

Bumping my arm against Xander's, I lean in and ask, "Can I catch a ride home with you?"

He looks over at me, nodding. "Sure. You didn't drive?"

"Nah, I rode here with Shooter and Sterling."

Xander unlocks the Subaru, and we both climb in. "Such a clean car," I tease. "Whoever washed it did a fabulous job."

Shrugging, Xander replies, "Eh, he did okay, I guess."

"Shiiit. I bet he did more than okay. He probably looked fucking sexy doing it, too."

Xander snorts. "Now, *that* I can confirm. While his car washing skills were a little mediocre, he did look hot doing it."

We glance at each other, sharing a smile, before his eyes return to the road. It only takes about five minutes to get home, and before long, Xander is parking his aunt's car in the driveway. He doesn't turn the engine off, nor does he make any attempt to get out. Neither do I.

The heat is turned on, the inside of the car toasty warm, even though I'm still chilled, and he's got his phone hooked up to the Bluetooth, playing some rock song I've never heard of on low volume. The air between us crackles, and I don't think it has anything to do with the temperature.

"Glad you came today," I tell him, turning my body in the seat to face him better.

Mimicking my position, his blue eyes lift to meet mine. Heat flares in them, and I feel it in my stomach. "Watching a bunch of hot cowboys get wet is hardly my idea of a bad afternoon." He chuckles, the sound melodic and rich.

Goosebumps raise on the flesh of my arm, heart beating a little faster, and despite the damp clothes I'm still wearing, my body feels like it's on fire. Our proximity, the way his face lights up when he smiles, the scent of whatever body wash or laundry soap he uses…all of it goes to my head, making me dizzy. Making me want to launch myself at him. Making me want to try things I've never done, but somehow know I'll enjoy because they'd be with him.

Instead of behaving like a horned-up neanderthal, I shrug, tossing him a cocky grin, and mutter, "What can I say? We're here to please the masses."

Xander hums, lids hooded as he watches me with his lip tucked between his teeth. He looks beautiful, face lit up on the faint glow coming from the dash. He makes my stomach twist and flip and squeeze in a way that's so foreign to me. I feel like I'm fifteen all over again, experiencing my first crush, only this time it's…more. It's what a crush *should* feel like.

Sitting in his presence, watching him, it reminds me of what they describe in movies. My fingers itch to reach out and touch him, my lips tingle with the need to taste him. It's all-consuming and heavy. It's a hazy mind and a steady vibration of need just below the skin. This feeling, while unsettling and different, is intoxicating.

Does he feel it, too?

Surely, he does. Or why else would he be looking at me the way he does? Like he can't tear his eyes away. Like he can't get his fill with a look alone.

Couldn't tell you who moves first, but one minute we're both relaxed in our seats, backs propped against the doors, and the next we're meeting in the middle, faces so close, our breath mingles. My hand slides up, cupping the side of his face, similar to how I did that night at the ranch, only this time, when I lean in and brush my lips softly against his, he doesn't pull away. He doesn't stop me.

In fact, he wraps a smooth, warm palm around the back of my neck, whispering a breathless "finally" against my mouth before fusing our lips together. His tongue slips into my mouth, curling around mine, and I revel in the taste of him—the taste I've been dying to try. It's minty and fresh from his gum, but also sweet. Addicting—and the feel of his lips against mine. This kiss feels like no other kiss I've experienced before. It feels like I've never truly been kissed before now. Like everything else was just practice, but this… This is the real deal. The sound that comes out of him is soft and heated, and it goes straight to my groin. Somehow, with all the grace in the world, Xander manages to unbuckle his seatbelt and climb into my lap, all while I seamlessly recline the seat, making room for him between the dash and myself.

Xander fits so effortlessly on top of me, his body the perfect size to curl up against me. Arms wrapping around his waist, I duck under his hoodie, trailing my fingers up his spine, loving the feel of his body reacting to mine. Between the shiver wracking through him, the goosebumps popping up under my touch, and the contented sigh he breathes into my mouth, I know he's enjoying this as much as I am. His hands roam up, threading through the hair on the back of my head. He tugs gently, nails raking across my scalp in a way that sends a bolt of arousal down my spine. I feel him growing hard against my stomach, and it doesn't freak me out at all, like I thought it might… It does the opposite. It turns me on.

We sit here like that for a while, making out and playfully touching and exploring each other, until the windows fog up and we can't seem to catch our breath. I've somehow lost my hat; it's probably laying in the empty driver's seat, and Xander's fingers are clutching onto the strands of my hair as his mouth moves against mine.

Eventually, and with all the willpower in the world, we pull away from one another, chests heaving, lips swollen and wet. Xander sits back on my lap, no doubt able to feel the hardness of my dick beneath him, and he swipes a thumb along my bottom lip.

"As much as I don't want to put a stop to this," he says breathlessly. "We probably should pump the brakes so we don't hook up for the first time in my aunt's driveway, in her car. Something tells me she wouldn't appreciate that."

I breathe out a laugh. "Yeah, you're probably right, but *goddamn*, do I not want to stop."

He leans down and captures my lips in one last kiss. "The feeling is mutual, cowboy."

Hearing him call me "*cowboy*" in his raspy, out-of-breath, just-kissed voice makes my cock throb behind the confines of my jeans.

Unlocking the door, he opens it, sliding off my lap and stepping into the night air. I climb out behind him, slipping my hands back around his waist and pulling him into me. Unable to help myself, I kiss him one last time, somehow managing to make it quick.

"I've got a shit ton to do before I leave for Vegas in a few days, so I probably won't get to see you much before you head down there. Want you to know it's not because I don't want to see you or because I'm freaking out about this. Pre-finals are always hectic, but I can't wait to see you there."

He smiles softly. "Me too."

After I make sure he gets inside, I make the short walk home, my mind reeling. By the time I make it inside my house, I can still feel the pressure of his lips on mine, and the one thing that keeps blaring inside my mind is how I've never had a kiss feel like that. Ever. And how I need it to happen again as soon as possible.

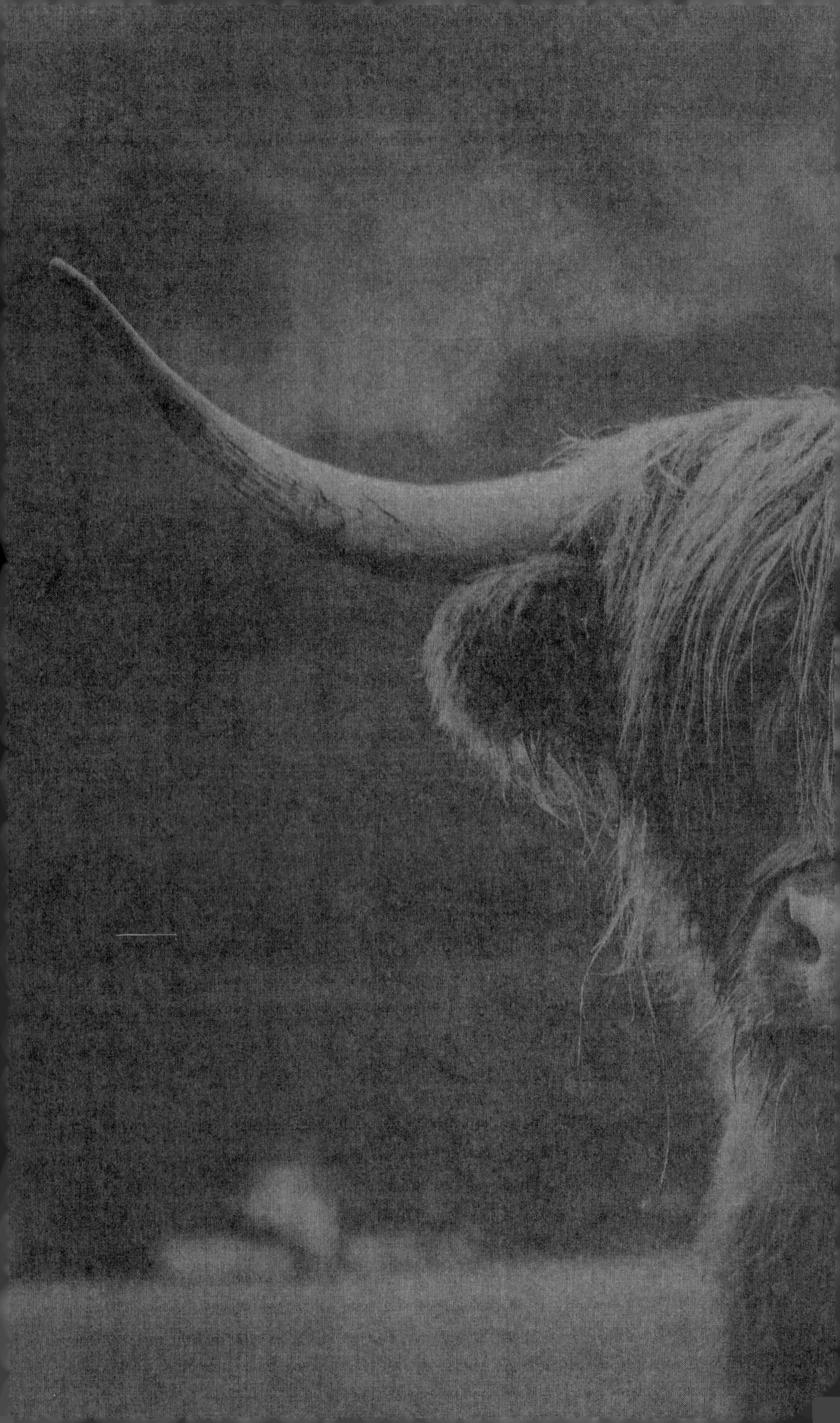

Chapter 18

Xander Dawson

True to his word, Cope was busy up until the morning he left for Vegas. The kiss we shared last week has been in the forefront of my mind ever since, and I can't help but wonder if it's been on his too. We've texted nearly every day. With everything he's got going on, it hasn't been anything in depth, but it's still something that makes me giddy, because I know that, regardless of how busy he is, I'm still on his mind enough for him to check in.

My plane landed in Las Vegas a few hours ago. After I checked into my hotel room and showered, I took an Uber to the arena the event is being held at. It's *massive*. There're so many people here, nearly every seat filled, and the crowd is rowdy and clearly very excited for the event to begin.

Cope was nice enough to make sure I had familiar faces to sit with in the stands. Prior to arriving, an unknown number texted me, which I quickly found out was Shooter. He told me where to meet him in the front of the arena, and when I got here, he and Whit were waiting for me. Everybody else in their group of friends is competing tonight, so the three of us are sitting together in the first row near the bucking chute—which I've since learned is the pen that the bulls and broncs are held in before it's their time to do their...thing.

Okay, so I'm not the best with the lingo yet, but I'm trying.

"You excited?" Shooter asks from beside me. He's practically bouncing in his seat, so it's safe to assume *he's* excited.

I nod. "Yeah. I've never seen anything like this before. I think it'll be cool to see Cope, uh, perform." My cheeks heat. "Is that what it's called?"

Shooter chuckles, but it doesn't feel mocking or like he's making fun of me. "Competing or riding both work," he corrects. "And Cope's damn good at what he does. You're in for a treat."

"I looked him up," I reply. "On YouTube, when he first told me what he does for a living, but I have no doubt seeing it in person will be even better."

"Nothing beats seeing them live," Whit offers from where he's sitting on the other side of Shooter.

"Do you travel with them?" I ask. "I mean, probably not with your clinic."

Whit shakes his head. "No, I don't. I probably could take the time off, but I generally don't prefer to do that." He nudges his glasses up the bridge of his nose before sweeping some hair out of his face. "But I watch them whenever they're competing at home."

Bareback is up first. All of this is a foreign language to me, but thankfully, Shooter breaks it down as simply as he can. There's a huge jumbotron screen that I watch, and every now and then, Shooter will point to the riders on the screen telling me what they're doing or how they're being scored. He explains the difference, other than the obvious one, between bareback—which is the way him and Sterling ride—and saddle—the way Cope rides—is that with bareback, the riders hold on to what is called a rigging, which I guess is a leather and rawhide handhold that's cinched on the horse, whereas, with saddle bronc riding, the riders only have a thick rein attached to the horses halter to hold on to.

Both seem like not a fun time to me, getting thrown around by this wild beast bucking underneath you while you get to hold on to a little bit of rope with only one hand, but at least with one you get to sit on a saddle, which has to be arguably more comfortable than sitting without one.

Truthfully, it seems like a crazy man's sport, and a concussion waiting to happen, but what the hell do I know?

The announcer booms over the loudspeaker, and the crowd goes wild. I'm assuming the festivities are about to begin. After the opening spiel is finished, and the national anthem is performed, the man behind the mic introduces the first bareback rider of the night. Music plays loudly, the lights flicker a bit, as the crowd stomps against the bleachers and cheers thunderously.

Rider number one busts out of the gate—err, I mean, *the bucking chute*—and everything happens so damn fast, I have no clue what I'm even looking at. Shooter does his best to explain what he can while we watch the riders come and go. That is, until it's Sterling's turn. Then Shooter becomes nothing but a loud and proud boyfriend, cheering him on. The grin on my face is wide and involuntarily as I alternate my gaze between Sterling on the writhing black-and-white beast and Shooter going crazy beside me.

As soon as the buzzer sounds, Shooter claps his massive

hands together, shouting at Sterling as he's pulled off the horse by another man on a different horse. Whether Sterling can even hear Shooter remains unknown, but he walks over to the edge of the arena, in front of where we are anyway, his smile blinding.

After that, Shooter leaves for a while, I'm guessing to go find Sterling in the back, and it's just me and Whit. We make a little small talk, but for the most part, I'm just observing everything and taking it all in.

Another few riders come and go before the man over the loudspeaker announces saddle bronc is up next. I don't know which number Cope is, but my stomach swirls with excitement and something else I can't place… Nerves, maybe? So far, nobody has gotten hurt, but what if he does? Shit, that's probably bad luck to even think, isn't it?

Eventually, Shooter finds his seat beside me again, arm bumping against mine as he plops down. "Cope's up next," he tells me, practically bouncing in his seat. "You excited?"

"Yeah," I reply honestly, a grin cracking through the façade I'm trying to put into place. Can't let his best friend know how into him I am, now can I? "You think he'll win?"

"Ah-ah." Shooter's eyes widen and he brings a finger up in front of his lips. "We don't talk about that inside the arena. Zip it."

When he makes a locking motion in front of his lips, I mimic it, then pretend to toss the key before returning my attention to the arena.

"He's in that chute over there," he murmurs near my ear, his arm outstretched, pointing toward the far side of the row of metal gates. "See him?"

"Barely."

I don't even know what I'm looking at, but once I focus my

eyes, I can make out the back of him as he lowers himself onto the horse. He's too far away to pick up on anything else. I *could* watch him on the jumbotron, but I'd rather watch *him*, even if it's a little hard to make out. We didn't get a chance to see each other prior to me coming here, so this'll be my first time seeing him in his whole done-up rodeo gear. Well, in person, that is.

"Alright, ladies and gentlemen," the announcer booms over the speaker, my gut twisting as nerves flutter through my body. A new song begins, one I'm not familiar with, but it's loud, even as the man continues. "Next up, we have a bronc rider here from Copper Lake, Wyoming. His fourth time joining us here tonight, let me hear it for Copeland Murphy!"

The words barely have time to leave his mouth before the chute is ripped open by a couple of guys and Cope enters the arena on top of a huge, fierce beast. My stomach's clear in my throat as I watch him on the edge of my seat, everything seeming to slow down. For the first time tonight, I'm actually seeing what's happening. Chestnut brown, with a thick, long mane to match, the horse looks strong and powerful as she bucks and kicks.

Cope's got a tight grip on the off-white rein attached to the horse's halter with his right hand; his left up above his head. The bronco jumps up, legs coming from beneath it as it lurches forward, all while Cope moves fluidly with her. Cope's feet move in a sweeping motion, forward to backward, from the horse's shoulder to flank. I remember Shooter telling me something earlier about the use of spurs on his boots, and how the movement, paired with how the riders hold the reins, helps them find rhythm with the animal.

The movement looks violent at times, making me queasy just thinking about being the one on the back of the horse.

When eight seconds are up, the blaring sound of the buzzer goes off, and the crowd erupts. I let out the breath I'd been holding as Cope is pulled off the animal. The moment his feet touch the dirt, he barrels over to the wall in front of us, his arms lifted above his head as he pumps them in the air victoriously. It's only then I realize I've raised out of my seat, along with Shooter, and everybody else around us. My cheeks hurt from smiling so wide, and I'm cheering so loud, my throat is no doubt going to feel raw later.

That was *incredible*. Confusing and kind of terrifying, but absolutely fucking incredible to watch. Holy shit.

The announcer shoots off Cope's overall score for the night—a ninety-four—but Shooter tells me we won't know if he won until the end. Even if he scores the highest tonight, they still have to take into account the earnings from the last ten days, add those up for all the riders, and then we'll have our winner. With it being the final night, the winner *will* be announced tonight, though. I know from listening to Cope talk about finals, and from what Shooter's told me since we've been here, there are several different winners and a multitude of prizes that will be announced and given out, but only one from each event will take the title of world champion. It's apparently a *large* cash prize, as well as a winning belt buckle, and bragging rights, of course.

After a few minutes, Cope has to go in the back so the next rider can come out. His gleaming eyes find mine once more before he does. His smirk grows, and he rips the hat off his head, giving it a swirl in the air like it's a lasso, and I swear I fucking melt. He bites down on his bottom lip, then blows a kiss my way before leaving.

"Oooh, shit, Xan-man," Shooter chirps in my ear, the smile

evident in his tone. He saw that just as much as I did. My cheeks and the tips of my ears heat up, and I don't even know why. It's not like I'm unfamiliar with hooking up, or with guys giving me attention. It's not something I normally get bashful from. But there's something—I can't even place what—about having Cope's attention, specifically...knowing he wants me, and then also knowing his friends notice it too. It gets me all warm and fuzzy inside. And maybe a little turned on.

Taking our seats again, we watch as the next handful of bronc riders comes out and do their thing. Watching them is not nearly as exciting as it was watching Cope, and this honestly probably wouldn't be anything that would pique my interest at all had it not been for him. Watching Cope out there was exhilarating. He gave his all tonight, and it was a rewarding thing to get to witness.

Once bronc riding is finished, they move on to the next part of the rodeo. All of this is so foreign to me; it's laughable at this point. My knowledge of the rodeo is so minute, that I thought it consisted of only bronc and bull riding. There's apparently a whole other section with a multitude of other events that I didn't even know about. In between events, Shooter explains everything in a way that's almost easy for me to follow along.

"Okay, so, there's typically seven main events that take place during a rodeo," he says, shifting in his chair to face me better. "They can be broken down into two different categories; the rough stock events—think bareback, saddle, and bull riding—and the timed events, which are your steer wrestling, barrel racing, tie-down, and team roping. All these events are point-based."

"And what's next?" I ask, feeling about as dumb as a box of rocks.

"Steer wrestling."

"Which is what, exactly?"

I wince when Shooter huffs out a laugh. "You may have heard it be called bulldogging. It's where a horse-mounted rider chases a steer—which is a male cow with his nuts cut off—and then wrestles it to the ground by grabbing its horns and pulling it off-balance."

My eyes, I'm sure, are wide as saucers as I gape at Shooter before peering next to him at Whit. "Holy fuck, that sounds awful. Doesn't the bull get hurt?"

Trying to hide his laughter, Shooter drags a hand over his mouth. It's an unsuccessful move because I totally see it. I've never felt so out of my element. Not even when I milked Tootsie for the first time. There's so much to this world I had no idea even existed. The rules, the events…everything. I don't think I could ever truly grasp the extent of it even if I tried.

"The bull's fine," Shooter replies to my previous question. "The livestock that are used in events like this are bred specifically for this. This is their job, and what they've been raised to do. And they're actually very well taken care of. The association has a ton of animal welfare rules to ensure the animals are receiving the best care. Honestly, a lot of these animals are treated better than even most dogs and cats in people's homes."

The three of us watch the rest of the events, with Shooter delving out more information each time. My head is spinning. When the barrel racers come out, I recognize Shooter's sister, Daisy, and their other friend, Jessie. Watching that was fun. By the time the last event wraps up, my head is crammed full of new information, and I feel like I could maybe hold my own in a conversation about the rodeo. *Big* maybe. I could at least pretend and half-follow along, and that's saying something.

The end of the night seems to drag on, but I think it's mostly because I'm so anxious to see Cope and congratulate him. I'm antsy to be near him. Knowing he's in this arena too, but I can't see him makes me feel stir crazy. Which is wild to even think, given that we've only known each other for a short while.

Not for the first time, I wonder how tonight's going to go once we all leave here. Will we kiss again? Do more? Maybe. Maybe not. But I'd be lying if I said I didn't want to. I haven't been able to stop thinking about that kiss since the night it happened. It's a continuous slideshow in my mind, the star of the show in my dreams every night. The way his lips went from timid and shy to hungry and sure, the taste of his tongue ravishing every corner of my mouth like he couldn't get enough. His large hands on my body, roaming and feeling and massaging.

I wanted more. So much more. It's a miracle I had enough sense to stop it before it went further.

The desire and the need to explore his body in great detail is immense, and it's only getting stronger as the days pass. Even from outside of his clothes, I can tell his body is a work of art. His muscles defined, skin taut over them. If I close my eyes, I can picture how the expanse of his naked back would look, the ridges between his abs, the firmness of his pecks. I can even imagine the tightness of his nipples. Would they be a pale pink like mine, or a darker shade. Images of me running my tongue all across his flesh. Through every divot and dip. The way his flavor would erupt on my taste buds. The slight musky taste from his sweat, mixed with the saltiness of his skin and the sweetness of whatever fresh soap he uses. It would be heady. My head would be swimming, and my groin would be aching.

Pulled from my very inappropriate thoughts when the crowd cheers vibrate through the bleachers, I shake my head free of what was running through it, bringing my attention back to the center of the arena, where they've started their announcements. They go through the scores in bareback, getting to the world champ title, and when 'Sterling Addams' is announced over the speaker, Shooter goes fucking apeshit next to me, cheering and hollering and making some *very* dirty promises to Sterling about later tonight. Laughter spills out of my mouth as I cheer right alongside him, feeling ecstatic for him even though we barely know each other. This is his first year pro, so it must be quite an accomplishment to take that title so early on in your career.

The energy all around us, and even just between Shooter, Whit, and I, is intense, and it only grows as the announcers move on to the saddle bronc portion. Sweating palms and shaky legs, I watch and listen eagerly as they go through everything, a level of nervousness eating at my gut as if it were me down there, waiting to find out how I did. He's won the title before; he told me as much when he was explaining the whole process. Last year, he won the average score, but missed out on the world champ title by a hair.

Watching him down there in the dirt, he looks confident. His shoulders are back, and he's standing tall. If he's nervous at all, he doesn't show it. He looks sexy as hell in his cowboy get-up, and I make no attempts at hiding my shameless perusal of his body, not that he can even see me up here. His tawny brown cowboy hat looks well-worn, and he's got on some type of leather vest over his black long-sleeve button-up shirt. The chaps hugging his thighs are black leather with a fringe that matches his hat, and his boots are covered in dirt, looking equally as worn as his hat. His vest, shirt, and chaps all have patches on them from his sponsors.

This is the first time I've seen him look like a true rodeo cowboy in person, and it's got my hands itching to get closer and touch him. *What would he look like in those chaps... and nothing else?* The way they manage to cup his groin—accentuate his bulge—so perfectly is downright sinful. Somehow, I'm able to redirect my thoughts, not allowing myself to go into *that* territory right now, just in time to hear the world champ winner for saddle bronc riding.

My chest tightens, heart thudding as Cope's name is announced. The entire arena erupts into a deafening roar, my feet leaving the ground as I jump up, Shooter's arms punching toward the sky at the same time. We turn to face each other, the pride on his face nearly knocking me over as we collide into one another in a short celebratory hug. Returning my gaze to the center of the arena, Cope's grinning ear-to-ear as he rips his hat off his head, tossing it in the air. He lets out a triumphed, *"Woooo!"* before running half around the arena until he comes to a stop in front of us.

"That's what I'm fucking talking about!" Shooter bellows beside me, the volume and the excitement causing laughter to erupt out of me as my gaze connects with Cope's. His chocolate brown eyes glint underneath the lights of the arena, his cheeks flushed, and the child-like giddiness present in his features makes me want to jump down and kiss him.

Shooter shakes me, with his hands planted on my shoulders, but I barely notice. Cope's got me locked in this bubble with him, the pride so thick swelling inside of me as I take him in has me feeling like I may burst at the seams.

"You did it!" I shout over the noise from the crowd. "You fucking did it!"

"Yeah, you fucking did, big boy," Shooter cuts in, causing

Cope to throw his head back and laugh. His laugh is contagious, both of us barking out one of our own.

By the time he leaves us to go do interviews or whatever the hell he has to do, my cheeks ache from smiling so much. Watching him work so hard tonight, knowing how hard he worked all season, and seeing him take that title, was extraordinary. I'm so happy I was able to come and watch this in person. I've gained a new level of respect for Cope, and all of his friends, seeing this with my own two eyes.

He's incredible, and I can't wait to show him that tonight if he lets me.

Chapter 19

Cope Murphy

The narrow corridor is no less than a hundred and five degrees as we make our way across the tan and maroon designed carpet. At least, that's what it feels like as the sweat beads above my brow, scaling across the nape of my neck, and dripping down into my shirt. It doesn't help that two hours ago, I was wrangling a bronc in a less than air-conditioned arena and haven't had a chance to shower yet, so I probably reek, the new sweat just adding to the already dry and marinated perspiration clung to my body.

My hands have a slight tremor to them, and my legs act like they don't want to work, like my knees could buckle at any moment. And I don't think it has anything to do with the exhaustion from bronc riding earlier and everything to do with the too-beautiful-for-his-own-good man walking beside me, his curly black hair flopping over his forehead and his icy blue eyes that heated with a flame that matched my own burning need before we left the bar a little bit ago.

Huge, world champion win aside, watching him has been

my favorite part of the evening. The way he flirted more and his cheeks flushed a deep pink with every beer he tossed back. The way he so effortlessly blended in with my friends. The way they so quickly took a liking to him—way before us coming to Vegas. The way he teased me when we played pool and I couldn't sink a ball to save my life because I was far too enamored with him. But most importantly, the way he leaned in real close to me near the jukebox, a playfulness dancing in his gaze as he said low enough for my ears only, "*Take me back to your hotel room, cowboy.*"

Those eight words carried the sultriest lilt that shot straight to my core, and I knew I'd do anything he asked if only he spoke to me like that.

So, here we are, walking side by side, wordlessly, down the never-ending, overheated hallway at the ritzy hotel I'm staying in for the week. Our arms hang by our sides as we go, close enough to brush occasionally, but not enough to full on touch. The electricity is still there, though, even from the small amount of contact. Every sweep against him sends shock waves through my body, a rich rush of anticipation for what's to come once we're behind closed doors.

I've thought about this for a while now. Thought of what doing more than kissing with Xander would be like, what it would feel like. And not even necessarily because he's a man—although, it probably is a little about that too, only because it's something I've never done before—but because of this strong, intense connection we seem to share. Intimacy for me has never been earth-shattering. It's never been something I felt like I *needed*, much less wanted. There's never been a time when it felt like I needed to experience what someone's body felt like against mine, when I craved tasting them, consuming them, on a deeper, filthier level. Sex has always been about a mix between expectation and release.

This need for Xander feels like neither of those things. It's carnal and deep and pure. It's about desire instead of obligation. A desire so strong, I'm choking on it. A need so thick, I can't see around it, and I don't want to. It's a blinding fog that I'll gladly welcome. I don't fully understand it, but I don't think I need to yet. I can learn as I go.

We stop in front of room 437, and with a shaky hand, I slip the key into the slot, waiting until it shines green before opening it up. My stomach leaps into my throat as that freshly cleaned hotel room smell hits us, the reality of where we're at crashing into me at full force, the jitters cranking up a couple dozen meters. Xander walks in before me, flicking the light on, and I follow, shutting and locking the door behind me, pressing my back up against the hard surface.

Xander turns, facing me, the bottle of liquor we took from the bar after slipping the bartender a fifty hanging from his grip. He looks sheepish. Even a little boyish as he peers at me through his long dark lashes. Neither of us makes any move, at least not right away. Our gazes locked, we revel in this moment. We drink it in. Let ourselves feel the gravity of it. After tonight, everything changes. There will be no more tiptoeing around this thing between us, no denying it's there—not that I've wanted to do much of that anyway.

With barely a glance to the side, he sets the bottle on the dresser before slowly taking a step forward. And then another. He's right in front of me, his lids hooded, his cheeks still splashed with color. "You look nervous," he states huskily.

Deciding to go with honesty, I give him a small grin. "I am."

His hand comes up, cupping the side of my neck, thumb

brushing along my jawline, and a shiver rolls through me at the gentle but sure touch. "Is this your first time with a man?"

Breathing a laugh through my nose, I ask, "Am I that obvious?"

He shakes his head. "Not obvious, but in the few times we've spoken about partners, it's always been women you've referenced, and I didn't want to assume."

Bringing my hands to his hips, I pull him into me, my mouth finding his, whatever nerves I was feeling a moment ago gone the second his lips part and my tongue slips inside. It rolls against his before licking my way around, savoring the way he tastes. The hand he has anchored to the side of my neck wraps around until his fingers are fisting in the hair at my nape. He tugs enough to add a bite of pain as he presses his hard body into mine.

Xander isn't as big or as muscular as I am, but even with my eyes closed, there's no mistaking that it's a man's body flush with mine. No mistaking it's a man's mouth I'm exploring, his scratchy five o'clock shadow rubbing against mine, and I can't deny how unbelievably hot it makes me. And again, not even because it's a man instead of a woman, but because it's *him*. Because it's *Xander* I'm tasting. Xander's the reason my heart is hammering, and why my dick is thickening.

Not a man, not a woman. Xander.

With there being zero breathing room between us, I can feel his erection as it rubs against my own, taunting me, and my pulse kicks up in speed, the blood roaring in my ears. I want to strip him naked and discover every inch of him, all night long. But first—"Wait," I blurt out, ripping my lips from his.

His hot breath fans my lips as confusion crosses through his eyes. "What's wrong?"

"Before we go any further, I need to shower."

Xander snorts. "I don't care about that."

"Yeah, but I do." I wince. "The first time we see each other naked, I do not want to be worrying about whether or not my pits smell like onions."

This makes him laugh. "You want to see me naked?" he asks, a knee-buckling heat flashing from his bright blue orbs once the laughter fades.

"I *really* want to see you naked," I reply and watch as a smirk lifts his lips.

"Good, because I *really* want to see you naked, too."

"Then I need to shower. I'll be fast."

"No problem," he says coolly, pressing another kiss to my lips. "I'll run and grab some ice for drinks while you're in there."

Going our separate ways, I slip into the bathroom and take what has to be the world's quickest, yet most efficient, shower known to man. Scrubbing all the right areas. I won't lie, though, I'd really hoped Xander would've snuck in and joined me. Although, I guess it might be a little weird to bathe together the first time we're seeing each other naked. Still, I can't help but feign a pout when I walk out of the bathroom with a pair of black briefs on and nothing else, finding Xander sitting against the headboard, a drink in one hand, his phone in the other as he scrolls through it.

Glancing up, he drops the phone into his lap when he sees me. A flash of what can only be described as hunger passes through his eyes as he rakes his gaze over my body in a way that I can feel over every inch of exposed flesh. "What's that look for?" he asks, humor lacing his words. He stands off the bed, grabbing a cup that was sitting on the nightstand, handing it to me.

I bring it up to my lips and tilt my head back, letting the

sweet cocktail drench my tongue, then I shrug, using the cup to hide my grin. "Maybe I was hoping you would've joined me."

His brows raise a little with surprise. "Well, had I known that was an option, I would've," he muses before reaching behind his head and pulling his shirt off in one swift go. My eyes immediately drop, wanting to take in every detail. Memorizing the sight of him. Miles of smooth, creamy skin stand before me, my fingers twitching to touch. My eyes dip a little lower, taking in his pretty pink nipples. They're taut, and have silver bars running through them. My mouth waters.

"Those are hot," I tell him, my words coming out airy and full of lust, looking up to find him already watching me.

Xander throws me a grin that's pure sex.

My dick twitches behind my briefs, and I reach down to readjust myself, letting out a groan. He gives me a breathy laugh as he closes the distance between us, taking the cup from my hand and placing it back on the nightstand behind him. His lips are soft and supple as they fuse with mine, his tongue gentle as it caresses mine, and he leads us back to the bed, where he climbs on backward, and I follow, our lips never severing.

As soon as we're situated on the bed, with me between his spread legs, everything intensifies. The air in the room vanishes, and with it goes any inhibitions I'd been subconsciously holding on to. Our movements become fevered, like neither of us can get enough. Xander's legs wrap around my waist while his hands find the small of my back as he tilts his head, deepening the kiss. He tastes amazing, my tongue can't seem to get deep enough, and when he moans into my mouth, I damn near combust from how fucking sexy it is.

Leaving his mouth, I work a hot trail across the sharp edge of his jawline, down to his neck where I nip the flesh there.

Xander's hips buck up when I do, a groan so chest-deep coming out of him, it sends a vibration through my entire body.

His neck is sensitive... *Noted.*

I take my time exploring every inch of skin, from his throat, to his shoulders, and even across his collarbone, before licking a path down between his pecs. My mouth waters before I capture the pretty pink, jeweled bud, flicking my tongue all around it before tugging on it gently with my teeth. He moans so beautifully the more I do it, getting louder and more desperate, and before long, he reaches up, guiding my head over to his other one, silently begging me to give that one the same treatment.

"Fuck, yes, Cope," he breathes, his chest heaving, hips rocking upward. I don't even know if he's aware that he's doing it.

The urge to sink lower, explore more of him is there, and it's heavy, but a pang hits me in my gut, keeping me from doing it simply because I don't know what I'm doing. I don't know what he likes, and I want to make it good for him.

Deciding to play it safe—at least for now—and gather myself, I sit back on my haunches, raking my gaze over him. And fuck, what a sight he is. His arms are now resting above him on the pillow, messy black curls a mess atop his head, bright blue eyes glazed over, cheeks flushed, and his top teeth are biting down on his full bottom lip in a way that's part innocent, part seductive. Lying before me, Xander is sex personified. He's gorgeous, and I don't even think he knows it.

Where I'm rough hands and weathered skin, he's soft and sweet. We're so different, in more ways than one, and I think that's what I enjoy the most. He makes my heart race in a way it's never done before. My body tingles, my stomach flutters, and it feels like it's hard to catch my breath when I'm near him…especially when he's looking at me like he is now. Like he, too, can't believe he's here.

Swallowing thickly, in a failed attempt at wetting my dry mouth, I run my fingers over his chest, eliciting a shiver from him. It brings a smile to my lips. "You're… Fuck." Words are becoming impossible. I'm overwhelmed in the very best way, and we've barely gotten. "You're beautiful, Xander."

The knot in his throat rolls as he watches me with soft eyes. They widen only slightly, as if that wasn't what he was expecting to hear. "So are you," he replies, his voice cracking. I can't help but wonder if he feels all of this too. If the weight of all of this, and the intensity of how much he wants it, is damn near choking him. I hope so.

My face heats under his compliment. Nobody has ever told me I was beautiful before. Hot or sexy or cute, sure, but never beautiful. Cowboys aren't seen as beautiful. They're masculine and rugged, and for some reason, the world thinks that masculinity can't also be beautiful. Like beautiful can only be feminine. That makes no sense to me, and it never has, because peering down at Xander, while he's not as built as I am physically, he's still quite masculine, but he's also one hundred percent beautiful. You can be both, and I wish more of society would catch up to that.

Blowing out a breath, with my stomach in my throat, I climb off the bed, needing to remove this restraining fabric from my body before my dick busts through the front. Xander's eyes track every movement, his lip between his teeth again as an inferno ignites in his blue gaze. I shove the material down my thighs, goosebumps spreading as the cool air of the room hits my flesh, but it's probably got more to do with Xander's eyes on me than anything.

My already hard dick juts out as the briefs pool around my ankles, and I wrap a fist around myself, giving a long, slow tug, the heat of his stare egging me on.

"Wow," Xander gushes, eyes lifting to meet mine, tongue sweeping across his lips to wet them. The sight sends a spark to my groin, a deep ache making itself home in my already full balls. "That's... You're *big*."

Glancing down at the dick in my hand, I shrug. "It's, like, average."

He gawks at me. "Cope, the average dick for an American man is about six inches long with an average girth of about five inches. You are *not* average, please be for real."

Chuckling, I reply, "You seem to know an awful lot about dick size, city boy."

"I'm...educated." He flashes me a blinding smirk.

"Mmhmm, I see that."

Xander scoots toward the end of the bed, slapping my hand away as he replaces it with his own. "And I'm about to learn a thing or two about yours here in a minute."

The blood roars in my ears, the sound deafening as the feel of his hand on my dick sends pleasure ricocheting through my body.

His fingers grip the base, pumping me nice and slow as his heated eyes bore into mine. He uses both hands, wrists flicking on the upstroke. The sensation is too good, and he's barely doing anything. The soft feel of his hands, and how they look wrapped around my length, it's such a contrast to my own hand. Xander leans in, wet pink tongue poking out as he rubs the slick, sensitive tip of my cock along the flat of it as he continues to stroke me like we have all the time in the world.

I've thought about this for weeks. Fantasized about what it would be like—what it would feel like—and if this is only the beginning, then I'm doomed. I'm not leaving this hotel room the same man I was when I walked in. My chest expands to full capacity as I try to drag in the breath that doesn't want to come; my lungs can't seem to get enough oxygen, greedy for more in the same way I'm greedy for more Xander. There's a low-simmering hum vibrating through my body. Through every limb, wrapping around my bones, intertwining with each muscle. A hum that's euphoric and addicting.

Full, plush lips close around my crown, pulling a long, low groan from my throat as his tongue swirls around and he applies the right amount of suction to make my toes curl. He lets out a soft moan, too, as if he's finding pleasure from making me feel good. A warm, sure hand drops to my balls, kneading and rolling them around as he sinks lower, taking more of my cock into his pretty little mouth. It's a fucking sight. Probably the sexiest sight I've ever seen in my life.

Xander's lips are stretched to full capacity around me, and I can't help myself. I bring my thumb up and trace where he's barely making me fit. His tongue pulsates along the underside of my shaft, his bloodshot eyes lifting to peer up at me from beneath his dark lashes. He looks like a fucking angel taking me, and my chest wants to cave in on itself with how much I'm feeling in this moment. The more he takes of me, the more he moans as he does it; the more I fall a little deeper. My blood heats, my heart pounds, my pulse races. The more he does—hell, the more he just simply fucking exists—the hazier my mind becomes. The hold he has on me is unreal.

Tears spring to Xander's eyes as he sinks the rest of the way, taking every last inch of me. My eyes roll back, and I can't stop myself from grabbing hold of the back of his head, fingers tightening against the strands. "Fuck, Xander."

I don't even recognize my own voice. The heat of it, the lust wrapped around every syllable, it's foreign and only turns me on more. He's been sucking my dick all of three minutes, and I'm already embarrassingly close to busting. This is too much. *He's* too much.

I can't fucking get enough.

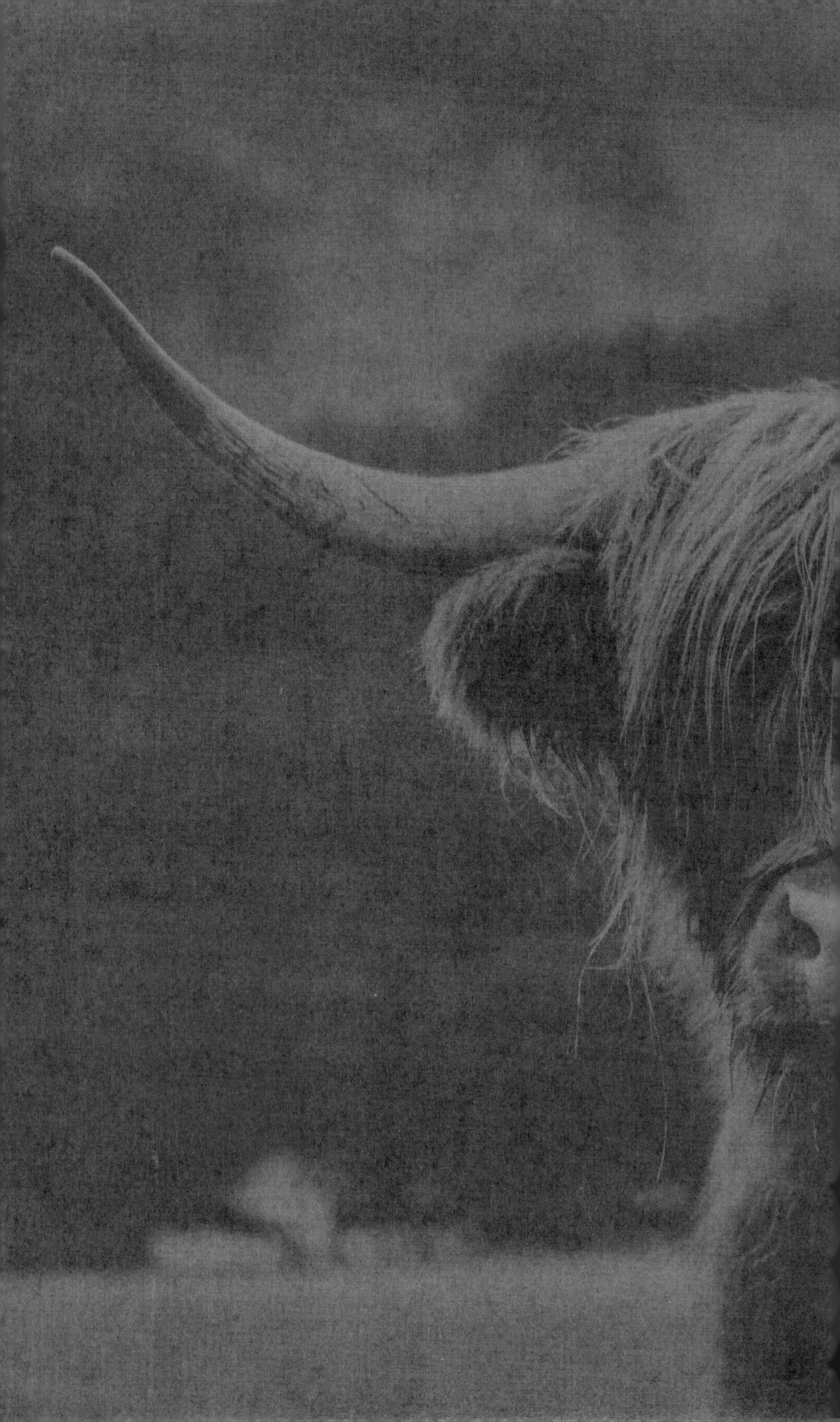

Chapter 20

Xander Dawson

I have died and gone straight to big dick heaven.

Cope's staring down at me like I'm the best thing he's ever laid eyes on as I swallow his *massive* cock. And I mean *massive*. Seriously, how is it fair that someone as good looking *and* genuinely nice as he is, is also graced with a dick nearly the size of my forearm?

Okay, that's slightly an exaggeration, but not by much.

His fingers are combing through my hair, and the way they grip feels so damn good. I'm going to look like a frizz ball by the time we're done, but I don't even care. I'm doused in all things Cope Murphy, and I'm drunk on it. His fresh scent is everywhere, the clean taste of his cock, the salty flavor of his arousal as it drips onto my tongue while he watches me take him. Breathing ragged, the noises he gives me as I suck him down are a symphony of my filthiest dreams. He's perfect.

I'm so hard, but I can't even think about pulling myself out and relieving the ache because all I can focus on is him…every last inch of him. By some miracle, I'm able to take his whole length in my mouth. It fills my throat and cuts off my air, but it's pure ecstasy. My nose brushes up against the trimmed hair at his base, the same color as that on his head. Nothing but the whites of his eyes shine as they roll back, his jaw having gone slack, only a breathless moan slipping between his parted red lips. Having this effect on him is surreal. It's heady. Powerful.

I want nothing more than to sit him on the edge of the bed as I climb on top of him, and ride him until he can't see straight, but I know he isn't ready for that. He may not even touch me tonight below the belt, and truthfully, I'm okay with that. I've always known I was gay; it was never a question, but I know, from witnessing friends go through this, that trying dick for the first time after only ever tasting pussy can be intimidating for some. We can go as slow as he needs as long as I get to keep making him feel like this.

And besides, it isn't about me tonight. We're celebrating *him*.

Cope gets louder the longer I suck him off, his grip on my hair turning painful, but I welcome it. I love it. Getting to see this side of him feels like a privilege. He's this hardworking bronc rider, a kind, helping neighbor, and a funny, laid-back, but always there for those who matter, type of friend. He's the man who would help an elderly woman out to her car and carry her groceries for her, or stop to help a wounded animal on the side of the road. He's multifaceted, but this side of him, I get the impression he doesn't show many people. This side is reserved for those lucky enough to earn their way in.

I can't help but wonder if he fucks hard and ruthless, or if he's kind and sweet. Maybe he's both, depending on the day or the mood. Maybe he'd find pleasure out of being the one to get fucked. While I prefer to bottom most of the time, as the feeling of fullness is too good to pass up, I do enjoy topping occasionally.

My hand finds his impressive balls again, and I work them around in my grip, moaning as I taste more of his flavor explode on my tongue. He's getting close, his hips undulating of their own accord. Just when I think he's about to unload down my throat, he pulls off, gripping himself hard at the base, staving off that impending release.

"Fuck," he hisses. "I don't want to come yet."

Cope hikes a hand under my arm, hauling me up, and crashes his lips into mine, tongue surging past the barrier and into my mouth. His desire is so potent, I can taste it dripping off of him as he owns me. The kiss is messy. It's sloppy and lacking any sort of finesse, but I don't care. Shoving me onto the bed, he moves in between my legs, fingers going to the waistband of my pants, and a flicker of something that vaguely resembles hesitancy flashes through his eyes, but as soon as he blinks, it's gone.

Fully hard, my dick springs out as soon as he pulls the material down, the swollen head slapping against my stomach. Cope's eyes zero in on my crotch as he wets his lips with his tongue. I'm not even sure if he realizes he does it. Once he's fully rid me of my clothes, he finds his place between my thighs again, hands pressed firmly down on them. With the way his eyes are wide and he's unmoving, I think he may be freaking out.

"We—We don't have to do this," I tell him shakily. My heart slams against my ribs, the tiny sliver of fear of rejection sneaking into my mind, making me want to cover myself.

But then… Well, then Cope's eyes snap up to meet mine, and the look I read as panic reveals itself clear as day as raw, hungry lust.

"I want to," is all he says. Doesn't make any attempt to move; maybe waiting for my permission. "Unless you don't want to?"

The way he phrases it as a question causes a pang right in the center of my chest. I nod. "No, I do. You just look...frozen. I don't want you to do anything that makes you uncomfortable. I know getting your dick sucked by a guy is a whole lot different than touching one yourself. If you need a minute—or longer—I'm okay with that. You don't, like, owe me anything just because I did—"

"Will you hush for a minute?" he interjects, taking me by surprise.

Pressing my lips together, I fight a smirk, waiting quietly for whatever it is he's about to say.

"Anyone ever tell you that you ramble an awful lot when you get nervous?" Cope breathes out a laugh, the sound settling something inside of me.

Indicating to my closed lips with my hand, I shrug, as if saying, *"Can't talk, remember, bossy?"*

He rolls his eyes, a grin tilting his lips. "And stubborn," he adds, to which I flip him off. "I don't need a minute, and I'm not freaking out. I just..." He breathes out another laugh, scrubbing a hand over his face. "Your dick's really hot. I wasn't totally sure how I'd react to seeing one in a sexual setting, and it caught me off guard how turned on it made me seeing it boing out like that. Seeing the glistening pre-cum on your stomach is...making me even harder." He shrugs bashfully before adding, "And I've also never seen an uncut cock before. It's cute, like a little hoodie."

My eyes go wide, a grin cracking on my face. "A *little hoodie?*" I all but bark at him, sitting up so we're face to face.

"Well, not *little*," he corrects, gesturing toward my dick. "Because I mean, come on, it's an impressive hoodie, if you ask me."

"*Copeland Murphy!*" I can't even get his name out without laughing at how ridiculous he is, and how he managed to lighten the entire mood in the matter of seconds. "My foreskin is *not* a hoodie."

He hums, lips twitching as he waggles his brows suggestively at me. "Kinda like it when you use my full name like that." Running a rough, warm palm up one of my thighs, he eyes me from underneath his lashes. "Would you prefer *sweater snake* instead?"

This time, I laugh so hard I snort before swatting his hand away.

"Turtle in a shell?"

"Oh, my God," I choke out.

"Peensleeve?"

"Stop talking," I demand, feigning exasperation, but I can't stop from chuckling. "You are ridiculous."

"Yeah, but you like it, though, don't you?" There's humor in his eyes and a crooked grin tipped up on his lips. Despite how unbearably horny I am, I can't help but give in to the playfulness.

Lifting one of my shoulders in a shrug, I mutter, "Eh, it's alright."

"Ha! Alright, my ass," he teases, rolling his eyes.

I bite down on my lip, trying to hide the smirk threatening to spread. A heated expression takes over his face as he rakes his gaze down my body, and suddenly, the playfulness is gone.

Finger hooked under my chin, he leans in, that damn panty-dropping smirk on his face before he presses a kiss to my lips. His tongue is gentle when it slips into my mouth, but he doesn't fail to steal my breath anyway. "Can I touch it?" he asks against my lips, the huskiness of his voice taking me by surprise. Gone is the teasing guy from a moment ago.

The intensity of his stare, paired with the way he's still gripping my chin, sends a thrill down my spine, a bolt of arousal burying itself in my rock-hard cock. I nod, unable to formulate a response. There's no hesitation, no moment to prepare himself—or me. When his hand wraps around my base and strokes upward slowly before rolling back down, it's an effort to not close my eyes. To not roll them back. His grip is firm, but not too much, and his lips are still a hairsbreadth from mine, so close I can taste him. So close I can *feel* how his breathing kicks up a notch. How it matches my own.

With a flick of his wrist, I moan, the sensation maddening. You'd never know, with the sure way he's pumping me and the heated way he's watching me, that this was his first time touching another man. If he's nervous, he hides it well. My heart rate kicks up, a rapid staccato against my ribcage, the air turning stifling in the room. Sweat lines my brow, the back of my neck, and my body lights up like live wire. I'm on fire. Every touch feels euphoric, and when his hand drops from my chin to the hardened bud on my left pec and pinches, I feel like I could come already.

"I'm gonna have fun with these," he rasps, flicking the barbell through the sensitive flesh but never taking his eyes off mine. His lips tip up into a grin that would make my knees buckle had I been standing.

Yeah, me too, I want to say but can't find the words. Nipple play is one of my favorite things. I've almost come from that alone before.

Blindly reaching out, I fumble a few times before I find his dick. I wrap a hand around his thick girth, mimicking his movement, knowing I won't be lasting. Honestly, I'm surprised I've even lasted this long.

"Cope," I cry out, the sensation beginning in my toes as it bubbles up like a volcano about to erupt. A chill racks through my body the higher it gets, the intensity enough to have me seeing stars.

"Me too," is all he says before crashing his mouth into mine.

The minute our tongues roll together, I'm done for. With my eyes slammed shut and my other hand gripping Cope's bicep, nails digging into his skin, I explode. My dick pulses, balls throbbing as I shoot thick ropes. He swallows my cries as his muscles tense and I feel him let go. Neither of us stops stroking the other until we're both too sensitive to handle it anymore, and after Cope gets up and wets a towel for us to clean off with, we collapse onto the bed, sated and exhausted.

Nerves begin twisting in my gut the longer we lie here, as I wonder how he's handling all of this internally—hooking up with a man for the first time. On the outside, he seems perfectly fine, but I can't help but worry he'll freak out once it all sets in. I don't have a clue how he'll be in the morning when the moment's passed, but for right now, I'm going to enjoy the way he wraps an arm around me and buries his face into my neck like he can't breathe without being near me.

I'm going to enjoy it in case it never happens again.

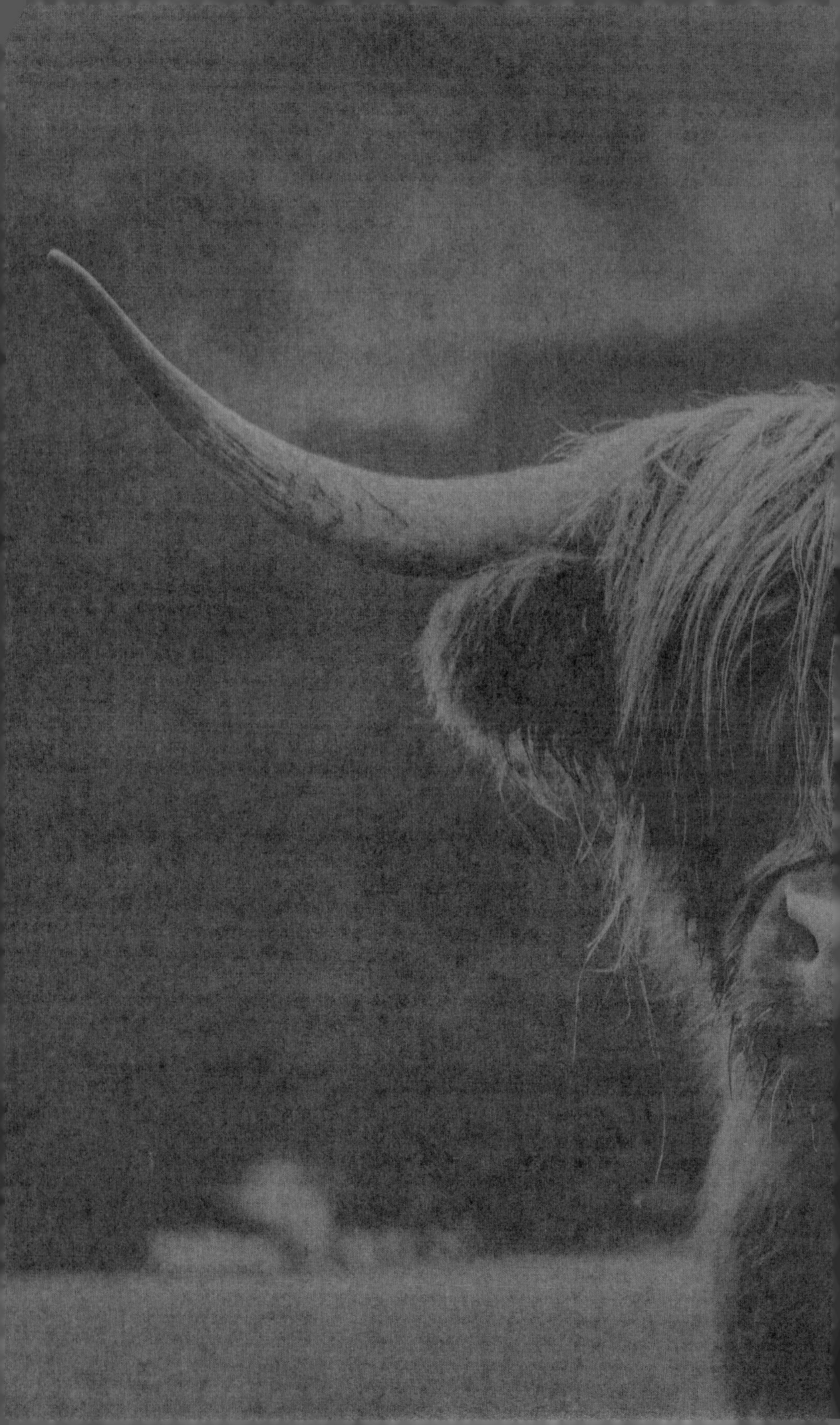

Chapter 21

Cope Murphy

My mind wakes up before my body is ready to. I'm far too comfortable, lying in this plush bedding, wrapped around the warmest, coziest pillow known to man. Only when I peel an eye open and take in the relatively dark room, thanks to the blackout curtains, I see it isn't a pillow at all that I'm curled around.

It's Xander.

Then the memories of last night replay in my head, and a smile tugs on my lips, remembering all that we did. Xander's back is tucked against my front, our bodies perfectly aligned. With the way his breathing is even and steady, it's probably safe to assume he isn't awake yet.

Looking inward, I search for a morsel of regret, or even that daunting feeling of dread that typically comes after I hook up with someone. There is none. No panic rising. My chest feels light, my mind still riding that rush that came from being with him, and my body really, *really* wants to do it all over again. Last night felt right, and I can't even begin to explain why.

Xander brings out something in me that I didn't know existed.

Subconsciously, I tighten my arm around his middle, hauling him even closer as I bury my face in the messy black curls on the back of his head. My senses come alive, breathing in his scent. I could easily lie here all day, doing just this, and I'd be content. Xander's body stirs a little, and I hear him inhale deeper, signaling he's waking up. A shot of unease hits me in the gut, not knowing how he's going to handle everything this morning. What if it's too soon after his breakup and he regrets it?

Sure, it was his idea to come back here last night, but we were both under the influence, so it could've been the alcohol talking. But I don't think either of us were *drunk*.

"Are you freaking out?" Xander asks, his voice thick with sleep, startling me out of my thoughts.

Brows pinching together, I say, "No, not at all, why do you ask?"

"Because you're stiff as a board—and I don't just mean the morning wood poking my thigh—and your grip on my stomach is kinda painful."

"Oh, shit. Sorry." I didn't even realize I'd tensed up. Forcing myself to relax, I rub on his stomach and breathe in the scent of his hair again. He brings his hand up, placing it on top of mine, lacing our fingers together on his abdomen. My heart squeezes.

"So, no freaking out about last night?" he asks again.

"None," I reiterate. "You?"

"God, no." Xander snorts out a laugh, turning around to face me. One of his hands is stuffed under his cheek on the pillow while the other rests flat on my chest. "I very much enjoyed it."

The blanket is pushed down to our waists, so his entire naked torso is exposed to me. My eyes greedily drink in his creamy skin as I reach out to finger the barbell through his left nipple. He groans, eyes rolling back. Goosebumps bloom around the area I'm touching, and I secretly love the way his body responds to me. Tugging gently on the metal, Xander hisses before it melts into another moan that sends a shiver down my spine. My body flushes hot, the sensation settling low in my groin.

My gaze lifts, finding Xander already watching me. His features are soft, blue eyes bright, and his lips part just enough that I can see the top of his straight row of bottom teeth. His breathing comes out in quick pants the more I play with the pierced pink bud.

"That feel good?" I ask hoarsely.

He nods, a groan falling from his lips. "Don't stop."

I bring my other hand up, teasing the right side at the same time. The temperature in the room feels like it's raised to a toasty level, and my dick is so hard it hurts. With the blanket covering him, I can't tell if he is too, but I'm willing to bet he is.

The rustling of the blankets is the only noise in the room as he scoots over, wrapping his arm around my neck as he nestles his face against my skin. I bring my hand around to the small of his back as he fists the short hairs at the nape of my neck. Shivers rack through me when I feel his hot, soft lips press down in the area between my neck and shoulder. One turns into two, and then into three until his lips pepper anywhere they can touch.

Xander hooks his leg over mine, somehow lining our erections up perfectly. The feeling of his velvety, hard length rubbing along mine is erotic and sensual, the sensation out of this world. Before long, both of our hips are rolling, chasing the high we're giving each other. Hot breath fans my neck as

I bring my hand lower over the swell of his plump ass, fingers digging into the flesh, needing him impossibly closer.

The sharp bite of incisors sinking into my neck pulls a groan from my throat as I buck into him harder. "Fuck, Xan," I breathe, my pulse kicking up to rapid speeds.

He hums, tightening his grip on my hair, and swiping his tongue across the area. Next, he brings his attention to my ear, flicking his tongue over the lobe, then tugging on it gently with his teeth. Xander nips along my jawline as the hand gripping his ass controls how hard he thrusts into me. Bringing his hand down to my cheek, he guides my mouth over to his.

Fireworks go off as our lips mold together. It's heated, our tongues fighting for dominance. I roll onto my back, taking Xander with me, and he wastes no time grinding on my lap. We're both making a mess, our dicks leaking the more we rub together. I could easily come like this, and if he keeps at the pace he's going, I will soon.

Unfortunately for me, the universe has other plans. The hotel door bursts open without any warning, and Xander jumps off me like he got burned while he fumbles with the blankets, yanking them up to cover us.

"Rise and shine, fuckers." Shooter walks into the room, and Sterling trails behind him. My eyes meet his first, and he shoots me a silent *"I'm sorry,"* before I narrow my eyes in front of him at his boyfriend and my pain in the ass best friend.

"What the fuck are you doing here?" I bark at him, sitting up and making sure I'm fully covered.

A mischievous grin slides on Shooter's face as his eyes bounce between Xander and me. "Well, well, well," he drawls. "What do we have here, my friends?"

"Uh, how did you even get in here?" Xander questions

beside me. At some point, he's pushed himself into a sitting position too.

"Cope gave me a key." Shooter holds up the white plastic square as if to prove his point. "Duh."

"I gave it to you in case I locked myself out again. Not so you can barge in here bright and early like you own the place, asshole."

He shrugs. "Semantics. Now, get up and get dressed, lovebirds. I'm starving."

"You couldn't have texted like a normal person?" I ask.

"I did. Twice. And called you. Now, up and meet us in the lobby in five minutes, or I'm coming back up here."

They turn around and leave, the door offering a quiet *click* once they're gone. Tossing a look over at Xander, we both laugh. "I'm sorry about him. He can be…"

"Intense?" Xander finishes for me.

"I was going to say a dick, but sure, let's go with that."

Xander tosses the blanket off of us, glancing between our now half-hard dicks. "Think we have time?" He raises a brow as he looks up at me.

Laughing, I say, "Absolutely not. He, one hundred percent, will come back up."

He dramatically rolls his eyes, a grin spread on his face. "Fiiine," he groans, climbing out of bed, and I follow to do the same.

Twenty minutes later, the gang's all sat around a huge circular table at some diner off the strip, and we've already ordered a ton of food for the group.

"How're you feeling after that win last night, Sterling?" Xander asks from beside me. He's mixing some cream and sugar into a hot cup of coffee.

"Sore, but so freaking good." The smile on Sterling's face is blinding, and I can't help but mimic it. It's not only his first world champ win, but it's only his first pro season. That's gotta feel fucking incredible.

Our food comes and we all dig in, most conversation coming to a halt. We all head back to Copper Lake later on today, and I'm excited to get home, but at the same time, I'm nervous. I don't know what's going to come with Xander once we're back. As far as I can tell, Colette is getting stronger by the day, and Xander is technically only here to help her while she needs it. There's no logical reason for him to stay if she doesn't need his help, but I can't ignore the pit that forms in my gut when I think about him leaving.

Whatever this is between us is new—way too new for me to expect him to uproot his entire life in the possibility that something real could be here—but fuck if I don't wish I could. Hell, for all I know, this was just a one-night thing for him. He may not even feel the same way I do. I'm hoping once we get back home, we'll be able to sit down and talk. I don't know what I'd even say, but I need to say something because this connection I feel with him is too strong to ignore.

I went from being perfectly content being by myself, assuming I'd never know what real, intimate feelings are like, to helping him out on the side of the road and wondering what it'd be like to get to know him.

After we all finish eating, Shooter kicks me under the table. When my eyes lift to meet his, he asks, "Wanna go outside and have a smoke with me really quick?"

"Sure." Glancing over at Xander, he's deep into a conversation with Whit about who knows what. Nudging his arm, I lean in and whisper into his ear, "I'll be right back."

He nods but doesn't look my way, too enthralled with what Whit's rambling on about.

Outside, Shooter lights two cigarettes, handing me one. We take a few drags in silence, watching the cars and the pedestrians pass us by, but I know he wants to talk.

Sure enough, not even a minute later, his blue eyes—a shade much darker than Xander's—drag to meet mine, a grin on his face. "So, last night," is all he says, waggling his brows suggestively.

Barking out a laugh, I shake my head. "What about it?"

"You fuck him?"

Shooter knows no boundaries, and he's the definition of blunt, but I can't really fault him because we've always been close. From the time we were little kids, we've had the type of friendship where we shared everything. I can't expect him to hold back now. Not that I really care and, to be honest, I could use his advice.

"We hooked up," I offer.

Bringing the cigarette up to his lips, he takes a drag, his features softening as he watches me. "Yeah, how was it?"

I can read between the lines. He isn't asking me that, looking for all the juicy details. He's asking me, as my friend, wanting to make sure I'm okay after having my first man-on-man experience. There're so many sides to Shooter, and for most of the world, they only see the one side. The bronc rider and son of the Graham legacy. Not many people get to see the caring, supportive side of him that I do.

Before I can even answer, a smile breaks free. I don't bother trying to hide it. "It was…really good."

"Man, had I known you batted for our team, I could've told you how great dick was a long-ass time ago."

Chuckling, I reply honestly, "I didn't know. You know how I am. Sex is the furthest thing from my mind most of the time, so it never even occurred to me that I may not be completely straight."

"And you aren't freaking out about that?"

Shaking my head, I exhale a cloud of smoke. "I think if it were anybody else, I probably would. But I don't know…he feels different. I probably sound ridiculous."

"Sooo ridiculous," he teases, rolling his eyes and smirking. "No, but for real, you don't. Sometimes people just click. There's no explanation or reason for it, it just happens."

"Yeah, but I don't know what to do. Eventually, he'll head back to Washington. He's only here temporarily. And then what? Just forget about him?"

"Not if you don't want to," he murmurs. "Have you talked to him about it?"

"No, and you barged in this morning. When would I have had the chance?"

"Oh, fuck off." He laughs. "You two were *not* talking when I walked in. You both looked frazzled, like you just got caught with your hand in the cookie jar."

My face heats, which gives everything away. Shooter chuckles, taking another drag before putting out the cigarette with his boot.

"Talk when you guys get home. If you both don't want it to end, then don't, but you never know until you talk."

"Since fucking when are you so wise?"

"I've always been wise, my friend. You've just been blind to all my awesomeness."

"Oh, for fuck's sake." I bark out a laugh as we head back inside to join the rest of our group. As ridiculous as he can be, Shooter's right. We need to talk. I just hope we're on the same page, because I don't know how I'm supposed to go on living life after experiencing something as incredible as what we did last night.

After we finish eating, we all head up to our rooms to pack before heading to the airport. We're all on the same flight, which is nice. As soon as Xander and I get back into our room, I'm hit with an urge to finish what we started earlier, but I know we don't have the time. Based on the flirty looks Xander is sending my way, I'd say he probably wants to as well.

Thankfully—but also, unfortunately—before I can try to talk myself into thinking we do, in fact, have time, my phone rings. Grabbing it off the bed, a grin spreads on my face when I see it's my parents calling. I hit accept, putting the call on speaker and setting it back on the bed so I can continue to pack while I talk.

"Hey, guys!"

"There's our world championship winning son," my dad's deep, gruff voice booms through the speaker. I turn my gaze to Xander and find him smiling over at me.

"Honey, we are so proud of you!" my mom gushes. "And we're so sorry that we couldn't be there to watch you in person."

"Thank you, and it's more than okay, Mom. There will be other ones you can come to."

"You're darn right there will be." I can hear the pride in her tone, and it makes my chest squeeze.

"You back home yet?" my dad asks.

"Not yet, we're getting ready to head to the airport now."

"We?" my mom asks. "Are you rooming with Shooter again?"

I can't help the laugh that bubbles up as my eyes find Xander's again from across the bed. "Nah, actually, my, uh, friend, Xander, came to watch me compete. We shared a room."

"Is he there now?" she asks. "Can he hear us?"

"Yup, he can hear you."

"Hi, Xander," my mom coos through the speaker, the smile evident in her tone.

His cheeks pinken. "Hi, Mr. and Mrs. Murphy. It's nice to, er, meet you."

"Oh, please, call me Pearl," my mom corrects before my dad adds, "And you can call me Clint. It's nice to meet you, Xander."

"Are you in the rodeo too?"

"No, ma'am—I mean, no, Pearl." I bite the inside of my cheek to stop from laughing. He looks so uncomfortable, but then his gaze flits to me. "Your son is incredible. He kicked some serious butt out there. It was amazing to witness."

My throat tightens, and what I'm sure looks like the goofiest grin spreads across my face. The four of us talk for a little while longer before we eventually end the call in favor of getting to the airport on time. The whole time we're packing, we keep sneaking glances at one another. The air is charged, and I'm craving to taste him one more time before we leave.

"I'm glad you were able to come this weekend," I tell him as I zip my suitcase.

He smiles warmly. "Me too. It was really cool to get to watch you in action."

"And what came after was pretty great too, right?" I toss him a wink.

"At the bar? Yeah, that was fun too." His lips twitch as he tries to hold back laughter.

Rolling my eyes, I mutter, "Not what I meant, city boy."

Xander rounds the bed, wrapping his arms around my middle. His blue gazes locks onto mine. "What came after was *perfect*."

When he leans up and seals his lips to mine, it takes all my self-control to let this be just a kiss. We pull apart, and I drag in a steadying breath, replaying what I talked to Shooter about.

"Let's set aside some time when we get home to talk about all of this," I mutter softly.

Xander smiles. "I'd like that."

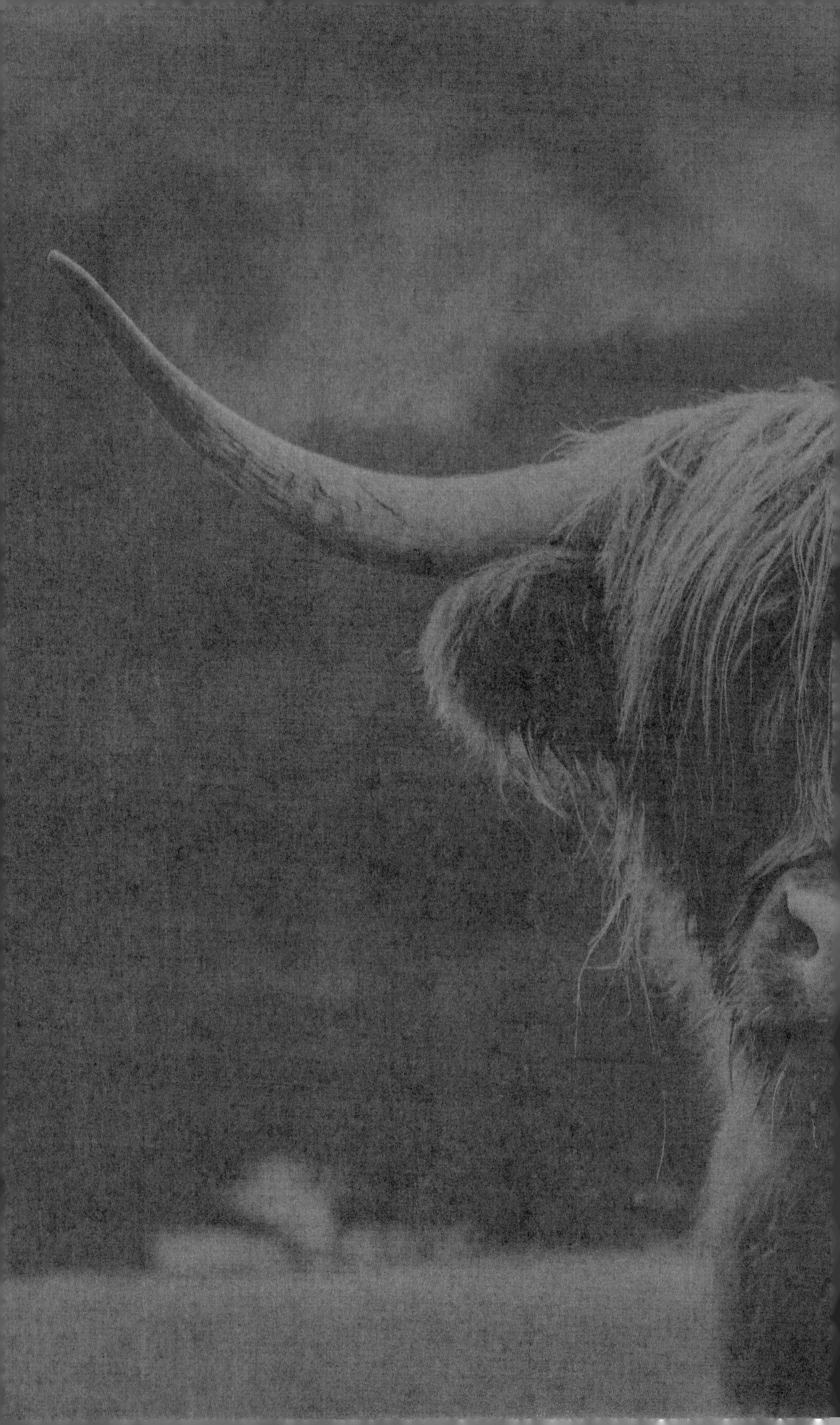

Chapter 22

Xander Dawson

The week since I've been back in Copper Lake has been a mess. One wrong thing after another after another. First, the morning after I got back, Aunt Colette slipped on the icy stairs on the back porch as she was heading down to feed the animals, fucking up her hip *again*. I took her to the doctor, and thankfully, nothing major was wrong with it. He instructed her to take it easy for a few days, ice it, then put some heat on it, and not overdo it.

He has clearly never met my aunt before. She's been a pain in the fucking ass to keep still, but somehow, I've managed to do it. Gemma told me she was just as stubborn while I was gone. Not surprising. My sister's flight ended up leaving a few hours before mine landed, so I wasn't able to see her in person, which was a bummer, but it made me feel a whole lot better that she was here.

Then, as if that weren't bad enough, a couple of nights ago, a skunk came into the yard and sprayed Aggie because, of course, she couldn't leave the little guy alone. In her haste, trying to run away from the stench that was actually *on her*, she, too, slipped on some ice in the form of a frozen puddle in the yard. It was clear she'd hurt herself, but I didn't know how bad. Panicked, I called Cope, freaking out at, like, eight at night. Like the fucking gem he is, he came over right away and called Whit, asking him to come take a look at her.

Thankfully, she just twisted her ankle and it'll heal on its own. Getting the skunk stench out of her was a whole different situation. That wasn't fun. There was no way I was going to ask Cope to help me with that, on top of everything else he had already helped with, but he insisted. We spent *hours* doing that, and by the time we were done, we were both so exhausted, we ended up going our separate ways, and I went back inside and passed out.

Cope's also had his own shit going on. When he was here, helping me give Aggie a deep cleaning, he told me his bathroom had flooded the night before. Apparently, some lever broke on the toilet, and it overflowed before he could turn the water off. If I believed in it, I'd say us hooking up was a bad omen.

Because of all of this, we've barely had time to talk, let alone hang out again. We've sent texts here and there throughout the day, but it's never anything of substance. I want more. I don't know where his head's at after everything we did in Las Vegas. The morning after, he was behaving normally, and when he came over for Aggie the other day, he was his usual cheerful self. He even kissed me. It wasn't drawn out or heated in any way, probably because the stench of skunk was everywhere, but it was nice. I'm sure it's simply a matter of lack of time on both our parts, and not anything deeper than that.

At least, I hope so.

Finishing up evening chores, I head back inside and take

a long, hot shower. Once I'm finished, I slip into some flannel pajama pants and a plain black long-sleeve shirt, and climb into bed. I turn on Netflix, picking some random, top-rated show, and I zone out, watching episode after episode until I look at the clock and realize several hours have passed in the blink of an eye.

It's after midnight, and I'm knee deep in the drama of this cheesy show, not a wink of sleep in sight. I've got way too much on my mind to relax enough. It's getting to be time for me to head back to Washington soon. My business partner, Bastian, and I have been looking into opening another bud store, and he thinks he's found the perfect location for it.

The last week since I've been back here, I've been going over all the figures, and I know we have enough to buy out our investors, which is great. That's what we want. But in order to do that, that means paying off Henry, too. After the couple of years we spent together in a relationship—no matter how not serious it may have been—it feels wrong to pay him off and go my separate way without at least sitting down and having a conversation with him. We haven't spoken since I dropped him off at the airport. Not that I expected we would. In fact, I'm glad we haven't, but I do think there are things we *should* talk about, but it should be face to face.

I don't want to go. At least, not for good. I'd like to maybe come back once I get everything figured out in Washington, but who knows how long that'll be. While my aunt has been doing better, I do think she could still use the help around here, especially since she *just* fell again. She's getting older, and while she's stubborn and would never admit it, I think she appreciates having a second set of hands around here to help with the weight of it all. And if I'm being honest, I've kind of grown to love this place. Not even because of Cope either. I'm not the type of person to make a huge life change for a guy. He would be a nice plus, though, if I did down the road decide to stay here.

Who knows. I'm getting ahead of myself. It's not even close to a fully fleshed-out idea. It's just something that's been on my mind a whole lot for the last few weeks. I've lived in Washington for most of my life. It's never occurred to me that I would want anything else. I'm happy with where I'm at in my life, but I've never felt overly fulfilled. Something about being in Copper Lake feels good. The small-town feel, the friendliness of the residents, getting to know my aunt a bit better, and the animals. The animals are a big part of it. I've grown attached to them, and the idea of never seeing them again makes me sadder than I'd care to admit. Even my kitty has grown to…tolerate Aunt Colette and this house.

Another thing that's surprised me a lot is how much enjoyment I've found in of taking care of them and the yard. When I first got here, I thought for sure I'd end up dreading my chores every morning and evening. Sure, they're a lot of work, and sometimes I kind of want to relax instead, but for the most part, I look forward to it. They're so full of personality, and most of them get so excited when they see me. I don't know if I want to leave them for good.

Part of me thinks I'm going crazy. I'm almost thirty, and I'm rethinking my entire life. Who does that? Well, probably a lot of people, but I never thought I'd be one of them. This trip here has been eye opening.

My phone vibrates on the bed beside me, startling me out of my thoughts. Confused at who would be texting me this late, I grab the phone and unlock it.

Cope: I can't sleep.

Smiling as I imagine him lying in bed, thinking of me, I thumb out a response as flutters swirl around in my stomach.

Me: Me either. I'm on episode who knows what of this dumb Netflix show.

Cope: I'm watching TV too, but it's not holding my attention.

Me: Same. *eye rolling emoji*

Cope: Wanna go for a ride with me?

Me: What? It's after midnight.

Cope: I know. Sometimes when I can't sleep, I like to hop in the truck and drive. It helps settle my mind.

My heart slams against my ribs as I consider his offer. It's late, but it *is* the perfect opportunity to talk to him about everything like I've wanted to do. Not to mention, I'd get to see him. Which that, in and of itself, is worth climbing out of bed in the middle of the night.

It's a no-brainer.

Me: Sure. I can walk over to your place. Give me five minutes, and I'll head out.

Cope: Nah, I'll drive over there. It's cold out, I don't want you walking.

Something that small shouldn't make my chest tighten, but it does. It's thoughtful without even trying to be. Gentlemanly.

Me: Sounds good.

Climbing out of bed, I don't bother changing. I'm sure he'll be in sleep clothes too. After I grab a beanie and my jacket out of the closet, I send a quick text to my aunt in case she wakes up, so she knows where I'm at, and then I head out front where his truck is already waiting for me.

Nerves have me feeling like I could hurl. Lord help me, I'm

ASHLEY JAMES

so gone for this man.

Chapter 23

Cope Murphy

The entire cab of my truck smells like him. It's intoxicating. My hand resting on the gear shifter itches to reach over and hold his. Lace our fingers together. Feel his skin on mine again. But I don't know if that would feel too intimate for Xander. I don't know what all of this means to him yet—although, I'm hoping we clear that up tonight—so I don't. It's below freezing outside. It hasn't snowed, but it looks like it may. The heat's blasting as we drive aimlessly down an empty backroad.

Music plays through the speakers softly, and despite the frigid air, I have the window rolled down about an inch. The heat counteracts the cold air, but I love the freshness of it hitting my face when I drive. I'm doing my best to keep my eyes trained on the road, when all I really want to do is turn to face Xander and drink him in. He's in a pair of dark green, white, and black plaid pajama pants. His black jacket isn't puffy, but I can tell it keeps him warm. He has it zipped all the way up to his throat, and he's wearing a lime green beanie on his head with some logo on it. If I had to guess, I'd say it was his store's logo. His messy black curls dip down underneath the hat, hanging over his brows, making him appear younger than he is.

We haven't seen each other much since Vegas, so having him in my truck right now, all to myself, is more exciting than it should be.

In my periphery, I watch him glance over at me. "Where are we going?" he asks, voice quiet.

"Nowhere in particular." I allow myself to look over at him, just for a moment, before returning my gaze to the dark road, lit up only by my headlights. "On nights like this, I don't normally have a destination. I just drive, letting my mind clear."

"What's on your mind tonight?"

"Well, full honesty..." I glance over, meeting his gaze. "You are."

He smiles. "What about me?"

"My mind keeps replaying Vegas, and what it all means."

Xander's quiet for a moment. My heart kicks up a notch at his silence. Shit, what if he's not wanting to talk about that? What if it didn't mean anything to him? I know I've never explored anything with a man before, but with women, I can usually tell if they're into me. The signs surely are the same no matter the gender, and I could've sworn I got more than just hook-up vibes from him. I guess I could be wrong.

Finally, he says, "I've thought about it a lot, too."

Letting out the breath I'd been holding, I grip the gear shifter tighter, fighting the smile trying to show on my face. "Glad it's not just me, then."

Turning off the road, I pull into an abandoned church, leaving the car on but putting it in park. I lower the volume on the music a little, turning to face Xander.

"What do you want it to mean?" he asks, going back to my original statement.

"I don't know, but I do know I don't want it to end."

The vulnerability of that statement leaves me feeling naked and exposed, and not in the fun way. Especially since I can't read Xander's facial expressions in this light. I'm nervous we aren't on the same page and he's about to let me down easy. Although, I suppose I'd rather know now before the feelings get stronger.

But then Xander smiles at me, and my whole body warms from the sight. I have such a visceral reaction to him. He leans over, grabbing the front of my shirt, and presses his lips to mine. The kiss is sweet and tender, and it makes my stomach somersault. I don't think I'll ever get over how incredible kissing Xander feels. It doesn't last long, and when he pulls away, I'm already craving another taste.

"I don't either," he says simply. "I like you, Cope. You've been a breath of fresh air since I first got to this town, and you never fail to make me feel happy and welcome. You're upfront and honest about how you're feeling, and not even once have I had to guess where I stand with you. It's refreshing."

Feeling relieved, I breathe out a sigh. "I like you too."

"But—"

"No buts," I insist with a chuckle, holding up a hand. "Buts in this instance are never good. Unless it's your butt. Then I'll allow it."

Xander laughs, the sound light and airy. "*But* there are a few things we should put out in the open," he finishes.

"Okay," I reply slowly, the conversation feeling heavy all of the sudden. "Like what?"

"Well, for starters, prior to meeting me, you considered

yourself straight, right?"

I shrug. "Yeah, but I'd never felt any reason why I'd need to question that."

"Is this just an experiment to you?" The question takes me off guard, and I sputter on my own spit. Xander reaches out and covers my hand with his. "I don't mean it to be an insulting or out-there question, but I have to ask. You'd be surprised by the number of *straight* men who dip their toes in the queer pond, and then are more than happy going on their merry way, pretending like it never happened. Not that I think you would do that. I care for you, but I also don't want to end up getting hurt. If my relationship with Henry taught me one thing, it's that communication is key. I don't ever want to be in another situation where we want different things.

"But in the same breath, I can understand how hard it can be coming to terms with this new revelation for you. You may not be ready for anything, especially not out in the open, with you being a public figure in a way. I'm not trying to get too serious and say we have to figure it all out right now, but I would like to sort of know we're on the same page."

Once he finishes, he lets out a deep sigh, like he didn't allow himself to take a single breath the whole time he was talking, and he looks down at the hands clasped together in his lap. The silence sits like its own presence in the cab of my truck as I think over everything he said. None of this even crossed my mind before now, but he's right. This is the stuff that *should* be talked about from the get-go. And I can see why he'd need to ask me about what this is to me, especially after what he just went through with his last relationship.

Reaching over, I take his chin between my thumb and index finger, turning his head until his bright blue eyes meet mine. There's trepidation in his gaze. "I want you, Xander," I say simply before continuing. "And I don't just mean physically. I don't just mean for a few fun nights. I don't give a shit that you're a man and not a woman. That doesn't matter to me. It's never been about that. Yes, if someone had asked me about my sexuality before, I would've said straight because I've never been given any reason to believe otherwise…until you. My feelings for you have always felt right. It's never been about your gender. Never been about what's between your legs. I don't even know what I'd say my sexuality is now because I've never been attracted to another man before you, but I'm *very* attracted to you, so I'm clearly not straight."

"I'm not asking you to define your sexuality, Cope," he breathes out.

"I know you're not, but I want you to know where I stand. I don't care that you're a man, or that I've only ever dated women. Hell, I've barely even dated women. I like *you,* and I don't want this to be something we just do for fun. I'd like to explore this and see if there's more here. Like with any relationship, I'd prefer if the entire world didn't know until we knew what the hell we were, but that has nothing to do with your gender and everything to do with being a private person. As far as our friends and family go, I don't care if they know. I'd prefer if they did because I enjoy being around you, so they'll obviously see that. And as soon as we know if there's something real here, I'd be happy to shout it from the rooftops that you're mine—you know, if you want to be. Please believe me when I say that my newfound discovery of my sexuality is not going to be an issue for us. I'm not some in-the-closet guy who's afraid to come out because of trauma or fear or anything. I simply just didn't know what I wanted until I met you."

His Adam's apple rolls on a rough swallow, and he's got his bottom lip tucked between his teeth. He looks adorable sitting in my passenger seat...like he belongs there.

"Have you ever heard of the term 'demisexual' before?" he asks.

My brows slash together as I shake my head. "No, I don't think so."

"Now, again, I'll never ask you to define your sexuality, and you should never be made to feel like you have to fit inside one singular label to be accepted, but hearing you explain all of that made me think you could possibly be demisexual."

"Is it like a demigod?" I waggle my brows as he snorts.

"Not exactly," he responds with a laugh. "People who identify as demisexual often only feel sexual attraction to someone after they've formed a strong emotional bond with them." Xander shrugs awkwardly before adding, "I'm not trying to label you, by any means, but I know sometimes when you're figuring yourself out, it can help some people to put a name to what they're feeling or why they're feeling that way. I'm not trying to shove you into a box—"

"No," I cut him off, my heart suddenly hammering inside my chest at what he's saying. "That actually makes a lot of sense. I've never heard that term before, but it sounds like me and how I've always felt. It would explain why I've never felt much sexual connection with anyone before or why I've never felt the way my friends seemed to feel about sex."

"You don't have to figure it all out now, or really, ever, if you don't want to," he reiterates.

"Thank you," I say softly. "You always seem to know the right thing to say to make me feel at ease."

His cheeks pinken and his lips tilt into a small smirk.

"Well, since we're putting it all out there tonight, I should tell you something." He meets my gaze, looking nervous, which makes my heart beat faster and not in a good way.

"Okay..."

"It's nothing bad," he hurries to say when I'm sure he can see the panic in my eyes. "At least, I don't think. Obviously, I still live in Washington. This was supposed to be something temporary to help my aunt." My stomach bottoms out, not wanting him to say what I think he might. "She's getting stronger now, but I still think she needs help. She's getting older, and it's a lot to maintain everything. I need to head back to Washington in a couple of weeks to handle some things with the business. We're wanting to buy out our investors and then open a second store. Bastian, my partner, has been on the hunt for the perfect location, and he thinks he may have found it, but I have to be there to deal with all the legal stuff, and get everything running."

"So, you're moving back home?"

How is that nothing bad?

"I'll be back," he says in a hurry. "I only plan to be there for as long as it takes to get this situated. A couple months, maybe. But then I'd like to come back to help my aunt. It'll only be temporary."

"You want to move here?"

"I don't know. It's a big move, but I'd be lying if I said it hadn't crossed my mind. And I don't want to freak you out and think I'm doing this because of you, because I'm not!" I chuckle at the rushed way he said that. "I've really fallen in love with this place, and knowing that my aunt probably needs help she's too damn stubborn to ask for is a large reason for my consideration. And of course, there's you too." Even in the low light, I can see the red splashing his cheeks. "I'm not ready to walk away from you for good. Not without at least trying. And if we try and realize it doesn't work out, then fine, but I'd rather know than always wonder. I'd just need you to know I'd be in Washington for at least the next month or so. But if you're okay with continuing this while I'm there, then I am too."

If we try and realize it doesn't work... Why wouldn't it work? I don't know why my mind is so hung up on that part, but I internally shake my head of those thoughts, knowing I need to give him some sort of a formulated answer.

"When do you leave for Washington?"

"I haven't bought the plane ticket yet, but probably in a week or so. I'm meeting with some guy on Monday to see about hiring him to help my aunt around the farm while I'm gone. She doesn't know I'm meeting him yet, but I want to make sure he's a viable, competent option before I bring it up to her. So, once I have that squared away, I'll book my ticket."

"Well, tomorrow night, a couple of the guys are coming over to my place to watch the Copper Lake U playoff game. I'd love for you to come if you're free."

"What time?"

"The game starts at seven, but everyone will probably get there a few hours early."

"Okay, I'll come. It sounds fun." He gives me a warm smile. "I have something to do with Whit in the afternoon, but I can come after."

"Whit?" I ask, my brow arched. "As in the vet, Whit?"

Xander snorts. "Is there any other Whit?"

"No." I laugh. "I just didn't know you guys hung out."

"We haven't. Except the times I've been with you and he's been there. But when he came to check out Aggie's ankle, while you ran to the store to get the stuff for her bath, we got to talking about highland cows and how much I've grown to love them since being here. Whit ended up telling me about this farm on the outskirts of town that he occasionally makes house calls to that, I guess, has a whole herd of them. We swapped numbers, and he texted me this morning, telling me he has to go out there tomorrow and asked if I wanted to join." He shrugs when he's finished.

Why wasn't I invited? I like cows. I'd like to see Xander's excitement when he gets to hang out with a bunch of them. *What the fuck, Whit?* Although, I do love that he's making friends—even better that they're my friends too.

"That works out because Whit and his boyfriend are supposed to come, too." There's too much distance between us in this truck. It's time to change that. "C'mere," I tell him, opening my arm, indicating for him to scooch over. "Let's cuddle."

Rolling his eyes and breathing out a chuckle, he slides across the seat and into my arms. He fits perfectly, like he's made to be there, and he lets out a contented sigh as soon as we're wrapped up in each other, like it's what he's been waiting for and needing this whole time. I turn up the music a little, then pluck the beanie off his head, and after some argument with him about it, I nuzzle my nose into the hair on top of his head, breathing him in. His scent, his feel, his everything, calms me. I don't even know how long we sit here like this, wrapped up in each other. After a while, we make out for a little bit, but for the most part, it's just about the cuddling. The connection that seems to go so much deeper with him than sex.

At one point, we both doze off for a while. The heat on, the music playing softly, his head on my chest. I'd love to sleep with him like this all night again, but in a bed. The one time in Vegas was not enough. By the time I drop him off at his aunt's, it's after three, and I already cannot wait for tonight.

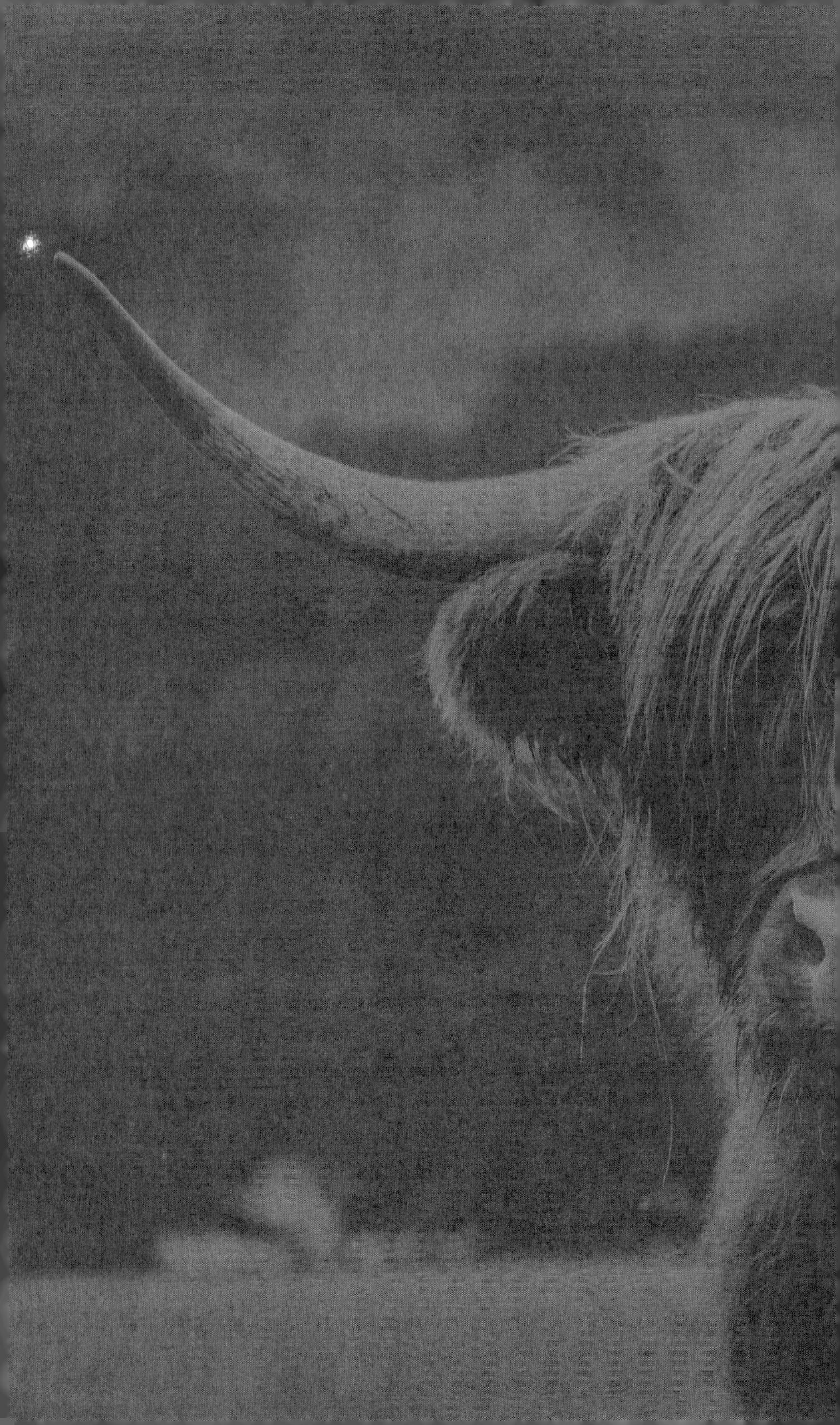

Chapter 24

Xander Dawson

Note to self: Don't stay out with hot cowboys until the early hours of the morning ever again. I clearly forgot that I'm no longer in college and that shit doesn't fly anymore. Three cups of coffee later, I'm only half-zombie as I climb into Whit's truck. No amount of exhaustion could keep me from doing what we're about to do, though. The giddy feeling growing in my stomach reminds me of when I was a kid on Christmas morning. Glee and anticipation practically drip out of my pores.

"Morning," I mutter as I buckle my seatbelt.

Eucalyptus and something sweet that I can't place fill my nostrils. It smells nice, but different.

Shooting a glance over at Whit, he smiles, eyes squinting behind his thick-framed glasses. "Good morning. Excited?" he asks.

"Very."

The few times I've been around Whit, he's always given me hardcore grandpa vibes, which I know doesn't totally make sense since he can't be that much older than me. He's always dressed in slacks and some type of nice cardigan or sweater that I know if I touched would be soft as hell. He's also the type people would say has an old soul. That term hasn't always made sense to me, but as soon as I met him, I understood it.

It's freezing outside, having snowed overnight. The ground and trees are all coated in a thick layer of white, and the corners of the truck windows are all iced over. From everyone I've talked to about the weather—which arguably isn't a lot, just my aunt and Cope—they say it's been an unusually warm year. We're approaching Christmas next week, and last night was the first real snow of the season.

Twenty minutes later, Whit pulls off the road and onto a long, one-lane, gravel road. The powder covering the ground goes on for miles, and I wonder if all this land belongs to the cattle owner. It's insane how much property people own here. It's the complete opposite back in Desert Creek. Several houses line whole blocks, so close we're practically on top of one another, and if you have a backyard, it's big enough for a grill and a swing set, and that's about it.

I never thought I'd enjoy living in the country. Living shoulder to shoulder with my neighbor never bothered me, but it's all I've ever known. Getting to wake up every morning, sit in the rocking chair on the back porch, and watch the sun rise with a cup of coffee in hand has genuinely become one of my favorite things. Add in Aggie's fluffy self coming to greet me with her version of bedhead, and it's perfection. I love it. It makes the idea of going back to Washington and not coming back sound even more dreadful than it already does.

But that would be crazy…right? Leaving everything I've ever known—leaving almost all of my family—to move here, somewhere I've been for all of two months. Yet somehow, I've managed to get more attached to this town than I was attached to any place in Washington my whole life. How is it possible that somewhere you've never been before now can feel so strongly like *home*?

Whit parks the truck in front of a huge weathered red barn, and after he grabs his supply bag, we climb out. The owner of the farm greets us and shows us where to go, but other than that, we don't see much of him. On the ride over, Whit told me one of the highlands is pregnant, so he's here to check on her and the baby, as well as the others. My eyes widen as I take them in. There's five total that I can see, some looking like babies.

"Whit, look at them!" I practically shout and growl at the same time. "They're so fucking cute and fuzzy, and there's so many of them!"

He laughs. "They are cute. And they're such a friendly breed. It's hard not to like them."

"You have the coolest job," I tell Whit as I inch my way closer to one of the smaller ones. A dark auburn-colored calf, so little she doesn't even have horns yet. I kneel, and even though she's watching me warily, she lets me pet her before licking the palm of my hand. "Oh, my gosh. I'm in love. I want them all. Can I please take them home?"

Whit chuckles from behind me. "Trust me, the job isn't always this cute. And I think Mr. Olsen would be pretty upset if you stole all his cattle."

"I'm sure he'd understand. I'll even ask real nicely, and say please."

"Let me know how that works out for you," he teases.

Whit examines a few of the animals, working in relative silence—something I've noticed he does a lot. He doesn't seem to be one for small talk—while I stay put in highland cow heaven.

"Don't they get cold out here in the snow?" I ask him once my fingers start to turn stiff from the cold weather. Thankfully, I remembered to shove some gloves into my coat pocket. Suddenly, I want to wrap them up in giant sweaters and shove beanies onto their heads. With horn holes, of course.

"Not really. The cold weather and snow have little effect on them. They're from the highlands of Scotland, which is cold and windy, and they're a common breed up north in Alaska and the Scandinavian countries because of this. It's why they have the fancy-looking bangs. It keeps the wind out of their eyes. They're quite adaptable animals."

I nod, not that Whit can see me.

"So, you and Cope, huh?" he asks after a few moments of silence.

Before I even know that I'm doing it, a grin splits my face, and I'm suddenly thankful that my back is toward Whit. "Yeah. It's new, but I like him."

"You know, he texted me all pissy that he wasn't invited today."

"No, he did not." I laugh, glancing over my shoulder. "Jealous because I got to see all these cuties and he didn't, huh?"

Eyebrow arched, he says, "Think it had less to do with the animals, and more to do with you."

"I doubt that." I brush him off. "We just saw each other last night."

"You'd be surprised. I've known Cope for a long while," he murmurs, almost as if to himself. "Never seen him like he is with you."

Replaying the sentence, I swallow hard. "What do you mean?"

"Smitten," is all he says, the hint of a smirk playing on his lips as he gets back to what he was doing.

Smitten. Is Cope smitten with me? Why does that make my stomach flutter like I'm free-falling? I bite back a grin, returning my attention to the baby highland in front of me. "Smitten," I whisper to her, the smile breaking free. "What about you and your man?" I ask Whit. "How long have you guys been together?"

"Not long. We met right before summer."

"He's cute."

"Yes, he is." I can hear the smile in his voice.

"You've lived here your whole life?" I stand up and make my way over to him, examining what he's doing.

"Pretty much. Copper Lake is the type of place that you come to and end up never leaving."

"So, you like living here?"

His eyes lift to meet mine. "I do. It holds a lot of memories—some good, some not so good—but I couldn't imagine myself living anywhere else. You're from Washington, right?"

"Yup, sure am."

"How're you liking it here?" he asks. "I'd imagine it's a lot different than what you're used to."

"That it is." I laugh. "I'm liking Copper Lake a whole lot more than I thought I would, if I'm being honest. Everyone's so nice, and it's beautiful here."

"I think it's great what you're doing for your aunt." His words take me by surprise. "I've been up to her place several times over the years to check on her animals, and even though she's one of the most stubborn women I've ever met, I can bet she's appreciative of your help."

Whit finishes up what he's doing, and about thirty minutes later, we're on the road again. The snow's coming down a bit harder now, but it looks beautiful falling over the trees and the wide-open fields.

"You're coming to Cope's in a few hours, right?" Whit asks as we pull up in front of my aunt's house.

"Yeah. I'll probably shower and do a few things around the house before I head over. You?"

"Yeah, Reggie and I will be there. Thanks for coming with me today. This was fun."

"Yeah, it was. I'll gladly come with you any time you have to go up there again." Hopping out of the truck, I spin back around and add, "And I'm dead serious."

Whit chuckles. "Alright, I'll see you in a few hours."

True to my word, a couple of hours, a hot shower, and some housework later, I'm walking over to Cope's house, excitement steadily buzzing in my gut. The snow has been falling all afternoon, and I'm bundled up with a puffer coat, gloves, a scarf, and a beanie, and I'm still freezing my ass off. When I texted Cope to let him know I was coming, he offered to drive over and pick me up, but I told him that was ridiculous because he's right next door.

I should've accepted the offer.

Of course, I could've taken my car, but it drives like trash in the snow, go figure, or I could've taken my aunt's Subaru, which probably excels in this type of weather, but I don't feel comfortable driving anybody else's car in the snow. I'd feel awful if I wrecked it, even though—again—I'm only going next door.

Climbing up the few steps on Cope's porch, I kick the snow off my boots before knocking on the door. He opens almost immediately, and the sight of him in the doorway is enough to take my breath away. He's got on a Copper Lake U football jersey. The school colors are red and gold, and they look damn good against his tan skin. A black backwards trucker hat sits on his head, and he's wearing a pair of straight-leg, *tight* Wranglers, and nothing more than a pair of black socks on his feet.

He clears his throat, and my head snaps up, gaze meeting his as my cheeks heat from him catching me checking him out. Smirking, he steps to the side, letting me pass by, but as I step over the threshold, before I can step too far into the house, he wraps an arm around my middle, hauling me into him. His scent envelops me; he smells so fucking good all the time. I would be perfectly content burying my face in his chest and inhaling for all of eternity.

My pulse races as I glance up at him from beneath my lashes. He's not *that* much taller, but he's got a few inches on me. He smiles warmly, and I swear I could melt right here from the sight. My frozen face long forgotten.

"You look cute all bundled up for the snow," he rasps, his face so close to mine, his warm, minty breath fanning my face.

"Thanks. Channeling my inner Frosty."

He laughs, the sound deep and throaty, before pressing his lips to mine. His tongue teases the seam before I part and let him in, and he explores my mouth, tasting and caressing so thoroughly, I forget we're standing in the entryway of a house filled with other people. My glove-covered hands fist his shirt as he kisses me, my head floating into the clouds at how good his mouth feels against mine.

"Get a room!" somebody calls out before chuckling.

The kiss ends, both of us breathless, and when we glance down the hall, it's Shooter walking by, a shit-eating grin on his face. Cope flips him off, and I busy myself with kicking out of my shoes and removing my outerwear. The house is warm, and it smells like delicious food, my stomach rumbling the farther we walk inside. I haven't eaten anything since this morning before Whit picked me up.

This is the first time I've been inside Cope's house. Even though it's right next door to my aunt's, it looks completely different on the inside. Another vast difference to where I'm from. Not only are the houses close together, but they also all mirror each other, inside and out. Cope's is a two-story, whereas my aunt's is a rambler style. The walls are a simple cream color, and everything is decorated in a very minimalist style. There're a few pictures in frames that adorn walls of him with his friends, and some with a couple who must be his parents.

"What do you want to drink?" Cope asks as we step into the kitchen, throwing me a glance over his shoulder.

"Whatever beer you have is fine."

"Xan-man!" Shooter strolls back into the kitchen, Sterling following behind him, that same grin on his face from before. "Nice to see you again, now that you're not sucking face with my best friend."

"Shut up, Shooter," Cope growls, flicking the hat off Shooter's head as he passes him to hand me the ice-cold can.

There's a ton of food already set out on the table and the countertops, so I grab a plate full, probably taking way too much, but I'm starving. There's a handful of people in the living room when we make it in there, and surprisingly, I recognize all of them. Whit's already here, too, with his boyfriend. Cope has a ton of furniture in here, including the biggest sectional sofa I've ever seen. There's room for everyone. He takes a seat on the chaise side of the sectional, pulling me down beside him. We're close enough that our legs press against each other, the area where they touch lit up like electricity.

I don't know shit about football, much like I didn't know anything about the rodeo, but to be honest, it's not really the game I'm focusing on anyway. It's the man beside me who smells good enough to eat, and who has his arm rested on the back of the couch behind me. I want to sink into him, toss my leg over his, and let my head fall on his chest. I'm not sure who all here knows about us, or if he wants them to, so I don't do any of what I want to. Although, he *did* kiss me in the entryway, where anybody could've caught us—hell, someone did catch us—and Whit knew about us already. I'd rather play it safe, though, and let him make the moves rather than do something and potentially make him uncomfortable.

One beer turns into two, which then turns into three. The room becomes rowdy once the game starts, and it's amusing to watch. From what I've gathered, it's a pretty important game. I think Cope mentioned it was a playoff game when he invited me over last night.

During halftime, I go outside with Shooter and Cope to smoke, but it's freezing. I swear, it's dropped like twenty degrees since getting here. Even with my coat on, I'm still shivering. Cope must notice, because he pulls me into him, his body heat doing wonders at warming me up.

He presses a kiss to the top of my head before bringing his lips to the shell of my ear. "Stay the night," he tells more than asks me.

An icy-hot shiver rolls down my spine, and I don't know if it's from his hot breath against my cold skin or the idea of getting to spend another night next to him. Probably the latter.

I glance up at him, his brown eyes nearly black, and I nod slowly. "Okay."

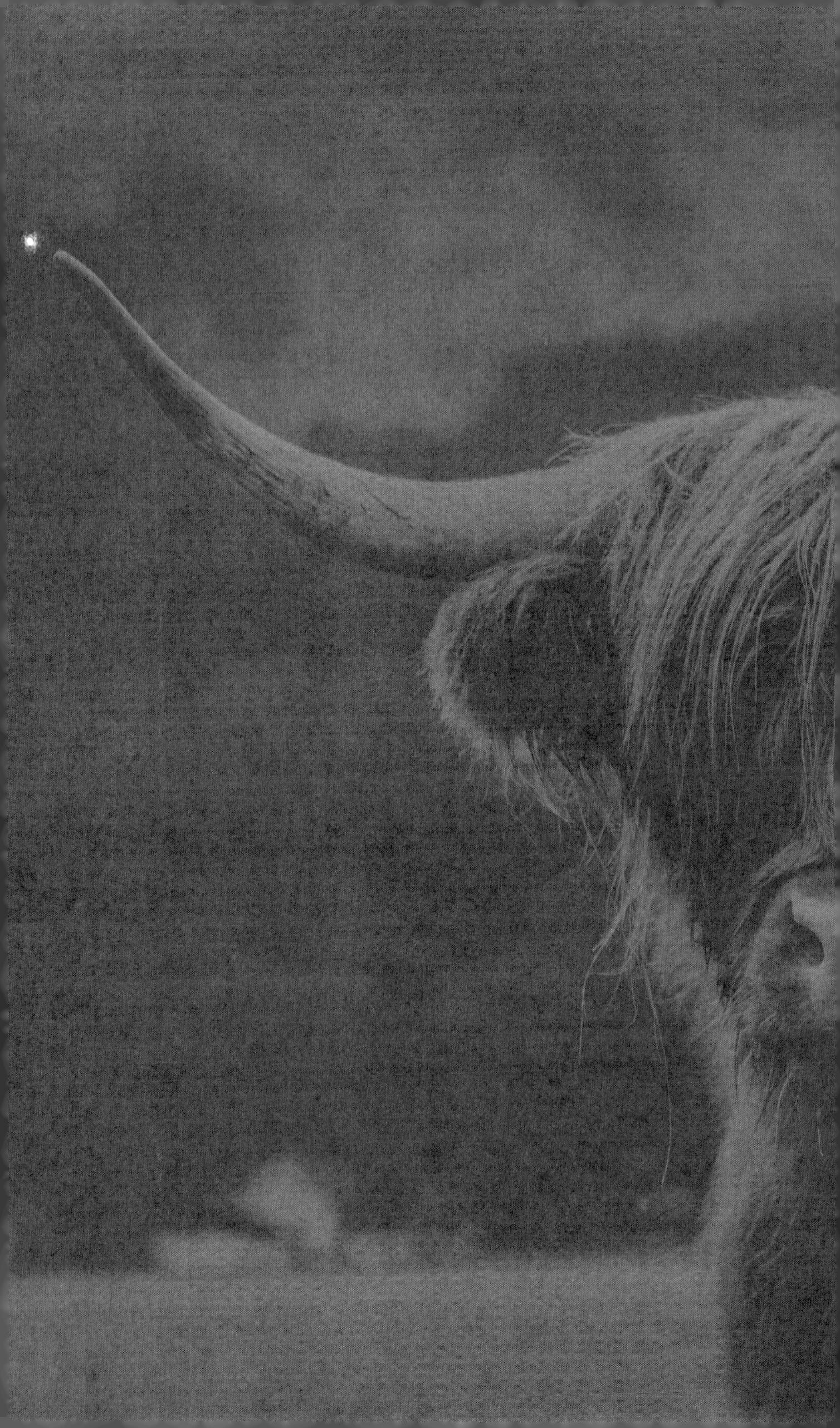

Chapter 25

Cope Murphy

If I didn't know any better, I'd say my friends were purposely trying to cockblock me. It's nearly nine o'clock by the time they all leave. The game ended hours ago, but we all got caught up in talking about this or that. Don't get me wrong, it was a fun evening, but I'm more than ready to get Xander alone. This is the first sleepover we've had since Vegas, and to say I'm antsy would be an understatement.

Whit and his man, Reggie, are the last to leave. Sliding the deadbolt into place, I turn, resting my back against the heavy wood door, and my eyes find Xander's immediately. He's at the end of the hall, butt propped against the entryway table, eyes filled with what can only be described as hunger. The air has shifted, becoming more tense. More supercharged. The chemistry between Xander and me still takes me by surprise. The way my body viscerally responds to him, the way it feels like I may actually die if I don't touch him, kiss him, be near him.

My entire life, I've gone through the motions, thinking that everybody who explained a feeling like this was exaggerating or flat-out lying. That there's no way the movies have it right. And then I meet Xander, and it's like it all clicks. My body immediately recognized his, immediately wanted him even before I understood it.

My feet carry me down the narrow hallway as I stalk closer to Xander. His top teeth bite down on his bottom lip in a way that makes me want to replace his teeth with mine. By the time I close the distance between us, I can barely breathe. The energy between us is stifling. Neither of us makes any move for a few moments. Eyes taking each other in, I can feel his want. His need. It's as potent as my own.

Xander moves first, but barely. His hand reaches out, gripping the hem of my shirt as he pulls me into him. His other hand comes up, knocking the hat off my head. We both breathe out a laugh when it hits the floor. Confident fingers thread through the hair atop my head as his baby blues alternate between my eyes and my lips. What feels like an eternity later, he takes my lips with his, and the whole world disappears. Our tongues meet in the middle. They dance and caress sensually. They taste greedily and explore wantonly.

"Take me to your bedroom, cowboy," Xander says against my lips.

The request sounding so similar to what he said in Vegas sends a thrill down my spine. Lust dripping off of his every word is a shot of desire straight to my core. Taking him by the hand, I lead him down the hall, toward the staircase. With each step we take, nerves and anticipation clutch my insides. A warmth settles in my chest once we cross the threshold to my room. I don't have any expectations, nor do I know what will or won't happen tonight, but intuition and the way he was looking at me earlier tell me it'll be more than we've done before.

That thought excites me and terrifies me in equal measures. Not only is he the first person I've hooked up with in quite a while, and not only is this brand-new territory for me with him being a man, but because of how deeply I care for him already, I want to make this good for him. I want it to be memorable in his eyes, and not because I was a fumbling, nervous moron. That fear takes me by surprise because it's not one I've thought about until this very moment, but I realize how strongly I feel that way.

We stop right next to my bed, only the lights from outside illuminating the area. My heart is thrashing against my ribs as I turn to face him, and he's looking at me like he can hear my every thought. I inhale a deep breath and decide to stick to what we've always done…honesty.

"I'm nervous." The words come out hushed, but I know he heard them. One thing about Xander is that I've never, not even once, felt an ounce of judgement come from him. Through every step of the way with whatever this is between us, he's been patient and sweet.

Xander gives me a sweet smile. "We don't have to do anything you don't want to do."

"No, I want to," I hurry and say, probably much more enthusiastically than I should've. Clearing my throat, I add, "I want to…to do it all, but I'm just nervous. This is uncharted territory, and I don't quite know how to lead here."

Pulling me in for a kiss that steals my breath away, he cups the side of my face in his soft, warm palm as he holds my gaze. "You've spent the last couple months teaching me," he says, his voice taking on a husky tone. "Showing me how to look after my aunt's farm, teaching me about the rodeo, showing me how I should be treated by a man. It's my turn to show you a thing or two, cowboy."

My cheeks flame, and I know without even looking, a flush spreads from my neck, to my face, all the way to the tips of my ears. My cock throbs behind my jeans, and I reach down to adjust myself, Xander's eyes tracking the movement, a smirk ticking up on his lips.

"First thing's first…" The hand cupping my face moves down to my shoulder, applying the smallest bit of pressure as he continues. "I'm gonna need you to drop to your knees, open that pretty mouth, and show me that tongue."

Fire shoots through my veins at his demand. At the hunger in his gaze as he steps back the slightest amount to give me room to obey. And I do. Without any hesitation, as if my body is moving of its own accord, my knees collide with the soft carpet, I tilt my head back slightly to look up at him, and I relax my jaw, sticking my tongue out exactly the way he asked. My flesh prickles with arousal, my body flushed hot, and my dick aches where it's still confined behind too many clothes.

The pleased grin that slides onto Xander's face fills me with a sense of pride, knowing I did that. I put that smile there. One handedly, he flicks open the button on his jeans, dragging the zipper down, the sound audible in the quiet room, and he pulls himself out. Suddenly, I'm face to face with the very appendage I've fantasized about since the first and only time I got to see it. It's even more beautiful than I remember. My mouth waters at the sight of the slightly pulled back foreskin, the glistening tip poking out from beneath it, and the thick veins running along the shaft. A dot of pre-cum beads at the slit, and I've never wanted to taste anything more than I do right now.

Glancing up from beneath my lashes, I lock eyes with Xander, and as if he can read my mind tonight, he steps forward, placing only the tip of his cock right on my tongue. My taste buds awaken, taking in the salty flavor of his arousal, and before I can even stop myself, a groan rips from my throat. His blue eyes darken at the sound, and I watch as his jaw clenches tightly, like he's trying to restrain himself.

I want to reach down and pull myself out. Stroke it. But I don't.

Xander then slides the underside of his shaft along the flat of my tongue. I don't wrap my lips around him yet. Instead, I let him use my tongue for a moment. He drags it up and down the length, his lips parted with pleasure, as my body comes alive under his watchful gaze.

"Fuck, that feels good," he breathes out. His eyes are hooded, cheeks pink, and from all the way down here, he already looks so beautifully wrecked. He reaches up, working his fingers through my strands again, gripping them at the scalp. The pinch of pain only adds to the arousal bubbling inside of me. "Close your lips," he instructs me hoarsely.

Doing as he asks, I let my tongue swirl around the tip, dipping underneath the foreskin too, before I hollow my cheeks and suck. He groans before thrusting a little more of his length into my mouth. After a few inches, my gag reflex kicks in, and tears spring to my eyes. Xander backs off for a moment, letting me focus once again on the tip. We do this back-and-forth game for a while, and eventually, I'm able to take more of his length into my mouth. Every once in a while, a salty burst of flavor will drop onto my tongue, right around the time his eyes will roll back and he lets out a groan. The sound is music to my ears, and I desperately want to hear more of it.

Xander works himself in and out of my mouth, the pleasure screwing up his face. I feel him swell slightly, and I know he has to be getting close, but before he can finish, he pulls out. His chest is heaving with heavy breaths, as is mine, and he wraps a tight fist around the base of his dick.

"Take your clothes off and get on the bed," he orders, reaching behind his head and pulling off his shirt. With his pants already undone, he shoves them the rest of the way down until they pool around his ankles.

Rising to my feet, I waste no time ridding myself of my clothes as I watch him climb onto the bed and position himself against my headboard. His hand lazily strokes himself as he watches me, the weight of his gaze intoxicating.

Right as I finish undressing, and before I can climb onto the bed, he stops me. "Do you have a condom and lube?"

A fresh wave of nerves washes over me as I nod, reaching into the drawer of my nightstand to retrieve those items. *Holy fuck, this is happening.* I toss them to the left of Xander before crawling on top of him. He happily spreads his legs for me, and I love how we look together like this. I fit perfectly against him. Leaning down, our lips meet, and this time the kiss is passionate and long. Our tongues stroke, hands roam, my heart beating so fast, I'm sure he can hear it.

Xander wraps his legs around my waist, and our cocks line up, rubbing together in a way that makes my toes curl. He sighs into my mouth, lips falling open, and I take the opportunity to move my focus down to his throat. My teeth nip at his Adam's apple as it rolls, and I pepper his neck with kisses, sucking the skin into my mouth, knowing that I'm leaving marks. I want him to look in the mirror tomorrow and see them, remembering what we did. I've never been a possessive guy. Never cared much about flaunting anybody as mine. But with Xander? I want all of that and more. I want people to know where I've been. I want them to know what we've done. I want to claim him as mine and me as his.

I sit back on my haunches, hands roaming around his chest before my fingers find the little silver barbells through his rosy nipples. Twirling, pinching, rolling. I love them. Love the way they look on him, love the reaction he has when I play with them. I'm enamored by the piercing. By his body. By *him*.

"You gonna fuck me, or am I fucking you?" he asks, words doused with lust and need.

My eyes dart up to his face, tongue thick, mouth dry, as I swallow thickly. "What do you want?" My voice is unrecognizable, even to my own ears.

I won't even act like I haven't thought about this, whether I'd be giving or taking in this instance. Both ways have played out in my head in extensive, erotic detail. I've even beat off to the idea of both ways. It's hot, the idea of Xander and I coming together as one, no matter how it happens.

"I want to do whichever way you're most comfortable with," he replies, hand still steadily stroking his cock.

Xander is sexy. He is mouthwateringly, unabashedly confident when it comes to his body and sex. Gone is the flustered man I met on the side of the dirt road. Gone is the unsure man who hadn't a clue how to take care of farm animals. In the bedroom, Xander is confidence embodied. It's hot as fuck, and despite how fucking nervous I am for what's about to happen—regardless of *how* it'll happen—his confidence is such a turn on to me. It calms my frayed nerves just being in his presence. Knowing that no matter what we do, he'll guide me through it without judgement, and he'll look at me like I'm the center of the universe while doing it.

I chew on my bottom lip as I think over what I want, and

while I do, Xander reaches out, wrapping a tight fist around my dick, stroking it while he does the same to himself with his other hand. He flicks his wrist, a move that has my breath catching in my throat.

"Either way, I think I'm okay with," I finally say on a groan.

His fist tightens on my dick, and I let out a hiss through my teeth. Eyes zeroing in on mine, he clicks his tongue at me before saying, "Which do you want, Cope? Don't give me the 'I'm fine with either' spiel. How. Do. You. Want. Me?"

"I want you to fuck me," I blurt out, taking us both by surprise.

Xander's eyes widen, his lips parting. "You do?"

Words failing me, I nod, my cock twitching in his grip. His eyes dip down, as if remembering what he was holding on to.

"Not gonna lie," he mutters. "That wasn't what I expected you to say."

"Me neither." I breathe out a laugh.

"Switch spots with me." Xander scoots over, letting me lie in the spot he was just occupying, and he situates himself between my legs, similar to how I was with him. His palms rub up and down on my thighs, the feeling sending sparks throughout my body. "Have you done anything like this before?"

"To myself," I admit, feeling my cheeks heat up as I do.

A sultry little grin tugs on Xander's lips. "Yeah, I'm gonna need to see that happen soon," he growls, pumping his cock again. "But on a serious note, when you did it to yourself…you enjoyed it?"

I nod. "I did."

He grins at me. "Well, in that case, give me the lube, and let's get to prepping this fine ass for my cock."

Chapter 26

Xander Dawson

This isn't where I pictured the night going. At all. Sure, I figured there would be sex; I've been dying to have sex with Cope, but *never* in a million years did I think he would suggest *me* topping *him*. That came out of left field, but I'm not complaining.

Am I slightly freaking out about it, though? Absolutely.

Hungry lips devour mine as I blindly flick the cap to the lube, pouring a glob onto my trembling fingers. My heart pounds voraciously as I bring my slick digits between his crease, using my other hand to stroke him slowly.

A shiver racks through Cope's body as the cool gel makes contact with his skin, and he breathes out the sexiest moan. His chest is rising and falling with his shallow, rapid breaths, his entire body coiled tight. I can't tell who's more nervous in this moment; him or me.

"Relax for me," I say against his lips, massaging the pad of my index finger around his tight entrance. It puckers under my touch, and as I swipe my thumb over the tip of his cock,

I notice how much he's leaking for me already. My mouth waters as a thought flits through my mind; a sure-fire way to relax him enough to stretch him for me.

With a gentle shove to the chest, silently telling him to lie down, I allow myself a moment to drink in this hard, fit, naked man before me. And fuck, what a sight it is. Cope is a gorgeous fucking man, and *all man* he is. A light smattering of hair covers both his pecs, down the center of his abdomen, before it thickens and gets darker underneath his navel, where it leads down to a full, trimmed patch of hair encompassing his impressive length. His Adonis belt is sharp and defined, and I can't help but trace it with my finger, loving the way he shivers as I do.

Pupils blown, his eyes look obsidian as they peer up at me from beneath heavy lids. His tongue pokes out, wetting his bottom lip in a way that shouldn't be as tempting as it is. Hell, everything Cope does is tempting and erotic, and I doubt he even realizes it. He's a sex symbol to the rodeo world—strong, talented, good looking—but it's *me* who gets to see him like this. Disheveled and needy. My chest swells at that realization.

I lean down, and with my eyes still locked on his, I drag the flat of my tongue along the underside of his large, heavy cock where it sits against his lower stomach. Even in the low lighting, I can make out the clench of his jaw and the flare of his nostrils as his dick thumps against his belly with pleasure. Closing my lips around his flared, red crown, I flick my tongue around, groaning at the flavor before hollowing my cheeks and sucking him down. Hands immediately find a place in my hair as he gasps the lower I sink. With his massive girth and length, it takes me a few tries before I can take all of him, but as soon as I do, I apply a bit more pressure on his hole, eventually breaching the tight muscle.

Cope's steely thighs wrap around my head, the muscles tightening as I work my finger in deeper, all while keeping a steady rhythm on his cock. One finger quickly turns into two, crooking them just so to graze that sweet button inside of him that makes him cry out. As I work a third digit into the mix, I double down on my efforts with his dick, sucking him hard, fast, and messy. When I glance up at him, his neck is pulled taut as his head is thrown back, and the noises escaping him are enough to make me blow my load.

Once I'm sure he's fully prepped, I pull my fingers out and sit back, finally stroking my own aching length. I grab the foil wrapper that's lying on the bed, ripping it open with my teeth, then slide it on before covering myself in a generous amount of lube. Bringing my slick hand up to his cock again, I pump him slowly as I inch closer to his body. His glassy, hooded gaze alternates between my hand, my sheathed cock, and my face.

Cope looks *gone* for this, and I love that.

"Ready?" I ask, spreading a firm globe with one hand, gripping myself at the base and lining us up with the other.

He nods, tongue swiping out across his lips once more. "Do it."

With that, I ease forward, only the tip at first. Cope's so goddamn tight, my eyes want to cross at the pressure and the heat and the force in which his ass sucks me in. Gritting my teeth, I focus on what little restraint I have left, and force myself to not sink in all at once, putting myself out of my misery. This is Cope's first time with a man, and I need to make it good for him.

His brows knit together, teeth clamped down on his lip, and he's clearly holding his breath. I close my fist around his length, giving him a few firm strokes. "Breathe for me," I tell him softly. Cope glances up at me and nods, exhaling a deep breath. "You okay? I can stop."

"Don't stop," he replies in a hurry. "Just go slow."

So, slow we go. With each inch I sink into him, the more wrecked I become. My entire body is lit up for him, pleasure seeping from my pores. His large hands fist the comforter beneath us, and his jaw has gone slack, dark eyes focused on where we're connected. And I can't help but look too. It's an erotic sight. After what feels like an eternity, I bottom out, my pelvis rubbing up against his ass. His tight warmth squeezes my cock, the feeling heaven sent.

"Look at us," I murmur, fingers tracing where my cock enters him. "Look how perfectly you take me."

I peer up at Cope, taken aback by the look in his eyes. It's fervid and intense, but it's also so much more than that. That one look has my heart thumping to a different beat. It takes my breath away. It has me leaning down, crashing my mouth against his. His hands come up, clutching the hair at the back of my head, like he's been dying for me to kiss him like this, and his tongue surges forward, grazing mine as he licks everywhere he can reach.

Easing out of him until only the very tip of my dick is inside of him, I bite down on his delectable, plump bottom lip as I sink all the way in again. A choked sound gets lodged in Cope's throat, his fingers tightening on my hair, and his legs wrapping around my waist. He's giving himself to me in a way he's never done before, and that knowledge has a rush of unexpected emotion barreling through me.

"Fuck, Xan." His words breathless against my lips, and when I open my eyes, my gaze locks with his. My hips rock a steady rhythm into him, picking up the pace once I'm sure he can handle it, all while never breaking eye contact. Overwhelmed with pleasure and emotion, I reach up, hand wrapping around the side of his neck, thumb underneath his chin, keeping his head up, our lips brushing with each thrust.

Sweat lines the back of my neck, dripping down my back. My body is an inferno while his is mine for the taking. As our bodies move together, flesh against slick flesh, this moment feels larger. It feels *more*. The way he watches me, the deep-throated groans pulling from his chest, the way my body moves so fluidly in and out of him. It's deeper somehow. It's something I can't explain, but my heart aches like it wants to break through my ribs and wrap around his. It's a blinding, burning need. An all-consuming type of yearning. It's being as deep into his body as I can physically go, and it's still not enough.

Cope's eyelids flutter, as if unable to stay open, and his hair slicks to his forehead, hands clutching at my sides like he never wants to let me go. "You feel so…fucking…good." He can barely get the words out, and when I change my angle ever so slightly and his head throws back, exposing his taut neck to me, I know I've hit his prostate. A guttural groan sounds from him, a noise so loud, it vibrates through my body where we're connected.

Dropping my head, I bury my face in his neck, dragging my tongue along the salty flesh as my hips snap into him harder, faster.

"Touch yourself," I growl against his throat. "Get yourself there, because I'm so fucking close, Cope."

With how flush our bodies are, I'm surprised he can even get between us, but he does. His hand moves feverishly, knuckles brushing against my abdomen as I pound into him, his body coiled tight and writhing beneath me. My release hits me hard and fast, spreading from the base of my spine, down into my balls, and when I let go, spilling into the condom, my vision goes black, stars dancing behind my eyes as I don't slow down. If anything, I speed up, knowing he's getting close if the continuous moans and heavy breathing right beside my ear are any indication. And sure enough, a moment later, I feel hot spurts coat my chest and his body jerks against mine.

Once he's done, I sit back and drag my gaze over him. His blissed-out eyes, rosy cheeks, and the evidence of what we've just done covering us both. "Fuck, look at the mess you made," I rasp, my mouth salivating with the need to clean it up. So, I do. I lean down, drag the flat of my tongue along his torso, gathering every last drop I can find, his flavor immediately taking over my sensations.

He groans as he watches me lick him clean before muttering, "Goddamn, that's fucking hot."

You have no idea.

After he's good as new, I slip my softening cock out of his ass, tugging off the condom and tying it at the end. Cope gets up and disappears into the bathroom, coming out a moment later with a washcloth for the mess on my chest. As I'm cleaning up, I keep waiting for the awkwardness to settle in. The cloud to trickle over and hang over our heads as Cope panics.

It never comes.

Instead, he wraps his burly arms around my middle, nuzzling his face into my throat, pressing hot, wet kisses against my skin. I swear, my heart swells twice the size.

"Was that okay?" I ask, not meaning for it to come out sounding so small.

"It was more than okay," he replies, face still buried in my neck. "That was fucking amazing, Xander."

"Yeah?"

"Yes. Ten out of ten recommend." I can't help but chuckle

at that. He joins in before adding, "I really fucking enjoy your skin, Jim."

He can barely get the words out before he's snorting out a laugh. One so contagious, I can't help but join in.

"*Skin Jim!* How long have you been waiting to drop that one?"

"A while," he says, looking entirely too pleased with himself. "I have one more."

I roll my eyes, feigning a look of annoyance, but we both know I'm full of shit. "Out with it, cowboy."

"Pig in a blanket." Cope practically chokes, trying to keep a straight face.

"You've lost your damn mind," I reply in between laughs, tears springing to my eyes because of it.

He peeks down at my now soft dick, a genuine smile taking over his face. "I think I'm in love with it."

My heart thumps at his choice of words. Even knowing he didn't mean it like that, I still can't help but love the sound of it.

"In love with my dick, huh?" I ask.

"Maybe obsessed?" The way he phrases it as a question as his gleaming eyes look up and find mine has me chuckling.

"Kind of obsessed with yours too. Not gonna lie."

"Even with no hoodie?"

Scrunching up my face, I shrug lazily. "Eh." Cope's eyebrows shoot up and his mouth drops open. I can't help the laugh that bubbles out of me. "I'm *joking!* Yes, your cock is perfect just the way he is. If I could make a molded statue out of it and set it on my dresser for me to admire daily, I would."

"Probably could work that out," he replies with a waggle of his brows. "Next time, I wanna do you, though. We can take turns."

"I'm a hundred percent down with that idea. Then maybe one time we can both fuck each other in the same session."

Pulling back, eyes widened, a grin takes over his face. "That's a fucking great idea."

Shrugging, I mutter, "I know. I'm full of the good ideas."

"Yeah, you are," he growls before his lips devour mine.

It's not long after we find ourselves bundled up in his comforter, sitting on the back porch, eating leftover food. The temperatures have dropped dramatically, but in these blankets with Cope, I can't even tell. The stars shine brightly in the sky, the moon nearly full, and there's a symphony of crickets filling the silence.

It's perfect.

This entire day has been perfect. From the cows with Whit, to getting to hang out again with Cope and his friends, to the sex. Couldn't have asked for a better day. There're no unsure feelings, only comfort. I love how silly we can still be, even when we're intimate. It's rare—at least for me thus far it has been—and it's a breath of fresh air.

"I'm leaving in a few days to head back to Washington," I say softly, without looking at him. Suddenly, the trip back home seems harder than before. It feels unfair to leave him after what we just shared.

"You don't know how long you'll be gone?"

I shake my head, throat thick and my mouth dry.

He glances over at me in my periphery, and when I turn my head and meet his gaze, he smiles at me. It's warm. "We can keep in contact while you're gone and see where it goes." A look of brief uncertainty passes through his eyes before he adds, "If you want to, that is."

"I definitely want to, Cope. I'm not ready to end whatever this is."

"Alright." He grins again. "It's settled then."

Hopefully, a little time and distance doesn't tear us apart. Though, with the way he's looking at me, there's a large part of me who thinks that's not possible.

I sure hope that part of me is correct. After tonight, it's safe to say I'm falling for Cope much harder and much faster than I could have ever expected.

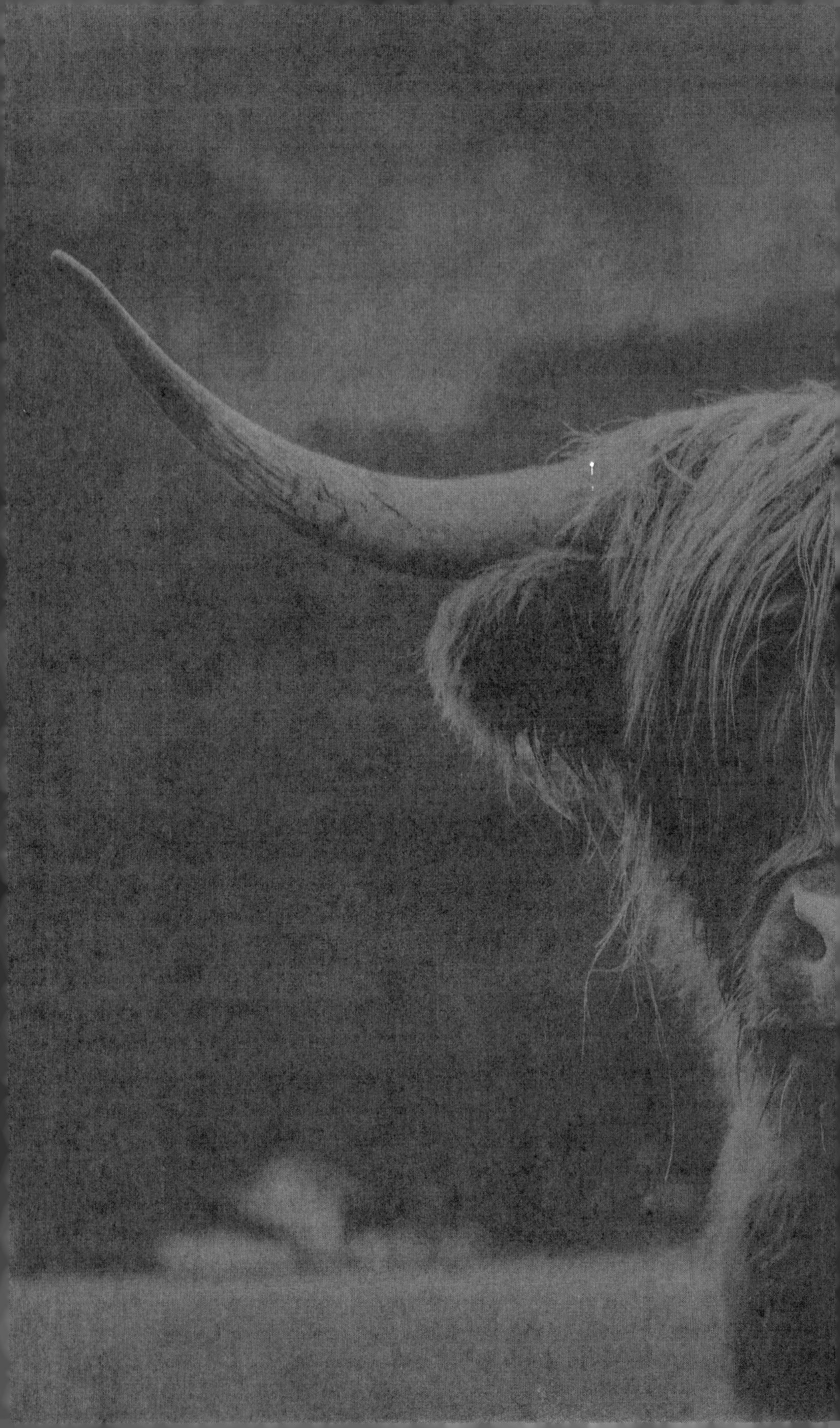

Chapter 27

Xander Dawson

"Hi, welcome to Tiffany's Table. For one?"

Smiling at the woman who looks entirely too chipper to be standing outside behind a hostess stand in the near-freezing temperatures, I reply, "No, I'm meeting two people who're already here. Can I go in and find them?"

"Of course. Enjoy!"

A rush of warmth hits me as soon as I pull open the door, a shiver wracking through my body at the harsh contrast. I don't know how it's possible, but I swear, it's colder here than it was when I left Copper Lake. For technically being a desert, the eastern part of Washington state is bitter, chilly, and dry in the winter. An obnoxious combination of chattering teeth and chapped cheeks. I landed in Washington the night before last, but it was so late, I spent the entirety of yesterday being lazy as fuck in bed or on the couch, watching re-runs on Netflix, except for the brief couple of hours Bastian stopped by.

My to-do list is a mile long while I'm here, but the one thing

I'm doing before getting started on that is meeting my friends for yummy food and mimosas. Sunday Brunch is something me, Travis, and Charlotte, Travis's sister, used to do on a regular basis. It's one thing I miss about being back here—probably one of the only things, if I'm being honest with myself.

Travis and Charlotte are easy to find once inside the dining room area. They're in our favorite spot in the far-left corner, right beside the window that has a gorgeous view of the Columbia River. Travis and Charlotte are carbon copies of one another on the outside. The same blonde hair. The same deep blue eyes. The same little button nose. But personality wise, they couldn't be more different. While Travis isn't necessarily what I'd call docile, he is a lot more laid-back and go with the flow than Charlotte is. I love my best friend, but he's been known to be quite the doormat in the past, and his sister would never allow that type of behavior.

Charlotte spots me first, a warm smile tipping her lips upon my approach. "There you are. Started to think you were standing us up," she teases.

"Ha ha," I deadpan as I slide into the open seat. "I needed to take a shower, and it wasn't until I was fully undressed and had the water running that I realized I didn't have any shampoo. So, I had to get dressed, run and grab some, and then head home to get clean."

"Mmhmm. Probably too busy talking to your *boyyyyfriend*," Travis interjects with a snigger.

"What are we, in elementary school?" I laugh, instantly feeling lighter being around these two. "And he isn't my boyfriend."

"But you were talking to him this morning?" Travis presses with a knowing grin.

"Well, yes, but it was on my way to the store. He's not why

I'm late."

It's the truth. Cope was getting up and ready for the gym when I called him during my walk to the store down the block. I've been gone a couple of days, and I already miss him. Which is wild to me, seeing as how I was away from Henry for weeks, having barely talked to him, and I didn't miss him, even if I tried like hell to make myself believe I did. I guess it goes to show how different relationships can be. Not that Cope and I are in a relationship…although, I don't know what else to call us. We're not just friends. That ship sailed. And both of us *did* say we wanted to see where this goes, so maybe *relationship* is the right word.

Our server comes up and drops off a glass of water and a mimosa to me before she takes our order. As soon as she grabs our menus and walks away, Travis pins me with a look. "Okay, spill. What's been going on with you and Mr. Rodeo?"

"Yeah, do tell," Charlotte chimes in. "Because Travis has been skimpy as hell with the juicy details."

"I told you everything I knew!" he exclaims, to which Charlotte rolls her eyes, clearly not believing him. I'm sure he's telling the truth, because I haven't told him much lately.

Giving the Cliffs Notes version, I dive in, filling them in on everything that's happened with Cope and me. By the time I finish, our food's arrived, and we all dig in. After laying everything out, I'm suddenly nervous about what they're both going to say. Their approval is important to me, and I want them to like Cope and this thing we have going on, especially since neither of them cared for Henry at all. Anybody who's ever dated somebody their friends hate can understand how straining and stressful it can be.

Travis washes down his bite of French toast with a swig of

mimosa that is far more champagne than orange juice at this point. "Sounds like you got it kinda bad for this guy, Xan."

I shrug, feeling about two feet tall and frayed wide open. "I mean, yeah, I guess. It just has felt like things with him and I have been magnetic since the very first meet, and that's hard to ignore."

"But realistically, how much longer are you staying in Copper Lake?" Charlotte asks. "If you start something with him, are you prepared to do the long-distance thing? That's not exactly ideal, nor is it as easy as some people think."

"Yeah, I know," I reply as I push my eggs around my plate, avoiding eye contact.

But Travis is smarter than that.

"Holy shit," he mutters, breathing out a laugh.

My head snaps up, gaze darting to meet his.

Charlotte looks between the both of us. "What?"

A grin splits his face. "You want to move there, don't you?"

My stomach lurches clear into my throat at the question, unsure about how they're going to take it. I've never been much of a liar, though, so with a deep breath, I nod. "Yes, but not because of him."

"Bullshit." Travis chuckles.

"I'm serious," I huff out. "I mean, sure, he's a big plus, but I started considering a change before I even realized I had feelings for him."

"How big of a plus?" Travis asks teasingly, waggling his brows at me.

Laughter bubbles out of me as I dramatically make a show of holding my hands a wide distance away from each other, waggling my brows right back at him.

"You're full of shit," is all he says as Charlotte giggles in her seat.

"Full of something," I quip back.

"Alright, alright," Charlotte cuts in, trying her best to appear serious. "We're in public. Let's not traumatize the poor patrons of this restaurant."

"Buzzkill," Travis and I both grumble at the same time before erupting in a fit of laughter.

"Okay, but on a serious note," Charlotte says. "You're really thinking of leaving Washington?"

"Maybe." I shrug.

"If not because of the cowboy, then why?" There's zero judgement in her tone, or in the way either of them is looking at me.

"I don't know… I've been here my entire life, and I guess I just don't feel like it's meant to be my home. I know that probably doesn't make sense, but I want more. Like, I could live in Desert Creek for the rest of my life and probably be happy. Be fine. But I don't want to be just happy or just fine. I want to be fulfilled."

"And you've felt like this for a while?" she asks.

"Maybe? I don't know." I blow out a breath, running my fingers over the beanie covering my head. "Not consciously, no. But I think deep down, I've felt like something was missing for a while, and I assumed it was what was lacking in my relationship with Henry, but I don't think it's that. I think it's more." A self-deprecating laugh creeps out at how ridiculous I sound. "I'm not making sense, but it's not one thing I can put a finger on. It's a *feeling*. A feeling I've felt since the moment I drove into Copper Lake." My face screws up. "Okay, maybe not since the moment I drove into Copper Lake, since my car broke down and that was embarrassing as fuck, but definitely since at least the morning after when I sat on my aunt's back porch and watched the sun rise above the picturesque view of the mountains in the distance and the miles and miles of open field, and Aggie came and stood beside me, looking adorable and imploring and welcoming all at once."

They're both quiet for a moment before Travis blurts out, "Who the fuck is Aggie?"

I snort at the confusion written all over his face. "She's a highland cow my aunt owns. Her name is Agatha, but I call her Aggie."

"A what?"

Rolling my eyes, I pull out my phone and find a picture of her. "A cow, you dumbass."

"*Wow.*" Travis whistles, handing me the phone back. "You're already channeling your inner cowboy, aren't you?"

"I am not." I laugh. "She's so cute, though." Flipping through some more pictures, I show them about a dozen different shots of her doing random cute shit. "She sits beside me—well, stands—every morning when I drink my coffee, and she follows me around while I do the morning chores. Oh! And she chases the chickens around the yard, pissing them off. She's quite the character."

Charlotte has a soft smile on her lips as Travis huffs out a laugh through his nose. "Okay, Farmer John," he mutters.

"Quit picking on him," Charlotte says. "I think it's cute. And things don't always have to make sense. Sometimes following your heart is the best you can do. It'll all piece together, eventually."

"What about the dispensary?" Travis asks.

"Bastian came over yesterday afternoon and we talked about it all. We're wanting to expand anyway, and I would become more of the background man, handling all the numbers and ordering and stuff, so it would still work out."

"Expand, as in open another store?"

"Yeah, it's something we've wanted to do from the beginning, but we had to find our footing first. Bas found a location up in Seattle that'll be available in about a month that we think would be the perfect spot to open a second store."

"That soon?"

I nod. "If everything goes according to plan, yeah." Bringing my water glass to my lips, I let the ice-cold liquid fill my mouth before I swallow and continue. "We want to buy out our investors before we open the second location, but it's been something we've been saving for, for a while now."

Travis arches a knowing brow at me. "You mean Henry?"

"And the other investors, yes."

"How's that going to go over with him?"

"Fine, I'd imagine." I shrug. "We're meeting after this so I can tell him."

Travis eyes me warily. Probably thinking that meeting with Henry can only lead to drama, but I'd like to believe that Henry and I are both capable of being mature adults about this. We've always managed to keep our personal lives outside of business, and there's no reason that should change now.

When I texted him asking to meet to discuss the investment, he agreed quickly and without a fight. That has to be a good sign.

"Please, just be careful," Travis finally says to me.

"It's going to be fine," I assure him.

"You say that, but I know how he can be."

"He's not Nathaniel." I hate bringing up Travis's narcissistic, cheating ex, but I know that's where his concern comes from. When they broke up, Nathaniel went through annoying efforts to try to lure Travis back under his spell, and while Henry is no saint, our split was also pretty amicable. "I think some time apart has shown him how the breakup was for the best."

We finish up our meal, and when our server comes and drops the bill off, Charlotte hurries and pays. Travis and I both give her shit, but she grins like the cat that got the canary. "You got big investors to pay off and another store to open," is all she says.

"Yeah, but I can pay for my food, Char."

"I know you can, but I wanted to." Her blue eyes soften around the corners. "I'm proud of you, Xander. You seem genuinely happy, and you've come so far from the broke college kid I once met. If this move is something that you truly want, I think you should do it. We'll miss you, but you shouldn't ignore your intuition."

"She's right," Travis chimes in. "I'm proud of you too, man."

Clearing my throat in an attempt to stave away the lump threatening to choke me, I smile. "Thank you, guys. That means a lot to me."

Travis arches a brow before adding, "But you better fucking come back and visit."

We all laugh together at that. "Obviously," I mutter, rolling my eyes dramatically.

My palms are slick with nerves and sweat as I walk through the lobby of a mid-rise building that's owned by the company Henry works for. After checking in at the front desk, and subsequently sending a text letting him know I'm here, I sit in one of the navy-blue cushy chairs, a plastic cup filled with water in hand as I suck down the liquid, trying to bring moisture back into my mouth.

Up until five minutes ago, when I was parking out front, I was cool as a cucumber. Wasn't nervous about seeing him or about this meeting, but now it's like everything's hitting me in full force. Glancing around, I take in the bleak, minimalist surroundings. This isn't the first time I've been in this building, but it is the first time I'm taking the time to really look. If I'm being honest, it's kind of boring and almost…clinical. Whoever designed this place should be fired.

A subtle vibration goes off in my pocket where my phone's at. Reaching in, I pull it out, the screen lighting up with a new text. A smile tugs on my lips as I read it.

Cope: Good luck with your meeting. Call me when you're finished if you want, I'll be home the rest of the evening.

After brunch with Travis and Charlotte, I went home and FaceTimed Cope. He walked over to my aunt's place and let me say hi to Aggie, and he didn't even look at me like I was crazy for asking him to do it. I've only been gone a few days, but I already miss everything. Him, Aggie, all the other animals. Hell, I even miss my stubborn old aunt. It's crazy to me how somewhere can feel like home after such a short amount of time, when somewhere I've lived my entire life doesn't feel like that.

Charlotte's words come back to me… *"trust your intuition."*

"Sir." I glance up, my gaze connecting with the receptionist. "Mr. Darby will see you now."

I nod, raising from the chair and heading back toward where I know Henry's office is. My heart pounds painfully, pulse deafening in my ears the closer I get. A very large part of me truly believes this conversation will go fine, but now that I'm here, about to face the music, a small little voice in the back of my mind can't help but worry something will go wrong. Not with the business, because Henry is smarter than that, but with us, personally. The last thing I want to do is end up in some screaming match with him, here, of all places.

My hand reaches for the cool brass knob on the door, and with a slight twist, it clicks open. Henry's office is bright and airy, the wall behind him all window. It overlooks the view of the river, and with the sun out today, his office is bathed in warmth. He's typing on his keyboard when I walk in, but his eyes lift to meet mine once I close the door.

"Hey, Xander," he offers, a forced smile tugging at his lips.

"Hey, hope I'm not pulling you from anything pressing." I take a seat in front of his desk, my hands fumbling with each other in my lap.

"No, you're fine. I'm finishing sending this email and then I'm all yours."

Sitting in front of Henry now, I can't help but notice—not for the first time—how different in every single way he is from Cope. Henry is all clean, tailored suits and soft hands, whereas Cope is dirt-covered Wranglers and rough, weathered skin. Henry is dark hair, bright green eyes, whereas Cope is blonde hair and eyes so dark, they almost seem bottomless. They're both hardworking, but in two very different ways—both admirable in their own ways. But where Cope can put his work away and be silly, embrace his inner child, Henry is married to his job and rarely allows himself to let loose.

Until I met Cope, I never realized just how much I needed that carefree silliness in my life. How much I craved it in a partner. In the intimacy. As I sit here now, I realize that while I was happy enough with Henry, while he made me smile, I now know with full certainty that we never could've been end game. I never would've felt fulfilled with him for the rest of my life. I think maybe Henry needed me in his life because he needed something carefree too, since he lives such a buttoned-up, stuffy day-to-day, but over time, he started to disregard me, just like he did with his own playful side. Maybe even resented me for it. What I have with Cope is still new, and we may not even end up together, but in the brief time we have known each other, he's shown me what I want and what I need. And somehow, despite how new it is, Cope feels like a much more significant part of my life than Henry ever did.

I need someone I can be fully myself with. Someone I can go on a drive with in the middle of the night when we can't sleep, talk about any and everything under the moon. Someone who isn't afraid to show me off, or who isn't afraid to admit to how they feel. And that someone never would've been Henry… and I'm okay with that now.

Henry finishes up his email, and we dive into the reason I'm here. He listens intently when I tell him how we're going to be paying him, and the other investors, off, and our plans to open the second store. He seems genuinely happy for me, and it's a thousand-pound weight off my shoulders.

"Are you back from your aunt's place for good?" he asks when we finish up the conversation.

I shake my head. "No, I'll be heading back once Bastian and I get everything settled. Even if she won't admit it, my aunt's in over her head and still needs help."

"For good, or are you coming back here?"

"Maybe for good. Maybe not. I'm not sure," I reply honestly.

Henry nods, his lips pressed into a thin line as he observes me. When he opens his mouth and speaks again, it's not at all what I expected him to say.

"For what it's worth, I'm sorry for how things turned out

with us," he admits. "I care about you and could've done more to ensure you knew that."

"Henry, don't." My voice comes out surprisingly steady. "You weren't the only one to blame in our relationship and, to be honest, it probably never would've worked. We're too different."

His green eyes watch me as he rubs a hand over his full, dark, cropped beard. "Yeah, well, that may be so, but I'm still sorry."

"I appreciate that."

We both push to a stand, and Henry extends his hand for me to shake. The finality of this moment is stifling but freeing at the same time. "I wish you the best of luck, Xander. I'm proud of you for all that you've accomplished and all that's to come."

Coming from anybody else, it would probably feel fake, too professional to be genuine, but from Henry, I know he means it, and something like pride swells in my chest. Not because of who he is to me, but because he's one of the smartest, most savvy businessmen I've ever met.

"Thanks, Henry." I shake his hand back. "Wish you all the best in life too."

I leave his office with my shoulders held high. That meeting was closure that I didn't even realize I needed. It was a door closing to a part of my life that meant a lot to me but no longer serves me. It was the start of a new beginning. A new outlook.

Chapter 28

Six Weeks Later

Cope Murphy

The SeaTac airport is a chaotic shitshow if I've ever seen one. It's huge and busy and loud, and I have to wait entirely too long at baggage claim, and then even longer at the checkout counter for my rental car. Once I finally have the keys and climb into the too-small vehicle, I then have to spend an embarrassing amount of time trying to find my way *out* of the airport parking lot.

I've been in Washington for all of an hour, and I already miss home. But even the chaos and stress couldn't dim the excitement I feel at knowing that, in three hours or less, I'm going to see Xander again for the first time in a month and a half. The grand opening for his new store is this afternoon, and I couldn't be prouder. When he asked me if I'd want to fly out and come to the opening a few weeks ago on FaceTime, there was an obvious note of apprehension in his voice, like he thought I might decline. I've never booked a flight so fast in my damn life.

It's coming at a perfect time too. Training and practice

have amped up since we're getting closer to rodeo season, but it was easy to take a few days off to come here. I'm hoping he'll get to fly back to Copper Lake soon—before I leave for the circuit—but I don't know for sure, so this was a great way to ensure I get to see him in the flesh before I leave.

My flight was delayed due to a huge snowstorm we had back home. They had to de-ice the plane and the runway, I guess. Wyoming isn't a stranger to cold, snowy weather, though, so I'm not sure why something like that would cause a flight delay, but whatever. I'm here now. Had I arrived on time, I would've had time to see Xander *before* his grand opening, but that's okay. I'm excited to see him in his element.

Despite both of us being pretty busy—him with the store opening and all that goes into that, and me with training and rodeo prep—we've managed to keep in touch the entire time he's been gone. Part of me wondered if our connection would wither with him so far away, if maybe his attraction to me would dim with him not being next door, but that didn't happen. We've texted every single day since he left Copper Lake, and we've even managed to talk on the phone or FaceTime at least a few times a week. Honestly, his need to see me or talk to me so frequently gives me that warm, fuzzy feeling in my stomach that, prior to meeting Xander, made no sense to me, because his need matches my own.

I've still been going over his aunt's house at least once a day, to check on her and make sure everything is getting done with the help they hired. Not only do I know it helps put Xander at ease—he's been nervous about how she's doing because he knows she wouldn't tell him if anything was wrong—but I also have become really fond of Colette and her farm full of animals. She can be a stubborn woman who has a hard time accepting help, but her face always lights up when I come over with goodies I've baked. Me and Larry have been bonding as well. He's always sitting in the window when I walk up the steps, and he stretches and meows when he spots me. When Colette opens the door, he brushes up against my legs until I pet him. But Xander was on the nose... Colette and Larry *do not* get along. He wants nothing to do with her, and it's pretty funny. She tried to get him back from the door the first morning I went over there, and he hissed at her and slapped her leg before scurrying off.

The drive from the airport to his new location in Seattle, with traffic, takes me about an hour, and the grand opening is already in full swing by the time I park the rental car. The parking lot is full, and I had to park on the street about a block up from the store. My heart is pounding, palms shaky and slick, and what can only be described as butterflies take over my gut as I approach the shop. The neighborhood is nice, and has a cute small-town feel to it. Rows of businesses go on for blocks. Xander's is sandwiched between two. From the outside looking in, I can't tell exactly what they are. They aren't open yet, whatever they are.

Standing outside are two tall, large men. They're checking IDs of everyone coming in. Reaching into my pocket, I pull out my wallet, and have my license ready to give them when it's my turn. The line moves swiftly, and a few minutes later, I'm stepping inside.

The scent of marijuana hangs in the air—not overwhelming, just present. There're a couple of different rows of glass countertops; the type you'd see in a comic book shop or a bakery. The space in here is larger than you'd think looking in from the outside, and it's packed with people. Chatter fills the air, and looking to my left, down toward the other side of the building, I spot Xander.

A smile tugs on my lips as I watch him. He's talking to a few guys, animatedly using his hands. His black hair is styled and out of his face, and he's got a wide grin that feels like a physical force wrapping around the organ in my chest. He's too far away for me to hear what he's saying, but whatever it is, he's passionate about it. Xander's dressed in a long-sleeve black shirt, tight jeans, and a clunky pair of Doc Martins. It's a simple outfit, a plain one, that on anybody else, I probably wouldn't even look twice at. But on him? Oh yeah, it fucking works for me.

I don't even know how long I sit there watching him, but he eventually notices me. Bright blue eyes drag from the people in front of him, to meet my gaze, and when he does, the grin on his face intensifies. Excusing himself, he crosses the room, over to where I'm standing like a love-sick puppy, and I swear my heart tries to jump out of my chest and cling to him as he approaches.

"You made it!"

His clean, fresh scent envelops me as he comes to a stop a few inches in front of me. My fingers itch to reach out and touch him. It's been too fucking long.

"Sorry, I'm late," I tell him. "My flight was delayed, and then there was traffic getting here."

"It's all good." He waves me off. "Wanna go out back with me?"

I nod, a smile splitting my face. The dopamine hit I feel coursing through my blood at the thought of being alone with him is similar to the feeling of being a kid on Christmas morning. It's wild. *Does he feel that way too, seeing me?*

Xander leads the way, and I follow him behind the counter

and into a back storage area. Back there, there's a door that leads to an alleyway. Nobody else is out here. Once we're outside, Xander puts a stopper in the doorjamb so we aren't locked out, and when he turns to face me, what can only be described as nervousness flashes through his eyes. As it always is when we're around each other, the air thickens. It intensifies. The sparks, the chemistry, that's ever-present with him makes itself known, and I suddenly wish we were truly alone.

"How was your flight?" he asks, pulling out a joint, placing it between his lips, and lighting it. I do the same, only with a cigarette.

"Wasn't bad," I reply honestly. "How're you feeling about all of this?"

"It's awesome." Xander's excitement is contagious. "Way more people showed up than Bastian and I thought. I even think a couple of my college friends might come too."

Unable to keep my hands to myself anymore, I step up to Xander, my hand going around the back of his neck. "Okay, I can't be near you any longer without kissing you first."

He huffs out a small laugh, a hot puff of air brushing my lips. "Then kiss me, cowboy," he murmurs, before I do just that.

Xander's lips part on a groan, and I take the opportunity to slip my tongue inside, rolling against his. He tastes so damn good, and when his hand comes up, slipping underneath the hem of my shirt, fingers brushing against my bare skin, I can't help the shiver that rolls through me. Xander walks us backward until my back hits the brick wall. He presses his body flush with mine, and the kiss grows hungrier from there. Six weeks is too long to go without this, that thought blowing my mind almost as much as his touch is.

I've gone most of my life without a connection like this,

and I was surviving just fine, and now, not even two whole months without him has me crawling out of my skin with need. The distance has only intensified things between us. All the text messages sent, the hours spent on the phone together, or on FaceTime where we got to see each other but couldn't touch. Talk about fucking torture. But it gave us the chance to truly learn about each other. Things we never would've thought to talk about had we been in the flesh. The random likes and dislikes we have, various childhood and adolescent stories shared, hopes for the future for ourselves. So, while the distance sucked, it also gave us the opportunity to learn about each other on a deeper level. On a less physical level.

If possible, I feel closer to him now than I did when he left for Washington. I can say with one hundred percent certainty that what I feel for Xander goes so far past a crush. I care for him in a visceral, intimately deep way. And I'm almost positive he feels the same.

I hope so.

After a few minutes, we manage to pull ourselves apart before it becomes way too inappropriate for a public place. We finish smoking and head back inside. Xander grabs my hand as he leads me back through the building, throwing me a glance over his shoulder. "There're some people I want you to meet," he says with glee.

We walk up to a group of three people: two guys and a girl. The same group he was talking to when I got here. All three sets of eyes turn to us as we approach, and it's quite clear that one of the guys and the girl are related. Suddenly, nerves rush through my veins, tickling my gut. These people are obviously important enough to Xander that he wants us to meet, and I want to make a good impression. My friends love him. I want his to love—or at the very least, like—me.

"Guys, this is Cope." I don't have to look at Xander to know there's a grin on his face. It's heard loud and clear when he speaks. Warmth spreads through my chest. "Cope, this is Charlotte, Travis, and Travis's fiancé, Mateo."

They all take me in, grins on their faces. I extend my hand, shaking all three of theirs. "Hey. It's nice to meet you guys. Xander's told me so much about you."

"Yeah, it's great to meet you, too, man," one of the guys, Travis, replies. He's Xander's best friend. His Shooter. Probably the one I've heard about the most. "How long are you in Washington for?"

"Just until Sunday."

"If you guys don't have anything else planned, let's all grab dinner tomorrow night," Travis suggests, eyes sliding over to Xander.

Xander nods, looking at me. "I'm down, if you are?"

It's my turn to nod. "Let's do it."

"Cool. Well, we gotta get going, but it was great to meet you, Cope. And Xan, so fucking proud of you, dude."

As soon as they leave, Xander gets pulled away by a few customers who have questions. I busy myself, strolling around, looking at all the items inside the glass and on the walls. It's all foreign to me, and honestly, mind-blowing seeing in a store like this. Wyoming is still very much a weed illegal state, and while I've tried smoking a few times in high school, it was never something I got into. Despite not being around it much, I *do* believe it has some incredible medicinal qualities, and think it should be as legal everywhere as alcohol is.

I love that Xander found something he enjoys, something he's passionate about, and he was able to make a career out of it. While I don't necessarily believe in the statement 'if you find a career you love, you'll never work a day in your life'—because loving it or not, it's still hard work—I do think enjoying what you do goes a long way in making it not *feel* as daunting and mentally taxing.

"Have you tried any of those yet?" someone asks, pulling me out of my thoughts.

It's not until I turn my head and meet a forest green gaze looking back at me that I realize he's talking to me. A man about my height stands before me with buzzed, short blond hair and a warm smile on his face. His nose is pierced with a black hoop, and he's got tattoos scattered all over his arms.

"Oh, no. I haven't tried any of these." I huff out a laugh before adding, "I don't even smoke weed, actually. I can't, really, because of my job."

The guy's brow quirks, lip twitching like he's trying to fight a smile. "Well, you're standing in front of the edibles, so you wouldn't smoke those."

I glance down at the contents inside of the counter, nodding as my neck heats, the warmth spilling into my cheeks. "Ah, yeah. I knew that."

It's a lie. He knows it, I know it. "Right. So, what do you do for work then?"

"I'm a professional bronc rider."

Thick, dark brows shoot up on his forehead. "No shit? That's fucking cool, man. You know, I run an art studio, and I've been wanting to—"

Whatever he was about to say is cut off when Xander walks over, slapping him on the back, a huge grin splitting his face.

"Aston, you came!"

Shifting to fully face Xander, the guy gives him a bro hug.

"You're in my neck of the woods. How could I not?"

Just then, another guy who's a smidge taller than Aston, with brown, slightly curly hair, significantly more tattoos, and the worst case of resting bitch face I've ever seen, steps up beside him, his eyes trailing from me to Xander.

"What's up, Xan," he rasps, his voice deeper than I thought it would be. "Nice place you got here. Thanks for the invite."

Xander practically preens under the compliment. All smiles. "Thanks. And thanks for coming." His hand lands on the small of my back as he looks between me and the two men. "Cope, these are friends from back in college. Aston"—he gestures toward the blond one—"and his husband, Knox," he mutters, regarding the unfriendly looking one. "Guys, this is Cope. He's my…"

Voice trailing off, he glances over at me, seemingly coming up short on how he should introduce me. It's not something we've talked about, but I save him the trouble as I extend my hand to the blond guy first and say, "Boyfriend. It's nice to meet you two."

The three of us shake hands, and beside me, I can see in my periphery that Xander is grinning, but I don't look at him. I don't know where that came from, but I'm not taking it back. I love the way it sounded rolling off my tongue.

"How'd you two meet?" Aston asks. "Do you live around here, Cope?"

"Nah, I actually live in a small town in Wyoming," I reply. "We met there when Xander's car broke down on the side of the road."

"I drove down there to help my aunt with her farm when she had surgery," Xander offers. "He stopped to help me when he saw my car on the side of the dirt road."

"What a gentleman," Aston says with a grin as he gives me a once-over. Glancing over at his husband, he says, "Cope was telling me that he's a professional bronc rider."

Knox's eyes widen, a devilish grin tugging on his lips. "Really? A rodeo cowboy, huh?"

I chuckle. "Yup, that's me."

"How'd you get into something like that?"

One of my favorite things when meeting new people is getting to talk about the rodeo. A smile splits my face. "Oh, man, the rodeo's been in my blood since I was little. It's something I always wanted to do as a kid, and couldn't picture myself doing anything else. My dad was part of the rodeo, and it's a big deal in my hometown, so I was exposed to it a lot."

Knox whistles. "Damn. I've never been to a rodeo, but it sounds badass."

I nod. "Thoroughly recommend checking one out, at least once. There're some that pass through Washington, or, I know it's kind of far and probably unrealistic, but if you guys ever find yourself in Wyoming, let me know, and I'd be happy to bring you to one."

"Hell yeah," Aston replies. "That'd be cool."

The four of us stand around, making some more small talk for a while before Knox and Aston excuse themselves. Xander eventually has to go mingle with the other guests while I happily sit and watch him from the outer corners of the room, thoroughly enjoying getting to see him in his element.

I'm dying to get him alone and get my hands on him, but in the meantime, watching him like this isn't a bad way to pass the time.

Chapter 29

Xander Dawson

By the time we're stumbling into the hotel room, we're all grabby hands and hungry lips. I'm honestly surprised I was able to keep my hands—mostly—to myself on the drive here from the dispensary. It wasn't an easy feat, though. It's been a *loooong* six weeks since Cope and I have seen each other, and I feel like I'm going out of my skin with this raw, carnal need for him.

Fingers grapple with our shirts as we yank them over our heads, pulling away only long enough to toe off our shoes before we're fumbling with the buttons on our pants, shoving them and our boxers down. There's no finesse to our movements, no grace period where we work our way into this moment. It seems we're both on the same page, needing to be skin to skin as quickly as possible.

My hands fly to the back of Cope's head, his to my hips, as our lips crash together in a fury of lust. We walk backward, his legs meeting the edge of the bed as we topple on top of it. Shimmying his way up toward the head of the bed, I follow, loving the feel of his thick, powerful thighs wrapping around my waist, pulling me in.

"Fuck, I've missed you," he admits, hot breath fanning my lips a moment before they're fused together again.

One thing I can't get enough of with Cope is how open he is with his feelings. He doesn't shy away from them. Doesn't play hard to get. He's not afraid to say exactly how he feels, even though I know this situation with us is new for him. Cope wears his heart on his sleeve, and I admire that. And from my corner of things, it seems like he's accepted this so gracefully. I may be the first man he's ever been with, but I haven't seen a freakout in sight. It's like he met me, realized he may have feelings for me, and said, *"fuck what society thinks, I feel how I feel."*

My sexuality has never been an insecurity of mine, but I also knew what I preferred from a very young age. I can imagine it can be quite jarring going your entire life, thinking you liked things one way, only to find out that may not be the whole truth.

I've never felt like a dirty little secret to Cope. Never felt like he was trying to hide me—or worse, hide his feelings for me. I mean, shit, earlier, when he met Aston and Knox, he introduced himself to them as my *boyfriend*. When that word spilled out of his mouth, I nearly choked on my own tongue. I'm surprised I was able to behave like a functioning human being after that. It took me by surprise, but at the same time… also, kind of not. It's on par for Cope. On par for everything I've seen of him thus far.

And the way that word—that title—sounded… Yeah, I could get used to that.

"I missed you too," I admit, my voice coming out breathy, revealing just how gone I am for Cope already, and we've barely gotten started.

Hot, slick lips leave mine, and trail along my jaw, his scruff scratching at my freshly shaved skin, causing a shiver to rack through my body in the very best way. I want to wake up tomorrow covered in beard burn because then I will get to replay this moment and what's to come for days after he goes back to Copper Lake. As much as I would love to follow him back there when he leaves Sunday, it's just not feasible with everything I still need to get settled here.

I've made up my mind—Washington isn't for me anymore. It's not home. It's not where I want to lay down roots. I plan to tell Cope tomorrow morning over breakfast, and I'm hoping I'll only have to be here a couple more weeks before I can make the move official. I'm thankful I can continue with my two businesses remotely. In this instance, it pays off to be the brains behind the operation. Not that Bastian is dumb or anything, but we both know I've always handled the numbers, while his strength has always been in the store and around our staff.

Sharp teeth nip at my clavicle, goosebumps blooming all over my flesh as I inhale a sharp breath that quickly melts into a groan when he runs the flat of his tongue over the area. My hips roll into his all on their own. We're both already hard, but I can tell, like me, he wants to take his time. We have all night… and then all day tomorrow too. I plan to become intimately familiar with every inch of Cope's body—every freckle, every line and dip of muscle, every last erogenous zone—by the time he has to jump on that plane and leave all over again.

Glancing over to the bedside table, I spot the bottle of champagne on ice I requested earlier, a grin tugging on my lips as I sit back on my haunches and grab it. Water droplets fall from the bottle onto Cope's exposed chest as I work the cork out. He hisses as the cool liquid lands on his skin. Once the bottle's open, I bring it up to my lips, tilt my head back, and down a few swallows.

Cope lifts his head slightly, allowing me to pour some into his mouth too. His dark, heated eyes stay firmly on me as he swallows, his throat rolling as he does. With the angle he's in, a few dribbles spill out of his mouth, and with a smirk I know he catches, I lean down, swiping my tongue along the side of his chin that's wet with champagne, gathering it up. An idea pops into my head, my cock twitching at the thought as I reposition myself between his spread thighs.

The sight before me is enough to make my mouth water. It's one I want to seal to memory and never forget. Cope is laid out in front of me, miles and miles of golden tan skin on display, not an inch of clothing covering his beautiful, hard body, and he's wearing the sexiest smirk that makes my heart pound harder. He is gorgeous. All man, and according to him, all mine.

The thought tips my lips up into a grin. "So, boyfriend, huh?"

Cope breathes out a laugh, his cheeks heating to a brilliant shade of pink. Bashful looks good on him. "Yeah. That okay?"

"Oh, cowboy…" I drag my finger from the base of his throat, all the way down his torso. "It's more than okay. In fact…" I tip the champagne bottle until a steady stream pours out of the lip, onto Cope's bare chest. It funnels downward until it pools in his navel. Leaning down, I peer up at him from beneath my lashes before I continue. "I kind of love the sound of it…don't you?"

Before he can answer, I flick my tongue over the dip, slurping the champagne out before dragging it up, making sure to clean up every ounce of spilled liquid across his chest. He groans, the sound vibrating against my mouth.

"Me too," he gasps. "I love the sound of it too."

I kiss and suck my way across his neck, trailing along his jaw, before brushing my lips with his. It's not a kiss. Not yet, at least. It's me, breathing him in. Letting my senses fill up with him until I'm drowning in Cope. His tongue flits out, gliding along my barely parted lips, grazing my bottom teeth. Pulling back teasingly, I watch a pout protrude from his mouth, his brows pinching together in a lusty frustration.

"I need you," he breathes.

"You have me."

A noise that can only be described as a growl rumbles up his throat.

"Know what I want?" I ask, the words coming out raspy and hoarse, my arousal evident in my tone.

"What's that?"

"I want *you* inside *me* tonight," I reply, climbing into his lap. His hands easily find my hips, his erection brushing along the crack of my ass. "Want to ride you, and feel you until I can't think around how full I am."

Cope whimpers, fingers digging into my flesh, no doubt leaving a mark. "Yes," he moans. "I want that too."

Our lips collide brutally. There's nothing gentle about this kiss. We're both so turned on, both aching for the pleasure we can give each other, and it's clear we're both done waiting. The slow, the teasing, it's over. Cope's tongue thrusts into my mouth, licking around, telling me without words just how desperate he is for me.

And I feel the same.

My arms snake around his neck, his around my middle, until our chests are flush. My nipples harden as they brush along his body, and my hips roll, loving the feel of his length caressing my ass. I'm so horny for him, I wish I could put his dick in me now, but I know I need to get myself ready. Not only has it been a while since I've been fucked, but he's also *huge*, and I know he could seriously hurt me if we aren't careful. But I'm not ready to end this yet.

I don't know how long we sit here, making out like we can't get enough of each other, but by the time we break apart, we're both breathless, and my head feels light. Cope's lips are red and swollen, slick with our shared spit, and his eyes are glazed over, pupils blown.

My chest warms as we watch each other, his attraction and the severity of his feelings for me evident in the way he looks at me. The way he doesn't falter. He says it all with his eyes. It's heady.

Leaning over, I reach into the drawer, pulling out the contents I stored in there, tossing the box onto the bed beside him as I keep the bottle in my grip. I climb off his lap, sitting in front of him as he watches me with part confusion, part intrigue.

"Give me your hand," I instruct Cope, to which he does. I flick open the cap on the bottle of lube, pouring a dime-size amount into his palm. "Play with yourself while you watch me work myself open for you."

If possible, his eyes darken even more, an obsidian sea of his desire all for me. His full lips part as he brings his hand to his stiff length. Letting the cool liquid drip from his palm onto his shaft, he spreads it around with his fingers before wrapping a firm grip around himself. The sight of Cope, this big, strong cowboy, pumping his cock in his fist is as sensual as it is filthy. And I can't tear my eyes away. I allow myself a few moments, simply watching and enjoying the view before I slick up my own fingers, spread my legs wide open, getting to work.

Cope's gaze very quickly leaves my face, raking shamelessly

down my body, until it locks on the spot between my thighs where my one finger turns into two, fucking in and out of my entrance. The heat of his stare ignites my blood, setting off a wildfire through my veins. His gaze is a physical entity, something that can be felt on every inch of my skin. I'm high on his attention, and I never want to be without it. The hunger written clear as day on his face fuels the flames.

Curling my fingers, I graze the sweet spot inside of me that makes my cock leak. I imagine his dick hitting that spot instead. How good that'll feel.

I need it.

I need him.

I need our bodies to be connected in a way that makes it impossible to tell where Cope ends and I begin.

Once I'm sure I've worked myself open enough, I reach for the box of condoms beside his hip, ripping it open, and grab one out. Tearing the foil with my teeth, I roll the rubber onto his hard, veiny length, desperately wanting to feel him bare inside of me one day. I slather his condom-clad cock up with a generous amount of lube before climbing over top of him. His hands, once again, easily find their home on my hips as mine rest beside his head on the pillow.

A rush of anticipation and nerves swim through me as I line his tip up with my hole. As soon as the flared head brushes along my tight pucker, a shiver rolls down my spine, goosebumps erecting all over. My skin feels alive, as if my body is one long strip of live wire, set off by his touch alone. Our gazes are locked, the entire world melting away as I lower myself onto him, inch by inch. The stretch feels unbearable at first, tears springing to my eyes as I try to close them. Before I can, Cope grabs my chin, forcing me to look him in the eye.

My heart nearly leaps out of my chest when I see the intensity in his gaze. Eventually, the stretch gives way to something much more pleasurable, and by the time I'm fully seated, I know without a doubt, Cope has ruined me for anybody else. Not that I want anybody else.

His teeth are gritted and bared to me, brows knit tightly as his nostrils flare on a harsh exhale. "Fuck, Xan," he gasps. "You're so fucking tight, strangling my cock."

I lean down, pressing my lips to his, giving us both a minute to adjust. It feels like he's going to split me open, with how full I feel. It's both overwhelming and mind-blowing at the same time. When I do finally start to rock on his lap, it's slow, his hands guiding me, our faces mere inches apart. We're breathing each other in, fully submerged in this moment, neither of us wanting to miss a thing.

The air thickens and everything about this feels right. With how close our bodies are, the underside of my dick drags along his abdomen with every bounce on his cock. The double stimulation is incredible, and when he reaches up, taking my pierced nipple between his thumb and forefinger, rolling and pinching, I swear, I see stars. Cope keeps his free hand firmly planted on my hip, pushing me down as he fucks into me from the bottom. His jaw is slack, as is mine, and we're both panting heavily as our movements speed up. I'm stuck between never wanting this moment to end and needing to come more than I've ever needed anything in my life.

"I love the feel of you deep inside me," I moan, my eyelids fluttering closed at the pleasure. "So big…so *good*."

He growls, flipping us without ever pulling out, until he's towering over me, plundering into my body. My legs hike around his waist, eyes rolling back as the new position has his cock dragging across my prostate, lighting my entire body up like an explosion of fireworks. Time stands still as we ride out this wave of pleasure together, our bodies moving as if they're made for each other. Sweat drips down my nape, lining my brows, and I can see the perspiration glistening on Cope's chest too.

"Oh, my God, Cope," I moan, my head thrown back onto the pillow as he relentlessly drills into me. "Yes…fuck, *yes*! Don't stop!"

Cope reaches up, grabbing ahold of the headboard as he fucks into me harder, the cords in his forearm protruding under the strength he's using, and I could fucking die a happy man at the sight. He's powerful and sexy, and all of that is on display above me, and I can barely hold back. With his other hand, he wraps a tight fist around my throbbing, leaking cock, stroking me to the same rhythm he's using as he slams into me.

"Give me your cum, city boy," he grits out. The rasp to his voice and the way his muscles are tensed up, I know he's getting close too.

All of my senses are heightened in this moment, and before long, the start of my release creeps in, building from the base of my spine, and I know there's no holding back.

"I'm close!" I cry out. "I'm gonna come."

Cope growls, the sound downright animalistic as he maintains his speed but seeming to somehow get deeper, peg my prostate a little harder. It does the trick, and on a choked sob, my dick erupts. Thick, white ropes coat my hand and my chest. The sight must set him off because his movements get jerky, his breathing stuttered, as he stills, spilling his own release into the condom with a moan that makes my cock twitch.

We're both out of breath and drenched in sweat by the time

he finishes. Shoving his arms under my back, he collapses on top of me a moment before he shifts us until we're both lying on our sides, our limbs remaining connected. "I fucking missed you," he rasps, his face burrowed in the crook of my neck.

Breathing out a laugh, I press a kiss to his forehead. "Missed you too."

We stay like that for a while; long enough for the cum on my body to start to dry and get itchy. After we begrudgingly climb out of bed and take a quick shower, we order delivery, and spend the rest of the evening lying in bed, drinking champagne straight out of the bottle, and eating an array of food.

It's genuinely the best way to end the night.

Chapter 30

Three Weeks Later

Cope Murphy

"Cope, you really didn't need to pick me up," Xander grumbles from the passenger seat as we sit at a red light. "I could've taken an Uber."

I glance over at him incredulously. "Please, be for real right now, Xan. The drive from the airport to Copper Lake is too far for that to be feasible, and how often do you see Uber drivers around here?"

His brows furrow. It's adorable. "Well, then I could've asked my aunt."

"Now, why would you do that, when I'm here and perfectly capable?"

"Uh, maybe because you were in the middle of helping Conrad rebuild one of the horse stables."

It's a lie. One that I have to bite the inside of my cheek to keep a grin from slipping out about. Xander is so concerned about being a nuisance or interrupting our work, when he really has no idea what he's talking about.

"Yeah, but it's no big deal. I'll stop by there on our way back to your place. That's okay with you, right?"

He nods. "Of course, that's okay."

Pulling onto the highway, I take out my phone and unlock it.

Me: The eagle has landed. I repeat, the eagle has landed.

Smirking to myself, I set the phone in my lap, switching lanes. "How was your flight?" I ask, glancing over at Xander.

Turning his head, resting it against the back of the seat, his dark curly hair peeking out from underneath the baby pink beanie on his head, he shrugs. "Not bad. Happy to be back, though."

My face splits with a toothy grin. "Me too."

A text comes through, vibrating in my lap, and when I glance down at the screen, I have to fight against a chuckle.

Conrad: Just say you've picked Xander up.

Me: Where's the fun in that?

Conrad: Goodbye, Cope. Quit texting and driving.

Chuckling, I lock the phone, setting it in the cup holder, then I reach over, placing my hand on the top of Xander's thigh. He thinks we're going to Conrad's so I can help him finish the stables—which I *did* do…last week—but in reality, we're going there for his surprise *Welcome Home* party, because as of twenty minutes ago when he landed, he's an official resident of Copper Lake, Wyoming.

When I was visiting him in Seattle, the morning after I got there, he dropped the good news, telling me he already spoke to his aunt about it. He's moving in there to help her around the farm. I couldn't be happier—even if I'd rather he move in with me. But that's probably a little soon, so I'm burying that thought. Or trying to. Next door really isn't *that* bad, I guess.

Rodeo season starts in about a month. So, that kind of sucks. Not the rodeo itself, because I'm really looking forward to that, but us being apart again after I just got him back. I'm hoping I can talk him into coming with me, even if only for a little while.

When we get to Grazing Acres, there are a few cars scattered around, but it doesn't look like Xander suspects anything. A steady thrum of excitement builds in my gut as I park the truck and we get out.

I round the front of the truck, meeting him, and I extend my hand for him to take. As soon as his soft palm slides against mine, I feel like a middle schooler with my first crush at how warm and fuzzy this makes me. Clearing my throat, I smile and say, "This is our first time holding hands."

Xander gets a far-off look, like he's thinking back over the time we've spent together. "Yeah, you're right, it is."

"Kinda love it."

He chuckles. "Me too."

I tip my chin in front of us and say, "Come on. Think Conrad's in the barn already."

There's a low hum of chatter from inside the barn, and Xander glances at me with a confused look on his face moments before everyone collectively yells, *"Surprise!"* Shooter jumps out, two party horns in his mouth, simultaneously going off as he blows.

Xander's eyes widen, laughter bubbling out of him as he looks from everyone to me. "What's all this for?"

"It's a welcome home party," I reply. "You know, since you're a Copper Lake resident now."

Surprise and something like appreciation crosses over his features. "You guys didn't have to do all this."

"Sure, we did," Colt chimes in. "Cope would've kicked all of our asses if we didn't show up with literal party hats on." He points to the triangle hat on his head that I—nicely—insisted everybody wear.

Whit steps up to Xander, pulling him in for a hug. "Colt's being dramatic... Sort of. The truth is, we're all so happy you've decided to stay. A party was definitely in order."

It's then I notice Reggie behind Whit. Schooling my features, my eyes flit to Conrad, not in the least bit surprised to see his narrowed on Whit's boyfriend. When I invited Whit, I figured he'd come, but I really didn't think he'd bring his new man to his ex-husband's house. They've been dating for a while now, and any time there's a get-together here, either Whit comes alone, or he doesn't come at all.

Guess there's no time like the present to make the introduction. I make a mental note to check in with Conrad about it later—even if he shuts me down immediately.

After a round of celebratory tequila shots, Conrad fires up the grill, getting started on the burgers, while Sterling and I head inside to cut up the fruits and veggies and get the side dishes ready. When I started planning this party, I originally thought to have it at my house. There's plenty of room, especially outside, but Conrad insisted we have it here. He comes off grumpy more often than not, but I know he enjoys having us all together.

This ranch goes back in his family several generations. When his folks died a few years ago, Conrad took over the responsibility and has run it ever since. He's an only child, and from my understanding, doesn't have any remaining family left around here. His grandma is still alive, I'm pretty sure, but she lives in Greece, and has for many years. If I had to guess, Conrad enjoys having us all here because it gives him a sense of family he doesn't have anymore. I'd imagine it gets lonely out here all by himself.

Once the food is done, we all sit around the bonfire, eating, drinking, and chatting. Glancing around the huge circle of us all, my chest squeezes, seeing everybody who's here for Xander. The way they accepted him so easily. But how could they not? He's incredible. He's sitting over by Whit currently, a paper plate topped high with food resting on top of his thighs as he talks animatedly to Whit and Reggie. I can tell by the wide grin on his face, and the fierce way he's using his hands, he's telling them all about the new dispensary.

After we all eat, it doesn't take long for the rowdy cowboys to come out and play. The sun sets, the music cranks up, and the liquor flows freely. I'm smoking a cigarette when Xander comes over to me, a goofy grin tipping up on my lips.

"Hi, boyfriend."

Xander sniggers, pulling out a joint, and placing it between his teeth, lighting it. "Hey, boyfriend."

"Having fun?"

I hold my arm out, silently telling him to *come here*. He does, pressing a quick, soft kiss to the side of my neck. Goosebumps blossom immediately, and my body awakens for him.

"I am," he confirms, voice raspy. "Thank you for doing this."

"It's no big deal." I shrug.

Pulling back enough to meet my eyes, he arches a thick, dark brow at me. "It's not no big deal. It means a lot to me, Cope."

I nod, emotion suddenly thick in my throat. What we have is still so new, but that doesn't stop me from wanting to jump feet first into the deep end anyway. The way I feel about Xander, I've never felt before. Everything about him, and about us, feels so undeniably right.

Clearing my throat, I say quietly, "Well, I'm really glad you're here."

A soft smile grows on his face as he leans in. "Me too," he whispers before capturing my lips in a kiss that warms my entire body.

His tongue licks along the seam of my lips. When I part them, he dips inside, and I can taste the sweet, earthy flavor of his weed mixed with a taste that is all Xander. One of his arms snakes around my middle, as I bring one of mine up to wrap around the nape of his neck, fingers brushing the soft curls sitting there. We fit together, physically and otherwise, perfectly. Like he was made specifically for me, and vice versa.

Xander breaks the kiss first, our foreheads rested against one another as we breathe each other in. Blame it on the excitement from today, the liquor I've consumed, or the arousal and need vibrating through my body, but I'm spilling words before I can stop myself.

"Move in with me."

His eyes fly open, widening comically as he peers up at me. "What?"

A pang of nervousness unfurrows in my gut, but I shove it away. "You heard me," I reply with a smirk, pulling back to take in his expression.

A deer in headlights…that's how Xander looks right now. I have to bite the inside of my cheek to keep from laughing at how adorable he looks, taken by surprise for the second time tonight.

"Cope…that's ridiculous."

"Is it?"

"Y-yes," he stutters. Even with the daylight nearly gone, I can see the flush on his cheeks.

Quirking a brow, I ask, "Why?"

"Because…" Xander breathes out a laugh. "Because we're new, and that's insane. People don't move in together after knowing each other for, like, five months."

"Sure, they do," I counter. "And if it feels right, who cares? I don't know about you, but every single thing about you and me has always felt right."

His features soften at that. "They have for me too."

"Okay, so, move in with me, city boy."

Rolling his eyes at the nickname, he fists my shirt, pulling me in for another kiss. This one's quick, over entirely too soon. After being away from him for weeks and weeks, I really was a dumbass bringing him straight here instead of taking him somewhere where we could be alone for a while. I'm craving a repeat of the last time we were together. And him being inside of me. Maybe both in the same session. *Oh, that could be fun.*

"You're thinking something dirty, aren't you?" Xander grins, peering up at me.

"What makes you say that?"

"Well, your eyes got all glossed over, and I definitely felt your cock twitch against my stomach just now."

I throw my head back and laugh. "Okay, yeah. But can you blame me? I'm so fucking horny for you. It's been *sooo* long."

Xander's lip ticks up into a sultry grin as his hand brushes over the growing bulge in my pants. "I mean, if you want, you can use my throat for now."

He squeezes my growing erection, and I hiss through gritted teeth. "Like, right now?"

"Right. Now."

My blood heats up, a thrill shooting down my spine at the idea of Xander getting on his knees for me right here, where anybody could see us. I'm about to agree to it because the visual is just too hot, but then a voice slices through the air, killing the moment.

"Cope!" Shooter hollers. "Where the fuck are you?" He rounds the corner of the barn, gaze landing on us, a knowing smirk lifting on his lips. "Oh, there you are. Let's go."

I blow out a frustrated sigh at his horrible timing. "Where?"

His gaze dips down briefly to where Xander's hand is still cupping my crotch. "Boone had to take off. So, you two are playing against me and Sterling in cornhole. You can fuck later."

He walks away, and I can't help but chuckle, eyes dragging over to meet Xander's. "He's such an asshole."

"I'll say," Xander mutters, reaching down to adjust himself. "Let's go play some cornhole, *boyfriend*."

The label falling from his lips has me smiling like a fool at his retreating form. Love the sound of that.

Chapter 31

Xander Dawson

The early sun hugs the mountain tops in the distance, shimmering dewdrops clinging to the grass, and while it's clear spring is in full swing, the air's still got a chilly bite to it this early in the morning. The mug in my hands warms me up as the steam from the freshly brewed coffee billows. Aggie is standing beside where I'm sitting in the rocking chair on the porch, and with the way she can't seem to get close enough to me, I'd say she's happy I'm back.

And I gotta admit, I am too.

Starting my days like this can't be beat. The last couple of months have felt lackluster every morning when I woke up and had my coffee on the porch of my house in a residential neighborhood, with the sounds of early morning traffic in the distance—or worse, in a hotel room with no balcony. There have been brief moments of doubt regarding this move, which I think is normal for such a big change. I wondered if I'd regret upending my entire life and moving several states away, or if maybe I wouldn't have what it took to make it in a place like this.

I've been back not even a full twenty-four hours, but I know with absolute certainty that I've made the right call. My soul is so much happier here.

The creaking back door opens, and I glance over just in time to watch Aunt Colette amble out, fuzzy pink slippers on her feet and a robe draped over her pajamas. "Welcome back," she says softly as she takes a seat in the rocking chair beside mine. "What time did you get in last night?"

"Not until after midnight."

Last night was so much fun, and completely unexpected. Knowing that Cope took the time to organize something like that for me makes the flutters that are ever-present in my stomach because of him intensify tenfold. It's such a genuinely sweet gesture, and it's so Cope. He's always showing up for me, always proving how much he cares.

When we got back here after the party, we fooled around for a little while in his truck, but I was beyond exhausted from traveling, so we didn't get very far.

"Did you have fun?" my aunt asks, pulling me out of my thoughts.

"I did." A smile grows on my lips before I take a sip of my coffee.

"He came over here and invited me."

That doesn't surprise me. Cope is such a genuinely nice guy, and even before I came here and we met, I know he'd come over and help Colette out from time to time. "Why didn't you go?"

She shrugs. "Wanted you to have your own fun. You don't want your old aunt tagging along."

Clicking my tongue at her, I reply, "That's not true. I would've loved for you to be there."

Her eyes soften as she takes a drink of her coffee. "I'm

happy you're here, you know. In Copper Lake. It's nice having family around."

"I'm happy I'm here too, Auntie."

Cope's invite to move in comes back into my mind, and my heart beats a little harder. I'm certain he was probably just swept up in the moment and from drinking. I meant it when I said it was a ridiculous idea… Yet, why can't I stop thinking about it then? Picturing it—picturing us, living together. Going to sleep beside each other, waking up together.

What Cope said—how we've always felt right—was spot on. But we couldn't move in together this soon…could we?

"What's got you looking so introspective this morning?" Aunt Colette asks.

It's right there on the tip of my tongue to blow her off, or lie about what I'm thinking about, but I don't. Maybe she could smack some sense into me. "Cope asked me to move in with him last night."

My cheeks heat as soon as the words leave my mouth.

If she's surprised by what I said, she doesn't show it. The only giveaway that she even heard me is the small smile playing on her lips as she brushes a hand over Aggie's soft coat. "And you don't want to?"

Huffing out a laugh, I say, "It's not that I don't want to. It's just…we've only known each other for a few months. That would be crazy, wouldn't it?"

She sits in thoughtful silence for a moment. I'm half-expecting her to tell me yes, that would be crazy. But she doesn't. "When I was twenty, I used to enjoy going to a small, quiet park by my home. I'd go there to think, read, sometimes do crossword puzzles. One afternoon when I was there, a gentleman came and sat beside me. He looked about my age, and he was cute." She smirks, wagging her brows at me. "Very cute. Anyway, he didn't say anything to me. Simply sat beside me. This went on for weeks. Finally, I couldn't take it anymore, and one day, introduced myself. We grabbed coffee that afternoon, and it turned into a daily thing. Our relationship moved quickly. The way I felt about him was unlike anything I'd experienced before."

When she doesn't say anything else for a minute, I ask, "Well, what happened?"

My gaze is laser focused on the side of her head as she stares out into the yard. "About six months after meeting him, he had to move across the country," she replies. "Military."

"He left?"

She nods. "He did, but he asked me to come with him. Asked me to marry him."

My eyes widen. "What did you say?"

A cold laugh leaves her mouth before her gaze drags over to meet mine. "I told him he'd lost his mind. Told him we barely knew each other, and I couldn't possibly uproot my entire life for a man I hadn't even known for a year."

My pulse races, the blood roaring in my ears as I listen to this personal story she's offering to me. "You didn't go?"

"No, I didn't go. I never did see him again, either." I don't know why that answer guts me as much as it does. There's a sadness in her eyes as she recounts this memory. "And you know what?"

"What?"

"There's never been a single other thing in my life that I regret more than not going with him. You know why?"

Chewing on my bottom lip, I shake my head.

"In the many, many years that have passed since he left,

I've never met anybody who made me feel even half of the way he did in the short time we knew each other. Time doesn't mean shit, Xander. Not when it's real." My aunt sets her coffee down on the table between us, bringing her gaze up to meet mine again. "Now, I'm not telling you to do anything you're not ready for or don't want, but if time is the only thing stopping you, then I urge you to get the hell out of that head of yours, and trust your heart. Trust your gut. If I could go back to that moment when he asked me to leave with him, I would say yes in a heartbeat."

My mouth's dry and my heart hammers in my chest. "But I'm here to help you," I offer pathetically. "And he leaves for the rodeo soon."

She tsks. "Those are just excuses, boy. I refuse to be your excuse. Refuse to be the reason you hold yourself back. It's right next door; there's no reason you couldn't still help out with the animals over here. Not to mention, I have that boy who helps out around here now, too, thanks to you."

Grabbing her coffee mug, she rises off the rocking chair, glancing around the yard before down at me.

"Do what feels right, Xander. Fuck the time."

And then she's gone, leaving me stunned over everything she just shared, and then her sweet parting words. Such an eloquent speaker, that one.

Once I finish my coffee, I get started on the morning chores. As usual, Aggie follows me around the yard while I do them, and I love it. Aside from Cope, she was who I missed the most while I was back in Washington. It's late morning by the time I finish up and take a shower. When I get out, I have a text waiting for me.

Cope: Horseback ride… You free?

A smile graces my lips as I type a response.
Me: Sure. Come over. I'm just getting ready.

Sliding off the horse, I take in my surroundings. "I don't think I'll ever get over how beautiful and serene it is up here," I mutter to Cope as he comes to stand behind me, his arms looping around my middle as he holds me close to his chest.

We took the trail ride and came up to the same spot he brought me to the first time we went on a ride together. The river is below, shimmering in the afternoon sun, and the mountain peaks surround us as far as the eye can see. It's like something you'd see on the front of a postcard.

After we make sure the horses aren't going to sneak off on us, I lay a blanket down as Cope grabs the food he packed from his backpack. Some meats, cheeses, and fruit in various Tupperware containers sit before us. Everything my aunt said to me this morning still replays on a loop in my mind as we eat in a comfortable silence, both of us taking in the view. It's relaxing being up here with him; something I could see myself getting used to.

Once we finish eating, we put the empty containers back in his backpack, and I move to lay in between his legs, my back to his front. His arms wrap tightly around me, his masculine scent enveloping me. I love the way we're able to spend time together without filling every moment with useless small talk. We can simply exist, enjoy the presence of one another.

The air's a little chilly, but I'm nice and toasty warm here in Cope's arms.

"I told my parents about us," Cope says softly beside my ear.

It surprises me, and when I turn my head to meet his gaze,

a grin slides on my face. "Did you now?"

He nods, a mirroring smile on his face.

"What did you tell them?"

"Just basic stuff," he says. "Where you're from, what brought you here, how we met, how much you mean to me." That last part has my stomach fluttering.

"What did they say?" It's not until this very moment that I realize how important it is to me that his parents like me. When he introduced us over speakerphone, they couldn't have been kinder. He's so close with them, their opinion obviously matters a lot. If they hate me—or worse, hate that I'm a man—it could ruin any future Cope and I have together.

"They said they could tell something more was going on after we all talked. They're excited to meet you," he says, leaning in to press a kiss to my forehead. He must sense the internal panic I'm feeling.

"They don't care that…I'm not a woman?"

Cope's brows crease together. "Not at all. My mom was giddy as can be and my dad was supportive, as always. They're happy that I'm happy. It's truly all they really want for their child."

Some of the panic subsides. "I'm happy that you're happy too," I murmur before capturing his lips in a quick, but deep kiss.

"When do you leave for the rodeo?" I ask him when we pull apart.

"In about a month." His deep voice vibrates from his chest, through my back that's pressed against him.

"You excited?"

I feel him nod. "Yeah, but it sucks that I have to leave you." Pressing a kiss to the side of my head, he murmurs, "You should come with me."

Laughter bubbles out of me. "You're just full of ideas lately, aren't you?"

"I'm serious," he goes on. "It doesn't have to be for the whole season. I know that's not feasible, but maybe for a little bit."

My aunt's words come back to me. About my excuses. About the farm hand she has now, and her insistence that I shouldn't use her as a reason to not go after what I want. What feels right.

"I'm sure I can come for a little while," I finally say quietly.

"Yeah?" I can hear the smile in his voice.

Nodding, I smile too. "Yeah. I'd love to get to see you in action."

Cope's hands sneak under the hem of my shirt, palms caressing my bare skin. A chill races through me, the touch sending a shot of arousal to my groin. "I'd love that too," he murmurs huskily, lips right beside the shell of my ear.

And just like that, the air around us shifts. It thickens as my need for him grows. He must be able to sense it, because the next moment, one of his hands is trailing lower until he reaches the waistband of my jeans. With skilled precision, he flicks open the button, sliding the zipper down, and he dips his hand underneath my boxers, palming my hardening cock. My head lolls against his shoulder, a deep-throated groan sounding as bolts of electricity ping-pong through my body.

"Cope…" His name leaves my lips on a breath as his fist begins to move ever so slowly up the length of me.

"You like that?" he asks, lust drenching his tone.

I nod, a whimper falling off my lips.

"I fucking missed you," he rasps, fist tightening. "Missed this." *A tight stroke. A flick of his wrist.* "Missed being near you." *Stroke. Flick of the wrist.* "Touching you."

My eyes roll back, hips lifting as he uses his other hand to work my jeans down my legs enough to free my dick. The cool air hits it, but there isn't a single part of my body that's cold. I'm burning up from the inside out with the way he's touching me. Cope reaches down, cupping my full balls, and I gasp *loudly*.

"Yeah...let me hear you, city boy." *Fuck*. "I love the sounds you make. Love the way your body responds to me. How mine responds to you. You're fucking made for me."

Holy shit. Cope isn't usually silent in bed, but this...this is so hot. I never want him to stop. I can feel his own erection against my back, and I desperately want to turn around so I can pull him out too, but it'll have to wait.

Hot lips press down on the overheated flesh on my neck, placing wet kisses all along the skin. His teeth graze the area, sending a shiver down my spine, just as he wraps a fist around my cock again, squeezing and stroking in a way that has me leaking. I feel his touch everywhere. His physical touch, but also the way he's touched me emotionally. Our connection is bone deep, and he's now a part of me in a way I never want to live without.

I turn my head, lips finding his, and I swear, it's like fireworks go off inside of me the moment his tongue grazes mine. His taste, the feel of him, his hands on my body... *Him*.

"Cope," I gasp against his mouth. "Fuck! Don't stop."

He reaches up with his free hand, underneath my shirt, fingers easily finding my hardened, sensitive nipple. He tugs on the piercing, pinching the bud, and I lose it. Cope is my undoing, and I can't hold back. My release barrels through me, taking me by surprise. Toes curling inside my shoes, limbs stiffening, I cry out against his lips as I unload all over my stomach.

I don't give myself any time to come down from the high he just gave to me before I'm sitting up and spinning around. Pressing a hot, fast kiss down on his lips, I run my fingers through my release, gathering as much of it up as I can.

"Pull yourself out," I order him, the shameless need clear in my voice. I need to make him feel as good as he just made me feel. Thankfully, he seems about as desperate as I am. As soon as his cock is freed, I lift my cum-soaked hand up to his face. "Spit."

A growl sounds at the back of his throat as he holds eye contact, adding his saliva to the mess in my hand.

Bringing my hand back down, I fist his hard length, stroking slowly at first, quickly getting more fevered. His dark, endless eyes drink me in, lids hooded and heavy, his cheeks bright pink and radiant. He looks exactly how I feel, and I can't get enough of it.

"God, you look fucking beautiful right now," I admit breathlessly.

A smile tugs on his lips, the flush deepening on his face. I lean in, capturing his full lips with mine. Straddling his lap, I pump my fist while my tongue thrusts into his mouth, licking every crevice I can reach. His burning arousal is a potent flavor on my tongue. I can't get enough.

Within a few minutes, I can tell he's getting close. His breathing has kicked up, and his groans are getting louder. Needier. The fingers of my free hand find their way into the hair on the nape of his neck, and I breathe against his lips, "Come for me, cowboy."

"Fuck!" he gasps before doing just that. His hot seed coats my hand as he grunts and moans into my mouth. At some point, his hands found their way to my hips, fingers digging into the flesh as I work him through his release. I can't help but smile, thinking about the marks that'll be there later.

Reaching behind myself, I grab the napkins he brought with us, using them to clean up the mess we made. We both tuck ourselves back into our pants before reaching for our waters, chugging them, and trying to catch our breath.

"Don't think I'm dropping the moving in with me thing."

He eyes me, and I throw my head back, laughing. "Didn't think you would," I reply.

"I'm serious, Xander."

"I know you are." My heart steadily beats as I take in his expression.

"So, will you?" He's looking at me with the cutest puppy dog eyes I've ever seen, and I nearly melt at the sight. "Please."

Biting the inside of my cheek in an attempt to ground myself, I watch him. I really, truly see him.

"Look…can we make a deal?"

"If the deal is you saying yes," he teases, a sly little grin slipping into place.

"I'm not saying no," I confirm, holding up a hand when I can tell he wants to butt in. "But can we wait until after the season is over before we make a final decision? Give ourselves time to get used to what we have. Get used to being together—and being apart. I don't want to rush simply because it feels good, you know? I want to…more than you know. But I'd feel better if we waited until you were back. Let us find our groove together. Okay?"

Cope's brows are pinched, his lips pressed into an unamused line. But eventually, his features soften. "Okay," he replies. "I respect your point and can see why waiting until I'm back is a better choice. But let the record show, I don't like it."

Chuckling, I nod. "Noted."

"I'm serious about you coming on the road with me for a little while. I'm not budging on that."

Tossing him a wink, I reply, "Deal."

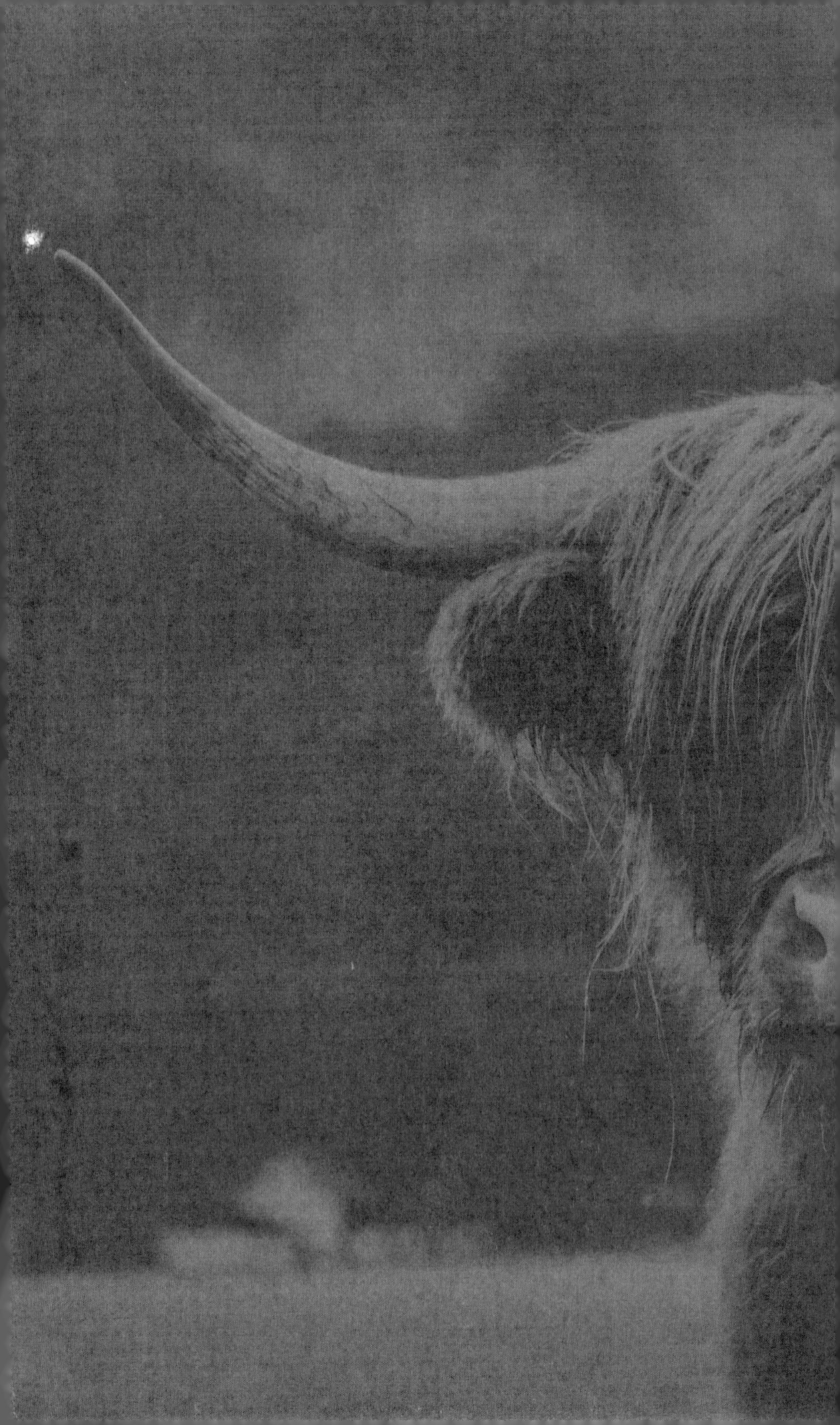

Chapter 32

Four Months Later

Xander Dawson

"I'm gonna grab another beer." Raising off the bleachers, I glance down at where Grady, Boone's brother-in-law, sits with a bouncy Suzy on his lap. "You guys want anything?"

"Ice!" Suzy bursts with her hands thrown into the air and big, cheeky grin on her face.

I look at Grady, chuckling from her enthusiasm. "Is it okay if she has one?"

"Yeah, but make sure it's small or she won't sleep tonight. Can you grab me a bottle of water? I got cash in my—"

"Don't worry about it," I cut him off. "I got you."

"Thanks, man." Grady's smile is warm and appreciative when I turn and head toward the concession stands.

We're in Dirks, Colorado, this weekend for a back-to-back rodeo night at the county fair. Aside from last week, when everybody was home for Stampede Days, this is only the third time I've been able to see Cope compete this season. I was hoping to get to travel with him a bit more, but the new store opening has been a lot more work behind the scenes than I was anticipating, and then the farm hand we hired to help my aunt ended up breaking his arm, and he was pretty much useless there for a while. It's been a mess, but his arm's healed now, and my stores are running smoothly.

Grabbing the drinks, I head back to the stands, not wanting to miss anything. The bareback bronc riders just finished up, meaning Cope's category is up next. He's had a phenomenal season so far—I know this because I've been studying up on the sport and the rules, so I feel like I semi know what I'm talking about now. At least in comparison to the first time I watched him compete in Vegas back in December.

As soon as my ass hits the uncomfortable metal seats, the announcer booms over the loudspeaker that we'll be starting the saddle bronc portion, and my insides flutter with excitement. I never thought I'd be the type of guy who enjoyed the rodeo—and I guess I don't, per se, but I *do* enjoy watching Cope. Well, and the other riders from Copper Lake, too, but especially Cope.

A couple of riders go before him, but as soon as I see him lower himself onto the bronc behind the gate, my heart beats harder. Even from all the way over here, I can tell he looks damn good in his outfit. A black leather vest covered in sponsor patches, a teal pearl snap shirt, a faded pair of Wranglers that I know cup his tight, firm ass nicely, covered in a pair of black leather chaps with teal fringe that matches his shirt almost perfectly, and even though I can't see his feet, I know he's got on his regular pair of well-worn boots.

A true cowboy.

And fuck, there's nothing sexier than that.

"Alright, ladies and gentlemen." The announcer's loud,

boisterous voice echoes around the arena. "Let's give it up for our next saddle bronc rider of the evening. Here from Copper Lake, Wyoming, last year's world champ, Copeland Murphy!"

The crowd goes wild as Cope busts out of the bucking chute. Like every time I watch him, everything happens so fast. The bronc jumps and kicks and bucks, and Cope moves with her with such precision, one hand gripping the reins, the other held up above his head. He moves with the writhing beast almost gracefully, which is humorous to say, since looking at them right now, there's nothing graceful about how she's jerking him around, but it's true.

He moves in a way that proves how talented he is. His body is loose, allowing him to move *with* her, like he can predict her next step. They look like a well-oiled machine, even though this is probably the first time he's ever ridden her. It truly is an art as much as it is a dangerous, adrenaline-filled sport. When the buzzer sounds, and he's pulled off the horse, I know without the announcer even reading off the score that he did an exceptional job.

Cope's gaze finds mine as if he knew exactly where I was the entire time. A smile splits his face as he points at me before blowing me a kiss. My chest warms, and an obnoxiously wide smile tugs on my lips as I return the gesture. He exits the arena shortly after that, and the next rider comes out, but I don't pay them any attention because my phone buzzes with a text I know is from Cope without even looking.

Cope: Sterling, Shooter, and I are walking over to the campsite to take showers before the rodeo is over. I'll come meet you in the stands once we're done.

I send him a thumbs up, shoving my phone back into my pocket. Shooter's back this season after taking part of last season off. From what I can tell, he's doing really well, and the fans seem happy that he's back.

About twenty minutes later, the three of them are walking over to where we're sitting, and we watch the rest of the show. Bull riding is the last event always, no idea why, so we stay to watch Colt and Boone compete. They're both badass and incredibly fucking talented, but every time I watch them ride, I'm thankful Cope rides broncs, and not bulls. Not that bronc riding is *safe* by any means, but it's definitely not as wild as riding an angry bull.

Once the rodeo's over, we all head back to the campsite we're staying at for the weekend. It's kind of fun to me how they all travel from location to location, towing their campers. I'm sure by the end of the season, they're all ready to sleep in their own beds, inside of a real house, but the idea of spending the spring and summer camping with your closest friends like a bunch of nomads is interesting to me. I love it, and I'm excited to get to be a part of it this weekend.

Boone grills us all some hamburgers and hot dogs, and we sit around the burning fire, eating, tossing back beers, and listening to music, while a steady hum of chatter and laughter keeps me smiling. It's a warm, clear night, the sky splashed with glittering stars, not a cloud in sight. I've had several beers at this point in the night, counting the ones I also had at the arena, so I'm feeling quite toasty.

Cope nudges me with his elbow, leaning in, lips hovering over the shell of my ear. "Did you have fun today?"

I nod, turning my head to meet his chocolate brown gaze. "I did, but I'm even happier now that you're here with me, and not on the back of a bronc."

Originally, I was going to drive down here since it's only

about a seven-hour drive, but my car's been acting up again. It was giving me hell about starting earlier this week—it's time to finally get rid of it and buy something more reliable. I can't keep putting it off—so, I booked a last-minute flight for this morning. Of course, because I'm me and have the worst fucking luck with flights, it was delayed. Because of that, I wasn't able to see Cope before the rodeo like I'd planned to.

Thankfully, my flight home isn't until Sunday morning, so I have all day tomorrow with him before his next rodeo, and then tomorrow night too.

Cope smirks, leaning in to capture my lips with his. My entire body lights up immediately from the contact, and when my lips part and his tongue slips inside, rolling with mine, I don't even try to stop the groan that reverberates from my chest.

"Is it too early to have you take me to bed?" I hum against his lips.

Chuckling, Cope pulls back and says, "I thought you'd never ask, city boy. Let's go."

He stands from the folding chair he was sitting in, holding out his hand for me. His palm is warm and rough as I slip mine into his grip and let him pull me into a stand. With a quick glance around the fire, I note that everybody is occupied and paying us no mind. Not that I really care one way or the other.

I'm fucking my man tonight, whether they're aware of it or not.

Cope and I practically sprint to the camper, ripping open the door once we reach it, and as soon as we're both inside the dark space, our bodies collide and our lips fuse together. My hands fly to his face, his to my hips, as he pulls me flush against him. A groan rips from my throat as I taste his desperation. I'll never get tired of how unabashed and open Cope is with his need for me.

Fingers finding the hem of my shirt, he rips his lips from mine long enough to yank the shirt over my head. As soon as I'm free of the material, I reach for his and do the same. Right before we're about to resume the making out, a gasp that doesn't belong to either of us sounds inside the otherwise quiet camper. My head turns, eyes flying in that direction. There's a blanket or a sheet—I can't tell with how dark it is in here—hung up toward the back of the camper, and the sound *definitely* came from back there.

I glance back to Cope questioningly, and he just smirks. "Hi, Shooter. Hi, Sterling," he calls out.

My eyes widen as I hear Shooter's distinct chuckle. "Sup, fucker."

Then I hear a much quieter Sterling. "Oh, my God."

Cope sniggers before taking my hand to lead me over to the front where his quote-unquote room is at. Staying rooted in place, I hiss, "What are you doing?"

He throws me a confused look over his shoulder. "Uh, taking you to bed?"

"Cope, we are interrupting them clearly trying to hook up. We cannot stay in here."

Cope snorts, continuing to lead me into his room. As soon as we're in there, he slides the little makeshift curtain over the door area, giving us a sense of privacy. Pulling out his phone, he unlocks it, and a moment later, music filters through the small speaker. He pulls my body into his, nuzzling his nose into my neck. Goosebumps bloom over my skin as I hear—and feel—him inhale deeply.

"There, music to drown them out. They don't fucking care that we're here," he mumbles against my flesh before pressing a hot kiss down on my throat. "This is not the first time I've been in this camper while they hook up."

I pull back, arousal shooting through my core. "Have you ever...you know," I ask, making a jacking off motion with my hand.

Cope's head falls back onto his shoulders as he laughs. "No, perv. I haven't jacked off to my friends fucking before."

Waggling my brows, I say, "But you've wanted to, huh?"

He growls, wrapping his palm around the back of my neck and hauling me into him. "I plead the fifth, city boy. Now shut up and let me touch you already."

Our lips collide with blistering heat, tongues slashing together in a fight for control, our hands coming down to our pants, seeing who can get the other naked the fastest. Of course, because I'm not wearing an obnoxiously large belt buckle, Cope gets my pants undone before I can get his, and he gladly shoves them down my legs, dropping to his knees before I even have a chance to push his down.

My cock, which is already hard and throbbing, bobs as soon as it's freed from my boxers, the cool air of the room sending a shiver down my spine. His hot, wet mouth closes around my tip in an instant, and I can't help the moan that falls from my lips. It's only been a week since we last hooked up—with him being home for the festival last week—but I swear, I'm insatiable when it comes to Cope. I can never get enough.

His tongue pokes underneath my foreskin, swirling around the sensitive crown in a way that has my eyes crossing. At some point, he figured out how much I love that, and I swear, now he does it just to make me squirm. A large, calloused palm cups my balls, rolling them in his grip as he takes more of my length into his mouth. My hands find his hair, threading through the strands, and gripping enough to guide him how I want.

"Fuck, Cope," I hiss, peering down at him now that my eyes have adjusted to the darkness, watching in awe as he takes me down his throat. He looks fucking stunning like this, and I can't get enough. He sucks me deep and hard and sloppy, spit dribbling down his chin, the sounds obscene, and as soon as he gets me right to the edge of exploding, he fully pulls away, and stands up. "You're a dick," I grumble, but the grin on my face gives me away.

Finally, he undoes his pants, shoving them and his boxers down, until I'm graced with his long, thick, veiny cock. I'll never get tired of seeing this beast. It's huge and sexy, and he most definitely knows what to do with it.

"Wanna fuck me tonight?" I ask, wrapping a fist around my aching dick and giving it a few pumps.

Cope grins, leaning in to press a row of kisses along my neck. "Actually, I was hoping we could take turns this time." A bolt of pleasure rips through my body, landing in my balls. When he pulls back to meet my gaze, his arousal and how much he wants this radiates off of him. "I prepped in the shower," he admits with a sultry little smirk.

God, that's fucking hot.

"Did you now?" I purr, reaching down to take his hot, hard length in my palm.

He nods, groaning as I stroke him. "I thought of your cock filling me up instead of my fingers while I did it," he admits.

"You like when I fill you up, don't you, cowboy?"

He nods again, eyes glazed over.

"Top or bottom first?" I ask, needing him in any way I can get him.

Guiding us over to the bed, he shoves me down before

blanketing my body with his. "I wanna fuck you first, but I don't want to come until you're inside of me."

My blood heats insurmountably at that, and all I can do is nod and watch him as he positions himself between my spread thighs, grabs the bottle of lube from underneath his pillow—and I snigger thinking of him stashing it under there in preparation for tonight—immediately getting to work stretching me. Despite the music still filtering out through Cope's phone, the noises at the other end of the camper get progressively louder the longer we're in here, and I won't lie… it's fucking hot. Knowing they're getting off at the same time we are, neither of us able to see the other, but we sure can hear, is filthy.

Cope reaches for the foil packet he pulled out with the lube, but before he can rip it open, I reach for his hand and say, "Fuck me raw."

Biting down on his bottom lip, he rakes his gaze over the length of my entire body. "You're sure?"

"Um, yeah," I reply with a chuckle. "I've been dying to feel you inside of me with no barrier."

Not needing anymore encouragement, Cope tosses the unopened foil packet onto the bed before reaching for the lube. He coats his bare cock, rubbing the rest over my hole, before lining himself up. A shiver racks through my body as I feel the blunt tip of his head press against my entrance. Entering me slowly, he leans down over my body, hands resting beside my head on the pillow, and he holds my gaze as I feel every last inch of him split me open. The pressure is intense, the burn something I've come to crave from him. He's so big, when he first gets inside of me, it always feels impossible.

Cope gives me a few minutes to adjust before he sits back

and gets to work. After that initial stretch and burn dissipates, there's nothing gentle about the way Cope handles me, and I fucking love it. With his hands pressed down on the backs of my thighs, he snaps his hips into my ass, the sound of sweaty, slapping skin fills the small space. At the same time, a very similar sound, paired with a very distinct moaning, comes from the other side of the camper.

I can't help the smirk that grows on my face as my eyes find Cope's. "Harder," I bite out, fingers fisting the sheets beneath me.

Huffing out a sound between a laugh and a groan, Cope picks up the pace, fucking me hard and fast, grazing my prostate with every roll of his hips. My head throws back, neck pulled taut as I cry out from the immense amount of pleasure flooding my body right now. He's relentless in his attack, my cock leaking a puddle onto my stomach the longer he fucks me.

I slap a hand over my mouth to try to keep quiet, the pleasure too fucking good, but Cope reaches down and rips my hand away before growling, "No. Let them hear you cry for me."

"Holy fuck," I gasp, chest heaving, sweat coating my body.

He's got my thighs practically sitting on top of my chest as he pounds into me, his teeth bared and his eyes wild. He looks and sounds purely animalistic as he towers over me, cock thrusting into my hole. It's so fucking good, and way too much. My release builds, sensation growing stronger and spreading through my entire body, and I know I need to put a stop to this before I come too soon.

"Stop, stop!" I rasp, pressing a palm to his slick chest and shoving him away.

The hard set of Cope's brows as he pulls out of me tells me he was as close to combusting as I was, and something about that turns me on even more. Getting up onto my knees, I bring my gaze to Cope's deep, bottomless eyes, cupping his cheek, and rubbing my thumb over his full bottom lip. I lean in, sealing my mouth to his as I lick into his mouth, savoring the flavor of him on my tongue.

Without ever breaking apart, I shift us until he's lying flat on the bed and I'm between his legs. Blindly, I reach for—and successfully grab—the bottle of lube, flicking the top open, and pouring a glob onto my fingers. Even though he told me he already prepped earlier, I still want to work him open a little more before sticking my dick in him. The last thing I want to do is unknowingly hurt him, especially since he has to compete again tomorrow night.

Once I'm sure he's good and stretched, I coat my length with the cool gel before lining up and slowly easing in. We both groan a sigh of relief and pleasure once I'm fully sheathed. His channel is hot and so fucking tight, it's a fight to not come on the spot. My movements are slow at first. Long, deep thrusts, loving the feel of Cope's hole squeezing my cock. Relishing the feel of him surrounding me with no barrier.

Both of my hands go to the back of his head, cupping him as our bodies are nearly flush, hips rolling into him. At this angle, our faces are mere inches apart, and we're breathing in the same air. It's so much more intimate than it was a moment ago, especially with how strong our eye contact is, and it makes my chest crack wide open for him. The sheer strength of my feelings for Cope is staggering. It nearly knocks me on my ass constantly. It's suffocating how deeply I care for him…but in the very best way.

Sex with Cope isn't just about physical pleasure. It's not just hot or amazing. It's so much more than that. Sex with

Cope feels like more than just our bodies are connecting. Like a piece of me that I wasn't even aware was missing has been mended. It's deep. Soulful. Pure, raw intimacy in its truest form. It's something I didn't even know existed before him. The way we fit together, physically and emotionally. It's the way he looks at me like I hold all the answers. The trust we put into each other.

I can't fully describe it, but it takes my breath away. It brings tears to my eyes. It's *everything*. He's everything.

The intensity of this moment has the air around us thick and heady, and based on the faraway look in his eyes, I know Cope feels it too. Our bodies are slick and hot, and I'm teetering so close to the edge, I know neither of us will last much longer. He reaches a hand between us, wrapping around his hard length, pumping his fist to the same rhythm I'm fucking him with. Our movements are sensual and meaningful, and it feels like our bodies are saying worlds more than our mouths can right now.

"Cope..." I breathe against his parted lips.

His brows scrunch and he nods, desire and something *more* swimming in his gaze, as if he understands everything I'm not saying. "I'm close," he croaks, teeth chomping down on his full bottom lip.

"Me too."

Pressure builds and spreads from my lower back, coiling around the base of my spine, and swimming through my veins. It's a heated rush, an earth-shattering throb burrowing deep in my balls, and as Cope lets go, a cry falling from his lips as his beautiful big cock explodes, his ass squeezes the life out of my dick, sending me crashing into my own release. As soon as my orgasm hits, I seal my lips to his, kissing him like my life depends on it—and in this moment, it feels like it does.

My body is boneless by the time I finish. I collapse on top of Cope, not even bothering to pull out of him, as we both catch our breath. The smell of sweat and sex hangs in the air, and the realization that Shooter and Sterling are still in here and heard all of that comes back to me, and I bust up laughing, my face buried in Cope's neck.

"What the hell is so funny?" he asks groggily. I'm sure he's feeling just as exhausted, if not more, than I am.

"I can't believe we just did that with them in here."

Cope chuckles, the sound vibrating from his body into mine as his chest shakes. "Hey, you guys done?" he booms, loud enough to be heard across the camper.

"Yup!" Shooter replies cheerfully. "Bravo performance, you two."

Cope laughs as I groan, wanting the ground to swallow me whole. "You guys, too," he offers, humor lacing his every word.

"Obviously," Shooter drawls. "I aim to please."

The sound of bare feet padding across the floor sounds moments before the makeshift curtain to Cope's space pulls open. Shooter's grinning mug travels from Cope's face to mine, then down to our still naked and exposed bodies.

"Shit," I hiss, falling off of Cope, accidentally flashing his dick to Shooter while I scramble for the blankets—which he's lying on top of.

Shooter chuckles. "Don't worry, Xan-man. I'm not looking at your junk. Get dressed, guys. Let's go smoke."

And then he's gone.

Glancing over at Cope, I groan. "He's got no boundaries."

Laughing, he says, "Not even one."

Shamelessly, I watch Cope get dressed, loving every dip,

muscle, and curve, feeling my cock twitch all over again.

"Quit ogling me, perv." Whipping my leg with his shirt, he chuckles. "Up you go."

I'll never quit ogling you, Copeland Murphy.

Chapter 33

Cope Murphy

We've stayed at these campgrounds before. A couple of times, actually. It's like that with a handful of the towns we stop in; either there's only one option due to the town's small size, or there's only one good option. This one's the former, but the views are gorgeous, so I don't mind. It's a quarter past seven, the air is crisp, birds are chirping in the trees all around us, and I can already tell it's going to be a scorcher. But for now, it's comfortable.

Shooter and Sterling are cooking a big breakfast for everyone back at the campsite before we start the day. There's some well-known zoo here that apparently has baby red pandas. When Daisy heard that, she was all over the idea, so that's what we're all doing before we have to hit the arena later on. For now, though, before breakfast and before we gotta get a move on, I'm taking Xander to a spot just off the beaten path that I think he's going to love.

He's slightly ahead of me as we hike the short distance to where we're going and, of course, I can't help but check him out. The soft blue sleeveless shirt he's wearing gives me a teasing peek at his chest. From the right angle, I can even see his jeweled nipple. It makes me want to take it between my teeth and play with it with my tongue. A pair of black athletic shorts sit right above his knees, and his Vans are white and in pristine condition. The top of his head is free of any type of hat, his black curls sleep tousled and beautiful, and with the way the sun is sitting in the sky, his profile is highlighted by the soft glow, all his sharp lines and smooth skin accentuated.

Xander tosses me a look over his shoulder, totally catching me checking him out. A sly smirk tugs on his lips. "Quit ogling me, perv," he parrots my words from last night, causing us both to chuckle.

"Can't help it, city boy." I shrug innocently. "You're just so damn sexy."

He rolls his eyes, trying to hide the smile that brings him. His cheeks pinken from the compliment, and it's moments like these I especially love how he wears his every emotion on his face. He can't hide it from me because his expressions give him away every time.

Almost to our destination, I reach out, slipping my hand into his. Xander glances down at our joined hands before meeting my gaze, a softness overtaking his eyes.

"Come on," I say, clearing my throat of the sudden emotional lump building. "It's right over here."

We veer to the left, coming to a clearing through the tall, thick trees. Xander scans the area for a moment before whispering, "Wow."

This place is nowhere near as beautiful and special as the spot I've taken Xander to back home, with the mountain peaks and the river below, but it's an easy close second. A shallow, rocky river runs through surrounding trees. The mountains sit in the far distance, and the sun peeks out from behind them, basking the sky in a rich, orange glow. The sound of the water trickling over the rocks is a calming one, and there's a wide-open area we can sit on. Slipping my backpack off my shoulders, I unzip it and pull out the blanket I stuffed in there so our asses don't get wet from the dewy grass.

"This place is beautiful," Xander mutters as we both take a seat.

"Isn't it?"

"You've been here before, I'm guessing?"

I nod. "A couple of times. I found it a few years back."

Xander leans over, wrapping his arms around my middle as we both lie back. He nuzzles his nose into my neck as I look up at the clear sky, trying to swallow down the feelings rushing through me. Sometimes it takes me aback how strongly I feel toward him—and in a relatively short amount of time. It hasn't even been a year since I met him broken down on the side of the dirt road. Hasn't even been a year since he unknowingly rocked my world in a way I didn't even know possible.

Being away from him this season has been hard. A lot harder than I thought it would be. He hasn't been able to come out nearly as much as I'd hoped. All I keep doing is telling myself that I'm biding my time. This is temporary, and hopefully, at the end of the season, he'll take me up on my offer to move in.

It's not something we've talked about much since I first asked him before I left for the circuit. He told me he wanted to let our relationship progress without the added pressure, and I've tried my best to respect that. But as the days go by, and the more I learn about Xander, the harder I fall. The more I feel.

Heat spreads through my body as his lips press down on

the sensitive area between my neck and my shoulder. It's not meant to be sexual, and I know he's not taking it any further than that, but I can't help but replay last night in my mind. How connected I felt to him—and not just physically. It's like our souls were aligned in a way they've never been before. Sex with Xander is always incredible and unlike anything…but last night was next level. The way he was looking at me felt like the weight of a thousand unspoken words, and it was right there on the tip of my tongue to admit just how deeply I've fallen for him, but I knew in the middle of sex wasn't the right time for that.

Pulling back, Xander glances down at me, his forearm rested on my shoulder. "What're you thinking about?"

It's like he can read my mind. Like he knows exactly where my head's at, and he's taunting me to spill my guts.

"You."

The lines around his eyes crinkle with a smile. "What about me?"

My heart pounds in my chest, and it feels like I may throw up with the knots in my stomach and the lump in my throat. I feel uncomfortably vulnerable right now, but the want in his eyes, mixed with the nervous way he's chewing on his bottom lip, makes me think he's feeling it too.

Everything about this moment is screaming at me that now is the right time. Ignoring the way my pulse is racing, I drag in a deep breath, holding it for a few moments before blowing it out.

And then I do it.

"I…love you, Xander."

He sucks in a sharp breath, his bright blue eyes widening for a second before almost immediately turning glossy. "What?"

The single word comes out no louder than a whisper.

Stomach doing a somersault, I reach out, palm cupping the side of his face. "I'm so in love with you, it feels unreal sometimes. Like maybe it's a dream, and I made it all up. Basically, my entire life, I thought I was content by myself. I thought maybe being in love wasn't for me because I've never felt anything close to it. I thought the movies and the books and the TV shows were overly exaggerated and, surely, there's no way people actually felt like that in real life. The jittery feeling. The butterflies. The endless hope that sits in your chest when you look at them and think about your future."

Xander's top teeth graze his bottom lip, the moisture filling his eyes nearly spilling over. The tip of my nose burns, and my throat aches, but I force myself to keep going. I need to get it out and off my chest.

"I know we haven't known each other all that long in the grand scheme of things, but somewhere along the way, I realized with an undeniable certainty that it's you." A fat tear falls hot down Xander's cheek, and I swipe it away with my thumb. "You are the feeling that everyone has always talked about. The feeling everybody is always chasing. The one you see in the movies, in the great love stories. The feeling that I've never understood… until you." My voice cracks, and I have to swallow around the enormous lump of emotion clogging my throat.

"From the moment you came into my life, it's like, deep down, I knew. Subconsciously, I knew. Things with you feel right. They feel sure, and they always have. I'm not saying I'm naïve to think that things with us will always be a walk in the park, but I believe that even during rough times, you'll still feel right. You'll feel like home." Nervous laughter bubbles out of me as I blink hard, causing a stream of tears to spill.

"Damn you, Cope." Xander laughs, sitting up and wiping his wet cheeks with the back of his hands. "I was not expecting this level of sweet so damn early in the morning."

Sitting up too, I toss my head back and chuckle. "Sorry about it," I mutter.

He looks at me, arching a brow. "No, you're not."

"You're right, I'm not."

His bottom lip quivers as he sits with what I said. My heart thumps, my fingers tingling with the need to reach out and touch him. But I wait. And fuck, is it worth it.

"Cope, if I haven't made it more than obvious, I'm fucking crazy about you. You popped up in my life at a time I didn't even realize I needed you. I was lost and empty but didn't know it. Didn't know how much I needed you until you were in front of me. You're *everything*, Cope. Everything I've always wanted, and everything I never knew I needed."

Moving between my legs, his hands wrap around the back of my neck, fingers stroking the hair at my nape. His icy blues dip down to my lips before leaning in and capturing them with his own. My entire body tingles from head to toe at the feel of his mouth moving against mine. At the feel of his hot, wet tongue teasing along the seam, begging for entrance. My chest swells—and so does something else—at the sensation of our tongues tangling. At the taste of him. The feel of my hands around his waist.

When he breaks the kiss and pulls back, his tongue lazily brushes over my spit-slick bottom lip, eyes tracking the movement before they lift, meeting mine. "I fucking love you too, cowboy."

The organ in my chest swells, expanding to twice the size it should be. At least, that's what it feels like as I replay those words over and over in my head, a wide, toothy grin splitting my face.

In all my years, I never knew it could be like this.

And now it is, and I feel like the luckiest man alive.

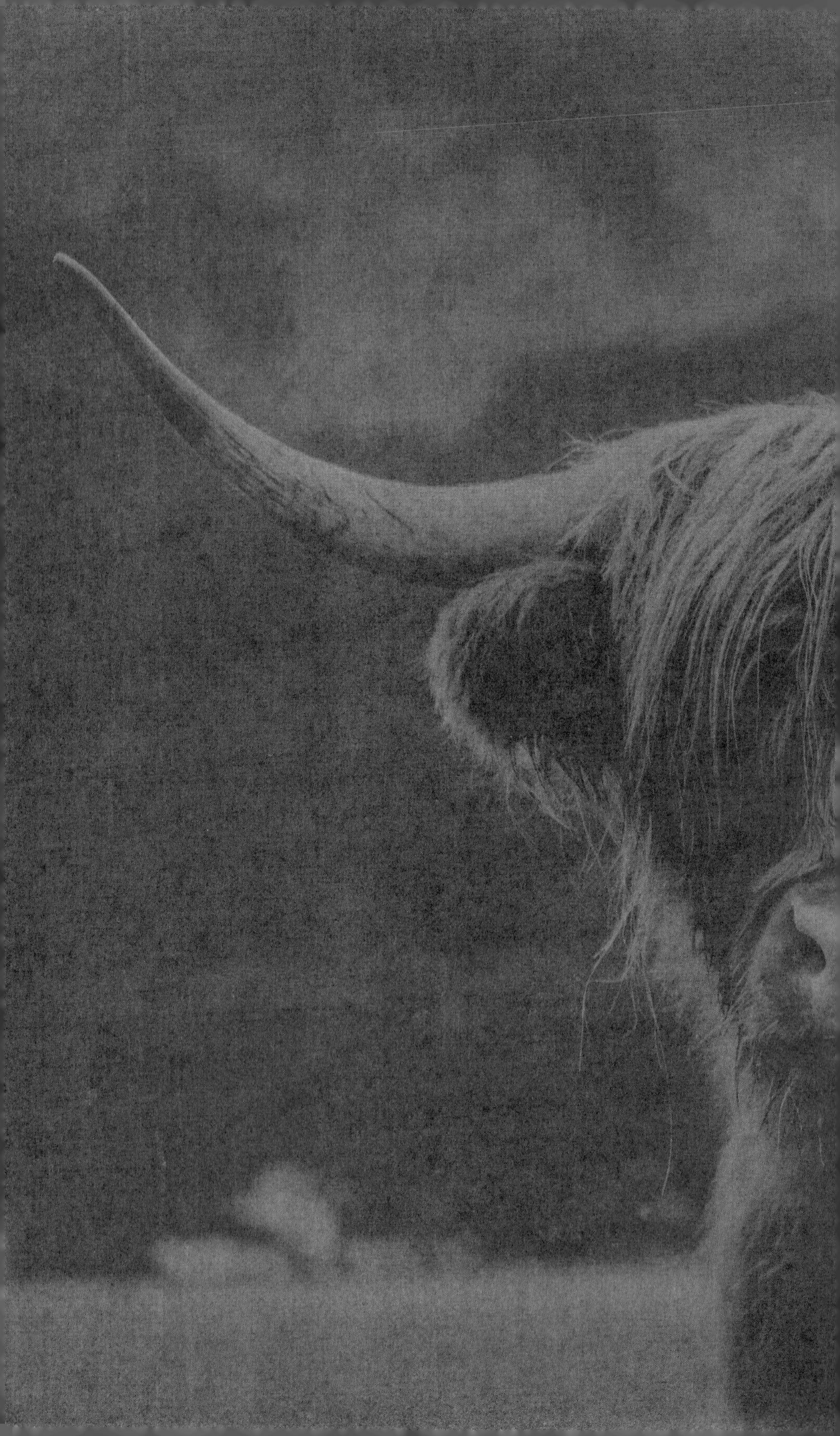

Epilogue

Four Months Later

Xander Dawson

"**W**ake up..." Cope's gravelly voice filters through my state of semi-unconscious. The bedding around me is warm and pillow-soft, and I'm so comfortable, it pains me to think of peeling even one eye open. But then I feel the blankets shift, and a nudging hand on the inside of my thigh, gently spreading me open. A brief moment passes, then a hot puff of air kisses the skin around my groin, and a deep groan reverberates from my chest. Suddenly, the idea of having to wake up doesn't sound so bad after all.

"Mmm, g'morning," I rasp, lifting the comforter, revealing a mischievous grin and miles of golden tan, muscled skin from my sexy boyfriend.

"Morning, birthday boy," he sing-songs, dragging the pads of his fingers up the front of my thighs, stopping dangerously close to an area dying to be touched.

I grumble, bringing a hand up to scrub over my face. "Don't remind me."

"Why?" he asks, a dark brow raised, and a shit-eating grin on his face. "Because you're thirty, flirty, and thriving?"

"Copeland Murphy!" A fit of laugher bubbles out of me. "Did you just quote an early 2000s chick flick?"

Cope laughs and shrugs. "Maybe. Now, can I give you your birthday blowjob already?"

I rock my hips upward, a shot of arousal shooting down to my core. "By all means…"

Any trace of humor fades from Cope's face, his eyes darkening with lust as he watches me from beneath his long, dark lashes, and drags the flat of his tongue along the underside of my cock, from base all the way to my sticky tip. Pulling the foreskin back, he licks all around the flared crown, gathering every last drop of pre-cum.

My hands fist at my sides as I watch him take me in his mouth and sink lower. The urge to rock my hips up into him is strong, but I don't. I let him do his thing. And fuck, does he do it well. Watching my thick cock disappear between his cherry red, full lips is a sight my wet dreams are made of, and the moans he lets out, muffled by my dick, like he can't get enough of me, drive me absolutely fucking wild.

His hand replaces his mouth, pumping me at a steady, mind-blowing rhythm while his lips and tongue tease my balls. Sucking one into his mouth, swirling that skilled tongue around, before doing the same to the other one. Easing my legs back until I'm spread wide open for him, Cope teases along my taint before spitting on my hole, causing my cheeks to flame from how fucking filthy it is.

The pad of his finger circles the tight muscle before pushing inside. I gasp, then moan, my body thrumming with the need to come. He dribbles a little more spit onto the area, inserting a second finger. Taking my cock back in his mouth, he works me over from both ends, and it's fucking maddening.

He's not holding back anymore either. Taking me to the back of his throat, he hollows his cheeks, sucking me hard as his head bobs. Fingers crooking inside of me, he grazes that sweet spot that has my balls drawing up tight to my body and me crying out.

"Oh, fuck," I gasp. "Fuck, Cope. Yes, *fuck*, I'm gonna come."

He moans around my length, the vibration of it my breaking point. My entire body tingles and shakes with pleasure, muscles coiled tight, toes curled, as I fucking *shatter*. Balls throbbing, I unload my release into his mouth, his fingers in my ass never letting up. It feels like it goes on forever, and he slurps up every drop.

Once I'm done, he withdraws his fingers, sitting back on his haunches. I sit up, too, bringing my thumb and forefinger to his chin. "Stick out your tongue. Let me see it," I say huskily.

Cope's lips part, his pink tongue sticking out, a pool of my release sitting right there on top, and the sight has my cock twitching all over again. He smirks, like he knows exactly what it does to me, before he leans in and crashes his lips into mine. I groan, my hands flying to the back of his head as his tongue surges into my mouth, the salty, heady flavor of myself mixing with the taste of him too.

He kisses me until I'm dizzy. Until there's no more evidence of my release in either of our mouths, and when he pulls away, his eyes are hooded and dark, and we're both out of breath.

"What a way to wake up," I rasp. "Let me return the favor."

He shakes his head. "We don't have time. Get up."

"Don't have time?" I question, confused. "We aren't doing anything today."

"I have a surprise for you," he announces vaguely. "Now, get up and get dressed unless you want company to see you butt-ass naked."

"Company?"

"Xander!"

"Okay, okay." I climb out of bed, stretching my arms above my head, breathing out a yawn. "I'm up."

"Oh, hold on. I'll be right back while you get dressed." Cope scurries out of the room, leaving me confused, but I do as he says, getting dressed. He comes back in with a gift-wrapped box, a grin on his face as he hands it to me.

"What's this?" I ask, my chest tightening as I take the box from him.

"Well, open it and find out."

My heart rate kicks up as I tear off the teal blue birthday wrapping paper. A shoe box waits for me, and when I open the lid, I'm met with a gorgeous pair of saddle brown boots that match a pair Cope has. "You got me my very own pair of boots?" I ask, emotion thick in my throat as I meet his gaze.

That same grin grows even wider as he nods. "No more Vans on the farm."

I can't help but laugh. He *hates* that I still wear those. "Thank you, Cope. These are amazing. Does this mean I'm a real cowboy now?"

"Funny you should say that," he mumbles, mostly to himself, before pulling out his phone and checking it. "Okay, come on. He's here."

Still confused, I follow Cope through the house. Larry is sitting on the custom kitty window perch Cope had installed when we moved in. He looks like the King of the Castle, watching us stroll by. We go down the steps on the porch, and go into the yard, watching Whit's truck drive up the driveway, a trailer attached to it.

"What's he doing here?" I ask. "I thought he had to work today."

"He does," Cope replies. "He is."

I glare at the back of his head, not loving how mysterious he's acting.

Whit parks his truck and hops out, a huge grin splitting on his face. "Happy birthday, Xan!"

"Thank you." Padding down the steps, I walk toward the trailer he's heading to, wondering what he's doing. Cope's behind me, I can hear his footsteps on the gravel. I toss him a look over my shoulder, and he just smirks and shrugs. They're in on something together, I just know it.

"What's going on?"

"I don't know what you mean," Cope replies innocently.

Whit opens the door to the trailer, and when I round it, my eyes widen as I take in what's inside. My heart races as I look from Whit to Cope, both of them seeming pretty pleased with themselves.

"Is this what I think it is?" I blurt out, my voice coming out higher than I mean to.

"Well, if you think it's a highland cow, you are correct," Whit drawls, pushing his glasses up the bridge of his nose with his pointer finger.

"No shit, Sherlock. I'm not blind." Cope laughs, and Whit scowls at him. "Is she…for me?"

When I officially moved in here with Cope when he got back from the circuit a couple of months ago, my aunt insisted—much to my appreciation—that I take Aggie with me. Even though it was only next door, she knew that Aggie was more attached to me than anything. Well, that, and the first week I was here, we woke up one morning to find Aggie sitting on the back porch. She'd somehow Houdini'ed her way *out* of my aunt's yard and *into* our yard. It was adorable. Ever since then, I've been begging Cope to get some more animals. They are herd animals, after all.

"She's for you," Cope supplies, barely holding back his own excitement. "Happy birthday, baby!"

"Are you fucking kidding me?" I gawk at him, my limbs trembling with all the adrenaline and excitement coursing through my blood. "You got me a cow for my birthday?"

Cope chuckles, nodding.

My jaw drops open as an embarrassing squeal escapes. "Best birthday present ever!"

"Hey," Cope says, frowning. "What about what I just did? That was pretty great."

Before I can respond, Whit holds up his hand. "I don't wanna know."

Cope and I glance at each other and chuckle. I've grown to love Whit, and he's someone I would consider a good friend at this point, but he can be so fun to rile up.

"She's pregnant," Whit offers when neither of us says anything back. When I look at him questioningly, he continues. "Her previous owners have to relocate out of state and were needing to re-home their animals. I saw how much you enjoyed the cows when I took you to that farm, and when I brought it up to Cope, he mentioned how you'd been wanting another cow for Agatha. The whole situation was a stroke of luck with how close it was to your birthday and when they needed to leave."

Blinking at Whit, with my jaw still on the floor, I drag my gaze to Cope, who looks nearly as excited as I am. If I asked him, he'd one hundred percent say he was simply excited to get me this cow because he knew I wanted it, but I don't buy it. I've seen how he is with Aggie when he thinks I'm not looking. I think Cope is a big ol' softie and wants more just as much as I do.

"Do we get to keep the calf?" I ask, practically bouncing on my heels. "Please! Can we keep the calf? Cope! Can you imagine—oh, my gosh! Please!"

"Yes, we're keeping the damn calf," he replies, barely holding in a laugh. "Calm down before you give yourself a hernia. We're keeping it."

Closing the distance between us in three very large strides, my body collides with his, arms wrapping around his neck and squeezing. "Thank you, thank you, thank you! Best birthday *ever*!"

"Because of the blowjob too?" he asks, quiet enough for only me to hear.

"Yes," I reply, humor in my voice. "Because of the blowjob too."

Pulling back, I press a quick kiss on the tip of his nose before turning my back on both of them and focusing my attention on the pretty mama in front of me.

"Does this mean we can eventually get the other animals I want too?" I glance over my shoulder, finding his lips pressed into a thin line, like he knew this was coming.

Whit chuckles beside him, but has his nose buried in his phone.

"The little goats, and the chickens, and the—oh!—the sheep?"

Cope rubs a hand over his mouth, no doubt hiding his amusement before he offers me a dry, "Yes, dear. Eventually, we can do all of that."

I squeal again, startling the heifer. "I love you," I tell him, meaning it with every fiber of my being.

If somebody would've told me two years ago that I would end up in some small town in Wyoming, shacked up with a bronc riding cowboy, collecting large animals to create my own little farm—and by choice—I would've told them they'd lost their damn minds.

Life has a funny way of spinning you for a loop and giving you everything you never knew you wanted. I never saw my life here, but fuck am I glad to be here.

Cope comes over, a big, adoring smile on his face, pressing a kiss to my forehead. "I love you, too, city boy."

The End.

Turn the page for a sneak peak at Burning the Midnight Oil, Copper Lake Book Three

Chapter 1

Grady Wilde

If I had to guess, I'd say it's too damn early to be awake right now. My eyes burn and my body feels heavy, but I know without even cracking an eyelid open, the sun is pouring in through the blinds. Grumbling and silently cursing the gods for being awake already, I roll onto my side, wanting to bury my face into the pillow and will myself back to sleep. Except when I roll over and swipe an arm across the bed to grab a pillow, it's a tiny body I find instead.

Giggles erupt in the otherwise quiet room. "Morning, Uncle Grady." The small, cheerful voice comes from right beside my head, sounding way too awake for how early I'm sure it is.

Peeling an eye open, I glance over at my niece, blonde bouncy curls falling over her shoulders messily, chocolate brown eyes staring down at me, with a wide grin on her face. She's wearing her usual Disney princess pajamas—today it's an Elsa nightgown—and she's got a tablet in her lap and her back pressed against my headboard.

"Morning, Suzy Q," I reply, voice thick and raspy from sleep. "Where's your mama?"

"Downstairs cleaning."

"And you aren't helping her?" I mock appalled.

"I put my cereal bowl in the dishwasher," she offers with a shrug.

"What a helpful girl you are."

"I know." Suzy giggles. "Can you please take me to the pool today?"

Scrubbing a hand over my face, I sit up, reaching for my phone on the nightstand. "What time is it?"

"I don't know."

I groan when the screen lights up and I see it's barely after eight in the morning. "Child, it's too damn early to be awake."

"You're not supposed to say damn, Uncle Grady."

I snort, tossing my legs over the side of the bed and standing up. "Yeah, neither are you."

"Where are you going?"

"The bathroom and then downstairs to talk to your mom."

It's been about three weeks since I left Bishop-Presley University for summer break. About a week before my classes ended for the semester, I called my sister last minute, asking if I could come spend the summer in our hometown, Copper Lake, with her and my niece. The original plan was to stay on campus because going home seemed like too much trouble, but the more that plan began to set in, the more I realized there is nothing I wanted less than to stay in Colorado in my dorm room for the entire summer. Especially because there isn't a single part of me that wants to return in the fall when classes resume.

Nobody knows that, though. Not even my sister. She

probably wouldn't have let me come stay with her had she known. Hell, the only reason she probably even said yes was because her husband is gone during the summer for the rodeo and she knew I could help with her daughter. Boone Stanton is a big, famous professional bull rider—emphasis on the big— and he travels four or five months out of the year for that. Jade, my sister, usually travels with him, so I was surprised to find her home at all.

After washing and drying my hands, I pull open the door to the bathroom and find Mabel, my sister's chocolate lab puppy, waiting for me. She's only six or seven months old, and come to think about it, she could be the reason my sister decided to stay home instead of traveling with Boone the way she normally does. I'd imagine it would be a pain in the ass traveling so frequently with a puppy.

"Hi, pretty girl." Her tail wags at the sound of my voice and she starts prancing in place like she's so excited, she can't contain herself. Throwing a quick glance toward the bedroom I'm occupying while I'm here, I spot the empty bed. Suzy must've already went to find her mom.

Meandering down the stairs, I rake my fingers through my hair, wincing when I snag on a knot. I need to take a shower and take a brush to my hair but it's too damn early for that. My sister and Boone's house is nice, the space open and airy. It was built for them but it resembles old farm style homes. The bottom of the staircase opens up to the living room, which has a wall of windows that overlooks their spacious backyard. I'm not sure how many acres they live on, but it's a lot.

White leather furniture fills the large room—which seems like a ballsy color choice to have with a toddler and a puppy, but what do I know—with various throw blankets and pillows laid everywhere. An all-black rocking chair that's only big enough for a child sits beside the couch. If I'm not mistaken, I believe Boone made that himself when Jade was pregnant with Suzy. A small Little Mermaid blanket is thrown over one of the tiny arms to the chair. There's a fireplace on the wall straight ahead, sitting below a huge flat screen TV mounted on the wall, and on either side of the fireplace is cream-colored wicker baskets; one that holds toys for Suzy, the other that holds toys for Mabel.

Padding across the space, the hardwood beneath my feet is cold, and I wish I'd slipped some socks on before I came down here. The dining room is on the other side of the wall that the fireplace is on, which leads right to the open concept kitchen that my sister is currently occupying. She's standing in front of the sink, the water running as she places dishes into the open dishwasher beside her. Suzy is now sitting at the bar, a bowl of mixed fruit in front of her as she watches whatever cartoon is playing on her tablet. Jade is pretty strict about tablet time during the day. She likes Suzy to play outside and run off some of the energy she carries inside of her, but morning times, I've noticed she lets her watch a little bit while they get ready for the day.

"Morning," I mutter as I grab a glass out of the cabinet and fill it up with water from the door of the fridge. Even though I know this water comes directly from the tap, it's still superior to sink water. Nobody can convince me otherwise.

Jade glances at me over her shoulder before returning her attention to the dishes again. "You're up early."

I snort. "Yeah, ask little miss Suzy Q about that."

Suzy giggles.

"Got any plans today?" Jade asks.

"Yeah, actually." I take a seat beside Suzy, plucking a strawberry out of the bowl in front of her before popping it into my mouth. Her brows furrow as she glares at me. "I'm heading down to the arena this afternoon to meet my buddy, Benji's, sister about a photography gig."

Jade turns off the water, grabbing a towel and drying her hands as she turns and rests her backside against the counter, meeting my gaze. "Hannah?"

"Yeah."

"What kind of photography gig?"

"That yearly festival…" I snap my fingers while I try and place the name that's clearly not coming to me.

"Stampede Days," Jade finishes for me.

"That's the one. They need a couple photographers to work that event."

Photography has been something I've enjoyed since I was a teenager. My parents got me my first camera for Christmas in middle school, and I immediately found it fascinating. Getting to show people how I see the world is special. Finding simple and otherwise ordinary things and bringing them to life, showing off their beauty, is something that brings me great joy.

For as long as I can remember, it's something I've wanted to make a career out of but never felt like I could. After years and years of my dad drilling it into my head the importance of having a real job—his words, not mine—that's stable and reliable, and having him point out time and time again that "taking pictures for a living" is anything but, I kind of just gave up the dream. The passion never left though; it burns inside of me.

I spent a lot of this year at college really thinking about what I wanted with my life. Where I wanted it to go. The closer I get to my senior year, the more dread fills me. I've never wanted to pursue a career in the field I'm going to school for. It was always something meant to appease my dad. Make him proud of me. But the more time that goes on, the more I realize I don't want to live a life appeasing anybody. The idea of finishing out my degree sounds about as appealing as swallowing shards of glass.

Photography is what I want to do. It's my passion. It brings me a sense of fulfillment. And I think I owe it to myself to at least try and see if I can make a solid career out of it. If I can't, then at least I gave it my best efforts. This gig at Stampede Days pays, and I took several photography jobs while at school, so I have money saved up. I owe this to myself. And besides, life isn't always about making the most money. Sure, money is great, and I'd love to have enough of it to where I won't have to worry about it. But happiness matters too. Doing something that fills your cup up.

"That'll be fun," Jade mutters as she takes a seat beside Suzy.

"When does Boone get home for the event?"

I don't miss the way Jade tenses slightly at my question. Interesting. Wonder what that's about.

"Sunday," she replies, not meeting my gaze.

"He'll be home for how long?"

"A week."

"Daddy's coming home?" Suzy asks, wide eyed, with a smile plastered on her face.

Jade smiles down at her, the sight warm and loving, as she brushes a hand over Suzy's head. "Yes, baby. Daddy will be home in a few days."

"Are you excited to have him home," I ask Jade.

Her eyes lift to meet mine, something passing through them I can't place before she nods. I'm excited Suzy will get to spend some time with him before he has to leave for the road again."

"What about you?" I ask. "Any plans?"

"I've gotta take Suzy to Mom and Dad's in a few hours. They're taking her for a couple nights. And then I'm meeting some friends for lunch."

"That sounds fun." Nudging Suzy with my elbow, I add, "Bet you'll have fun with Grammie and Pop-Pop."

She nods. Pop-Pop told me we could have ice cream sundaes and watch Moana after dinner."

"Hell yeah. That'll be a fun time."

"You're not supposed to say hell," Suzy says, causing Jade to glower at me from above her head.

"Yeah, well, neither are you, kid."

Before my sister can rip me a new one for swearing again, her phone goes off, Boone's name flashing on the screen. Instead of answering it herself, she hands it to Suzy. "Here, daddy's calling to talk to you before you go to Grammies."

Suzy takes the phone and runs into the living room. I can faintly hear the gruff, deep sound of Boone's voice filling the speakers when she finally answers.

"You don't want to talk to him?" I ask Jade.

She shrugs, getting off the bar stool and avoiding my gaze. "He's only calling briefly to talk to Suzy. I don't need to talk to him."

I watch my sister for a moment. "Are you okay?"

Throwing me a look from across the kitchen, her brows clash together like my question caught her off guard. "Yes, I'm fine."

"Are you sure?"

"Yes, Grady." She blows out a breath.

"Okay, but... you know you can talk to me, right? If you weren't fine."

"Why wouldn't I be fine?"

Holding my hands up, I reply, "I'm just saying."

Her eyes soften around the corners. "Well, thank you, but I'm—"

"Fine," I finish for her. "Yeah, you said that."

Jade rolls her eyes and breathes out a laugh, flipping me off before leaving the kitchen.

I laugh too, but can't help but feel like there's something she's not telling me. She seems off, and she has the entire time since I've been here.

Coming June 2024, Pre-Order Here

Acknowledgments

My daughters. They're the best little cheerleaders I could ever ask for.

My family. I'm so blessed to have such a supportive family. I'm so completely thankful for your love and support, even when writing seems to take up my entire life.

My bestie. My alpha. My person. Katie. This was a fun one, wasn't it? Thank you for always being there for me. For giving me the feedback I need and the reassurance to keep me going. And that cover! Ugh, you killed it. I'm so obsessed with these covers, and it's all thanks to you. I know I say this all the time, but thank you for always putting up with me, for sticking by me through whatever crazy idea I have, and for loving Xander and Cope so dang much. I love you!

Mads. Thank you for putting up with my control freak self. You're a PA who deserves an award for patience. Thank you also for beta reading and for loving these two.

Shann. Thank you, yet again, for putting up with my dozens of questions regarding the rodeo and farm life. And don't even get me started on your love for Xander. Thanks for all your help with this book. Your feedback means the world to me. ILY!

Jill and Becca. Thank you both so much for being incredible beta readers and amazing hype girls. Your commentary while reading made me so happy, and I just adore you both so much.

Kenzie. You're incredible. Thank you for all your help to make these two and this book the best that it could be.

My Amazing Patrons. Y'all saw every part of this story first, and your constant support means the world to me.

Getting to share them with you so early was such an incredible experience. I adore you all so much!

The Author Agency. Becca and Shauna—you ladies are outstanding. Literally invaluable I can't thank you enough for all that you do for me and my release. You're so on top of everything and so helpful. From the help with the PR boxes to being so organized... seriously, thank you. I've gained so many new readers with this series, and I know I have y'all to thank for that.

ARC Readers. Thank you to everybody who early read this book, everyone who reviewed and/or made gorgeous edits, and everyone who simply hyped the book up and shared teasers. I appreciate y'all so much!

Trista Boggs. Thank you for coming up with the name for Conrad's ranch—Grazing Acres. It fits so much!

All my Readers. Without y'all, I wouldn't even be here. I love and appreciate each of you more than you'll ever know. You're helping make my dreams come true, and that's still so surreal to me. So, whether this is your first book by me or you've been here since the beginning... thank you.

About the Author

Ashley James is an LGBTQIA+ author who enjoys writing (and reading) the toxic, swoony, broody, filthy talking, red flag men. She is originally from Washington State—and no, not Seattle—but now resides in South Carolina with her two daughters and her Sphynx kitties, Goose and Houston.

Connect with the Author

Books by Ashley James

The Deepest Desires Series
Barred Desires (Book One)
Forsaken Desires (Book Two)
Illicit Desires (Book Three)

Hidden Affairs Series
Brazen Affairs (Book One)
Storm Clouds and Devastation (Book Two)
Insatiable Hunger (Book Three)

Copper Lake Series
Eight Seconds to Ride (Book One)
Dirt Road Secrets (Book Two)
Burning the Midnight Oil (Book Three, Pre-Order Here)

Standalones
Kismet
Wounded
Say My Name
Whiskey Nights and Neon Dreams

Manufactured by Amazon.ca
Acheson, AB